Praise for *Boogie-Woogie*

"Moynihan's first novel is spectacular stuff: a frothy yet dark fiction about the New York art scene. It's fast, snappy, funny, and sick."
—*The Observer*

"A mature and very funny satire. Moynihan is pitiless about the foibles and pretensions of (mostly New York) dealers, artists, and collectors....This flamboyantly funny novel is an elegant warning not to take any of them too seriously."
—*Times Literary Supplement*

"Sharp and clever...[Moynihan] knows his territory well and writes with a jaded and melancholy insight....Anyone who has ever worked in the art world will recognize this as straight observation rather than caricature."
—*Daily Telegraph*

"Very funny."
—*Time Out* (London)

"A highly enjoyable satire."
—*Evening Standard*

"A smart and funny first novel...Vivid physical description is one of the marvelous strengths of this novel."
—Mason Kernan, *Modern Painters*

"Excellent. Sophisticated satire."
—*The Daily Mail*

"It is best to read the whole book in one sitting. Once you get going it is hard to stop."
—*The Spectator*

"A sophisticated take on what's going on in a trendsetting part of contemporary Western society."
—*The Independent*

"An elaborately choreographed dance to the music of modern art…An extremely entertaining book that is more revealing of the human side of the contemporary art world than a barrowful of scholarly texts."
—*The Irish Times*

"A sharply observed satire on the absurdities of the contemporary [art] scene…An impressive debut, stylishly written, and packed with sly in-jokes."
—*The Mail on Sunday*

"An elegant equation of the parallel games of sex and art."
—*Sunday Telegraph* (the Arts)

"A slick, ruthless satire…Moynihan writes in scalpel-sharp language, with a ferociously accurate ear for dialogue….Clever, competent, and cool."
—*Sunday Telegraph* (Books)

BOOGIE-WOOGIE

Danny Moynihan

Thomas Dunne Books
St. Martin's Press ✖ New York

THOMAS DUNNE BOOKS.
An imprint of St. Martin's Press.

www.stmartins.com

Cover designed by Damien Hirst
Art direction: Damien Hirst, Hugh Allan
Design: Jonathan Barnbrook and Jason Beard
Computer manipulation: Steve Warner
Photography: Mike Parsons
Cover layout: Sebastian Conran Associates

Cover artwork credits: Damien Hirst: *Away from the Flock*, courtesy of White Cube Gallery and *Chlorophyll B*, photo by Gareth Winters, courtesy of Science Ltd.; Sarah Lucas: *1-123-123-12-12*, courtesy of Sadie Coles Gallery; Marc Quinn: *Self*, courtesy of Jay Jopling Fine Art; Jeff Koons: *Rabbit*, photo by Douglas Parker Studio; Michael Joo: *Mongoloid Version B-29 (Miss Megook Decals 1–6)—detail*, photo by Marie Graziela Branco; Matthew Collishaw: *Bullet Hole*, courtesy of Lisson Gallery; Ashley Bickerton: *Seascape: Transporter for the Waste of Its Own Construction #3*, courtesy of Sonnabend Gallery, New York.

ISBN 0-312-27281-2

First published in Great Britain by Duckworth Literary Entertainments Ltd.

First U.S. Edition: February 2001

10 9 8 7 6 5 4 3 2 1

Contents

For my mother Anne Dunn

I would also like to thank: Hugh Allan, Katrine Boorman, Tom Hedley, Damien Hirst, Lizzy Kremer, Zoe Manzi, Jennifer Santos, Sarah Such, Amber Trentham and Ed Victor.

CHAPTER ONE

A SPRING MORNING,
ONE YEAR AGO

Brigid Murphy and Elaine Yoon-Jung Yi

When Elaine woke she immediately focused on the double row of shoes parked neatly against the wall. Her eyes wandered over the thick white shaggy carpet and up to a chest of drawers upon which was scattered a carnage of photographs in gold plastic frames. In the semi-darkness Elaine could just make out the array of faces peering down at her. It reminded her of the somewhat depressing homages to the recent dead in Italian churches; these simple yet powerful memorials together with the relics of dead saints had fascinated her when she had gone on a school trip to Italy the previous year. Now, the combination of shoes and photographs immured in this small dusky room conjured in Elaine's conceptual mind a work of art based on the lingering presence of the dead in everyday objects. There was definitely something to be made of it; however, her hangover was too acute for any constructive or useful theory and she soon tired of thinking.

'Holy Mary mother of fekin' Jesus,' Brigid thought to herself, 'what the feck happened last night?' Try as she might, she could not discern from the floating filaments of her memory the precise sequence of events from the previous night's escapade. At least she was home. It sometimes happened in this mad city that she did not wake up at home. Once she had woken up on a futon in Brooklyn. That is not to say Brigid was promiscuous, but the abandon of youth together with the three thousand miles or so that divided her from her neighbourhood church had to an extent liberated her moral obligations. Also, after twenty years in the Irish bog, New York had unlocked the doors of Brigid's imagination and thrown her into a wonderful unknown. 'Feckin' fantastic,' she kept saying to herself.

Elaine had met Brigid the night before at Sky Jell. She had taken advantage of her drug-induced state and seduced her. There had been an initial struggle but once she had got Brigid to take her back home it had been fairly straightforward. The sexual ambiguity of her hetero victims during the seduction process had become an obsessive challenge; the no aroused her more than the yes until her desire overwhelmed them into complicity. It was never easy. Her attempts were littered with failures, but success was a delicious prize. She kept them like hunting trophies, and Brigid was her beautiful red-headed Irish one.

Brigid closed her eyes tightly. 'I don't feckin' believe it,' she thought to herself. Her memory was unwinding, unravelling and connecting with alarming precision. Although she had been drugged up to the eyeballs with Ecstasy, Brigid could now envisage the evening and its final curtain call with uncompromising clarity. The Asian girl, some kind of artist. Was she still here?

Elaine had suggested a massage. She gave terrific massages. Those eastern ones with a lot of stroking and kneading of pressure points. Brigid had innocently agreed. As Elaine squeezed, pummelled and stroked Brigid's back, she'd felt the ambiguity coming on. She'd felt Brigid restraining herself. It was in the breathing. Drawing Brigid's dress up around her waist, she repeated the massage on her lower half. When her fingers manipulated the flesh around her buttocks, she could feel her victim quiver.

Brigid remembered turning over on to her back in an attempt to stop the proceedings but the Asian girl – and she could not for the life of her remember her name – had continued massaging her front. She had thanked her and was trying to get up from her supine position when Elaine began stroking her breasts. There had been the long explanation about not being gay but really liking her and how difficult all this was. Elaine had then explained that this was a tantric massage and although it was sensual, it was not a gay thing. Brigid had been really embarrassed and apologised for suggesting that Elaine was making a move on her, and the massage continued. Various items of clothing were removed for the purpose of this exercise and Brigid, a professional carer, was not too concerned about this requirement. She proceeded to fall into a dream state and before she knew it Elaine had removed her panties and was down on her. In the past making love to a girl had only occurred to Brigid as a complete turn-off, so it was a surprise when and at what speed she had reached an orgasm. Being of a generous nature, she felt it was only fair to reciprocate.

Heteros were usually awkward and predictable but Elaine had been surprised at the fervour of Brigid's love-making. Pretty much every possible position had been tried and several orgasms reached by the both of them. One more would be nice, thought Elaine. One for the road.

Brigid had to go to work. Although she felt intensely uneasy about the whole episode she determined to be polite and ask the girl to leave. She would be pleasant and pretend everything was quite normal.

Elaine decided to burrow under the quilt and surface between Brigid's legs. She calculated that the girl would wake up pleasantly surprised.

Brigid, who was lying on her back, felt a movement within the cotton world of her bed and opening her eyes for the first time, saw the quilt ripple like a snake and slither towards her. She no longer had the carefree, Ecstasy-driven abandon of the night before and now the Asian tongue felt more like a slug sliding across her genitalia. She lay there frozen, unable to react.

At first Elaine's tongue probed with the utmost delicacy, like a feather, hardly touching the lips which furled over the clitoris, but as her desire intensified so did the pressure of her tongue. For the first five minutes Brigid did nothing to suggest that she was enjoying this early morning attention but then a few tiny, almost imperceptible spasms confirmed Elaine's progress. She penetrated deeper, rolling her tongue fervently around and into Brigid's vagina.

Elaine's slug-like tongue had become an independent entity, forcing itself on her with overwhelming urgency. Her desire for politeness had lost her the only chance to extricate herself from the Asian advance. She ran her fingers through Elaine's cropped hair until she felt the skull curve into the neck and then, gripping the base of it, she pulled Elaine's head firmly

against her gyrating pelvis until a flurry of sharp currents thrust her up
against Elaine's mouth, nose and eyes.

Art Spindle

Art Spindle dabbed the thin film of moisture which had developed on his
forehead. 'Does he suspect anything, Jean? ... I know it's difficult. Jean,
listen to me ... listen ... calm down, just calm down and listen. There is no
way he could have seen us, just no way ... Okay, do you want to meet me
at the gallery first? ... Of course I love you ... No, I'm not just saying that.
I love you, okay ... You're asking me why? For all sorts of reasons, Jean ...
Well, ah ... you're a beautiful person and ... that too ... Yes ... You're very
beautiful, Jean ... Yes you are ... How many times do you want me to say
it? I love you ... See you at one.'

Spindle put the phone down and walked into the hall of his Park Avenue
residence. He adjusted his cravat and stroked his chin, checking for any
stubble which his razor might have missed. Stretching his arms out,
Spindle's dark-blue Armani suit opened up like an attacking cobra as it
dangled loosely over his wiry frame. The phone rang.

'Your hairdresser ... well ... Yeah ... Ah ... The ... Okay, Jean ... Ah ...
Okay ... Quarter past one then ... Yes I do ... Bye.' He gave out a deep
sigh and dialled the gallery. 'Is Beth in yet? The Frick Library, okay. Have
I got any appointments this morning? ... The Freunds ... In half an hour.
What did they want to see? ... The Tabor paintings. Right. Tell Jack to put
two in the small showroom, no more than two. You got that? Bye.'

Spindle cleared his throat and walked over to the kitchen where he
poured himself another coffee. 'The Freunds,' he said out loud, and liking
the resonance of his voice in the large and empty apartment he repeated,
'The Freunds.' It had been a while since they had bought anything from
him. He had played a reasonable round of golf with Mr Freund once some
years ago, he remembered. Golf was Spindle's passion. Every weekend he
shed his art dealer image and transformed himself, sporting garish chequered trousers and vinyl turtle-neck sweaters. He would drive out of New
York and spend the day chasing a small white ball around emerald-green

lawns and fusty-green fairways. He liked to take collectors with him because he would be able to enthuse them with some art work or other in-between the golfing banter. He once managed to sell a Picasso watercolour on the eleventh green.

Interrupted by the phone, he picked up the receiver and stood silently for a few minutes. 'Anyway, honey, anyway you like ... No, it's not that I don't care, I care very much ... Of course I do, Jean ... Yes ... Well, I like it when it's like, kinda messy. You know what I mean? ... Well, straight could be good ...'

Elaine's legs were wrapped about Brigid's limp body.

'I don't believe I did this,' sighed Brigid.

'What do ya mean?'

'You know, with a girl.'

'There is a first time for everything.'

'Right, I'll tell me children that. They'll say, "Ma, I did it with a donkey" and I'll say, "Well, there's a first time for everything." '

Paige Quale

A collection of birds competed noisily with the distant echo of Manhattan traffic. It was nine thirty on a cool May morning in Central Park.

Frozen in the middle of a narrow, tarmac path stood a pair of ten-year-old twins dressed in white skirts with rose-petalled blouses. The girls stared in disbelief at the oncoming figure of Paige Quale on roller blades. Their mother, a few feet away, moved to intercede, her knotted brow strapped above worried eyes which glared out of a thin, sallow face. Paige divided the twins.

'Ass-hole,' the twins screamed in unison.

'Watch where the fuck you're going!' the mother snapped. The words faded as Paige careered away and down towards a looming tunnel, her white T-shirt flapping in the wind. With a rush of adrenaline, Paige sped into darkness. The echoing noise of her blades cutting the roads accentuated her sense of omnipotence. Out of the tunnel she hurtled, curling round a tramp, then a pale-faced spotty youth and finally an old woman feeding a squirrel. Each one grimaced as she sped past them.

Jo Richards

When Jo Richards emerged over the crest of the hill, he looked up from the asphalt he'd been gazing at and smoothed his lank, inky-black hair away from his pale face. He observed Central Park gently fall away in front of him. The scenery reminded him of Robert Greene's paintings. He had never quite grasped the busy, almost fairy-tale images of people in scrubbed veridian and olive-green park landscapes; however, he couldn't help thinking that everything around him on this particular day, at this particular moment, was very true to Greene's vision. So much happening it was almost overwhelming, he thought to himself. Lowering his head again he walked down the gentle slope.

A small incline slowed Paige's speed and gave her time to take in the distant figure of Matt Dillon. Her heart raced. As he approached, she turned on her blades and with all the elegance she could muster, began a series of dance routines she had been practising lately. She raised her leg high above her waist and rotated on her blades with ballerina-like grace. He walked past. It wasn't Matt Dillon. She determined not to compound the humiliation of not being noticed and continued dancing.

Jo Richards walked past a girl dancing on roller blades on his left, while on his right, a masseur kneaded a crouching figure. This struck him as an interesting juxtaposition and it dawned on him that he had never been aware, intellectually aware that is, of peripheral vision. Finding it an interesting concept, he spent the rest of his walk through the park concentrating on the flux and flow of this other dimension.

Beth Freemantle

Beth Freemantle walks through the park on her way to the Spindle Gallery, where she is the angelic receptionist, a transparency-filer, a carnivorous invoice-maker, the coffee-maker, a door-opener, a verbal punch bag, an apologist; in other words a general dogsbody. She is everything and nothing, disposable and indisposable; a pawn in four thousand square feet of space. Above all, Beth Freemantle works for Art Spindle, the rabid top dog art dealer on Fifty-seventh Street.

'Hey, Paige,' sang a cockatoo voice. Paige turned to see Beth, an acquaintance from Sarah Lawrence and pal from Bar Six days, bound gracelessly towards her.

'Hey, Paige, like, so great to see you. How are you? You look so great,' Beth announced breathlessly.

'Hey, Beth, how you doin'?' replied Paige, grinding to a standstill.

'Just great. I'm working at the Art Spindle Gallery on Fifty-seventh Street, you know, and it is so great, you gotta come see the gallery. There's a real, like, interesting show of Duane Dyson, you know?'

'Ah ha.'

'So Paige, what's happening with you? Hey, how's Peter Crontin? Are you guys, like, still an item?'

'Didn't you hear about that, Beth?'

'Hear what?'

'He died in a car accident.'

'Oh my God! I didn't know. Jesus, I'm sorry, I'm like, I don't know what to say. Jesus, Paige.'

'We kinda separated a few months before.'

'Oh my God, I just don't believe this, I mean he was such a great guy, oh Jesus, oh my God.'

A few awkward seconds followed before Paige cheerfully announced, 'I just saw Matt Dillon.'

'No!' Beth exclaimed.

'Yeah.'

'No!'

'Yeah, he was, like, so cute.'

'Hey, I don't believe it!'

'Ah ha.'

'What was he wearing?' Beth asked.

'Black coat, blue shirt, you know that kinda thing.'
'Cool.'
'Ah ha.'
'Did he look at you?'
'And how.'
'In the eye?'
'Ah ha.'
'Did he say anything?'
'Ah ha.'
'What?'
'Hi.'
'Hi?'
'Yeah, "Hi."'
'Hey.'
Paige circled Beth on her blades. 'I'm in love.'
'Oh come on!'
'Ah ha.'
'Was he alone?'
'Ah ha.'
'What did you say?'
'Oh, you know, I kinda said "Hi" back.'
'Oh Jesus. I don't believe it, oh Gaaad. Then what?'
'He kinda walked on.'
'Did he look back?'
'Ah ha.'
'He didn't?'
'Yeah he did.'
'Jesus, what did you like, do?'
'Nothing.'
'Nothing?'
'Ah ha.'
'Oh Jesus man, that is like, so cool.' Beth suddenly changed expression and asked the time.
        'Ten,' Paige replied.

'I gotta get to work.'

'Okay.'

'Hey, like, come to the gallery.'

'Yeah, sure will, Beth.'

'See ya, Paige.'

'See ya.'

Paige jettisoned herself towards Fifth Avenue. Beth walked towards the Spindle Gallery:

It's a really beautiful day and I'm like, walking back from the Frick Library where I've like, been doing some research for Art Spindle and I bump into Paige Quale or like, 'Bitch Quale', as we used to know her at college. She's still on those blades and, like, makes a big thing about Matt Dillon who I, like, see all the time anyway. She is so, like, stupid. Anyway, I've decided to do it. I'm real excited about it but, like, real scared at the same time, you know? Can you believe, like, about Peter Crontin?

As Elaine was putting on her leather jacket she caught Brigid's reflection in the mirror. She was blow-drying her red hair, which dangled loosely over her face. Elaine absorbed her porcelain beauty: the white skin, the freckled white skin. When Brigid lifted her arms, the towel unhinged to reveal her firm ivory-white bosoms and small pink nipples. Elaine tingled at the spectacle until she found her own reflection looking into the mirror and in that split second Brigid looked up and caught her watchful Oriental eyes. Elaine looking at Brigid looking at Elaine who had been looking at herself. Brigid blushed. The hair-dryer hummed loudly as it blow-dried the wet strands into silken threads. Elaine smiled and sat down on the bed.

Art Spindle greeted Mr and Mrs Freund at the door of the showroom with robust familiarity. Smiling broadly and flirtatiously, Mrs Freund commiserated over the amount of time since their last meeting, inducing Mr Freund to make a jocular quip about their last round of golf in the summer of 1994.

Spindle invited the couple to make themselves comfortable on two Judd chairs. These had been chosen to impress, but their minimal austerity tried even the most corpulent of clients, and helped precipitate quick departures for those who were not serious art collectors. Special customers were sent to another showroom where cushioned thirties chairs had been installed. The Freunds weren't serious collectors, but tried to keep their hand in. An occasional purchase satiated several fields of concern, notably their need to feel *au courant*, as the French would say. One or two purchases a year usually did the trick. Equally important was to keep in with the dealers, who both held the functions and sat on the boards of those who held other functions. Two purchases a year over five years kept four to six dealers attentive and the invitations flowing. Artists were not that important but it was a bonus if they could be persuaded to attend one of their own events. Another aspect, although this wasn't of interest to Mrs Freund, was the appreciation in value of the art work. After a few drinks Mr Freund would gloat over his canny investments.

The Freunds settled themselves as comfortably as possible on the Judd chairs. Mr Freund sat back, allowing his large body to fill the chair like hot lead in a mould. Mrs Freund perched on the edge, leaning enthusiastically towards the great Spindle. Spindle effusively informed them that this was an interesting show which had drawn the attention of several publications, most notably the glowing review in the *New York Times*. The Freunds agreed it was an interesting show and were impressed, but not wholly convinced. Museum curators were queuing up for possible exhibitions and purchases, Spindle continued, elaborating on the theme. The *coup de grâce* came when Spindle dropped the bait, informing them that certain collectors of the Freunds' acquaintance had already made a purchase, illustrating that a veritable genius was now flowering in Spindle's gallery. The two men picked themselves up like farmyard cocks, straightening their spines, strutting the room, stroking their chins, waving an arm or two, accompanied occasionally by 'ummms' and 'errrs' between tense pauses. At these moments, Mrs Freund knew her place: she sat back, adjusting her limbs to the contours of her stainless-steel nest and waited for the next stage of the game. A twenty per cent discount was agreed upon. The tense atmosphere diffused and again became convivial. The next stage was Mrs Freund's domain. A choice had to be made between the two paintings available. Mrs Freund was not about to choose quickly; after all, if her husband was prepared to spend thirty thousand dollars, she had every right, as a shopping woman, to ponder her indecision.

This was a tense moment for the dealer: the shopping woman was capricious and quite capable of ruining the deal. Spindle became agitated; as far as he was concerned, silence and contemplation did more harm than good. He coughed nervously, scratched his forehead and moved around in his seat until Mrs Freund declared carelessly that she wished they could buy both. Her husband paled. Spindle couldn't believe his luck. Of course, he continued, they were welcome to accompany him to the MOMA dinner the following week. Mrs Freund realised her mistake, but the suggestion of a glamorous dinner invitation hovered like a ripe peach that oozed with the social implications of being seen at the Spindle table. Her enthusiasm escalated. Spindle, realising his deal was lightly hooked, delicately reeled in his fish. Mrs Freund was clearly won; she lay lifeless on the deck, her eyes glazed and staring vacuously into space, but the weight of her husband could ruin the catch. A twenty per cent reduction for the two works could easily be arranged, Spindle continued. A show next year in Japan and Germany would inevitably augment prices.

Freund felt he was losing control. Maybe he should reserve the second one? Spindle hated reserves: it was as good as throwing the fish back into the water. Freund could always resell at a large profit, he went on relentlessly, the Modern was sure to buy one. The more elaborately Spindle wove his web, the more entangled Mr Freund became. Now the buyer cast the familiar furtive glance towards his wife, the 'get me out of this one' glance. But it was to no avail. Then one final effort, a change of subject, golf on Sunday. Sunday? Spindle had collectors in from Texas to see the show, he didn't think he could hold the painting. Freund sat back on the Judd in a sweat. Spindle wiped his brow with his Hermès handkerchief. Mrs Freund sighed with satisfaction. A done deal. The deal done.

Brigid had dressed. She did not need make-up but all the same liked eyeliner and this she drew carefully along the rim of one eye. Her concentrated gaze excluded all but her face which was framed across a blurred bedroom landscape and included a haze of colours which constituted Elaine's crouched form on the bed. Elaine was turning over an idea in her mind about being observed and also being the observer. How strange it was that she hadn't been able to focus on both her own reflection and Brigid's at the same time. Yet there was something about the intensity of that split second – her looking at Brigid, looking at her, looking at herself in the mirror – that overwhelmed her. While on the one hand it had not been possible for her to focus on the reflections of Brigid drying her hair and herself simultaneously, on the other hand, in that moment when Brigid's eyes had locked on to hers in the mirror, they had almost brought into existence the phenomenon of seeing two things at once.

Brigid interrupted her chain of thought. 'Are you ready?' she asked, adjusting her blue and white nurse's uniform.

'Yep,' Elaine replied, getting up from the bed.

Mr Rhinegold and Dolores Ballesteros

In the corner of a darkly lit room lined with rows of mahogany shelves burdened with heavy tomes of the classics, Mr Alfred Rhinegold sat motionless in a 1955 Webster and Webster wheelchair, his spectacles catching both the refracted reflection of the Seventy-fourth Street traffic and a Mondrian *Boogie-Woogie* which hung next to the window. His cheeks, billowing with a wheezing tide of breath, and his open, downturned mouth gave the impression of a toad waiting for a stray fly to come its way. In fact, Mr Rhinegold was asleep. The monotony of the day wore on unnoticed in the library. The only disturbance to his peace might have been the siren of a police car above the drone of New York traffic or the occasional eruption deep inside his mucus-laden lungs.

Dolores Ballesteros walked into the library carrying in one hand a yellow bucket containing a number of cans, brushes and dusters and in the other the cord of a very old-looking vacuum-cleaner. Mr Rhinegold had parked his wheelchair by his desk. He looked moderately disgruntled. His body had shrunk into his clothes to such a degree that the shirt collar skirted around his chin, making his head resemble a periscope – which followed the approaching maid.

'Helloo, Mss Rhinego. Ee beauti day,' she chirped cheerfully in a Spanish accent. Mr Rhinegold grunted. Dolores slid the library steps to one end of the room. Once in position, and after removing the red feather duster from the bucket, she climbed the steps. The feather duster hovered over twelve volumes of Balzac, tickling their bindings before moving on to Dickens and the volumes of Dryden followed by Dumas. All volumes sprayed thousands of particles of dust which the morning light picked up as they gently lowered themselves to the floor. From here Dolores' General Electric vacuum-cleaner would soon be sucking them up into its rapacious bowel.

Dolores had an irritating habit of talking to her employer as she worked. On these occasions he would drift off, or pretend to, and stubbornly refuse to take any notice of her. To camouflage himself he would sink his head into his collar and, once nestled comfortably around the rim, close his eyes and forcibly drown himself in memories. Today he remembered the day when he walked into Alfred Stieglitz's gallery and bought his first work of art, a Marsden Hartley. He sold it in the late forties, but the thrill of buying and owning a work of art had inadvertently created an addiction. Stieglitz had become a guru until their row in 1933, when in the midst of a heated argument on whether or not photography was an art form, he had torn up two of Alfred's snaps. This action had been intended to prove that they were instantly replaceable, which however they were not, nor consequently was Stieglitz's friendship.

The man who would change Rhinegold's perception of art again was Dr Albert Barnes. He remembered being taken to see the Barnes Collection in the early thirties by the American artist Charles Demuth and how mesmerised he was when Barnes himself showed them his massive collection. At first he had disliked Barnes intensely, finding him grotesquely arrogant. However, the collector had taken an interest in him and a few months later Rhinegold received an invitation to stay for the weekend. Rhinegold took the train down to Philadelphia where he was met by his host and taken to the factory, where Barnes propounded on his theories of employment, expanding on art theory at dinner. It was an exhausting day. For a year or two Barnes continued to invite Rhinegold and his first wife Laura, who happened to have the same name as the collector's wife, until one day Rhinegold lazily questioned the genius of Soutine. Both the Rhinegolds were, in effect, shown the door, never to see or hear from Barnes again, despite many letters of apology for this momentary lapse of judgement.

As Jo Richards emerged from Central Park on to Fifth Avenue, ideas and conundrums regarding the peripheral were being formulated. His pace had quickened considerably, his hair had fallen back over his ears and hung loosely over his face. 'Peripheral vision, at a given moment, is comprised of things not completely defined by form but by presence,' Jo thought to himself. It was strange how much was taken for granted, interesting how space was defined by objects on the peripheral limits when they themselves were not specified as a whole. When he had reached the Whitney Museum, Jo put his hand up to one eye and then the other. Without the peripheral, he thought to himself, space would be indefinable. Peripheral vision – there was a work in there somewhere, he was sure of it.

Elaine Yoon paced the downtown platform of Union Square station, still chewing over the phenomenon of seeing two things at once. Maybe she could capture this notion in an art piece; video could be an interesting medium – a real flexible mirror. She could video short cuts from her life and then screen it and simultaneously record the people who were watching. This second video could then be shown together with a copy of the original running in sync in another room. Thus not only would the work play on that moment of observation, but both audience and artist would participate in the work itself. The teeth of the platform grille slid across to meet the train doors. Elaine caught sight of herself in the window amongst the crowd that was waiting to get on to the train. She could even video and record the art world. This could be a really cool piece.

The chime of a door-bell rudely echoed around number thirty-five, Seventy-fourth Street. Mr Rhinegold spluttered to consciousness as he groped the worn leather arms of his wheelchair in an attempt to verify his existence. A voice drifted into the library.

'I'm here to see Mrs Rhinegold,' said Jo Richards.

'I think you know the way, Mr Richards.' The manservant, Robert Freign's voice flowed with smooth clarity tinged with sarcasm. Rhinegold turned his chair towards the entrance of the library but was too late to catch Jo who was already half-way up the stairs.

Jo had befriended his ex-girlfriend's great-aunt, Mrs Alfreda Rhinegold, when they had been invited for tea at her residence on Seventy-fourth Street a few years ago. He had been astonished to see several important-looking paintings hanging on the walls. Although what he thought were paintings by Léger turned out to be by minor American artists of the thirties, there were some veritable masterpieces, including a real, *bona fide* Mondrian. It had been the first time Jo had seen such an important work of art in a private residence. His surprise and uncharacteristic effusiveness had charmed their hostess, who made him promise to keep in touch. Unfortunately, a few months later, his relationship with Mrs Rhinegold's great-niece foundered, thus severing his ties with her family and therefore Mrs Rhinegold. It was only after a brief flirtation with Art Spindle's daughter, which brought him into contact with the dealer, that the idea of establishing communication with Mrs Rhinegold resurfaced. He had confided his knowledge of the whereabouts of a certain Mondrian masterpiece to Art Spindle, who had become very excited at the prospect of acquiring the painting, even though there had been no suggestion that the Rhinegolds wanted to sell it. Spindle had dangled a carrot of ten per cent of the sale price in front of Jo, who had finally agreed to try to persuade them to sell. Jo was now making his third visit in as many months, though he had not yet dared to bring up the subject of the painting.

Mrs Alfreda Rhinegold

Mrs Alfreda Rhinegold sat upright on a faded pink settee. The silk had

worn thin on the arms. She spoke with relentless rapidity, like a forest bird.
'And Jo, how is your art going?'

'Well, I ...' Jo Richards started.

'It must be so hard for a young artist these days, although back in the
fifties it was tough-going. I remember Jackson always complaining at
private views in that drunken way he had.'

'Well, it's not going too ...' he tried to intercede.

'I mean, look at poor old Gorky. He had a terrible time, and Rothko.
Newman wasn't that badly off, I suppose, but there were some who were
perfectly wretched.'

'Yes, well, I can't really complain,' Jo managed to slide in successfully.
'I sold a couple of pieces last month which are paying the rent.'

'My poor boy. I must see your work sometime.'

'Yes, you must ...' Jo started enthusiastically.

'I remember meeting that fella, oh goodness me, ah de, ah, de ...
Koone.'

'De Kooning,' Jo intervened.

'That's right, de Kooning. He was always complaining about the rent,
most engagingly of course. I didn't buy anything at the time. I never really
approved of those squiggly women. What do you think of them?'

Jo frowned and cleared his throat. 'Well, I ...' he tried to continue.

'I mean, what a horrible portrayal of women. Anyway he wasn't ... he
wasn't American enough to my mind. Jackson was so much more, ah more
... expressive, you know.' Mrs Rhinegold gave a little twist of her wrist.
'Pizzazz as we used to say.'

'I see ...' Jo began.

'So, what do you like?'

'Well, I like the Minimalists.'

'Minimalist. How interesting,' Mrs Rhinegold crescendoed. 'And what
do they do, these Minimalists?'

'I suppose, well ...' Jo hesitated. 'I suppose it's, ah, what they don't ...'

'Oh, I see. A minimal amount, you mean?'

'Well, not exactly. I suppose you could say it was the space between
spaces,' he managed to explain.

'I see, very modern, beyond me, but very modern, yes, yes. And is your work, ah, what was it?'

'Minimalist.'

'Yes, that's it, "Minimalist".'

'Not exactly. I'm more on the conceptual side.'

'Oh, and what does that mean? I'm most awfully interested. You see, I only get the *Burlington* from England these days. It's rather, how would you say, old-fashioned, but it has its contemporary moments.'

'Ah …'

'I suppose you could say that the Mondrian downstairs is Minimalist.'

'Yeah, there is an element of Minimalism.'

Mrs Rhinegold gave out a piercing laugh. 'Minimalist sounds like a medical condition, don't you think?'

'Yes, I suppose,' Jo began enthusiastically before being interrupted by a soft knock at the door. Freign entered holding a tray arrayed with clinking china.

'Oh Freign, you are a darling,' Mrs Rhinegold chirped as Freign lowered the tray on to the Charles X side table. 'I'll pour today.'

'Yes, madam,' Freign replied. He glided out of the room closing the door noiselessly.

'Milk?' she questioned.

'Yes please.'

'Sugar?' she bellowed.

'Yes, that would be …'

'One lump or two?'

'Well, actually three.'

'Three,' she screamed. 'My goodness, that's not very minimal.'

'No, I suppose …'

'My husband,' she said while pouring the tea, 'always took a lot of sugar until his accident in 1961.'

'1961!' Jo said with a tone of surprise.

'Yes, it's been almost, almost … mathematics have never been my strong point,' she said, frowning.

'Thirty-seven years,' Jo calculated.

'Thirty-seven years, is it really? Good gracious. Well, I suppose he is ninety-five ... he was forty-something when it happened, I think, most unfortunate. Is that tea all right? Dolores isn't the best tea-maker, but it's usually passable.'

Jo took a sip. 'Perfect.'

'Mind you, with all that sugar it wouldn't really matter. Now what was it that you were saying – "con" something?'

'Conceptual.'

'Yes, conceptual, that was the word; conceptual. How awfully fascinating, all these new words.'

Robert Freign (the manservant)

Robert Freign dragged the glass along the wall until he was satisfied he had found the area which would afford him the most clarity. The sounds of Mrs Rhinegold and Jo Richards condensed themselves into the emptiness of the glass. More often than not the noises were so bland that they were unattributable, except perhaps by Robert Freign and his florid imagination. He stood perfectly still in a straight military posture, listening to each passage with expressionless concentration, his tongue the only physical manifestation as it rolled over dry lips. It reminded him of an undercover mission in Aden when he had used this technique to calculate the exact positioning of an Arab infidel. Shooting him through the wall had enabled the special services to uncover and eliminate a formidably virulent cell of insurgents.

'You see,' continued Mrs Rhinegold, 'we travelled so much after his stroke that we, well, we rather missed out on contemporary art. But Alfred went on buying the Moderns you know, under Alfred Barr's direction of course. As a matter of fact, the last thing we bought was that Braque from the Slava place, you know?' she said, pointing towards a small Cubist still-life of two lemons and a jug on newspaper. Jo narrowed his eyes on what he had taken to be a Picasso.

'The Slavanama Gallery,' he corrected her.

'That's the place. Just round the corner, in fact I sometimes peer in. No buying these days of course.'

'Not at all?' Jo queried.

'No, not for years. For one thing, my dear, we couldn't afford it. Anyway we've got enough paintings and sculptures as it is. Perhaps I should sell something and buy contemporary. What do you think?'

'I, ah, it sounds like a good idea, in fact ...'

'I could buy some Minimalist, and the "con" thing. Is it expensive?' Mrs Rhinegold inquired.

Meanwhile Dolores glided along the shelves and surfaces of the library, dusting and shining as she went. Every so often she shot a glance over at Mr Rhinegold who was pretending to sleep. She knew this ruse well because when he really was asleep he would emit a sort of gurgling wheeze – an alarming sound to the uninitiated – as well as letting his head collapse forwards like a dead bird. Mr Rhinegold at this moment had more of a set look. The muscles were operational and keeping his head afloat.

Both Barnes and Stieglitz had been responsible for Rhinegold's introduction to the American art scene and had to a large extent formulated his eye for Modernism. But it was initially Alfred Barr who was responsible for Rhinegold's most prodigious decade in collecting, via Barr's show in 1936 entitled *Cubism and Abstract Art*. Suddenly Rhinegold's old favourites receded to give way to a new wave of abstraction. At the time his company was making precision tools for dentistry and other engineering devices, and he was earning sufficient monies to be a real player in the art world. He had begun to buy many of the young artists such as Cavallon, McNeil, Ferren, Xceron, Green and Shaw, before Barr, hearing of his interest in contemporary art, shrewdly invited him to be on the Board of Trustees at the MOMA. He was, at the age of thirty, the youngest board member and with an energy befitting his youthful years he tackled his assignments with determined assiduity. Not a minute was wasted. He attended every art opening, visited every studio, went to lectures given by Hoffman, Helion and George Morris. He made it his duty to get to know every artist and thinker of his generation. By 1939 he was responsible for adding over thirty paintings to the museum's collection; however, in the same year he had a furious row with Hans Hoffman who accused him of collecting 'sterile and dilettante art'. This incensed Rhinegold so much that he decided only to follow the work of the purist, neo-plasticist and post-analytical Cubists. Unfortunately during the war a more lyrical and biomorphic abstraction was showing itself which was rooted not just in the work of Picasso but also in other art movements such as Surrealism. He had always been outraged by what he saw as the informality of both Surrealism and Dadaism, and refused to be part of anything that was influenced by it. By the end of the war, although still the youngest board member, and even though he had befriended Albers and Feininger, he was thought of by his peers as reactionary. However, he had remained friends with Barr and occasionally was able to help his friend out when the museum needed what he called a 'master verk'.

His previous friendship with Stieglitz and then Barnes had left their mark. Through their European connections he had managed to collect Braque, Picasso, Klee and Kandinsky as well as the home-grown talent of Hartly, Demuth, Sheeler and Davies among others, but these were lost in his acrimonious divorce case. Rhinegold's first marriage to Laura Bastovitz had been short and expensive. He had met Miss Bastovitz in 1934 at a meeting of New York Democrats. She was the daughter of a Polish count who had left Poland during the First World War. Miss Bastovitz was a formidable lady, not unlike Rhinegold's mother, with a sharp, east European intellect, which fostered more interest in philosophy and politics than in the arts. This lack of interest caused the breakdown of their marriage and, as if to prove the power of political will over the decadence of art, she stripped him of his most valued possessions, the proceeds of which, after a well-reported sale, she gave to some charitable urban project.

This last memory irritated Rhinegold enough to open his eyes again, whereupon he spotted Dolores on her ladder dusting the glass cabinet that contained his favourite sculpture: Medardo Rosso's *Bambino Malato*. Honsbeen, who ran the Peridot Gallery, found it for him in 1955. He could just see the wax face peering eerily out through the glass cabinet slightly to the left of Dolores' sturdy legs. He couldn't help but notice the edge of her frilly pink petticoat, which lingered with the ghost of a smile just beneath the dark recesses of her apron. It reminded him of Frau Springer, a pale, tight-lipped and rather disagreeable housekeeper in Berlin whose voluminous dresses would rustle ominously along the corridors inspiring awe and terror in all who had inhabited that house. As a child he had always wondered how the dress held its form, until one day Frau Springer slipped over, giving him a view of a metal contraption, not dissimilar to a flower stand, and stuffed with frilly-layered white material, which he was later to discover were called 'bloomers', the same name as his best friend at school.

Dolores turned to check on her employer, only to find him peering up at her lower half. She chuckled but he continued to stare quite undeterred. 'Much dusti, señor,' she said, trying to distract him. 'Uh,' Rhinegold grunted, aware his eyes had fixed somewhere up Dolores' skirt. 'Yah, much dust,' and, conscious that this could be the beginning of one of her marathon monologues, he closed his eyes to discourage any further communication and slipped back to his first divorce case. Quite why this was of any importance forty years later was beyond him. Perhaps he was searching for something that would irritate him more than Dolores' vacuum-cleaner.

Dolores smiled to herself as Rhinegold's head nestled back around his collar, and having finished dusting the books she bent over and turned on the vacuum.

After a cup of coffee at Three Guys, Paige Quale decided to go home. She wove through the pedestrians and, after crossing Seventy-sixth Street, picked up speed and glided along the east side of Madison, finally making a sharp turn down Seventy-fourth.

Freign removed the glass from his ear and gently replaced it next to the full bottle of Evian which stood on the bedside table. Straightening his waistcoat and feeling for the stiffness of his tie, the Rhinegolds' manservant opened the door of the guest room and once in the hallway closed it without a sound being emitted. Having glided down the marble staircase which swept down to the front hall, Freign made for the kitchen door.

'Frrreign!' Rhinegold's voice struck with aged severity from across the hall. He sat crouched, his wheelchair poking half-way out of the library door. 'Some vater, Freign.'

'Surely, sir,' replied Freign, steadying himself after the surprise rear-guard attack of this mechanical device and its wizened occupant.

'Ver is ze nurse?'

'Miss Murphy is late, sir.'

'Ze young are unrrreliable.'

'Indeed they are, sir,' Freign replied.

Mr Rhinegold winced and muttered. Clearly agitated, he wheeled himself to the window where a shaft of sunlight illuminated his cranium and accentuated the heavy rifts lining his face; like a Victorian geological map. This ancient, fish-like creature, with heavy lower lip and sunken eyes somewhat enlarged by thick spectacles, attracted the attention of a young girl speeding down the sidewalk on roller blades.

Paige picked up speed down the south side of Seventy-fourth. She could feel the cool breeze against her hot, perspiring skin. But just as she was admiring her reflection in the passing windows – a favourite occupation of hers – she caught sight of a small bespectacled and shrivelled face that hovered like a phantom behind the silhouette of her speeding body. Once, when Paige was aged eleven, she had experienced a similar sensation while studying her reflection on a lake in Vermont. Through her floating image, she had suddenly seen a large fish swimming in the murky depths. This unearthly monster's languid passage among the weeds and old tree trunks was enough to precipitate a piercing scream which alerted the attention of the other occupants of the boat. The vessel rocked fiercely as they all leaned over the side to observe the focus of her terror and consequently Paige lost her balance and fell overboard. Thinking she was about to be gobbled up by what was in reality a two-pound speckled trout she panicked and forgot the few rudimentary rules of swimming. Her arms flailed about and within seconds she began to descend towards her slippery companion. Had it not been for Uncle Gabriel's kiss-of-life she surely would have died.

Brigid Murphy, hungover and late for work, rounded the corner on Lexington and walked west on Seventy-fourth. As she neared the Rhinegold residence a girl came hurtling towards her on roller blades. Brigid admired the girl's elegance and agility but suddenly she saw her catch something in the pavement and lurch forwards, falling awkwardly to the ground.

The pavement came looming towards her in slow motion. Paige hit the pavement with deadening force, her right shoulder taking the full brunt of the impact. The right side of her face scraped along the ground until the volition and angle of the fall carried her body over into an awkward somersault. As she spun over, the right roller blade caught the back of her left thigh so that she landed on her right knee, twisting it around until it was almost at right angles with her thigh which now slid along the pavement, removing both her stocking and a layer of skin.

Mr Rhinegold found this most amusing. Adjusting his spectacles, he strained forward to view his prey and to his delight the design of her fall afforded him a view of her white panties. He chuckled until a coughing fit interrupted his mirth and he had to hold his chair to steady himself. By the time the seizure had left him, a crowd had accumulated round the girl. 'Meddling rrabble,' he wheezed to himself.

Paige opened her eyes to see several people looking down at her; they seemed distant, somehow separated from reality. A sharp pain momentarily lifted her out of her dazed state before once again she drifted into unconsciousness.

Dolores looked out of the basement window. All she could see was Brigid's back as she squatted on the pavement, the medic's face drooping down towards her, half a dozen pairs of legs and the wheels and undercarriage of an ambulance. The frustration at not being able to see the action elevated to exasperation when she saw Freign's familiar grey pleated trousers walk towards the scene. Now both Freign and Brigid were witnessing something she wasn't. It was almost too much to bear.

As Freign described the event to the almost blind Mrs Kravitz, a perky octogenarian from across the street who had once been Eleanor Roosevelt's neighbour, Brigid was dabbing Paige's forehead with a damp cloth.

'Do you know what happened?' the medic asked Brigid.

'She had a terrible fall,' Brigid whispered. 'I think her leg could be broken.'

An ambulance sounding its sirens hurtled about the place, and the room pulsated with rotating blue and red lights. White rooms and glittering surgical instruments filtered through into Rhinegold's imagination where they multiplied and evolved into several morbid scenarios, all of which reminded him of his own mortality. Hoping a distraction might cure him of the waking nightmare which had now engulfed him, Mr Rhinegold wheeled himself to the door of the library which led out into the hall. Just as he was calming himself down, he caught sight of a blurred figure descending the stairs. Gradually, as the figure came towards him, the features became focused until Jo Richards loomed larger than life in front of him.

'Good morning, Mr Rhinegold,' Jo cheerfully greeted the old man. Mr Rhinegold's expression turned into a parody of disapproval; his eyes constricted into beady bullets, his mouth extended downwards and, with what looked liked being a minor angina attack, his thin translucent cheeks inflated and deflated like the cheeks of an expectant toad.

Thinking he had not heard the first time round, Jo repeated his greeting. 'Good morning, sir.'

But Rhinegold only grunted back and with alarming strength turned his chair one hundred and eighty degrees, causing rubber and marble to screech. One thrust of the wheels hurtled man and machine back into the library. Jo watched the old man disappear into the gloom, then shot a nervous glance at the Mondrian hanging by the window and made for the front door.

Within the small world that Mr Rhinegold inhabited – the area between library, hall and bedroom – the sad mornings, long monotonous afternoons, short evenings and broken nights only saw the occasional fussing of Nurse Murphy, the familiar bustle of Dolores the maid, Freign's slippery passages or, and at most, the ranting of his more than familiar wife. As a result, this last half-hour was fast gaining epic proportions on a scale altogether too much for the old man: the noise of the front door closing and Freign's footsteps across the marble hall so compounded Mr Rhinegold's addled thoughts, that when Freign reappeared he could not quite discern who was silhouetted so regimentally against the doorway.

'Who are you?' Rhinegold barked.

'It is I, sir,' a familiar voice replied.

'Yah, yah,' and taken aback by the absurdity of not recognising Freign he added, 'I vill have some wasser now, Freign.'

'Yes, sir,' Freign said as he ceremoniously poured the water from a silver jug.

'Vere is Mrs Rrrhinegold?'

'In her room, I presume,' Freign replied forlornly.

'Zat fella vaz ere again today. I don't like it. I don't trrrust him one bit.'

'You mean Mr Richards, the young man?'

'Vat ?'

'Mr Richards was indeed here. Will that be all, sir?'

Rhinegold accidentally spluttered in his water. 'Ya, ya,' he managed after recovering his composure. Freign walked solemnly out, followed by Mr Rhinegold's beady eyes, and once he was out of sight he clawed at the inside of his jacket eventually extracting the butt end of a cigar. He slotted the brown stub into his mouth, in the way only seasoned cigar smokers do, and, after lighting it with some determined and breathless inhalations, he let the smoke curl about him.

Dewey Bozo

Dewey crouched in the bath until his ass touched the water. Too hot. Turning on the cold he circulated the water with the palms of his hands and when it was to his liking he lay back and let the water pour over his body until he was totally submerged. Dewey clawed his scalp, letting his curly black hair float on the surface of the water. After a while he eased himself out of the bath. A pool of water accumulated on the vinyl floor as he rubbed himself dry. The phone rang.

'This is Dewey Bozo's answering machine. Dewey's out right now but will respond to any message except if it's Johnny, Eric or the IRS.'

It was Elaine. Still naked, he dived on to the bed.

'It's me, hello,' Elaine said, blowing smoke through her nose.

Dewey picked up and rolled over on his back. 'Hi honey, so who was that number last night? She was real cute.'

'A nurse,' she replied lazily.

'A nurse!' Dewey exclaimed.

'Yeah, from Ireland.'

'Well, it was lucky Joany wasn't about. She would have tied you up and beaten your pretty little ass.'

'That sounds interesting,' Elaine laughed.

'How's ten-ton Joany anyhow?' Dewey asked.

'Same as ever; short-tempered, abusive, opinionated and in love with me.'

'You guys are so crazy together. Anyway, while you were bumper-to-bumper with your Irish number I had to deal with her friend.'

'Oh my Gaad,' Elaine sighed.

'She was like, all over me, honey. I told her I was gay but she just wouldn't take no for an answer. Then she was trying to kiss my neck, so I said, I like boys, *comprende?* Boys. You know what she said? "You can do it up me arse." '

Dewey pronounced arse in an Irish accent. Elaine burst out laughing.

'So I said, honey, that's not the point. I never, ever touch south of the border. She said, I'm a nurse, I know things you don't. I said like what and she said, I can find your G-spot, and I said, honey, I can find my alphabet without your help, and you know what she said?'

'What?'

'Not with a blow job at the same time. Honey, I nearly died.'

'What did you say?'

'I said, listen, honey, I said I don't feed nobody's monkey, and then she grabbed the family jewels. I could have screamed. I did. Jesus, she stuck to me like a fly to semen.'

'That's disgusting, Dewey.'

'Then she starting drooling,' Dewey screamed, 'she was walking around with her mouth open, drooling, and everyone was asking who my friend was. My credibility is shot, honey, thanks to you.'

'It was worth it.'

'You owe.'

'Okay ... I owe.'

'Oh my God, oh my God, Elaine, oh my God. I met the most glorious boy. I mean a Venus with a penis like you've never seen.'

'And did you?'

'Tender talent, my lucky day – he sprayed my tonsils, honey, until I was choking with love. My jaws are like ce-ment.'

'Oh Jesus, Dewey. Sprayed your tonsils. Where did that come from?'

'Where do you think?'

'Dewey, I think I'm in love.'

'What about Joany?'

'What about her?'

'You always want what you can't have.'

'Well, speak for yourself.'

'Honey, I get what I want ... always.'

'Always?'

'And all ways.'

'Well, Dewey, you should have seen the way ...'

'Don't disgust me, honey, it makes me sick.'

'What am I going to do, Dewey?'

'Ring her, ask her out, take her to Lot 61 or the theatre. She's English or Irish, isn't she? What have you got to lose?'

'A great pair of tits, an ass to die for and a tongue which will go anywhere.'

Dewey screamed with delight. 'Okay. But don't confuse that with luurve.'

'What are you talking about, that is love,' Elaine replied.

'Elaine, you are a sex machine.'

'Oh yeah? How many guys did you blow last night?'

'You know what happened to me as I was going home? This erector set queen with a full face accosted me on Tenth and Fourteenth ...'

'That's no way near home,' Elaine interrupted languidly.

'A small diversion, honey. Anyway, she turned out to be a real dumper, you know? So, she took me into her truck and was more than a little frank.'

'A little frank?'

'I gotta a few bruises, honey.'

'I wish you would be more careful, Dewey.'

'I just can't say no. You don't know what it's like. Everybody wants to fuck me.'

'Everybody?'

'It comes with the looks, darling. One look and they come.'

Screams of laughter.

'I want her, Dewey.' Elaine sighed. 'There's gotta be a way.'

A few minutes of peace went lazily by until a voice pierced through the haze.

'Good morning to ya, Mr Rhinegold.'

Through the enveloping smoke the familiar shape of Nurse Murphy loomed. He quickly put the cigar back into his jacket.

'Now you know what the doctor said ?'

'Ze doktor, ze doktor, always ze goddamn doktor. Vat is he? God?' Rhinegold cried, clenching the leather arm of his wheelchair.

'Sure, he's only doing his job, you know,' Brigid soothed.

'Yah, and I employ him,' Rhinegold muttered angrily, and added, 'Can't a man have five minutes' peace arrround here?'

'Come on now, time for your injection,' chirped Brigid, producing a large syringe. Mr Rhinegold surveyed the object with disapproval before being made acutely aware of his smouldering cigar.

'Oh, Mr Rhinegold,' Nurse Murphy teased as she reached into the folds of his suit, dextrously removing the glowing cigar. 'Now I'm wondering what this is?'

'Goddamn.'

CHAPTER TWO

LUNCH, SIX MONTHS LATER

Elaine had begun her magnum opus a few months back. Several small loans from a few girlfriends, and a much larger amount from an older lady who lived in the building and who had developed a powerful crush on her (a crush Elaine had ruthlessly encouraged), had soon enabled her to buy a sophisticated video camera. At first Elaine was so excited by the novelty of the contraption that she had shot every aspect of her life. Its flexibility, range and size facilitated clandestine footage and her unsuspecting victims were regularly caught at their most natural, vulnerable and uninhibited.

Elaine adjusted her New York Yankees' baseball cap so that her face was partly hidden from view, she shuffled around the lobby chairs and followed Brigid out of Mount Sinai Hospital on to the street. At a reasonable distance of forty or so feet she walked behind her subject until she got to a set of traffic lights. Casually Elaine turned her back and pretended to inspect a sushi menu stuck behind the window of a small Japanese take-away. In the reflection of the window she could see Brigid waiting patiently for the lights to change. She removed her video camera from a leather satchel and began filming Brigid's reflection. Turning slowly like a matador, she swept a hundred and eighty degrees until she caught Brigid about to cross the road. Quickly putting the camera back into her satchel, she slipped along the familiar route, the subway, the streets which after six months Elaine knew by heart, except for the days when Brigid adjusted her passage home. A street, perhaps a block or two, never a real diversion except once, after a particularly trying night-shift, Brigid had fallen asleep on the subway and missed her station altogether.

The Maclestones

'Jean,' Bob Maclestone called out above the ring of the door-bell, 'what do you think of the, ah, Brancusi, ah, in the, ah, hallway?'

Mrs Maclestone came out of the kitchen holding a pin in a towering heap of dyed blonde hair. 'Maria, the dog!' Her nasal voice pierced the Park Avenue apartment, and then lowering her voice she addressed her husband. 'What, honey?'

'The ah, Brancusi in, ah, here,' he repeated, opening his palm towards a wooden totem pole object rising up the hallway and encircled by a giant staircase leading to the next floor.

'It looks great, honey,' she answered and added, cocking her head, now firmly pinned down, 'Maybe a bit off-centre, yes, maybe a little bit to the left.'

Maclestone projected opulence: Versace suit, open-neck shirt, well-polished English-made shoes, a casual look, not too conventional, a big man. He bent down, putting his shoulder against the base of the sculpture, and pushed the wooden object sideways.

'Yes, that's ...' Jean hesitated and turned towards the drawing-room entrance. Raising her index finger she added, 'Why don't we put it next to the Basquiat in the drawing-room, honey?'

'I like ah, the space here, Jean. It gives p-plenty of ah, room. You know, Jean, it might be ah, a bit cramped,' he replied, taking his jacket off.

'I think it would look great next to the Basquiat,' Jean persisted.

'It's ah ...'

'I think Basquiat and Brancusi could look great together – they've something similar, you know, *je ne sais pas quoi.*'

'Okay, honey,' and bending down again he pushed the giant structure along the bleached maple floor towards the doorway of the drawing-room. The Brancusi glided noiselessly across the floor.

'It's not going to scratch the floor, is it?' Mrs Maclestone's voice pitched with concern.

'No ah,' Maclestone gasped as he strained to keep the momentum of the drive forward.

Jean Maclestone watched her husband with a certain disdain, her hands firmly planted on her hips, right leg thrust forward.

'What about the doorway, Bob?' She squinted, trying to calculate the distance between door frame and the bulbous notch at the tip of the sculpture.

'It should be f-fine,' he gasped. Finally they arrived next to a large black canvas on which was drawn a dog baring its teeth and various letters and numbers scribbled in different colours.

Spindle came in wearing his pin-stripe, his like, power-suit, only worn on days like, when there is like, a mega purchase or a mega buy. Apparently Jo Richards is coming in with someone real important. So this is like unbeliev-able – this lady is like crazy about like, shipwrecks and stuff you know? So Art is like reading a book on marine archaeology!

The buzz of the intercom disturbed Beth's train of thought.

'Beth, get me Hubert de Bougain at the Modern,' Art demanded.

'Sure, Art. Sally Saul is on line one.'

'I'll ring her back. Has Jo Richards rung yet? No?'

Art swept the thin wisps of hair down on to his head and then picked up the phone.

'Hubert my friend.'

'Art, how err u?'

'Just great, Hubert. It was great to see you and Françoise the other night. Just great.'

'It werse a gret pleshere, Art.'

'Now, Hubert. I have something for you.'

'Ah oui?'

'Hubert, this is one of the great masterpieces of the twentieth century. I've never seen anything like it.'

'Whert is iit, Art?'

'It's a *Boogie-Woogie*.'

'Un Boogie-Woogie?'

'A *Boogie-Woogie*, Hubert, a Mondrian to beat all Mondrians, and

according to documentation it was the last painting he completed. Jesus, is
it a great painting!'

'You ner, Art, the Musée ward be verrie intresssed.'

'I think you should discreetly find out from the board whether they
could raise that kinda money.'

'How murrrch is iit, Art?'

'Well, Hubert, I think it is going to be in the region of six or seven
million.'

'*Sept millions!*'

'Maybe, maybe more.'

Bob Maclestone raised himself slowly. He was flushed and his forehead
was noticeably moist from moving the Brancusi.

'Maybe.'

'May, ah.'

'No,' Jean Maclestone insisted. 'It doesn't work there.'

'I ah, no I ...'

'I never liked that Basquiat. Art's got a great one. What about next to
the Warhol?'

'You really think, J-Jean?' Maclestone said, unconvinced.

'Let's try it, Bob. I think it could work.'

Maclestone bent down again and slid the object along the floor.

'Mind the Hirst,' Mrs Maclestone warned, as she followed his shuffling
steps. The Maclestones and the Brancusi finally arrived next to the Warhol.
'That's better, don't you think, honey?'

Maclestone raised himself and took a few steps back until he stood next
to his wife. 'I don't know, Jean, I ah, I just think ah, maybe ah ...' but she
interrupted him before he could finish. 'You know, I never liked the
Warhol there. It's kind of cramped, don't you think?'

'Well ...'

'I think it should be in the hallway.'

Maclestone turned to look through the doorway. 'Ah ...'

'Andy would have preferred it.'

'Well, I ...'

'Anyway Art thinks so.'

'Art ah, Art. What do you mean, Art?' Maclestone raised his voice an octave and went a deeper shade of red.

'What's wrong, Bob?'

'Art this and Art that.'

'Well, I was only saying that he always says that Andy needs more space, Bob.'

'Mr Spindle seems to ah, have a lot of opinions,' Maclestone retorted firmly.

'Well, he's allowed them, honey,' she replied, noticeably flustered.

'I'm just saying that he ah, seems to be attached to every g-goddamn object in our lives.'

'Oh for God's sake Bob, that is an exaggeration,' Jean replied with marked irritation, and turned towards the hallway.

Maclestone shouted after her, 'I don't care. I don't care what he ah, he thinks, Jean. You un-understand?'

Jean turned towards him with a look of disbelief. 'Honey, I ...'

'I'm putting the ah, B-Brancusi in the ah, hall.'

'Well, what about how I feel about it?'

'You mean how Art f-feels?'

'What are you insinuating, Bob?'

'Well, he seems to feature a hell of, hell of a lot these days,' he shouted.

'Bob!'

Art held the receiver and pinched the tip of his nose, and then with the palm of his hand rubbed his right eye. 'Julian, I think we got you a show at the Walker.'

'I don't know if I like my work travelling so much. You know what I mean?'

'The Walker is a major museum, Julian.'

'Yeah, I guess so.'

'I think it's important.'

'You think?'

'Yeah, I don't think you should turn down the Walker, you know. Richard Flood has made it into one of the great museums.'

'What I really want is a retrospective, Art.'

'Well, I had a talk with Margarita Levels in Rotterdam who seems interested in doing a major survey of your work.'

'Rotterdam, where's Rotterdam?'

'It's a major Dutch town with some great museums.'

'Has it got Rembrandt and stuff?'

'Sure.'

'Sounds interesting. Maybe we should discuss it.'

'Okay. Lunch next week?'

'I'm in Chicago for the drawing show, back on Thursday.'

Freign walked up the back stairs of the Rhinegold residence until he reached a small door at the very top of the building. He opened the door. It was a sunny day and the window cast a parallelogram of sunlight across the oak floorboards. He walked through the shaft of light towards a trestle table in the corner of the room. It was covered with tubes of paint, small bottles, plastic containers, paint brushes and paint-soiled rags. A palette balanced on the edge of the table. He picked up the palette and looked intently at its surface. On one side lay a cold emerald-green, a musty olive-green, a warm Naples yellow, a cadmium-yellow and a violet. A mountain of lead-white rose up sharply above these colours and fell away on the other side into a valley of cobalt and ultramarine blues which in turn were bordered by carmine and vermilion. Freign armed himself with various brushes and his palette and walked to an easel that reached the ceiling. As he walked, the shaft of light momentarily caught the colours and illuminated them to their full intensity. Bolted half-way up the structure was a canvas measuring thirty by thirty-six inches. Next to the easel, resting on a small white table, lay several peaches in various stages of decomposition. Freign's mournful expression now metamorphosed into a concentrated, furrowed frown. His grey eyes turned blue and his pupils pulled to attention like those of a bird of prey. The sable brush, which had been soaked with a mixture of turpentine and linseed oil, now stroked the carmine until it was laden with colour and then, crossing the void in a great arch, landed gently on the curved back of a drawn peach.

'It's got this great red, real deep, you know, and then a light yellow that kinda sets it off in a real interesting way,' Art was saying to Bob Maclestone over the phone.

'Is there ah, any p-possibility of seeing it in the, in the f-flesh? You know I like to, ah, see it like, ah ... raw. You know what I mean?'

'I know what you mean, Bob. We'll have it in the gallery real soon. You're going to love it. It's one of the great twentieth-century masterpieces. I haven't had anything like this before, and you know how few are in private hands.'

'I wanna be f-first, the first, ah, okay?'

'Sure, Bob, no problem. No problem at all.'

'Okay, the f-f-first,' Bob reiterated. Art knew that Bob stuttered badly when he was excited. Bob was hooked.

Rhinegold opened his right eye, the left refused to respond. Dolores was dusting the Mondrian frame. If he warned her to be careful it would undoubtedly lead to a long explanation of some sort and so he peered at her discreetly in case she got too excitable with the duster.

Undoubtedly the Mondrian had been a coup. Guggenheim had a few works in her gallery which had intrigued him and through Harry Holtzman, a young artist he had met quite by chance at a lecture on American painting, a meeting was arranged with the master at Café Society, Mondrian's favourite bar. His English was not good, and Rhinegold's Dutch limited, so a curious blend of both was adopted which seemed to put the master at ease. Despite Rhinegold's enthusiastic attempts to bring up the subject, Mondrian didn't want to talk about painting. He preferred discussing the latest trend in music: Boogie-Woogie. This was not an area Rhinegold knew much about and its relevance at that time seemed trivial compared with the great intellectual issues of the day, such as the effect of Freudian theory on visual imagery or the conceptual conundrums of Duchamp, a popular French *émigré*.

Mondrian seemed disappointed that the young German collector did not know of any new clubs. Only later did this request strike Rhinegold as absurd, when he calculated that the painter was nearly twenty years his senior. The idea of going to clubs seemed frivolous to him when there was a bloody war raging across the Atlantic. Rhinegold was more interested in the contemporary classical scene, which at the time was being spearheaded by Virgil Thomson. Nevertheless, he was much taken by Mondrian's interpretation of these musical sounds, and had persuaded him to part with an example. Mondrian finally agreed and on a given day Rhinegold had taken a cab down to his studio on Fifty-ninth Street; a curious box-shaped room not dissimilar to one of his paintings. Mondrian insisted on a celebratory drink of tea, which was accompanied by all the artist's 'Boogie-Woogie' collection and a rather complicated explanation of how he applied each sound to colour and form. The Dutch-English narrative was occasionally illustrated by a sudden dance routine involving curious jerkings of limbs. Rhinegold mistook one of these physical contortions (a sort of doubling-up action) to be some kind of seizure, and as he got up to help Mondrian another spirited gesticulation succeeded in tipping him over one of the artist's home-made chairs. It had been an awkward and embarrassing moment. Finally a price was negotiated and it was agreed that Rhinegold should pay half then and the rest a week later. He remembered counting the cash in the corner of the room because Mondrian disliked the colour green. The master started a lengthy and elaborate packing procedure. This involved the canvas being wrapped in white paper with such perfection that it took Rhinegold several days to have the courage to unwrap it. He kept the paper for several years before the maid, mistaking it for rubbish, threw the wrapping out and her job with it.

A week later Rhinegold had contacted Mondrian's residence only to be told that the master had died that very morning. After the initial shock of hearing this sad news he remembered that he still held part payment for the painting. Rhinegold decided that he would take up the problem with the artist's dealer Peggy Guggenheim. Mondrian had complained on the first meeting that Guggenheim seemed so absorbed by the work of a young painter called Jackson Pollock that she had little time to represent him properly. Rhinegold himself had disapproved of her gallery ever since '42 when he'd seen a show where the paintings were hung on the ends of baseball bats and lit with lights that turned on and off every few seconds. He'd thought it sacrilege to treat art in this frivolous manner. Nevertheless, Rhinegold swallowed his prejudice and went down to the Art of this Century Gallery on Fifty-seventh Street to meet her. She sat at the front of her submarine-like gallery swathed in harsh fluorescent lighting. Her cold and distant manner vanished as she realised he was a serious collector. Before long she was trying to sell him the sub-Picasso paintings that hung on the wall. They were in fact the work of the artist Mondrian had been complaining about: Jackson Pollock. Rhinegold became more and more irritated until he stormed out of the gallery. Eventually he settled the matter with Harry Holtzman.

'Art, it's Leo on line one,' Beth informed Art over the intercom.
  'Hey Leo, how are you doing? What can I do for you?'
  'Art, I've got this great show coming up by an artist called Shume.'
  'Shume?'
  'Shume, John Shume. He's really great.'
  'What's the work?'
  'It's about design, you know.'
  'Design?'
  'Yeah, design, design and life and how our bodies are reflected in design. You got to see it. It's just terrific, Latchky bought five.'
  'Five!'
  'Yeah, Art. He was real excited.'

Elaine Yoon stationed herself just under a canopied Korean deli opposite Brigid Murphy's apartment building. She pointed her camera at the sliding blue-grey window situated on the tenth floor. Brigid's window turned a pale yellow as she turned on the light. In her room lay strewn clothes and shoes. Make-up, cream tubes and perfume bottles sprawled on the dressing table. An unmade bed suggested nights of fitful sleep. She yawned, looked

at her bedside clock, fell on the bed and shut her eyes. Outside and below
Elaine shut off her camera and waited. Brigid must've fallen asleep.

Given her restricted ability to walk long distances, Paige Quale decided to
compound the daily ten blocks prescribed by her surgeon after the accident, into visiting the Fifty-seventh Street galleries. It was about twelve
o'clock when she limped into the Levine show at the Mary Glades Gallery
on the eleventh floor of the Fuller Building. Levine happened to be an artist
whose elegant figurative paintings she admired, principally because they
were always being made into posters for her favourite clothing stores,
Calvin Klein and Armani; their slick manicured subjects, usually women,
fitting in well with the austere minimalist architecture and the soft angular
forms of the fashion. It was while she was looking at *Lulu IV* that an
alarmingly shrill voice resonated from the entrance of the gallery.

'And what about this artist?'

The reply was whispered and barely audible.

'How very interesting,' the shrill voice continued, 'and what would you
say these works represent?'

It was by overhearing conversations in galleries and falling in behind
tour groups in museums that Paige Quale had acquired her knowledge of
art. She was too vain and impatient to learn in the conventional manner.
Paige's attention was now concentrated on the response but again the voice
failed to gather sufficient momentum to reach her eager ears. She decided
to move closer to the entrance of the second gallery to gain visual contact
with the voices, and there, to the left of *Lulu V*, through the doorway and
looking at *Lulu II*, Paige saw the cone-shaped, vanilla-iced hair, spiralling
out of a white mink fur that cascaded like an ice floe, stopping an inch short
of the ground. Next to Mrs Rhinegold was a man with greased-back, black
hair who was wearing a bedraggled navy-blue coat. As the figures turned
towards her, she immediately recognised him as the Dillon lookalike from
Central Park six months earlier. Paige saw herself flush in the metal frame
of *Lulu V*. She quickly stepped out of their line of vision hoping to disguise
herself as a disinterested spectator. As Paige loitered at the entrance,
casually browsing over a few catalogues, she overheard the soft drone of

her idol informing his companion of their next port of call; the Art Spindle Gallery; four floors below.

Half an hour later Brigid was getting out of her bath. Steam poured from the white towel as she rubbed herself dry. The yellow window steamed over. Elaine raised her camera in time to catch a mottled shadow but no sooner had she done this than the shadow retreated. Elaine pinched the end of a Camel Light filter and drew it out of the packet, slightly dislodging the remaining firmly packed cigarettes. It was her second packet of the day. She turned her back against the breeze and bowed her head towards her illuminated cupped hands. Elaine inhaled deeply, then coughed violently and involuntarily towards the bright red apples that nestled in their violet paper tray outside the deli. The Korean grocer popped out of the shop and glared at her. Elaine switched on her video camera and turned it towards the unsuspecting shopkeeper.

'Yeah?' she questioned. Thinking Elaine was Korean, the grocer let out a flurry of his native language before retreating to serve a waiting customer. A few minutes later, seeing Elaine was still standing next to his apples, he came out again and continued his tirade. This is great street material, Elaine thought as she switched her camera back on, she could cut it with an opening or something.

The elevator door opened on to the foyer. 'The Art Spindle Gallery' was written across the frosted glass above the receptionist's desk marking the entrance of the gallery.

'This is a show of Tom Brane,' Jo murmured.

'And what is this all about?' his companion asked, as they were confronted by a large painting sagging under the weight of polystyrene, mannequin parts and baby dummies all encrusted with thick mottled paint. Jo peered discreetly at the label only to be confounded by the title: *Untitled*.

'Each component is a metaphor for, for ...' Jo began awkwardly.

'The environment?' Mrs Rhinegold cut in.

'Yes, well, I ...'

'Just like the Fraser show?' Mrs Rhinegold bellowed.

Jo cleared his throat and started a reply. 'Well, yes, ah.'

'I do think it is so important you know, the environment I mean,' she cut in again.

'Yes, it's the most important issue today I think,' Jo said with unusual certainty.

'You mean more than your art?'

'Well, ah …' Jo relapsed into uncertainty. 'My work does mean a lot to me.'

'More than the environment?' Mrs Rhinegold persisted.

'Yes, I suppose so,' Jo concluded, unconvinced.

'That's the problem, you see. Not with you because you're an artist and we need artists, but the environment will always take second place to man and second place is no place, is it?'

Mrs Rhinegold's high-pitched determination was beginning to arouse the curiosity of other viewers. Jo felt embarrassed. They moved on to a larger canvas sagging under even more debris.

'Ah, this is a delightful one,' she bellowed.

Paige hobbled to the safety of the Spindle Gallery counter. 'Hi, Beth,' she cooed.

Beth looked up and leaned back on her chair. 'Hey, Paige, up and about. How are ya? You look great,' she said without drawing breath.

'Oh, you know, okay I guess.'

Beth crossed her arms and asked, 'So, like, what's up?'

'Doing the galleries, you know,' Paige replied.

'Seen anything interesting?'

'Ah ha, I guess so.'

'Like what?'

'The Levine show. It's really great.'

'Oh yeah, I haven't seen it yet, like, I don't really go for Levine, you know.'

'Ah ha.'

Jo Richards looking like, totally smooth, accompanied by like, a divinely

*jewel-encrusted and totally-minked out lady, comes through the elevator
doors and Spindle is out there like, sliming across the room. So I'm, like,
craning my neck to hear what they're saying, you know, and who should
come in but 'Bitch' Quale.*

'So, what's it like working here?' Paige asked Beth.

'Paige, it's like the greatest, you know, like you meet like so many
interesting people, you know, like lots of artists and collectors and stuff.'
Beth's eyes turned towards the ceiling.

'Maybe I should work in a gallery,' Paige said.

'Paige, you would love it.'

'Ah ha.' Paige's eyes glazed over.

*I tell Paige I gotta work and she finally like, gets the message. So stupid. Like
now, you know, she wants a job in an art gallery. Can you believe that?*

'Jo, how are you?' Jo turned around to be confronted by Art Spindle.

'Art, ah, may I introduce you to Alfreda Rhinegold. This is Art Spindle.'
Jo gets out his longest sentence of the day.

'Mr Spindle, I am so enjoying the show.'

Spindle beamed. 'It's a pleasure to meet you, Mrs Rhinegold. Yes, he's
a great artist, don't you think?' he said, raising his hand to his forehead. A
moment of silence ensued as all three silently conjured up words for polite
but poignant opinions. Spindle cleared his throat and machine-gunned,
'We've been showing him for a number of years. Now he's getting more
involved with the texture of paint.' He paused, stroked his head and looked
at Mrs Rhinegold. 'We've had a great response to this show, just great. I've
got a great painting in my office.' Spindle was now leading Mrs Rhinegold
towards the back of the gallery and once he had manoeuvred them both
into a showroom he pressed the intercom and asked Beth to get Jack to
bring in the Branes.

'You're so kind,' Mrs Rhinegold said.

Spindle looked directly into Mrs Rhinegold's eyes. 'I always think it's important to show all the work there is to people who are genuinely interested.'

She smiled and replied, 'I see, well, Slavanamana used to just show one painting at a time.'

Spindle laughed. 'What a character he was.'

Jean Maclestone stormed out of the elevator towards the counter.

'Is Art in?' she asked abruptly.

'He's with a client right now, Mrs Maclestone,' Beth replied politely.

Jean scrutinised a translucent reflection of herself in the glass panelling behind the desk. 'Well, can you inform him that I'm here, please,' she demanded flatly.

Beth bit her lip nervously. This was going to be difficult. 'Mr Spindle told us not to disturb him.'

'Listen, honey, I think you will find that does not apply to me,' she said sharply.

'Yes, but like ...'

'Just get me Art Spindle, will you?!'

'But like, I was given like instructions, Mrs Maclestone ...'

Jean looked Beth in the eye and then marched around the desk. Beth stood at the mouth of the corridor watching Jean Maclestone's retreating figure stride purposefully towards the showrooms.

'Well, I think a painting of that importance would be worth a large amount of money. Off the top of my head it would be in the region of ...'

The door opened suddenly. All three were momentarily startled. 'Oh, Jean , urr ...' Art sprang up from his chair.

Without so much as a cursory acknowledgement towards anyone in the room, Jean demanded, 'Can I talk to you, Art?'

'Please urr, excuse me for urr, moment, urr, I urr, I will be back in a second,' Art faltered as he shuffled awkwardly out of the room.

'Mr Spindle seems very charming,' Mrs Rhinegold said. 'What do you think Alfred would do if I brought this painting home?' She pointed to the Brane in front of them.

'Well, I'm not ...'

'I think he would have a seizure, my dear.'

Jo laughed self-consciously. 'Yes, well, quite possibly ...'

Outside the showroom Jean flicked open her compact and padded her forehead. Art scratched the back of his head.

'Jean, I am in a very, very important meeting. I really don't appreciate this ...'

'Are we eating at Elaine's tonight?'

'Is that all you wanted to ask me? I mean Jesus Christ.'

Art walked back in and closed the door quietly behind him. 'I must apologise for the interruption.'

'Well, I'm sure you are very busy, Mr Spindle, we really should be on our way, do you not think, Joseph?'

'I ah ...' Jo began.

'Oh no,no, no,' Art implored. 'Another tea perhaps?'

'Well, that is most generous of you, but I must be getting back to my husband. You see, he is not very well and needs my constant attention ...'

When the old lady and Jo Richards go, like Art accompanies them to the door which he never like, normally does and I hear her name: Rhinegold. I look it up in the database, no Rhinegold, and then in the book, and there are like, at least thirty on the Upper East Side. She's like, definitely Upper East Side, you know what I mean? We got this like weird show on by an artist called Brane, right? Kinda like, environmental paintings. Art has sold them all as usual. The guy's a genius but like, the greatest is Anna Slant, she is so cool.

Art is not pleased. In fact he is like, really pissed off. He started shouting at me about letting Jean Maclestone in. I told him what happened. He said I should have been more assertive. I said I had told her several times. After a while he kinda calmed down. He was like, sweating real bad.

Art wiped his brow of the thin film of sweat which had developed over the last half hour. He could not believe Jean had walked in when she did. Beth should have told her in stronger terms. But on the other hand, Jean was kinda stubborn. Maybe he should get a new receptionist; like some big nigger with gold teeth. Spindle chuckled to himself, despite his fury about Mrs Rhinegold leaving.

'I love Matthew's new piece,' Jean was saying. 'Driver, go up Madison. It's so surreal and crazy. Hey, driver, I said Madison.'

'Eh,' the driver emitted.

'I said Madison, not Park, Jesus Christ. Oh forget it, just drive,' Jean said turning back to her friend Emille. 'What was I saying?'

'The Barney.'

'Driver you've just passed Park, what the hell are you doing?' Jean yelled.

The driver slammed on the brakes. Emille and Jean lurched forwards. 'You dun tark to mi lika thet,' he shouted back.

'What the hell was that?'

'Dun tark to mi lika thet,' he shouted again.

'I'll talk to you anyway I want, ass-hole. Come on, Emille, let's get out of here,' Jean said, trembling, but the doors were locked. 'Let us out now,' she shouted.

'Fi dollars,' the driver shouted back. Meanwhile a dozen or so cars had piled up behind them. The street echoed with the sound of horns.

'Jesus, fuck,' Jean said, as she put some dollar notes into the plastic drawer. She followed Emille out of the taxi and once she was on the pavement she stooped down and shouted, 'I'm taking your number, driver.' Slamming the door she added, 'Your job is on the line, baby.'

Brigid Murphy finally re-emerged out of her building. Elaine adjusted her brown leather bag over her shoulder and crossed the road, automatically measuring the distance between herself and her prey. It was a difficult job. A slow-down in pace or an outright stop meant a quick diversion was necessary. A clothes store or even a deli could provide adequate cover, but she could not very well window shop in front of CitiBank or a funeral parlour. Over the last few months Elaine had had to have her wits about her. She had a constant awareness not only of her subject but of everything around her.

Brigid hesitated in front of a Betsy Johnson outlet on Eighty-fourth and Madison. Elaine turned towards a bookstore and pretended to look at the flowerpot stand which was now shelving for one-dollar books. Out of the corner of her eye she saw Brigid slipping into the store. She then angled herself so that from a distance of thirty or so feet she had a view of a rack of the clothes in one part of the shop. In Elaine's viewfinder there were broken reflections of the murky, milky interior and flashing, fleeting figures and cars outside. Brigid occasionally appeared in shot as if trapped between all these forms. A décolleté gold dress had drawn her attention. Although one hundred and seventy dollars was outside Brigid's budget, she nevertheless slipped into it and, holding her breath, twirled in front of the mirror. The gold sparkled under the spotlight and her figure held firmly within. Without further hesitation she bought the dress. 'We only live once,' she muttered, handing over her Visa card.

Elaine had accumulated a huge variety of flea-market clothes which she used as camouflage. Sometimes she changed three times in the course of one day's detective work. She now removed her baseball cap and replaced it with an off-white wool hat with ear flaps. The reversible army jacket turned from jungle green to desert-storm beige. As she manoeuvred her clothes around she held her camera between her knees and clasped her baseball cap in her teeth. At the same time she kept a sharp look out on the store entrance. Brigid came out and walked down Madison, eventually crossing the street on Seventy-ninth.

Across the road, Emille de Grey and Jean Maclestone sat opposite each other in Luigi's. Emille, who was Jean's childhood friend, wore a pleated, black Issey Miyake two-piece ensemble, which made her look like a character out of *Babylon 5*.

'How are the kids, Jean?' she asked, picking up the menu.

'Ernie is setting up an art editions web site. It is such a great idea,' Jean replied.

'A web site, Jean?' Emille queried.

'You know the internet, Emille?'

'Oh Jean, everybody's talking about it, but I just don't get it.'

'It's very simple. You plug your computer into the telephone and then there's all this information you can get.' She looked sharply across the room to where the waitress was chatting with the barman and started waving her arm. 'Jesus Christ,' she muttered.

'It's that simple?' Emille asked. Jean stopped waving when eventually the barman noticed and pointed her out to the young waitress.

'It's that simple, Emille. Honestly, I don't know what all the fuss is about,' she replied impatiently.

As far as Elaine was concerned buses were the most dangerous form of transport. Firstly, lines were a problem, but once on the bus all sorts of other problems arose, like if a group of disabled or Japanese tourists were to come aboard, and Elaine, for want of space, was pushed into Brigid's orbit, or if the groups were already on the bus and they got off at the same time leaving them alone. Confined spaces were precarious; Elaine was afraid of being recognised – not because she thought Brigid would realise she'd been followed but because it would make her project that much more difficult. A second sighting would probably give the game away.

'Alfred, my dear, why don't we buy some contemporary art?' Alfreda Rhinegold chirped enthusiastically. Mr Rhinegold lifted his head which had been hanging precariously close to his soup and glared disdainfully across at his wife.

'I think it would be rather jolly, don't you?' she continued. 'I mean, we haven't bought for years, darling.'

A spoon of soup hovered near Rhinegold's open mouth. 'Vith vat?' he asked incredulously.

'Well my dear, we could sell a painting,' she said, so quickly that Rhinegold couldn't quite catch the latter part of the sentence.

'Sell, sell vat?'

Alfreda pressed the button for Freign. 'A painting, Alfred.'

Rhinegold dropped his spoon on his side plate, making a loud clatter.

'A painting,' he growled as Freign entered the room. 'Vat painting?' he asked, softening his tone.

Freign hovered over Mrs Rhinegold waiting for some kind of instruction which she seemed to be deliberately keeping from him. Freign, knowing that he had a restraining effect on the old man's temper, knew also that his presence was a necessary condition to the discussion of any difficult subject. This was as much a medical precaution as anything else.

'As a matter of fact, I thought the painting you gave me,' she replied, daintily wiping her lips.

Rhinegold visibly changed colour and clasped the arms of his wheelchair. 'Ze, ze,' he gave out a series of shallow breaths, 'Mondrian,' he finally wheezed.

'Well, I think these days it would fetch a tidy sum, Alfred. Just think what fun we could have visiting all those galleries filled with all this new art, it would be like the old days. You would adore it. I've been reading all about conceptual art and it is absolutely fascinating. I think it would be ...'

'Sell ze Mondrian!' Rhinegold repeated as he wheeled himself to the window. 'I have had ze painting for vorty, vifty years, vifty years it hadz been un ze vall, I paid der master himself, and now you vant to zell.' He paused and brought his fist down on the leather arm. 'It is a masterverk, Alfreda.'

Although Spindle felt he had an unspoken understanding when it came to his relationship with Jean, he could not help but sense that there was always an underlying hostility there. Bob Maclestone, on the other hand, accepted Spindle's relationship with his wife as it gave him the security of a domestic life as well as the freedom to have his own gratifying but inconsequential affairs. It also gave him the upper hand in his business dealings with Spindle, who would always give him first choice as well as large discounts on important purchases. The advantages for Spindle were that he had both a large slice of the deals with one of New York's most prominent collectors and also an introduction to the younger contemporary world which Maclestone made it his business to keep up with. This in turn gave Spindle the opportunity to make early, lucrative investments and to keep pace with his downtown colleagues.

'Bob, this Mondrian is a great modern masterpiece. Probably the last of its kind in a private collection,' Art said, pouring Bob Maclestone a glass of Chardonnay at Luigi's. Bob fingered his chin and looked at the waitress who was gliding towards him. He could time this right, he thought to himself. 'How much, Art?' he asked, anticipating her arrival. As the waitress neared their table she bent over and picked up a napkin. 'Around eight million,' Art said, stroking his head. Missed. Bob, determined to have another cast, hesitated until the waitress had approached the table and repeated, 'How much was that?'

'Eight million,' Art replied, looking down at the menu.

'Are you ready to order, gentlemen?' the waitress asked with a smile.

The woman on the bus was probably in her early forties, thin and gaunt with black, greasy hair and a pale yellow face. One of her front teeth was missing, her lips creased in a deformed grimace. She stared at Elaine, who upon seeing her out of the corner of her eye, pretended not to notice her.

'Hey you!' the woman suddenly barked. Elaine continued to take no notice and turned her face towards the window.

'I'm talkin' to you, miss.' She nudged Elaine on the shoulder. Elaine turned around and looked at the menacing woman. 'Yeah you, I'm addressing you, bitch.' Some passengers began turning their heads, putting down their newspapers and stopping their conversations. Brigid recognised Elaine immediately. Brigid looked away quickly and bit her lip.

'Lay off, honey,' Elaine said to the crazy woman.

'Don't honey me, you fuckin' bitch. Just because you're fuckin' Chinese doesn't fuckin' mean you can look at me like that, right, right?' The woman squinted and then poked Elaine with her index finger. 'So, you killed any Buddhists lately, eh?' she whined sarcastically.

Elaine knew the game was up for today, Brigid had seen her; she could feel her tension from the other end of the bus and, although a chance meeting would have been a perfect way to reestablish a dialogue, her main motivating concern was with the video.

'Well, did you kill them, Chink?'

'I'll tell you some day, lady.' The bus stopped and Elaine pushed her way out of the door.

'So Art, are you going after Sch-Schneider?' Bob Maclestone asked.

'I think he's a great artist and we've always had a good relationship. Maybe. What do you think, Bob?'

'You should go for it. He's s-s-solid, good prices. No, I think he would fit in well with the gallery.'

'Yeah, I think you're right, Bob. Do you think you could talk to him one of these days? It's always good coming from a collector, you know what I mean?'

'Sure, Art, I think Jean's invited him to d-dinner next week,' he said. 'That girl's kinda s-sexy.' Maclestone changed the subject and pointed to a red-headed number sitting down at the bar of the restaurant.

Brigid had only been at Luigi's for a few minutes and already several customers were making furtive glances in her direction. She was suddenly aware that she was being seen as single. Prey. It was just a matter of time before one of them was going to sidle up to her and deliver some slippery comment or two.

'Did you hear that the Glades Gallery wants to take on Schneider?' Emille de Grey said urgently.

Jean Maclestone leaned forward. 'Mary Glades, no way, that's a rumour.'

'Well, Dannini told me.'

'Dannini told you?'

'Yeah, he said Glades offered Schneider five hundred thousand dollars,' Emille said.

Jean looked quite put out. 'Five hundred thousand?'

'Half a million dollars,' Emille confirmed triumphantly.

'I'm sure Art will offer more.' Jean Maclestone looked up at the waitress.

'I'll have a macchiato.'

'Macchai ...'

'A macchiato,' she repeated irritably.

'I don't thin ...'

Jean interrupted her quickly. 'Listen, honey, I have a macchiato here every other day, right.'

'Is not ...'

'Get me the maître d'.'

The waitress turned red and swung away from the table.

'They come to this country and can't speak the language. I mean, how many taxi drivers know where Prince Street is?' Emille de Grey said in a loud whisper. Jean sipped her Perrier and shot a glance at the counter where the waitress was talking to the maître d'. 'It's such a bore when they change personnel. One has to be nice all over again until they get used to one.'

'Jacques was so great, you remember Jacques, Jeannie?'

'Of course I remember Jacques. I wonder what happened to him?'

'Alphonse told me he was opening a restaurant downtown.'

'Alphonse told you that?' Jean said, sounding pained. The maître d' was now hovering behind Mrs Maclestone, waiting for a break in the crossfire. Perceiving a pause, he stooped a little and delivered in a silvery Italian accent, 'Signora Maclestoo, I sorry but eee waitress first day and no understand.'

'Oh Alphonse, I wanted a macchiato.'

'A macchiato, of cor, signora.'

'Oh Alphonse, you didn't tell me Jacques was opening a restaurant,' Jean said sternly, shaking her head from side to side.

'May or maybe na, you know hee mama give money and ee find a place or maybe in Trenton.'

'Trenton!' Emille exclaimed. 'I thought you said downtown?'

'Veri expensive and he no much money, but he has uncle in Jersey might givee you know, but he clever he ...'

'Well, thank you, Alphonse. I'll have that macchiato now,' Mrs Maclestone interrupted, perceiving that Alphonse was about to entrench himself at their table, and just to make sure he got the message, she ruthlessly changed the subject. 'Bob bought the greatest piece yesterday.'

'He did?'

'Either they talk too much or not at all,' Jean said as she followed Alphonse gliding away between the tables towards the espresso machine. *'Uno macchiato po cinqo,'* she heard him say.

Spindle looked at his watch and moved uneasily in his chair.

'I have an appointment at the gallery, Bob. I'll pick up the tab, okay?'

'No, I'll do it, Art.'

'No, I insist. I'm sure you paid last time.'

'No, no, no. This is on me, Art.'

'Okay, Bob, thank you. So I'll see you next week?' Art said, putting his hands on the arms of his chair and leaning forward. Bob was looking over at the bar and wiped the side of his mouth with his napkin. 'I think I might have a coffee at the b-bar,' he said.

'Okay, Bob, and if I get an image I'll ring you.'

'You do that.'

Elaine drew herself up on a bar stool. She became aware that she was in a room full of lemons. One small lemon and an orange sat seductively on a white plate, below a bottle of red wine, against a lime-green background. Two sides of a lemon on a chopping board. Several lemons nestled among the folds of a light blue table-cloth as if they had been lazily thrown on to an irregular surface in Morocco. A very large lemon was painted at close range. A tree laden with ripe lemons luxuriantly hanging against a sumptuous deep red background. An unripe lemon, looking suspiciously like a lime, balanced precariously on a shelf against a cold white background. She was in the Lemon Bar on Sixty-third and Third. It was two forty-five.

'You want another drink, lady?' a voice broke in.

'Yeah, I'll take a Bud.'

'Right.'

Of obvious Irish descent, the barman, a large man with a round face, looked as if he could either love you or kill you. He had blue watery eyes and light reddish hair, and strode up and down behind the counter like a rugged quartermaster. Elaine got off from the stool and almost disappeared from view. She dug into her jeans and drew out a wad of well-used dollar bills, which she threw on to the counter before hauling herself back on to the barstool.

'You got nuts or something?' she inquired aggressively, as the barman picked up the crumpled notes. He made another journey down the bar, returning with a small plate of peanuts which he slid disdainfully towards her.

'Thanks,' Elaine sneered.

Bob Maclestone sat down a couple of stools away from the attractive redhead and ordered a cappuccino. He proceeded to search through the spirit bottles against the mirrored wall behind the bar until he found Brigid Murphy's reflection between the Baileys Cream and advocaat bottles. She was probably Californian or Floridian, he guessed. She wore a white shirt and tight-fitting blue jeans. Bob noticed the amount of rouge that clung to her cheekbones and, glancing down, the fashionable vamp nail varnish on her fingernails and the cheap-looking rings clamped around her fingers. A crucifix swayed gently away from her chest as she leaned forward to suck from a straw. He presumed that she was waiting for someone from the way she occasionally glanced at the door and consulted the clock above the bar. Then again, the fact that she was eating alone suggested otherwise. He also sensed a certain anxiety besetting her each time she heard the thump and brush of the revolving doors. Perhaps this was his chance to stir up some kind of conversation.

Brigid felt the man's eyes boring into her. She had already noticed that he was middle-aged and rather corpulent. She knew he was going to start talking and decided to look as if she was waiting for a friend. With any luck this tactic could deter him from making an approach. Brigid did not feel like a conversation.

It was now or never. Bob Maclestone mulled over several different forms of approach. While on duty in 'Nam his colleagues had taught him a variety of direct but seductive conversation starters, but as he'd grown older these seemed to be less appropriate. The bravado, the cocky, flirtatious hustle should now be replaced by a more gentle and sophisticated approach.

'Hey, haven't I seen you before?' the rotund character sitting a few seats along to her right finally managed.

'Jaysus Christ,' Brigid muttered to herself, and turning towards the man she replied brusquely, 'No.'

'This is my, ah, my local, I come here sometimes for lunch or l-like a drink. I'm sorry, I thought you must have been here before,' Bob said, reddening as the words were slowly delivered.

'Oh.'

'Yeah I-I ah, I like it here.'

'Right.'

'Can I ah, can I buy you a drink?'

'That's very kind of ya but I'm okay. Tanks.'

'Ah you from ah Ca-Canada?'

'Ireland.'

'Right. Ah, Ireland, right. Where ah, where?'

'Dublin,' Brigid cut in sharply.

'Dublin, that ah, that ah, in ah …'

Dolores Ballesteros plugged the sink, reached for the dish-washing liquid, squirted some into the basin where it landed in the form of a thin green worm, and turned on the hot water. She added cold until satisfied that the temperature was even but hot enough for the dishes. She filled the right basin with cold water. The Rhinegolds did have a dishwasher but these were hand-painted Meissen plates that could only be washed by hand. Before she could slip all the plates into the hot water, the two wine glasses had to be carefully washed and rinsed. Dolores drew each plate up out of the water and wiped them with a sponge. The Rhinegolds had only had soup to start, with salad and ham for their main course, so the plates were not too dirty and the salad oil came off easily in the soapy water. Mr Rhinegold's side plate was another matter; the camembert had dried and adhered so stubbornly that Dolores had to use the bristly side of the sponge to remove it. Coffee cups came next, posing no difficulty at all. The dishes were placed in the rack and by the time she had finished she was pleased to find the glasses and plates were almost dry, requiring only a brisk wipe before being put away.

The washing-up completed, Dolores tugged at the fingers of the yellow plastic gloves until she had enough of the material to grip on to and pulled them off. She then placed them, together with the Joy, under the basin where she took the opportunity to take out the Pledge can. Having armed herself with this product and a spanking new cloth, bought by Freign the day before, she made for the dining-room. After making sure that all the crumbs were removed from the mahogany table, she sprayed the wood with polish and burnished until her blurred reflection became visible.

Paige Quale lay on the sofa in front of the television watching the Jerry Springer show. Some guy had had an affair with his mother and was complaining that she'd raped him. She drifted into a fantasy in which Jo Richards burst through her apartment door. He tore her clothes off and kissed her passionately. His hands were caressing her naked body. Paige took her clothes off and positioned herself in front of the mirror. She stroked herself all over until her nipples were hard. Matt Dillon was fervently sucking at her breasts. She could feel his hands sliding up her legs. Jo kissed her passionately. She went down on her knees and began sucking Jo off. Meanwhile Matt took her from behind. Paige lay on the carpet in front of the mirror with her legs wide open. Now Jo was down on her and she had Matt in her mouth. Paige inserted two fingers inside herself with one hand and pinched her nipple hard with the other. As she was about to come the phone rang.

When Jo Richards got home he rang Art who was out at lunch. He lay back on his bed with a pencil in his mouth and with one foot relieved the other of his black slip-on shoe, then he repeated the process with his other foot.

Elaine crunched at the last of her iceberg lettuce and tomato salad. Her fork dangled over her plate while her right hand was controlling the video camera. She was mentally editing her morning's work. So far the voice recordings of the Korean and the Johnson store were the only things worth keeping.

'Coffee?' the Irish man grunted.

'Yeah,' Elaine replied without looking at him.

Paige lay on the sofa half-listening to her father on the phone. 'Your mother and I are both concerned that you haven't found a job yet,' he growled. Paige held the cordless phone in one hand and played with herself with the other. 'I went for an interview today, Daddy,' she whined.

'What kinda job?' Mr Quale asked.

'Like it's for an art gallery receptionist on Fifty-seventh Street. It's a cool job. I really want this one, Daddy,' Paige replied enthusiastically.

'How did it go, angel?' Daddy's voice softened.

'Okay, I guess. I feel real optimistic about it.'

'That sounds promising, honey. So, what else are you doing with yourself in the Big Apple?'

'This and that, I'm going to museums a lot and baking cakes for this coffee shop on Fifty-third, you know, and, oh Daddy, can you hold a second?'

'Sure, honey.'

Paige pressed the hold button and turning the portable over on to its smooth side, she placed it between her legs and slid the device back and forth. Her breathing quickened before turning into a flurry of sighs. Her body jerked forwards. Paige gave out a muffled cry after which she removed the hand-set from between her legs.

'That was the gallery, Daddy. They want to see me again.'

Brigid wrote her number on a match box the barman had given her earlier.

'It's been nice to meet ya, Bob,' she said.

'I'm going to hold to my promise,' Maclestone said, getting up from the stool. 'I'm sorry about ah, your friend standing you up.'

'It's no big deal as you's Americans say,' Brigid replied, putting her coat on. 'I'll get over it.'

Seeing Elaine on the bus had brought back memories which she'd sooner forget but she couldn't deny there was also a part of her that had wanted to meet her, to somehow exorcise the ghost which haunted her every so often. Now the ghost loomed larger than ever.

Jean patted her lips delicately. 'We're having a down period, you know, Emille? Bob is kinda distracted, I don't know, maybe he's having an affair?'

Emille gave a concerned frown. 'You think so, Jean?'

'We're arguing a lot, no sex, a lot of business trips, you know that kinda thing.'

'Gees, that's a bad sign,' Emille said, sipping her coffee.

Jean stiffened noticeably. 'What do you mean, Emille?'

Emille took up a bedside-manner expression; the head slightly tilted to one side with a kind of benign smile. She leaned over and took Jean's hand which lay on the table half-holding her coffee cup. 'That was the beginning of the end for Roger and I,' she said, looking into her eyes. 'Of course, it went on like that for years, but you know, Jean, it was a bit like flogging a dead horse. I knew there was another woman, of course.'

'You did?'

'There were all the tell-tale signs: the old perfume, a faintly acrid but distinct smell of another person's skin, the very-good-wine breath, and then later, after having hired a P. I., I discovered that Roger's business trips were not the kinda business I thought they were. You know what I mean? He'd come back from Dusseldorf with a tan having failed to get the Toyota ad, that kinda thing.'

'Men are such lousy liars,' Jean smirked, looking out of the window. 'Bob keeps coming back smelling of stale smoke, and we know how he feels about smoke.'

'So, what's his excuse?'

'In a bar with some artist or dealer or something.'

'Oh my dear,' Emille sighed.

CHAPTER THREE

AFTERNOON, THREE
MONTHS BACK

The sun on this icy day had not managed to thaw the frozen stalactites that hung majestically from the air-conditioning units clamped along the backs of buildings. There had been a mini-heatwave the week before, but today a cold snap had left a thin layer of snow on the steel-grey pavements.

Rachel wore a green woolly hat, matching mittens and a dark grey overcoat the sleeves of which, it having been a man's coat, were rolled up to her elbows. Elaine wore khaki pants and a black leather jacket. Both had galoshes over their sneakers. 'I've been doing this really weird piece,' Elaine said, as they walked across Third and up Lafayette. 'Oh yeah?' inquired Rachel, squinting as the sun momentarily lit her face.

'Yeah, it's kinda like, collage with video, right.'

'Right.'

'I shoot real personal things and then like, other stuff.'

'Right.'

'Then I'm gonna de-structuralise it and kinda put it together again so things are like, juxtaposed against each other.'

'You mean everything is all jumbled up?'

'Umm, yeah, kinda like, it like makes sense, but then it doesn't, you know what I mean?'

'Yeah, kinda.'

Half a block away a black mass hit the ground with deadening force followed by an echo like the crack of a circus whip. A lifeless body lay on the ground. 'Oh my God!' Elaine exclaimed. 'Gaad!' Rachel followed suit.

'Is that like, weird?'

'Maybe we should cross over.'

'Yeah, I am like totally freaked.'

'Do you think that was a wipe-out?'

'Totally.'

'Jesus H Christ!'

'That is totally, totally weird.'

'Fuck, fuck.' Rachel's throat had tightened and her words were high pitched.

Elaine removed the camera from her satchel and began shooting.

'Elaine!' Rachel exclaimed.

'What?' Elaine asked as she moved towards the body with the camera firmly in her eye socket. She began bending down as she approached the body.

'Jesus, Elaine, let's get out of here. I don't fucking believe you're doing this. Elaine, let's not get involved for Christ's sake, come on. Jesus fuck.'

'Relax, man,' Elaine said, retreating back towards Rachel who was holding her pudgy white hands up to her face.

'I don't believe you just did that.'

As they started to cross the street, Elaine asked Rachel whether she wanted a coffee.

'I gotta get to a tutorial, Elaine.'

'Who you got?'

'Tom Tiller.'

'Oh well, I guess it could be worse.'

'He's okay I guess.'

'Did you see his show at Freedman's?'

'Yeah, kinda bla.'

'Yeah, kinda whatever.'

'Like Koons, you know, but like ten years later.'

'I'm always like, falling asleep at his lectures.'

'Yeah, he kinda like, drones on and on and on,' Elaine said as she pushed against the doors of the Cooper Union Building. 'And on and on and on,' Rachel added, in a low monotone voice. They both laughed as the doors swung back behind them.

'Is there any coffee, Mrs Ballesteros?' Freign asked mournfully.

He delicately wiped from his mouth the residues of his lunch – the apple pie had been particularly crusty – and looked across the kitchen to where Dolores' figure was slung obtusely over the sink. The insistent clinking of china fused with a hummed flamenco ditty.

'Si, si una minutas,' she replied, putting a saucepan onto the draining board. Whilst doing so she inadvertently juxtaposed the pan against another in such a way that the combination of weight and angle caused it to slip back into the sink. A loud clanging noise ensued. Dolores swore under her breath and retrieving the offending pan placed it more strategically. Having wiped her hands on her apron she filled the kettle with Evian water.

As he watched Dolores juggle with the coffee preparations, Freign's mind drifted back to the liberation of Paris in 1945 when, after entering Paris with his battalion, he had gone directly to the Louvre. Freign was proud to have been the first soldier in post-occupied France to visit the museum. How well he could remember marching through the great rooms and seeing the paintings that would change his life for ever: Géricault's *Raft*, the Rembrandts, Latours, and in particular, the Impressionist pictures which had been such a revelation; such an inspiration. On his way out he had caught an American G I removing a Flemish landscape from the wall. Freign had apprehended him and reported the soldier to his commanding officer. It was of great embarrassment to the victorious Allies but was soon forgotten amongst the festivities. The French government had quietly decorated him with the *légion d'honneur*; an honour that could be identified on the recipient by a subtle red ribbon worn on the lapel, but which was now confused with a similar ribbon worn by Aids sympathisers. A voice snaked itself into his consciousness, 'Café, Roberto?'

Dewey walked into the the Emmert Gallery. Five large paintings of body parts hung in a rectangular room. He picked up the press release.

'These paintings depict various parts of the human body isolated from their usual context and presented on a grand, iconic scale. They are

cropped and stylised images that concentrate on a particular feature. They
deny biographical potential and guarantee the subject's anonymity.'

Dewey slipped the press release into his briefcase and smiled flirtatiously
at the boy behind the desk. ''Bye-bye,' he called out.

Elaine would spend at least three hours editing every day at Cooper Union,
carefully joining the personal with the impersonal, the trite with the
serious, the violent with the poetic, weaving aspects of her own life with
aspects of the lives of those who filtered in and out of her life. What was
interesting to her was the way the meaning of the footage altered as she
dissected and juxtaposed it. Though she was the voyeur, the video was
autobiographical – a self-portrait almost. Elaine felt she was a spider in a
web.

Jo Richards stared out of the window of his Eighteenth Street loft. Each
piece he had conceptualised failed in its conclusion. They were either too
obvious, too vague or, in the case of those that worked, too dull, uninspir-
ing and commonplace. He entwined his hands behind the back of his neck
and, leaning back, tipped his chair on its hind legs. Art, he asked himself,
did it really mean anything in the real world? In the great scheme of things?
Or was it just self-indulgent crap?

Perhaps he been deluding himself all these years. Years spent conceptu-
alising what was real to create a metaphor for what was essential. 'From
the ore every minute take the gold from within it,' he quoted under his
breath. Alchemy using human blood, yes well, that was rather interesting
– blood, alchemy, essence, something could evolve here.

Dewey read the press release as he circled the gallery: 'These photographs
are extraordinary images created by the juxtapositioning of earthy images
and the brilliant coloration of man-made objects. Habankano has created
images, by manipulating, not contriving, social situation with unreal,
almost Surreal symbolism. His direct yet elusive approach gives these
photographs an intensely vibrant quality.' He furtively slipped it into his
leather briefcase.

Beth walked down down Fifth Avenue. *Is this crazy or what!? Like, I'm gorgeous. Gone is the nose, gone is the turkey chin, my buttocks are like, buttocks, and my tits are just to die for. I could do with like, a couple of extra inches, I guess. The bruising is clearing up, but you can still see a scar from the bridge of my nose down, but the ones below the nipples and like, on my buttocks are still real bad. (Don't have to show those quite yet.) I got to tell you it hurt. Like a rattlesnake has, like, bitten you in twenty different places. It was real bad for a week or so, and now it just kinda like, throbs.*

Even if I say so myself, I look kinda hot. I've lost like, twenty pounds, in like three months, not bad, right? I'm beginning to get some great vibes. Dad was real pissed. He said I looked like a cheerleader from Saskatchewan; 'all tits and ass,' like, is that an insult, or what? I guess for him it was both. Men are hypocrites. Mom didn't 'approve' before like, the operation, but since seeing the results, you know, she thinks it's totally great. I got Art to hire the 'Bitch' Quale. She's okay I guess.

Elaine had gotten great footage of Brigid at the hospital. She had managed to persuade a girl who was visiting her boyfriend in the ward where Brigid worked, to film her as she went about her duties.

There were shots of Brigid making a bed, looking at charts and talking to patients. It was the first time she'd got some vocals from her. Elaine had also got Cathy Steed to go down on her the night before. Elaine downloaded her rushes on to the school's Avid hard drive.

Paige Quale picked up her nail-file only to put it down again. 'The Spindle Gallery. Mr Spindle is very busy this week, but I'm sure if you send them in, ah ha. Mr Spindle always looks at transparencies. Who? No, he's very busy. Paige Quale, no, Quale. Q.U.A.L.E. Quale. You got it. I will make sure he sees them. Ben Toone. Ah ha. Yeah, I understand. Yes, Mr Toone. Ah ha. Of course. 'Bye, Mr Toone.' She put the phone down. 'Sucker,' she said, resuming her nail filing with quick, measured strokes.

'The Spindle Gallery. Hold on please. The Spindle Gallery. He's on another call, will you hold? Gladys Simms, yeah, I'll tell him. The Spindle

Gallery. I'll just put you through. Yes, we are. The gallery is showing Lawrence Walker. Ah ha. No, we're open till six o'clock. No problem. 'Bye-bye.'

Art Spindle held the receiver with one hand and scribbled something on to his note-pad with the other. Then, swivelling his chair so that it faced the Madison Avenue traffic, he grunted under his breath.

'I got this great-looking gal working for me. You know, she wears those real tight slinky dresses. Great butt, Jesus, what a body, Leo. You gotta come and check this one out.'

'Art, you're terrible!'

'You gotta have a good-looking chick at that reception, Leo. It pulls in the clients. Maclestone's in here every other day. He's crazy about her. Last week I sold him two Walkers.'

'So, what happened to that girl, ah, ah, what's her name?'

'You mean Beth Freemantle? I was going to fire her but she beat me to it, she resigned.' Spindle gave out a kind of cough-laugh, heartily accompanied by Leo.

'By the way, Art, have you heard about this boy, David Warburg?'

'You mean that young English collector?'

'No, no, he's an artist.'

'Oh yeah?'

'Yeah, he's got a show downtown at Sam's.'

'What's the show, Leo?'

'Well, Art, he does these ducks.'

'Ducks?'

'Yeah, ducks.'

'Weird.'

'Yeah, real weird show, Art. They're kinda all over the shop, like on the floor, on chairs, stuck on the ceiling, you know.'

'Real ducks?'

'No, wooden ones.'

'You mean like, ah, ah, what are they called?'

'Err.'

'Shit.'

'Decoys?'

'Yeah, decoys. So is it an installation or are they individual?'

'It's a piece, Art, you got to buy the whole goddamn lot.'

'How many?'

'About fifty.'

'Fifty ducks, gee, that's a lot of ducks.'

'Fuck of a lot of ducks, Art. Don't you think it's up Maclestone's street?'

'I don't think Jean likes ducks.'

'Ah well, fuck the ducks.'

'Yeah, fuck them.'

Between downloading her latest rushes, Elaine reviewed some cuts on the hard drive. Brigid on the corner of Lexington and Eighty-sixth Street waiting to cross the road. A man begins talking to her and continues to do so as they cross the street and walk up Eighty-sixth towards the park. Brigid is clearly trying to shake him off but the man sticks to her until she's forced to hail a cab.

The video cut to Brigid singing to herself while looking at a book on Tuscan gardens in Barnes and Noble. Cut to an opening of Uki Massuri at the Barbara Repo Gallery.

Brigid frequents a bar on Houston called Melones. Elaine rewinds the shots of her slowly getting drunk with all her Irish friends. She had such a cute smile.

Dewey Bozo coughed politely. Paige looked up from her computer.

'Can I help you?' she asked.

'Could I see Mr Spindle, please?' Dewey asked.

'I'm sorry, sir, he's with clients right now, would you like to wait?'

'Okay, I'll wait. Have you got a press release for this show?' he asked politely.

The phone rang, 'Sure.' Paige handed him a plastic folder while picking up the telephone. 'The Spindle Gallery. Mr Spindle is in a meeting right now. Can I take a message?'

Dewey sat in the foyer of the Spindle Gallery and read the press release. '*Sexual revolutions* is a feminist, revisionist history of a revolution that was fought at cocktail parties. These mixed media works are constructed family snapshots, framed – literally and figuratively – within the texts of the 1960s and 1970s sex manuals and feminist manifestos. The works contrast the middle-class, urban bias of these texts with the realities faced by working-class, rural women.'

In a basement showroom at the Barbara Repo Gallery Bob Maclestone and Repo stood in front of Ray King's new work. Although Maclestone was not tall, standing at five feet nine, he towered over Barbara Repo whose diminutive, skeletal frame hovered nervously beside him. 'It's an amazing new departure, don't you think? He always wanted to paint and now he's done it,' she commented. 'It's so great.'

'Yeah, gr-great development.' As Bob Maclestone nodded in agreement the few twisting white hairs which had been liberated from the pomaded curls glistened under the harsh gallery lights.

'People are crazy about them!' Barbara exclaimed, with startling passion accompanied by a firm yet uncoordinated fist action; a sort of dig into the air from the hip.

'Really, ah right, well how much, ah, how much are you, ah, asking for them?'

'Well, we're asking twenty thousand dollars for the large ones and twelve thousand dollars for the smaller ones,' she replied. 'But this one here has been reserved by the Modern,' she added, pointing at a confused mass of lines and boxes at the bottom half of a white canvas.

'I kinda l-like this one,' Maclestone said, pointing to an almost identical picture.

'Yes, I like this one too. I don't know why they chose that one,' she said with a perplexed look.

Maclestone's consumerist passion had altered his bored, melancholic expression into one of hawkish concentration. 'But maybe this one over here, yeah, this one, just great.'

'Yeah, that's a great painting. That's my favourite,' she said approvingly.

Maclestone left the Repo Gallery satisfied that he had bought the best painting.

Brigid doubles back into Agustino's; she must've forgotten something.

Since leaving Slant, Ivor Schneider had had offers from Barbara Repo, Mary Glades, Paul Dannini and Art Spindle. He was biding his time and playing one off against the other. Jean and Bob Maclestone had been early collectors of his work and continued to buy the occasional painting. However, the real purpose of Jean's visit was not as collector but as ambassador for Spindle, who wanted Jean to persuade Schneider to show at his gallery.

Schneider knew this and Jean knew that Ivor knew.

Schneider was wearing a sarong, a tank-top and cowboy boots. His hair was tangled, his voice broken and languid; as if he had just arisen from a deep slumber. He was talking about an episode of *The Simpsons* he'd seen the night before and equating its significance with his relationship with the Anna Slant Gallery, whose stable he had left a few months before. Jean Maclestone was in his studio ostensibly to view the new work.

'So you see, Slant is to the Art World what Homer Simpson is to the nuclear power industry.' Jean accompanied Ivor's jocular remark with a knowing chuckle.

'I'm real happy with this one,' he said, sliding a canvas across the room and leaning it against the wall. Jean held her hand to her neck and gasped. 'Ivor, oh Ivor, it's just, it's just superb,' she stammered. There was a reverential silence before Schneider inhaled his cigarette deeply and blew the tar stripped smoke towards the ceiling. 'They'd kinda look great at Repo's in that big space, don't you think, Jean?'

'Ivor, that ...' She paused. 'That is such a great painting,' she replied, oblivious to his last remark. 'So great, you know, I think ...' She paused. 'You know, I think Art should have a look at this.'

'You think so, Jean? I don't know, maybe, maybe. I'm showing it in May at the Delraye Gallery in Paris.'

'The Delraye Gallery?' Jean questioned.

'Yeah, he's this great guy I met at a Gagosian opening a couple of months back. We had a crazy night – went on till six in the morning. Jesus, I tell you,' he stroked his hair and blew his cheeks out, 'one not to forget.'

'What kinda gallery, Ivor?'

Schneider dragged powerfully from the butt end of his cigarette which he held between thumb and index finger and cupped in the palm of his hand. 'I'll show you a couple of catalogues,' he said, flicking the cigarette on to the floor and grinding it out with the heel of his boot. Skirting the shelves of art books, he eventually pulled out two slim catalogues. One was for a show of Balthus and the other for late Picasso.

'Isn't this Balthus at the Met?' Jean frowned.

'Yeah, he must have gotten a loan.'

One night Elaine filmed Brigid coming home with a tall, black-haired man. The man stubs the cigarette out on the pavement outside the main door. (Elaine had kept the butt.)

'Jay, it's Art Spindle.'

'My dear man, are you in town?'

'No, I'm in New York.'

'So how's it going over there?'

'Mustn't grumble. Preparing for Cologne.'

'Listen, Art, I'm so glad that you called, I have a marvellous new piece by Hirst which I thought would fit perfectly into your collection. Not for resale, old boy.'

'I've got a couple of pieces of his already, Jay.'

'Indeed you have, and two exceptional pieces they are, but this is one of the most important things he's done and I think if you had some loose change, it would be worth it.'

'What is it?'

'It's a geometrically perfect ruler called *Mortality*. It's an edition of three. I've sold one to Latchky and the other is on reserve to the Tate.'

'How much?'

'Forty thousand pounds which today is, wait a minute, is about sixty-six thousand dollars.'

'Expensive, Jay.'

'Well, you know, I think he's doing very exciting work. I think this piece is seminal in that it shows, in a wonderfully simple way, how we measure our lives by certain events and yet fail to recognise the finite.'

'Umm, interesting, yeah, umm, yeah.'

'I think it's an important piece.'

'Will you take fifty-five?'

'Well, Art, the problem is that it is very expensive to make. Hirst uses the head of Time and Measure in Paris to get precisely the right size and then it's constructed in Germany by precision engineers.'

'Jesus. Okay, what about fifty-eight?'

'I think sixty would be an excellent price.'

'Jay, you drive a hard bargain. I'll take it for fifty-nine.'

'I think for you that would be satisfactory. As usual you've made a wise decision.'

Some funny shots of Brigid attempting to roller blade in Central Park with her friend Trace.

A couple of blocks down, Bob Maclestone entered the Lovell Slim Gallery. As he walked in, the two receptionists whispered to each other and as soon as he had moved through into the main showroom, one of them scuttled back to inform Lovell Slim of his presence. The show consisted of curvaceous pink shapes made up of some sort of petro-based material, videos of men and women flexing their muscles all accompanied by a bizarre combination of music and incidental noise. Maclestone took in the show with rapid efficiency but just as he was turning the handle of the glass door to make his escape, Lovell Slim pounced.

'Bob,' he bellowed.

'Oh ah, hi, Lovell.'

'How are you? I was just saying to Sally that we hadn't seen you or Jean for a while.'

Maclestone cleared his throat. 'Great, just great, Lovell. I ah, I am ah, just doing the rounds, you know?' he said, still gripping the door.

'Oh Bob, I was going to ring you.' Lovell's voice fell to a whisper. 'This young artist we're showing is really interesting.' Putting his arm over Maclestone's shoulder, he swivelled him around towards the gallery. 'Latchky came in here the other day,' he said almost inaudibly, 'bought half the show.'

'Latch, Latchky, really?' Bob sounded crestfallen.

'He's a young guy from Toronto, Bob. On the way up. He's …'

Brigid takes her jersey off on a warm autumn day.

Jean Maclestone crossed her legs and straightened her skirt so it looped over the knee. Ivor Schneider sat back on a well-used fifties sofa made of goat's skin. His sarong was almost indecent, showing most of the hairy thigh of his right leg. 'You know what it was like in the eighties – that crazy time, man. We didn't know what was going on, you know, all the shows in every goddamn city. The collectors falling over each other for work. We didn't know where we were, man – it didn't really matter, you know what I mean? Then there was the crash and we kinda woke up. Woke up with a big bang. I had to rediscover myself, you know? Don't get me wrong, it was a good thing, but I don't wanna make the same mistake twice. I wanna be a free man. Free of that kinda commitment, that kinda crazy life. I know that Art and Barbara want to show me, maybe I'll do a show, but it's down to other things like space and time. It's down to the work now, not the profits or the politics, you understand, Jean? I wanna be my own agent at my own pace. You remember the crazy eighties, the crazy nights, all that wild stuff, those crazy guys, the mad rush, the madness, man.' Ivor smiled broadly and dragged at his cigarette. Looking up at the ceiling, he sighed. 'Free, man, free of all that shit – you know?'

Brigid trips on the Broad Walk, then regains her balance. Cut to the Korean grocer shouting at Elaine.

'There now, now that didn't hurt, did it?' Brigid Murphy said, drawing down Rhinegold's sleeve after the injection.

'Nuthing hurts zeez days, except zee regrets,' Rhinegold said.

'Ah well now, me Da used to say have no regrets. There's no room for regret in life, he'd say. Sure, life is for living, look forwards when you're looking backwards. I never knew what he meant till I come over here and then I realised you just have to take opportunities as they come.' As Nurse Murphy twittered on, Rhinegold's mind went back to the day in 1961 when he'd just had a celebratory lunch with Alfred Barr after the hanging of the great Italian Futurist exhibition at the Museum of Modern Art. He was striding purposefully down the street, deep in thought, when he started crossing the road, subliminally feeling someone doing the same next to him. He remembered flying through the air in slow motion; almost somersaulting over the cab.

'He was a fisherman me Da was, so he wasn't home much,' Brigid said sadly. 'He used to say that he was happiest at sea, he loved the beauty of the open sea.'

When he had tried to get up nothing happened. He lay there for what seemed like hours, a large crowd gathered over him, he had thought it was the end, he could hardly breathe and there was this deadening sensation.

'One day Ma got a phone call saying that his boat was missing off the coast of Connemara. I think Ma knew then, you know instinctively, but the weeks went by and I was full of hope. I was convinced he was alive, I mean completely. Then one day there was a letter saying that because he'd been missing for so many weeks like, that they were presuming him dead. I mean how can you presume somebody's dead? Sure I still think I'm going to bump into him on the street.'

Brigid buys a dress in Betsy Johnson's. Brigid buys some apples. Brigid walks into the subway. Elaine smokes a cigarette, naked.

'Dear Mr Spindle, Thank you for your letter concerning the Mondrian. I have in the past discussed with my husband the possible sale of this work. As you might be aware, my husband bought the painting from the artist himself and has understandably a strong sentimental attachment to it.' Mrs Rhinegold sighed and looked at Freign who was sitting bolt upright on the other side of her desk. 'I find all of this very difficult, Robert. I wish I'd never even contemplated the idea, it's just, oh, never mind.'

'It is your painting after all and ...'

'Yes, yes, I know, Robert. It's not the point. I agreed, that's the problem. I do hate going back on my word but I never wanted to sell it in the first place. It's almost as if Mr Spindle willed me into it. He's like some ghastly hypnotist.' She picked up her pen and looked out the window. 'On further consideration we have decided not to sell the painting. I hope we have not inconvenienced you in any way. Thank you so much for the flowers you sent the other day. They were most appreciated. Yours, Alfreda Rhinegold. P.S I am appalled at the raising of artifacts from the *Titanic*, aren't you? Although marine archaeology is of special interest I do feel it is like robbing a grave.' She spoke out the words as she wrote them and then passed the letter to Freign.

'I think this will deter him for the time being,' he said eventually, after reading the letter to himself. 'Although asking him a question is inviting an answer. Perhaps, madam, you should leave out the "aren't you",' he suggested.

'I'm not sure even doing that is going to deter him. He's an extremely determined man. I mean, in the last few months he has sent me dozens of unreadable books on archaeology and enough flowers for a funeral, not to mention all these letters. Really, Robert, they're almost love letters,' she said holding the latest.

'They are ... intimate, it must be said,' Freign agreed.

'Did I read you the last one?' she asked, picking up Spindle's note and peering down through her pince-nez. '"Your intelligence resonates like the echo of a sea shell," and again, "the elegance of your opinions stands out against the debris of modernity."'

'Maybe, madam, he has ah, strong feelings for ...' Freign started.

'Of course he hasn't, Robert, after all I could be his grandmother.'

'Not exactly, madam.'

Brigid talking to a fat lady on the steps of a building on Seventy-fourth Street. Elaine and friends smoking dope late one night.

Spindle clenched the receiver and leaned forwards, placing his elbows on the desk. 'Now you just listen to me,' he said, poking his finger aggressively towards the ceiling. 'I wanna see that consignment in my office by tomorrow morning otherwise I will sue your ass.' He slammed the phone down and, threading a long silk handkerchief out of his top pocket like a magician, he dabbed the tiny beads of sweat from off his brow.

'Art Spindle Gallery. No she doesn't. I'm afraid not. Ah ha. No we don't have a forwarding address. Ah ha. Ah ha. I'm afraid we can't give you that information, sir. He's on another call. Can he ring you back? Ah ha. No problem, Mr Toone. I can leave a message. Any time, sir.

'Ass-hole,' Paige murmured.

After a good hour Spindle reluctantly allowed Paige to let Dewey Bozo in.

'What can I do for you, Mr Bozo?' Art asked quietly.

'I'm curating a show downtown at Anna Slant's gallery called *Deviant Mythology*. I believe Jean Maclestone mentioned it to you. It's a show dealing with post-classical imagery in contemporary art. Anna is going to show the sculptural side of it and we thought it would be so great if you could do the kinda painting aspect, you know.'

Art caressed his head and frowned. 'Jean mentioned this to me?' he questioned.

'Yes, she said she was like, going to discuss it with you.'

'Oh, I'm sorry ah, Mr ah, ah?'

'Dewey Bozo.'

'Mr Bozo, I'm sorry, this is not a good time to discuss it. I have a meeting in a minute. Maybe if you could send me details of what you intend to put across in this show with a list of artists you're thinking of, I could look through it and come back to you.' Art tapped the edge of his desk impatiently.

'As a matter of fact, I have all the documentation with me, like the, the *raison d'être*,' Dewey giggled nervously, 'and a list of artists I would like to include,' he said shuffling through a large dossier. 'As you can see, I have Schnabel and Bickerton and Sherman.'

Art got up from behind his desk and extended his hands to receive the proposal. 'Okay, I'll look through this. Very nice to meet you, Mr Bozo. I'll give you a call, okay?' he said, patting Dewey on the back and leading him towards the door.

'It was great to meet you, Art. I hope that we will be able to work together.'

Elaine had dubbed her own sighing and breathing over Brigid walking up to a patient's bed with the board in her hand. Then in shot were Elaine and Joany making out with Brigid's voice dubbed over asking how a patient feels. 'How are you feeling today?' is repeated over and over as Elaine climaxes, dissolving to Brigid repeatedly bending over to make the bed with Elaine's sighing. She liked the effect, it was like a kinda visual Philip Glass piece.

Jo Richards gave out a long sigh as he got up from his desk. He walked the forty-one steps needed to get from the front end of the loft to the back where he had his living quarters; a bed, a chair, a bathroom- dressing room. He kept his clothes in the latter area. It was big enough for that, a room within a room. Jo went into the bathroom where he stood himself in front of the mirror. Then, as if he had noticed something out of the ordinary, he leaned towards his reflection and inspected a particular part of his chin. After a few minutes of self-observation, he turned off the light and strode back down to the front of the loft where he sat down at his desk. As soon as he had made himself comfortable, Jo ran his fingers through his hair and, with a sigh, got up from the desk and walked back down to the end of the loft where he entered the room within a room and removed a jacket from the makeshift rail. After some lengthy deliberations in front of the mirror he proceeded to the front door. He put his hand on the door knob and turned it slowly but after a moment's hesitation he went back to his desk where he picked up his pen and placed it in his jacket pocket.

'Richards evaluates death in *Murder* by using a void box that gives an impression of endlessness within a permanent structure. However, the show belongs to Lathers who deals ...'

Jo squeezed the bridge of his nose between thumb and index finger and sneezed. He got up, walked over to the window, and as he looked down at the traffic, rotated the coins in his trouser pocket.

On the four white walls – the common denominator of all New York galleries – hung six large paintings pulsating with the kind of pigment usually found after a raucous candle-lit dinner in some East Village apartment: cigarettes, cups, wax, dust collided on the canvas with careless abandon. Dewey lingered over each painting, scanning the debris within.

'*Muse 1* reminds us of love lost; an artificial landscape reflecting the chaotic nature of our aspirations and romantic illusions', the *New York Times* critic had written in an article now sanctified in a plastic folder on the receptionist's desk, together with a list of titles and prices. Having read the review and noticing that the blonde receptionist was busy on the phone, Dewey slipped the plastic folder into his battered brown leather briefcase.

Rachel, in blue denim overalls, manipulated a piece of soggy grey clay the size of a football. Elaine sidled up to her, hands dug deep into her combats, shoulders slightly hunched, and drawled, 'What ya doin', Rachel?'

'I was at the Marks Gallery and I saw this great piece by that guy who makes stuff out of real weird material, it was kinda amorphous.'

'You mean like Charles Long.'

'Yeah kinda, but like more shaped.'

'Shaped?'

'I mean sort of shapely,' Rachel corrected herself and nervously added more water to the clay mound. 'It had this strange quality which was real interesting,' she said, massaging the clay as it dissoved into a liquid form. 'Shit! What the fuck? Oh Jesus, Elaine. Just urgh.' Elaine looked seriously at the evolving mess. 'Hey, Rachel, I think it looks kinda great.'

Freign turned sharply in his chair as Brigid Murphy walked in saying, 'Right, I'm off, Robert. I'll see ya in the morning. Mind now you don't forget the new pills Dr Grout has prescribed. See ya.' As the door closed behind her, Freign contemplated the new addition to Rhinegold's already vast array of prescriptions. What a scam these medicines were, he thought to himself. Doctors seem to prescribe out of habit rather than necessity. When he had been in training in Malaysia, the sterilising effects of urine together with a few plants with naturally occurring medicinal properties had been quite sufficient to cure the severest of conditions. He remembered clearly being stranded for two weeks in the Sarawak region of Borneo, and having to sterilise an unpleasant laceration with his own urine. By the time he had emerged from the jungle the wound had completely cleared. For years his affliction in those harsh circumstances had been used as an example to young recruits.

Mr Rhinegold slept. His head was arched back on itself, his sharp aquiline nose pointed towards the ceiling like an American bittern. As Freign walked in, a pitched rasping noise was emanating from Rhinegold's chest. 'Sir,' Freign called out to no avail. 'Sir,' he repeated loudly. The wheezing spluttered to a halt, the eyes flickered open, the head sprang forward.

'Vat, ah it is you, vat is it?' Rhinegold gurgled, shuffling into a more stable position.

'Your medicine, sir,' Freign replied, presenting him with a glass of water and a few multi-coloured pills, which he was balancing on the tray.

'Pilz, alvays zi pilz, I am made of ze pilz,' he grumbled.

'It does seem excessive,' Freign agreed.

'Vat time?'

'It is five o'clock, sir.'

Dewey peered into a black box. 'Blutin's new work takes a more direct approach and employs surgical tools to dissect the skin which covers the mundane and exposes the intricate web of psychological implications which are hidden deep within our complex attitudes towards sexual ambivalence.'

'I'm going to Guppy's tonight,' Alfreda announced as she walked out of the library. Rhinegold grunted. He had met Alfreda in 1956 at a dinner party given by the Trustees of the Museum of Modern Art honouring Nelson Rockefeller. They had been placed next to each other and had discussed a variety of subjects. Alfreda was from an old-school, well-to-do Boston family and was down for the season, partly for her own leisure and partly as an associate of the Isabella Gardner Museum where she worked in public relations. It was a somewhat ambiguous title but one which nevertheless gave her sufficient station to be at ease within the echelons of New York society. Rhinegold had found her particularly receptive to his opinions on modern art. A few days later he had cabled her at her residence on Central Park West with an invitation to dine with him at the fashionable Pavillion restaurant on the top floor of the Waldorf Towers. After a fine meal sprinkled with clever repartee and some of his more amusing anecdotes, they had found themselves very much to one another's liking. Another few dates ensued before he asked for her hand in marriage. Alfreda Arrowsmith politely declined. Although stunned by her refusal, he swallowed his wounded pride, and continued to escort her to various functions.

'The subjects of these paintings range from the mundane to the profound, from everyday experience to the insistence of memory. Though the images can be read as significant, as indeed they are, the notation or way of the painting is crucial in its quest for autonomy. This uneasy partnership is developed mainly through the idea of repetition, with its possibility of disruption and absence.'

Dewey's next port-of-call was a group show at Flacks. Grace Ford had written an effusive review in the *Times* on a piece by Lathers entitled *Twenty-eight minutes*, which had somewhat intrigued him. Among the other artists was Jo Richards, whose work his new friend, Beth Freemantle, was going to exhibit in the spring.

Dolores waddled into the laundry room. She opened the dryer and pulled out a basket full of laundry, then refilled it with wet laundry and turned it on. The deep drone of the machine engulfed the room. The first item to be taken from the pink plastic basket was a crumpled white shirt which she shook irreverently before smoothing it flat over the ironing board. She picked up the iron, pressed the spray button to get the necessary dampness, and laid it flat on the shirt. The heat of the iron caused a puff of steam and a swishing sound, a noise Dolores always found satisfying; one day she had imagined it being like a small wave breaking over the sand and it had reminded her of home: a small fishing village called Rosas on the Costa Brava in Spain.

Rhinegold lit a small cigar and gazed out of the window. Spring had arrived. Rhinegold boldly invited Alfreda to Connecticut for the weekend to stay with Dr Grout, who had taken up his first practice in the small town of Westport. After some hesitation – it was after all the height of the season – she agreed, and on a sunny afternoon they motored down to the country. Upon their arrival Mrs Cliffe, the housekeeper, informed them that Dr Grout had been called away to Boston on an urgent matter and would be returning the following day. A fine meal had been prepared for them, accompanied by an excellent ChâteauTalbot '37, after which they retired to the drawing-room and sat in front of a blazing fire. Many subjects were discussed, apart from the one which was uppermost in his mind, before they both went up to their rooms. Rhinegold remembered lying in bed frantic with unrequited love until he could stand it no longer and, realising that if he did not act now he would probably never have this kind of opportunity again, he furtively made his way to her room. He found Alfreda fast asleep. Rhinegold's heart pounded with excitement and trepidation as he climbed in beside her.

Jo stood over his bed, straightened the comforter, removed all the creases, puffed up the two pillows and then bent down to pick up the *New York Times* from the floor. He walked back up to his desk. 'Richards evaluates death, in *Murder*, by using a void box that gives an impression of endless-ness within a permanent structure, but the show belongs to Lathers who deals with death as a measure against time in *Twenty-eight Minutes*, a video, projected on a clock, showing a man running against the second hand. The runner begins to lose ground against the second hand and is eventually overtaken by it, after which, he collapses on the twenty-eighth minute in front of the minute hand which ticks over him.' Jo put the paper down and looked at his watch. Beth should be here any minute, he thought to himself, looking around the loft to see if there was anything else to clear up.

In a darkened room ten seats were arranged in front of *Twenty-eight Minutes*. Dewey sat transfixed by the man running around the clock. The video had started with the athlete on the half-hour and the second hand on the hour. The first fifteen minutes he had lapped the hand several times but now, as the athlete tired, they were moving at the same pace.

'One is exhilarated by the pace of the runner as he laps all the hands of the clock as if they too were athletes, but after a while the second hand starts to catch up and finally, as the athlete slows with exhaustion, it overtakes him. Lathers suggests that human achievement and existence are in some way measured by the relentlessness of time and he leaves us feeling that we are only minute footnotes in an endless cycle.' Jo re-read the article.

Having ironed the back of the shirt, Dolores replaced the iron and arranged the folds so that the right side lay flat on the board, then she repeated the process. The collar required placing inside out across the end of the board, as well as more spray because the stiffness made it more difficult to iron. She always made sure that the inside of the collar was taut before applying the iron. When she was satisfied the shirt was creaseless, she laid it front up and fastened the buttons. After smoothing the shirt down with the palms of her hand, she carefully turned it over. Taking the shoulder of the right arm, she folded it so that the arm lay over the back making the fold straight down the centre of the front pocket. She straightened the sleeve which now lay on top of the tail of the shirt and then repeated this manoeuvre with the left side. Finally she pulled the top and bottom ends to straighten out any remaining folds and, with sublime dexterity, tucked her right hand under the tail end, drawing it over itself. After making sure that no creases had appeared, she repeated the fold. Now all there was left to do was to turn it over and place it flat on its back.

Dressed in a beige tank-top, Rachel stood next to the sink and placed her arm under the tap, letting the water wash away the soap lather. But the encrusted clay remained stubbornly attached to her. 'Let me help you,' Elaine said, drawing away from the bathroom door against which she'd been leaning. She went over to where Rachel stood looking despairingly at her arm. 'This clay is so sticky a sander couldn't take it off,' she said. Elaine held the soap tightly and pummelled it on to her arm, then, taking a Swiss army knife from her pocket, she opened up a blade and began scraping off the clay.

'Jesus, Elaine, that's kinda dangerous.'

'It's the only way, Rachel,' she replied, looking intently at what she was doing. After a few minutes all the obdurate patches had been removed and Elaine washed her arm down with a wet flannel. Suddenly Elaine splashed water in Rachel's face. 'Elaine,' Rachel giggled and splashed her back. Soon they were both soaked to the bone.

'Shit!' Elaine said, finally pinching her T-shirt away from her skin where it had adhered.

'Don't worry about it,' Rachel puffed, wiping the wet hair away from her eyes.'I've got some stuff you can borrow.'

After the second purchase of the day, Bob Maclestone decided to look into the Basset Building on Prince Street.

'I really love this artist. I think he's just great,' the girl with the nasal voice declared from behind the counter. 'He just had a really great review in *Art in America*,' she went on, 'and I think he's going to have a show at the Slap Gallery in Brussels.'

'The Slap Gallery,' Maclestone repeated.

'Yeah, and I'm taking him to Chicago this year,' she droned on.

'Chicago, right, great,' he said feigning enthusiasm.

Maclestone walked out of the Santer Gallery without a purchase and decided he had done enough shopping for the day. As he made his way uptown he wondered what Jean would think of his small buying spree and whether she'd like the skin-tinted plastic object he'd bought at Lovells. Maybe he should stop off at Billy's Topless for a quick drink.

Art Spindle's voice came through the gallery intercom. 'Paige, can you come into my office now?' Paige got up and straightened her short skirt over her slender thighs and sauntered through the gallery into Spindle's office.

'Oh Paige,' Spindle said without looking up, 'could you just take down this letter?' He got up and walked around the desk.

Paige crossed her legs and adjusted pen and paper.

'Dear Mrs Rhinegold. I am sending you this excellent account of the raising of the *Mary Rose*. I visited Portsmouth in the UK last year and was so impressed by the wreck that I eventually managed to buy this beautiful tabor pipe from a dealer over there. I hope you will accept this small gift as a token of my admiration and affection.' A moment of silence passed. 'Wreck sounds weird. Ring up Columbia or some place and find out the proper term,' he said, waving his handkerchief which he then applied to his forehead. 'To continue – as for the Mondrian I think we could get five and a half million dollars in the present market. Jo informed me that you would like a contract. I suggest that we get our lawyers to draw up an agreement that is mutually satisfactory. As Mr Richards may have told you, we take ten per cent of the sale price. I hope ...'

Mr Spindle rested his hand on Paige's shoulder. 'I hope ah, I hope that ah, no ah ...'

Now both his hands lay either side of her bare neck. 'Ah, I ah, hope you find this reasonable.'

Paige stiffened as Spindle tightened his clasp. She bent forwards to write the last sentence hoping that he would relax his grip. It worked. Spindle walked around his desk and sat down.

'Can you read that out?' he asked.

She read out the unfinished letter.

Spindle jumped up and walked back around the desk. 'May I say again how much I enjoyed visiting you and your beautiful collection. Please ah ...' Again Mr Spindle's hands groped Paige's shoulders. 'And ah, and ah, please send Mr Harper my regards. Yours etcetera etcetera,' he ended, pulling away from Paige abruptly and manoeuvring back to the other side of the desk.

Paige read out the letter again.

'That's great, just great. Now, Paige, could you take a look at these notes here? I want you to put these ah, in order.'

Paige walked around the desk and stood next to Spindle. He put his hand on the back of her thigh. 'Draw up a chair, will you. There's a lot of stuff here. I want you to sort it out.'

Paige drew up a chair and sat down, looking intently at the pile of papers Spindle was waving his glasses at.

'Now, this is a letter regarding the consignment from the Slater Gallery in Los Angeles,' he said, picking up a letter. 'Could you confirm that tomorrow, Paige, and ah, here is ah, oh by the way, Paige, how would you like a promotion?'

'Oh Art, that would be great.'

'I would like you to be my PA, Paige. I think you're doing a great job.'

I resigned from Spindle a few months back but not without the mailing list and a few like, prime collector and curator contacts. I'm just so excited. So I found this space in Chelsea which is totally, totally great. It's like two thousand square feet, I mean it's not Marks but hey, I'm just starting right. So this is the deal; the gallery opens with Jo Richards on May 3rd. Jo's a like, fantastic artist. He is right on the edge, you know what I mean? Oh yeah, I finished with Thomas Johnson, he was so like, preppie and we didn't like the same art. Milton Avery is like the most modern he's ever likely to get, you know what I mean? So there's just no way you can be like, be with somebody who's not into what you're into, right? Oh yeah and you know what the final thing was when I like, had everything done kinda thing? He just got freaked out by the scars. I mean he really freaked out. Why is it that men are so squeamish about like, blood and stuff? I mean when you have like, a period right, they are just so weird about it, you know?

Paige felt Art's hand on her knee. She could feel herself perspiring in disgust and yet she remained frozen; a promotion was on the line here.

'I want you to send all these slides back to the artists. I mean, Paige, you've never seen so much shit.' He followed this with a weasel-like laugh. 'What do you think I should do with this?' He held up a transparency to the light.

Paige leaned over and looked up at the transparency which dangled from Spindle's outstretched hand. 'Well ah, what is it?'

'It's a Picasso, Paige. I was thinking of buying it for my collection. What do you think?'

'A Picasso, gee, Art.'

Spindle's hand was now stroking the inside of her thigh.

'Art, I don't think this is a good idea,' she said.

'You don't like it?' he said surprised.

'No, I mean ...'

Spindle dropped the transparency and shot his other hand on to her bosom, pushing her back into the chair.

'Art, God, Art!'

'You're so beautiful, Paige, oh Paige.' His mouth tried to find her lips.

Paige choked. 'Art, no, this is, no, Art!'

Art Spindle was not taking no for an answer and his hand went up and under her blouse where he clawed greedily at her bra.

'Art, for Christ's sake!' she cried. 'No! Please, Art.'

Paige managed to roll over sending chair and Spindle crashing to the ground. She scrambled to her feet, ignoring the tearing of her black A-line Marc Jacobs skirt. Thinking she was finally free, she made for the door, but a hand had curled around her ankle and before she knew it her stockings were sliding down as Spindle attempted to draw her on top of him. She tried to wade away from him but the combination of his weight and the pain from her operation nine months before got the better of her and she was pulled to the floor.

'Art, please, Art, I don't want to, please.'

But Art was now firmly in position, his tentacles again sliding under her blouse and groping her breasts.

Paige looked down to see Spindle's liver-spotted head between her legs. She started to cry. 'Please Art, oh please don't.'

These small objects reveal our fear of pain and mortality.

A set of teeth made from chalk and hanging from a black board.

A tongue made of black felt.

An eye made of salt.

A heart made of fat.

A kidney carved of stone.

Each piece represents an inner fear by cleverly using metaphor and uncomfortable juxtapositions.

Dewey went from one object to another exclaiming to himself, until the idea of *Teeth and Black Board* made him hold his hand to his mouth.

Rhinegold pulled at his cigar. The Grout experience gave the relationship sufficient impetus for a reasonably long courtship before, yet again, Rhinegold asked Alfreda to marry him. Several days went by before he received a note asking him to meet her at the Pavillion. As this was where they'd had their first date, he felt it was a good omen.

When he arrived she was already waiting for him. She wore a rather formal two-piece tweed ensemble and a cap that dangled foppishly over her forehead. He remembered this well because, although it was a perfectly charming attire, she had the air of a headmistress, and he couldn't help but feel he was being interviewed for some job. For the next hour and a half she told him intimate details about her life. Among other things she informed him of her love for another man who, it seemed, was not at all suitable. As they neared the end of the meal, she apologised for not telling him before. She had wanted to but been afraid that he would not want to see her again. She did feel strongly for him but it would take time to adjust.

He remembered looking across New York that night and seeing the Empire State Building with its flashing vertex, which reminded him of a lighthouse: isolated and alone. It suddenly occurred to him that Alfreda's admission was a cry for help.

Freign came in one minute late, which gave Dolores great pleasure as he was usually so punctilious. She determined to needle him sufficiently to get a rise.

'Dolores, Mrs Rhinegold's tea,' Freign flatly demanded, pronouncing the last word with clinical precision.

'Latey Roberto,' Dolores said. 'It is latey.'

He glanced at his watch and then at the kitchen clock. It was five-thirty. He was not late. 'I am not late,' Freign said sternly. He was never late. It was a noted characteristic of his. His commanding officer had congratulated him on more than one occasion. In the Sudan, Freign had marched through the desert for one whole week on a particularly dangerous mission and although he had lost several men, he had succeeded admirably and arrived at the appointed destination precisely on time.

'*Si*, it is latey,' Dolores persisted. Freign raised himself and looking directly into Dolores' small cunning eyes he said, 'It is precisely five-thirty.'

Hatti Datzheimer, Jill Kleiberg, Guppy Dale and Alfreda Rhinegold combined in rotation for a bridge four. Tonight was bridge night, one of the few nights Mrs Rhinegold ever went out. One of the four ladies would entertain the others to an early evening meal followed by a marathon session of cards. Husbands, what was left of them, were not included. A stroke had paralysed Mr Dale's left side as well as, it seemed, half his memory. Mr Rhinegold's temper disqualified him from any kind of game. Mr Kleiberg had run off with his wife's best friend's daughter. Mr Datzheimer was dead.

In the bedroom Elaine and Rachel were both topless trying on T-shirts.

'What about this one?' Rachel suggested, holding up a black sleeveless T-shirt with the *X-Girl* logo across it.

'I hate logos.'

'What about the yellow one?'

'Yellow is not, is most definitely not my colour,' Elaine said, raising her eyebrows and adding, 'They're all kinda big, Rachel.'

'I'm a big girl,' Rachel said, holding her large bosoms in her hands. 'Big and sexy.'

'Yeah, they sure are. Not like my little nodules,' Elaine whined.

'Oh come on, honey, they're perfect tits, man, just beautiful and I luurve the rings, they're just so great.'

Dewey peered at a photograph of a pubescent girl with her legs open, her hairless vagina slightly open and protruding from between spread legs. A colour television quivering with milky colours reflected in the mirror behind her. 'What is pictured in these large format photographs backed on to aluminium are nudes which depict the restlessness and fantasy perhaps encouraged by a provincial boredom and the narcissism of adolescence that makes posing irresistible.'

Beth was half an hour late. Jo had begun to think that she wasn't coming, when the sound of the door-bell interrupted his reverie about the receptionist at the Paul Kasmin Gallery. Although the show had been organised and the dates set, it had seemed strange that she had not wanted to see him at all over the last month and a half. When Beth finally came through the door he did not immediately recognise her. 'Hey Beth, you ah, you look …' hesitating, he scrutinised Beth's face, 'kinda different.' She had transformed radically and, although the change was not unattractive, it would take him some time before he got used to the metamorphosis.

Freign knocked on the door. There was no reply. Nevertheless, he walked into the bedroom and lowered the tray on to a small side table. He could hear the shower in the bathroom. Mrs Rhinegold's silhouette could be seen through the shower curtain, broken only at the base where her delicate ankles were clearly visible. In one motion Freign leaned down, grasped an ankle and pulled it upwards. There was a dull thud like a large stone hitting the shoals in shallow water as Mrs Rhinegold's head hit the ceramic floor.

Beth Freemantle sat on a rickety, old Thonet chair which Jo had found for two dollars in the Grand Street market. Jo stood in front of her, clutching a ruler that was being waved at several drawings pinned on the wall.

He moved on to a drawing of a kind of mechanical device. 'Placed in a certain way and using this device the viewer can only be subliminally aware of the space around him. You see, Beth, I am real interested in the fine line between the reality of what we observe and what we don't. It seems to me there is a blurred area which can only be defined by both the seen and the unseen.'

So, I go to Jo's loft to see the work for the show. Jo looks great. He is so hot it is like UNBELIEVABLE – but I play it cool. Anyway the work is real interesting, you know? He's working with sight and like, perception. The show is going to be so great.

'Life,' Schneider pondered, 'life has just gotta be the greatest work of art, man.' He smiled with a look of earnestness. Jean sat back in her chair and smiled. It was as if this statement had liberated her in some way, as if perhaps she too was art in the making. 'Ivor, you're so right.'

This cold February day was now drawing to a close and the purple yellow light was hardening into a frozen indigo.

CHAPTER FOUR

EVENING, SIX WEEKS AGO

Having slid a stainless-steel spatula under the baked sole, Dolores lifted the cooked fish and placed it neatly on the serving dish. The yellowing cupboard door resisted her tugging until the brittle hinge finally snapped open revealing several piled-up plates of various colours and sizes. Dolores took one of these and put it next to the serving dish. She then selected a bone-handled fish knife from a red velvet-lined box and cut down the spine of the sole from head to tail. She carefully slid the knife under the flesh, separating it from the bones underneath, and removed both fillets. She then laid them carefully side-by-side on the gold-rimmed, oval plate before turning the sole over to reveal its underbelly, whereupon she repeated her neat and meticulous carving.

Freign came into the kitchen humming an army ditty. 'Ready?' he asked. The tray waited for him on the sideboard. '*Si, si, si,*' Dolores replied, as she let the baking dish slide into the sink of hot water. 'Quickie, quickie, e getti coldi,' she flustered. Freign lifted the tray and glided through the swing-doors.

Mendia Krew is showing downtown at Anna Slant's on Prince Street. It's an installation metamorphosing body parts into utilitarian objects. She does this by making moulds of various parts of her body and transforming them into everyday objects. The artist has, for instance, made a door handle out of a mould made from the inside of her vagina.

Elaine Yoon adjusted the mike which perched on her lapel.

'Testing, testing, one, two, three,' she mimicked before retrieving her recorder from the inside of her jacket. Her words echoed around the gallery bathroom like a voice in a tin drum. She then zipped her jacket up to her chin and walked into the exhibition.

'That sounds like a good price, Mr Spindle, but, as Mr and Mrs Rhinegold's lawyer, I think I should also get a quote from Sotheby's or Christie's before making a decision,' Mr Horovitz said.

'Of course, of course. Now, I would suggest ...' Spindle paused and then continued slowly, 'that you talk to Rebecca Fields in the Modern department at Christie's.'

'Rebecca Fields,' Mr Horovitz repeated.

'Yes. To my mind she is the expert in this field. Absolutely terrific person.'

'I'll ring her tomorrow.'

'As a matter of fact I have to ring her this evening on some other business. I could arrange for her to do this quickly. They can be quite slow.'

'That's very kind of you, Mr Spindle ...'

As Elaine stood looking down into a perspex case which contained wine glasses cast from the artist's bosoms, she became aware of a distorted reflection in the casing peering up at her.

'Excuse me, haven't I, ah, haven't I, ah, seen you before?' the faint reflection uttered. Elaine cocked her head sideways and was confronted by an unshaven man wearing a slate-grey Gucci suit, the elegance of which was lost on the owner's rotund figure. 'Maybe,' she responded indifferently, as she moved on to the rubber mould taken from inside the artist's teeth and made into a paper clip.

'I'm ah, I'm sure that ... ah, you don't remember, ah?'

'No, Mister, I don't, unless you go to strip joints or gay bars?' she cut in coldly, before spotting Dewey coming in through the elevator doors.

'No, I ah, no ...' he began.

'Excuse me, I've just seen a friend,' she said, and raising her plastic cup she skirted around his large body towards the gallery entrance.

'Ah, ah, okay. I ah ...' spluttered Maclestone as she drifted off. Elaine smiled to herself. That was a great take.

'Your dinner, sir,' announced Freign, placing the tray down on the walnut table designed for Rhinegold's solitary meals.

Rhinegold's head jerked up from its nest. 'Vat has she attempted today?' he asked in a slight but disagreeable voice.

'Sole, sir,' Freign replied, as he manoeuvred Rhinegold over to the table in the middle of the room.

'I prefer cod. Why not vie ...' the voice died away somewhere inside of him, 'vie cod?' he managed on his next breath.

'I expect the sole was fresh today,' Freign replied.

'Vat?'

'I expect the sole was fresh today,' he bellowed, and seeing Rhinegold was now shakily picking up his knife asked, 'Will that be all?'

'I vil have some vine,' Rhinegold said.

'Excuse me, sir?'

'Vine,' Rhinegold repeated irritably.

'But sir ...'

'Rebecca, I'm glad I caught you at this late hour,' Art said cheerfully.

'What can I do for you, Art?'

'Well, I'm thinking of selling my Miro.'

'The Miro?'

'Yeah, I love it but I think it's the right time to sell. What do you think?'

'I think you're right, Art. The market is very receptive to anything Surrealist at the moment. I think we could get a very good price for it.'

'That would be great, Rebecca, just great, and oh yes, I wonder whether you could do me a small favour?'

'Sure.'

'I have an old friend of the family who wants to have an insurance valuation on a painting they own.'

'Sure, no problem at all. What's the painting?'

'Well, it's a Mondrian – a pretty good one at that. They want a reasonable valuation, if you know what I mean. They don't want to pay a ridiculous premium.'

'Of course, I quite understand. Now Art, we have a very interesting sale coming up for your Miro ...'

'Hey Dewey sweetheart, thank God you're here,' Elaine said, smiling with relief.

Dewey clawed his hair back and blew his cheeks out, finally sighing with an exaggerated air of exhaustion. 'Sorry I'm late, baby, I had a meeting uptown. So, what's going on? Seen anyone famous or vaguely attractive?' he asked, glancing around the room.

'Some like, old perve, tried to pick me up,' she purred.

'Remember, honey, they don't fall off trees,' he said and added quizzically, 'Was he my type?' His eyes rolled in their sockets with anticipation.

'Everybody's your type,' Elaine replied coolly.

Dewey threw down his hands. 'Elaine, I am a democrat – what do you expect? How old?'

'Old. Like forty-five, fifty.'

'That's my cup of tea, as they say,' Dewey said, jolting his head back and clapping his hands together. 'Where is he?'

'He wants wine,' Freign said as he came into the kitchen. Dolores looked up with a startled expression. 'No vino por señor. E doctore say no winee.'

'You tell him,' Freign said, 'because I'm certainly not.'

Dolores threw a short arm in the air and emitted a guttural noise before exiting the kitchen. Freign squeezed his nose between thumb and index finger and sneezed through his mouth. Twice.

After his National Service, Freign joined the SAS. He had done his first year on the bleak windswept downs at Aldershot before being transferred to the Canadian army for training in the tundra. After two years, in which he excelled in undercover combat techniques, he and his battalion were sent to Southern India to exercise with a Gurkha division stationed near Goa.

Freign was a quiet, solitary man, regarded as aloof, even arrogant, by his comrades; consequently he usually spent his leave alone. During one leave he decided to trek through the Mysore region of Southern India and, while washing in a stream, he was bitten by a snake. When he regained consciousness a few days later, he found himself in a small hut. He discovered that he had been found by children and brought back to the village where he had been lying in a delirious state. Freign managed to explain that people were waiting for him, though due to the covert nature of the Ghurkas' mission, he could not elaborate further. A toothless villager who spoke enough English to translate adequately, told Freign that it would be quite some time before he would be fit. On no account, he warned, should he try and leave lest the fever from the snake-bite recur.

'You're Paige Quale,' Jo beamed, as he sidled up to Paige who was looking vaguely at a perforated mould of an armpit which had been transformed into a shower-head.

'Yeah,' Paige smiled back, pretending not to recognise him, 'and you are?'

'Jo Richards,' he said, extending his hand. 'I've seen you working at the Spindle Gallery.'

Jo had been seeing quite a bit of Spindle until Mrs Rhinegold's accident had scuppered their plans. He'd noted but had not as yet deigned to talk to her except for the occasional perfunctory greeting.

'Oh, yeah.' She let him shake her limp hand. Jo knotted his brow and asked earnestly, 'So what do you do there, Paige?'

'Oh, I'm a director of the gallery. I kinda do like, you know, look after clients, show them work, that kinda thing.'

'You're a director of the Spindle Gallery!' he exclaimed.

'Ah ha,' Paige confirmed with a distinct air of satisfaction. Her expression changed abruptly when she saw Beth Freemantle making a direct assault.

'Hey, Beth,' Jo purred affectionately. Beth kissed him on the cheeks but near enough to his mouth so their lips met at the corners. 'Jo and Paige Quale. Well, whaddya know?' She smiled, still holding on to Jo's hand.

Paige held her cup in both hands and smiled nervously. 'Beth, you look, ah, neat,' she stuttered. Paige tried to figure out what had changed but the look was almost too fundamental for a precise description.

'Well thanks, Paige. And I see you've met my *numero uno* artist.'

'Ah ha,' Paige replied. The nose had definitely changed shape, she thought to herself, and something around the chin was different.

'I hope you don't mind me taking him away, Paige,' said Beth with detectable smugness.

Paige put on her vacuous and disinterested look. 'Nope,' and then, looking at Jo, she said, 'See you later.'

Jo smiled flirtatiously. 'Sure thing.'

Dewey was talking to Andrea Rosen and Michele Landers.

'I bought this beautiful fifties vase on Twenty-sixth Street last Sunday. It's kinda bluey-green with this like, milky-white vein running through it. It is so unbelievably gorgeous and as we were leaving, we bumped into Ivor Schneider with this girl – I mean she couldn't have been more than sixteen, maybe even younger. Anyway as we were talking I had this like, great idea for a found object show, you know? Like, getting ten artists and doing a show of things they have found in a flea market or some place ...'

Beth looked across the room in Paige's direction and adjusted her glasses. 'Like, what were you doing with that rat bag?' she asked with mock anger.

'Paige?'

'Yeah, the "Bitch" Quale.'

'What's the problem?' Jo looked confused.

Beth cocked her head to one side. 'Like, why do you think she's got that job at Spindle's?'

Jo hunched his shoulders and slid his bottom lip over his top one making an 'I-don't-know' kind of grimace. 'What do you mean?'

Beth put her hands on her hips. 'She screwed Spindle.'

Jo contorted his face in disbelief. 'What!' he exclaimed.

'Yeah. The "Bitch" Quale,' she confirmed with disdain.

'She screwed Spindle? I don't believe it,' Jo repeated incredulously.

'Yeah, Jane Whale told me that she walked into Spindle's office one

evening after work ...' Beth paused and lowered her voice. 'And like
Spindle was going down on her.'

'Jesus. Why would she want to screw Spindle?'

'My job, dummy.'

'Bitch. I had no idea. She looks kinda innocent, you know what I mean?
Kinda attractive too.'

'Total bitch,' and then, catching sight of Maclestone across the room,
she added excitedly, 'Look, Jo, that's Bob Maclestone, one of the like,
big-time collectors. I want to introduce you guys.'

'Okay, Beth,' Jo said enthusiastically, glad to be off the Paige subject.

*I just don't get it, you know – Jo's kinda real flirtatious one moment and
like, real cold the next – it's just so weird and then he's like, awkward – I
don't know, I think he likes me but he's real shy.*

Freign was naturally anxious to get back to his battalion. After all, his
Commander could have been interpreting his absence as desertion. The
communist uprising in Malaysia was, at the time, of particular concern and
his action might be seen as politically motivated, especially when socialism
was rife on the British Isles and various communist agents were being
exposed in the press. Freign decided to leave the village, despite local
medical advice. He got up from his bed and walked out of his hospital hut.
The translator, who sat outside the hut, looked at him with astonishment.
Freign thanked him for all his help and asked him the way to Badami. The
translator, however, became most excitable and in no time at all he was
surrounded by a hysterical rabble. His next abode was more like a prison
than a hospital and the door of his so-called bedroom was firmly locked.
The translator's toothless face peered occasionally from behind the small
bars half-way up the door. Whenever he asked his guard as to the cause of
his predicament he was told he must rest, 'You rest, Sahib,' or, 'Sahib very
tired, he need rest.'

'You know Beth Freemantle?' Dewey asked, looking across the room to
where Beth was talking to Jo Richards and Maclestone.

'No,' Elaine replied, following Dewey's stare, 'kinda cute though.'

'She's so great. She's just had surgery,' Dewey said in his bitchy tone.

'Oh yeah, where?'

'Everywhere, honey. She was a mess. Now she's opening a gallery and showing Jo Richards, the guy on her left who's kinda good-looking, and then the guy on her right is Bob Maclestone.' Dewey pointed to the back of a man next to Beth who slowly turned round.

Elaine gasped.

Dewey joined his hands together as if in prayer. 'I luuurve hairy men, honey, and paunches and power, and the fat ones are always the best in bed.' Looking down at Elaine, he added, 'Beth was real fat, honey.'

A higher octave reflected Elaine's dismay. 'Why is he powerful, Dewey?'

Dewey looked astonished and then nodded his head from side to side. 'He's one of the biggest collectors in New York,' he said reverentially, eyes agog.

'Oh my God, oh my God, oh my God,' she said, burying herself into Dewey's chest and hitting his shoulder gently with her fist.

'Honey, what's with you?'

Elaine held her short hair in a fist and made a full circle. 'Shit, fuck, shit,' she said angrily.

Dewey put his hand to his chest. 'You didn't do an "Elaine"?'

Elaine looked mournful and shook her head in confirmation. 'I kinda blew him out.'

'Well, they say he likes young girls,' Dewey whined, raising his eyebrows. 'You could make it up to him I guess.'

'No way, Jose.'

Some days later, when he was fully restored to health, Freign asked his translator whether it would be safe to leave. The one-legged, toothless man smiled and adamantly shook his head. Freign tried to explain that it was very important that he should get back to where he came from, but the Indian hit his stick on the parched ground and declared, 'Sahib is very tired today.' Finally, Freign decided that an escape plan would have to be devised. Once a day he was led by an armed guard to an area where he could perform his ablutions. It was obvious to him that this was the only time he could attempt an escape, but he could also see that the village was far too populated to walk through without being noticed.

Having bludgeoned his guard into an unconscious state, Freign hid himself for the whole day under some foliage in the middle of the village. It was an old Red Indian method, taught while training in the Canadian tundra. He then witnessed the effect of his disappearance. The villagers, assuming he had left the compound, organised search parties: every member of the village was called up, put into groups and equipped with sticks. As one group came back another would set out. This continuous activity restricted Freign to his lair for the duration of the night. The next day, more men and women arrived from neighbouring villages and they in turn were grouped and sent out to look for him. At the end of the second day he saw the translator being dragged from his hut to a clearing not far from where he lay. A large circle formed around him. The sticks that people carried now descended upon the old man with inspired violence. Freign, against commando training, decided an innocent man could not be punished for his disappearance and without being noticed raised himself from his hide-out and walked stiffly towards the circle which, upon his arrival, parted in an almost biblical manner. An awed hush descended upon the crowd. Suddenly one of the village elders fell on his knees and knelt like a Mohammedan in prayer. One by one the crowd followed suit and began braying hysterically. Freign picked up the old translator who was lying prostrate and whimpering on the ground and perched him back on his sticks. Using his most authoritative manner, he signalled everybody to rise. With considerable caution, the villagers got up and bowed their heads in quiet reverence.

Dewey was speaking excitedly to John and Rachel Currin. 'It is so fabulous. It had this like, sensational living room with windows all along, looking over the East River, and the art! Oh my God the art!' He put his hand over his mouth and breathed in deeply, making a kind of high-pitched rasping noise. 'So fab ... u ... lous. There was this Katz all along one wall and this really cool Judd stack piece – you know, an early wood one with blue interiors, right, and a gigantic Andre covering the whole floor. John Ashbery was there and he recited a beautiful poem from his latest book ...'

Bob Maclestone is here. Bob is like, the biggest collector, right and what's so great is that he's been like real supportive about me opening a gallery. He's really great. The other day he walked into Robert Miller and bought like, three Kusama, just like that. He's gotta meet Jo.

Maclestone pointed a finger at Jo. 'So is this going to be your first sh-show?'

'I've been in shows, but not a one-man,' Jo replied.

Maclestone suppressed a yawn. 'Right.'

'Yeah, I'm really excited about it, Bob,' Jo said awkwardly.

'Well, I got to ah, see it. What kind of work?'

'I'm kinda Minimalist, I work with kinda dysfunctional objects and ...'

Beth adjusted her glasses nervously and broke in, 'They're really great, Bob. I'm real excited about the work. We're opening in May, did I tell you that, Bob? It's going to be so great,' she rattled on.

Jo added earnestly, 'Yeah, Bob, I would very much like to know your opinion.'

'Well, that ah, that's ah, sounds ah, great.' Maclestone coughed and shot a glance across at Paige who was standing a few yards away, 'Oh, there's ah ... I ah, have to ah ...'

'Sure, Bob, no problem,' Jo said as Maclestone made to go.

'Well, g-good luck, ah ah ...' Bob struggled to remember Jo's name before Jo reminded him of it. 'Jo,' he said, 'Jo Richards.'

'Jo, I'll be seeing you.'

'Thank you, Mr Maclestone.'

'Thank me?' Maclestone sounded perplexed.

'For the luck.'

'Ah yes, of, of course.'

'I'll send you a card, Bob,' Beth called out as Maclestone turned away.

'You ah, do that,' Bob replied.

Jo felt a wave of panic as Maclestone walked away. He felt that didn't go so well and for a moment this was confirmed in Beth's reaction. 'I just don't, like, fucking believe it,' she said under her breath, as Maclestone's outstretched hand found Paige's lean waist.

'What's wrong, Beth?' Jo asked guiltily as he prepared to hear the worst.

'Paige fucking Quale,' she replied. 'Men are so obvious.'

'Oh right,' Jo breathed a sigh of relief.

Singh, the translator, explained that this was a 'Thuggee community' and if it had not been for the discovery of a flute on his person implying he was a musician, a profession sacred under Thuggee law, Freign would have been eliminated. Singh managed to explain, with some difficulty, how Thuggee had sprung from a mixture of rogue Mohammedans from the Mogul invasion in the seventeenth century and Hindus who worshipped Kali, the goddess of destruction. The Hindus, he said, believed that in the beginning there were gods of creation and destruction and as time went on, the creative gods produced more quickly than the destructive ones could destroy. So to redress the balance, Kali created three or four votaries called Thuggees whose aim was to murder in the purest way.

'This is Elaine Yoon,' Dewey said.

Beth looked at her without hiding her curiosity for Elaine's various adornments. 'Beth Freemantle. I just love your rings.'

'Oh thanks,' Elaine replied glumly. An awkward silence followed before Beth said, 'So Elaine, you like the show?'

'Yeah, I think it's real interesting.'

'Are you like, an artist, Elaine?' Beth asked, trying to force her into a conversation.

Elaine looked puzzled for a second and said, 'Yeah, kinda thing.'

'You don't seem like, certain?'

'I go to Cooper Union.'

'You study art?'

'Yeah, and you?'

'I'm between jobs. I used to work at the Art Spindle Gallery and ...'

'The Art Spindle Gallery!' Elaine exclaimed.

'Yeah. The Art Spindle Gallery, but we like, parted company.'

'So now what?'

'Well, you know, Elaine, I'm gonna open my own gallery.'

'That's great ... where?'

'On Twenty-second Street next to the Dia Foundation. We got a fabulous space on the second floor.'

'Who are you showing?'

'We're opening with an artist called Jo Richards. He's like, so great. This is his first one-man show. I'm really excited by the work.'

'What kinda work?'

'He's doing this like, installation of kinda dysfunctional objects, you know, like household things.'

'Oh yeah?'

'Yeah.'

'Sounds cool.'

'Yeah, it's really great and then our next show is like, a works on paper show.'

Freign discovered his new-found friends and their peculiar ways rather to his liking and decided to explore this ancient religion and its practices. He was allowed to accompany the Thuggees on their many expeditions until he himself became one of them. One day, Singh sent word from Goa that he had gained the confidence of some American tourists who were visiting temples and that he was accompanying them as their guide the day after next to see the Vittala Temple. Freign selected a few Thuggees and set out for the temple where he waited for the group to arrive. Freign was casually inspecting the temple dressed in a white flannel suit, when Singh and five American tourists appeared. Occasionally, Freign would scribble notes in a little black leather note-book. It was not long before the insatiable curiosity of the Americans prevailed and a conversation was struck up. Freign's genuine interest in temples and architecture, enhanced by his considerable knowledge of the former, together with his easy charm and meticulous manners, soon seduced the Americans and in no time at all the old Texan couple were issuing invitations to Galveston and the Virginians insisted he visit them in Charlottesville. The fifth member of the group, a pretty Bostonian girl, wandered off among the ruins where she could be seen scrutinising various carvings and periodically consulting her guide-book. Freign explained that he was an archaeologist on his way through the area to a dig of some importance. After some more conversation he invited the group to dine with him at his camp.

Jean Maclestone and Art Spindle found themselves in the same elevator going up to the Mendia Krew exhibition.

'Jean,' Art cried, 'I was hoping I'd run into you here.'

Jean looked up at the changing floor numbers. 'You didn't ring back this afternoon, Art.'

'Oh Gaad, I'm sorry, Jean, I was at the doctor, I got back late and ...'

'Are you pregnant?'

Art laughed out loud. 'Am I pregnant?' After another two floors of laughter he repeated, 'Am I pregnant?' and, leaning forward, attempted to kiss her on the cheek, but Jean swayed to the left and just managed to retrieve her balance before the elevator doors opened on to the Krew show. As it happened, the first person she saw was her husband talking to a fair haired girl in a tight Dolce & Gabbana dress. Par for the course, she thought to herself, but Maclestone managed to score the first goal. 'Hello, ah, you two,' he insinuated.

'Oh Bob, how are you? And Paige ...' Art began.

Using Art's assist pass, Jean drove in the equaliser. 'All friends, ah,' she said deliberately and, extending her hand out to a bemused Paige, added, 'I'm Jean Maclestone by the way.' As she extended her hand, she looked at the two men incredulously.

'As ah, you must know, Jean, Paige works fo-fo-for Art here,' Maclestone slammed in to go one ahead.

'Sure does,' Art added, attempting to stabilise matters with gung-ho cheerfulness.

'That does not altogether surprise me,' Jean said sarcastically. Paige was beginning to realise she was the puck in the Stanley Cup Final and tried to withdraw. 'I have to speak to a client,' she managed.

'Oh, don't let us drive you away, we're all friends here, you know, in varying degrees, but friends all the same.'

Paige would have liked to use the reference to 'degrees' as a quip about the present atmosphere, but, remembering just in time that her off-the-cuff humour was limited, nearly always producing the opposite effect to the one intended, she resisted. Instead, Paige hesitated, and stumbling awkwardly, expressed how much she was enjoying the show before descending sharply into opinions about the work. Jean heard out Paige's attempts and then, aiming a cold dead stare at her sweating husband, asked, 'And have you bought something?'

'No, I ah,' Maclestone started.

'Surprising,' Jean commented sarcastically. Art and Paige managed to peel off on some banal excuse.

'Looks like shit to me,' Jean said, looking around the various pink objects on the wall.

'Art might per-persuade you otherwise.'

'At least he has some worthwhile opinions.'

But Maclestone saved this one in the nick of time. 'You c-call those opinions?' he asked.

Jean bit her lip and looked over Bob's shoulder pretending she hadn't heard Bob's devastating last quip.

'Somebody's videoing us, Bob. Do you know who that is?'

Bob turned around but Elaine's camera had continued on its passage around the room.

It was a warm evening and the sun cast long shadows in the clearing where Freign had chosen to set up camp. The tourists arrived, and after some polite introductions they sat down for dinner. Conversation flowed convivially as Freign's accomplices hovered discreetly in the background. He explained that they were hired diggers for a site he was to begin work on. Freign sat next to Miss Arrowsmith, the young lady from Boston, a talkative girl with disarming wit and at times quite outspoken. Gradually and much to his chagrin, he found himself feeling quite attached to her, an unfortunate occurrence as he had prescribed himself to be her murderer.

As the evening drew into the night and the moon rose and her pupils dilated, Freign's heart grew heavier. The hour was fast approaching when he would have to give the *jhirnee*: the signal for murder. Realising he would not be able to kill her himself, he decided to consult his trusted servant Singh, whom he had saved from certain death, and who was now always near his side. After a while he rejoined his guests, excusing himself for his absence, and continued to participate in the light-hearted and informal conversations now infecting them. After half an hour or so he called out calmly, '*Hooshiaree*,' the preparatory signal; the servants stationed themselves behind the guests, none of whom suspected their imminent fate; conversation continued until Freign finally gave the *jhirnee*: he cleared his throat and shouted '*Jey kalee*' upon which the so-called waiters stepped forward in unison and, with skilful dexterity, slung their kerchiefs around the unsuspecting necks, twisting the cloth in such a way as to snap the upper spine. The only sound made was a chorus of clicks like the snapping of fingers before the victims, without the slightest struggle, went limp. Once the thug stranglers were completely sure that they were dead they released their grip and the bodies slumped forward on to the table. Freign had done the same with his designated victim but as he whipped the kerchief around her delicate neck he had whispered to her to feign death. Being a quick-witted girl, she did as she was told.

'I'm sorry, Beth, but I had to get that,' Elaine said.

'Oh, why's that?' Beth asked.

'I'm doing this kinda video installation piece, you know.'

Dewey suddenly emerged between them again. 'You'll never guess who I've just seen,' he said excitedly.

'Elaine was just like, telling me about her video piece.'

'You are just going to love this piece, Beth. It is going blow everybody's mind. It is so fucking weird.' Dewey held his hand to his chest.

Beth had asked Elaine to join them for a drink but Elaine declined. 'I gotta work tonight, Beth,' she said despondently.

'You gotta work tonight?' Beth queried.

'Yeah, I got a part-time job in a bar.'

'You know, Elaine, I'd really like to see your work some day.'

'That would be great, Beth.'

'Gimme your number, Elaine.' She scribbled her number on a deli receipt she found in her pocket. Beth put the paper in her bag. 'I'll call you next week. It was great meeting you.'

'Yeah, great meeting you, Beth.' As they moved apart, Spindle tapped Beth on the shoulder. She swung around to be confronted by her old boss whom she had not seen since they parted company.

Spindle's greeting was dependent on the importance of the recipient. Beth was an ex-employee and would normally not merit more than a limp simper but, somewhere in the back of his calculating mind, he felt that she was going places, and so he gave her more of an elaborate welcome. Swathed in a broad and toothy smile, he approached her as if she were a long-lost friend. Grabbing her shoulders, he descended upon her; his pursed lips pressed silently against her skin before receding back into a hovering smile. His fingers then unclamped her forearms where they had fallen into a reciprocated semi-formal embrace. Spindle's eyes darted over her upwardly turned head, and finding there was no one of importance to distract him, he began a conversation.

'Do you think he'll do it, Jean?' Dewey said, looking over to where Spindle was talking to Beth.

'I'm working on it but you know he's so stubborn,' Jean Maclestone replied.

'It would be such a great show to do. I can't believe he's hesitating. So what did you do today? Did you hear about Ford and Francesca?' Jean looked inquisitively at Dewey, letting him continue. 'Oh my Gaad, you haven't?'

Spindle comes up to me, like real smarmy, with a big greedy grin and says in that smooth way, 'Hey, Beth, I always knew you had it in you to open a gallery.' Boy is he an ass hole, and then he starts like, congratulating me and you know what he said, 'So I expect you've got a real good mailing list.' As

*if like, insinuating that I had stolen his, which is totally right but you don't
say it, right?*

Elaine Yoon-Jung Yi slipped out of Anna Slant's gallery. As she was making
her way down Broadway she reached down into the inside of her leather
jacket and switched off her recorder. It had been a good evening's work.
Not only had she recorded a big-time art collector making a pass at her,
but she had also videoed his wife arrive with Art Spindle who was,
according to Dewey, her lover. It was all on tape. This piece was gonna
shake the art world. She'd also gotten Beth Freemantle interested in her
work. When Elaine turned right on Canal a freezing wind took her breath
away. She crossed Canal and a few minutes later she was pushing at the
door of Heaven Can't Wait.

'Jesus, it's Dewey Bozo,' Spindle mumbled to himself as Dewey approached him. Dewey had been pestering him about doing some show and
now, because he was Jean's new confidant, he'd become all over familiar.
     'Art, you look fabulous, I love the suit. Where is it from? No, wait – Paul
Smith – it's got to be with those lapels and,' he opened Art's jacket so that
the bright blue lining displayed itself, 'and the lining is always so neat ...'

'I'm sorry, Bob. My boyfriend is meeting me here and we're going out for
dinner.' Paige declined as she slid a fake-fur coat over her shoulders.
     'Well ah, maybe ah, we could have dinner another time, Paige?' Bob
asked awkwardly, reeling at the news of Paige's relationship. He had been
given the impression by Art Spindle that Paige was single.
     'That would be great, Bob,' Paige replied, smiling broadly. John Smythe,
a Brit banker from Wall Street, had taken her out a couple of times but had
not as yet made a move. He was a tall young man with fair hair and a thin
face. His aquiline nose supported a pair of gold-rimmed oval specs. He had
a surprisingly high voice with a slight lisp. They had met at Lorne's party
where he had talked intensely and eloquently about riding and mushrooms.
Paige, who had enjoyed his turn of phrase more than the subjects, had
quickly accepted an invitation for dinner. The first dinner was at a

charming French restaurant uptown named Le Figaro. He had described his family and ancestral background for most of the evening after which he had accompanied her back to her apartment. She had hoped for a kiss at least but John Smythe had merely raised her hand in his and, with a slight bow, passed his lips over her knuckles. When she had looked at her watch in the elevator she was surprised to see that it was only ten o'clock.

Elaine wore fishnet stockings, suspenders, black panties and a white tank-top cut just below her breasts. She turned away from her audience and placed her hands on the vast mirror which stretched across the dance floor and up to the ceiling. Keeping her legs straight she bent down, letting her hands slide down the mirror until her forehead touched the floor. Staring at her through her legs were the beady eyes of a sweaty-looking man with a moustache on which, she noticed, he had a ripple of beer froth. She slid the palms of her hands up from her ankles to the back of her knees and up to her thighs until she reached her buttocks which she proceeded to pull apart, revealing her G-string. The moustache slowly brought out a dollar bill and holding it between two pudgy fingers waved it as close to her fanny as house rules would allow. She pulled the panties strap, allowing him to slip the dollar between strap and flesh. Elaine rolled her tongue over her top lip and moved her hands over her ribcage and under her bosoms which she proceeded to hold firmly so that her nipples protruded between thumb and index finger. Half closing her eyes, she pinched her nipples and arched her back as if in ecstatic pain. A large black man in a voluminous bomber jacket leaned over from the bar, waving another dollar. She invited him to place the note between her bosoms. A Chinaman in his late twenties sat down next to the moustache. Having succeeded in tempting a few custom-ers from the bar to the banquette in front of her, she lay down in front of them and lifted her legs so that they were almost at right angles to her body before lowering them to the floor. She stroked the inside of her thigh before slipping her finger under her panties. The Chinaman broke into a toothy smile and took out a ten dollar bill. He stretched over so that it hung just above her crotch. She drew her hand and touched his, before removing the bill and placing it with the others under the suspender strap. The grinning Chinaman fixed his eyes on the indentation she was making in her panties. Elaine rolled over until she lay flat on her stomach and raised her ass so it was only a foot away from him. She leaned on her left elbow and smoothed her legs and thighs with her right hand before drawing a line with her index finger from the small of her back down across her ass. Finally, she pressed her finger on to her pussy which indented the panties sufficiently to reveal her shaven lips. The Chinaman stopped grinning and rummaged through his pockets for another ten dollar bill.

Old Singh was in charge of the disposal of the bodies once they had been searched and stripped of valuables. He made incisions in the abdomen of the corpses so that they would not swell in the ground once they had been buried, and then ordered them to be thrown into the pit which had been prepared the night before. Night had camouflaged any signs of life that Miss Arrowsmith might have betrayed and so, once she was thrown in, Singh ordered his men to search for all possible evidence before filling in the pit. As soon as they were out of sight, Singh ordered her to hide in the forest and wait there till morning.

It was an excellent haul: two thousand dollars had been found on their persons including rings and other trinkets as well as a large amount of gold from the teeth of the Texans. On Freign's insistence, the lady had been spared the indignity of a body search.

Jean and Dewey had decided to have dinner after the private view. 'I luurve Rialto, have you been there, Jean? It is so great. Let's go there, or maybe Balthazar. What do you think?'

'Balthazar is so noisy, I don't know,' Jean replied unenthusiastically, 'maybe Rialto.'

'I think you would really like Rialto, Jean.'

'Do you have to make a reservation?'

Dewey raised his hand over his shoulder. 'The maître d' is a really good friend of mine.'

Jo, Beth and the Force, as they were known, Yvonne and Carmen, decided to have a drink at Verruca's.

'Isn't Verruca a foot canker?' Jo asked.

'Urgh, a foot canker, no way!' Yvonne squirmed.

'Yeah, I heard that too,' Beth joined in.

'How weird to call a bar after a foot growth,' Carmen pondered. Jo laughed flirtatiously. He really liked Carmen.

John Smythe appeared at the elevator doors with head held high and proceeded to peruse the gallery. He looked for a moment as if he were trying to recognise the scent of something. Paige saw him first and excused herself from Bob's conversation.

'You made it?' she said cheerfully.

'It's very rare that I come downtown,' he said seriously, looking down at the wine glass cast from the artist's bosom. 'I find this kind of art extremely pretentious. Don't you?' he pronounced coldly. Paige noticed the artist was standing close by and flushed.

'I don't know, I kinda like it,' she replied.

'I'm not at all convinced,' he said sternly. John Smythe prepared to stand his ground come what may and was about to conjure a witty and cutting remark when Mendia Krew interrupted his deliberations.

'Paige Quale,' she greeted them effusively, 'so great you came. How ya doin'?'

'Great show, Mendia. This is Mendia Krew, the artist,' Paige introduced.

'John Smythe,' he grunted with a quick bow of the head.

The experience had been intoxicating. Freign fell in love with her and she with him. After a few months of travelling around India they arrived in Bombay where she was to take the boat to Cape Town and then fly back to Boston. Freign had, in effect, deserted the army and was technically a fugitive. They spent several days in a hotel agonising over his future.

Her knuckles could be seen as they moved back and forth under the black fabric. More dollar bills waved around her. Elaine could feel them being placed under her suspender strap. She noticed several men had gathered and were staring at her crotch. Men are such ass-holes, she thought to herself as she pouted seductively at the advancing Chinese man and his twenty dollar bill. Elaine let him slip the bill in her crotch but the tip of his finger remained between her knickers and her shaven lip. Elaine moved away. The Chinese man grinned until he felt the hand of the large black bouncer land on his shoulder and pull him back on to the stool. The two men looked at each other menacingly.

Freign had retained a passport from a Thuggee victim and had used it to enter Pakistan, Afghanistan, Persia and finally Aden where he paid a captain to smuggle him aboard his ship carrying spices destined for Marseilles in France. He spent several months living in a *pension* in the old port area and got a job diving for grey mullet with an old fisherman who would smoke their eggs and sell them in the market. After six months he had saved enough money to pay his way to Tangier where he boarded a boat with a cargo of dates going to New Orleans.

'I find your premise weak. What possible interest is it to anybody that these useless objects are in fact moulds taken from your body? I mean come on, old girl. It's pretentious twaddle,' John Smythe retorted aggressively.

'Who the fuck is this creep, Paige?' Mendia Krew asked angrily, turning to Paige who was flushed pink with embarrassment. 'You know what, your friend is a real ass-hole,' Mendia said emphatically.

'A part of the anatomy, my dear girl, that I presume your so-called art comes from,' Smythe shouted back.

As soon as the words had left his mouth he felt a sharp sting on his cheek. The artist had slapped him hard. It took him a few seconds to realise what had happened by which time she had walked away, much to the admiration of the gallery who were triumphantly clapping and whooping. Paige was mortified.

Miss Arrowsmith flew down to New Orleans where Freign had installed himself in the most luxurious hotel. They stayed for two weeks, almost all of which was spent in their room.

Rhinegold felt thirsty. He mumbled under his breath and manoeuvred himself so that he faced the door leading to the hall. 'Freign!' he called out. 'Frrreign!' A few words of German followed his second attempt. There being no response, Rhinegold made his way to the large mahogany desk and pressed a small red button.

A loud buzzing noise interrupted Freign's train of thought. He removed *British Administration in India 1800-1880* by Major John Sparrow from his chest, and got up from his bed. He put on his beautifully ironed jacket and made his way downstairs.

Elaine had made eighty dollars in one shift, three times the usual amount, and almost all coming from the Chinese man. It was customary for the girls to hang out at the bar with generous clients. Elaine disliked this part of the job intensely but under house rules she was obliged to participate in these conversations. The Chinese man would have to buy an extortionately expensive glass of champagne which was in fact soda with a drop of white wine after which she would have to pretend to be fascinated by his conversation. The man turned out to be a computer nerd and proceeded to explain how exhilarating it was spending eighty per cent of his life in front of a plastic box. Evidently he earned a fair amount of money doing so and towards the end of their talk he offered her five hundred dollars to sleep with him. What interested her was that his request was made with exactly the same effusiveness as the discourse on computers.

Having braced themselves for the outside, Paige Quale and John Smythe left the Basset Building and crossed over Broadway to Balthazar. The owner, Keith McNally, happened to be at the entrance. John Smythe greeted him in familiar fashion but McNally did not seem to recognise him and so Smythe reminded him of some occasion or other to which McNally responded with a muted smile and an 'Oh yeah' response. He obviously had no idea who Smythe was. Fortunately John had booked several days in advance and they were placed at a banquette for two at the back of the restaurant.

'Isn't this just divine?' Dewey said, having managed to get a table from his friend, the maître d. He waved at some friends and finally sat down with Jean.

'People,' he began with a sigh, 'there are just so many people in this world.' Dewey unfolded his napkin and broke a piece of French bread in half.

'What did you think of the show?' Jean asked, looking into her compact.

'I think it was kinda interesting. What did you think?'

'Kinda interesting …'

Bob Maclestone and Art Spindle ended up together at Da Silvanos. Larry Gagosian was there and greeted Bob effusively and nodded at Art with a wry smile. They did not like each other.

'So what did you think of the show?' Art asked as he fiddled with a bread stick.

'Kinda sexy,' Bob growled.

'Yeah,' Art agreed.

Jo spoke into Carmen's ear at Verruca's. 'What did you think of the Krew show?'

'I think we're going to buy a couple, she's so great.'

'She's original. I like that wine glass. You know Marie-Antoinette did that with her tits?' Jo said, smiling broadly.

'Really?'

'Yeah, maybe you should do some. I would definitely buy a set,' he said, glancing down at Carmen's chest. Carmen was about to reply when Beth interrupted, 'So what did you think of Mendia's new work?'

'We were saying how much we liked it,' Carmen replied.

'Oh really, ah.' Beth hesitated as she weighed up saying she disliked the show because Jo was so obviously flirting with her or agreeing because she and Yvonne might be clients in the future.

'I think there is like, something real interesting about the work, you know? Like tactile.'

'I feel I must apologise for my outburst, Paige, but I do stand by my opinion that this kind of work is absurd,' Smythe pontificated while cleaning his specs with a napkin. 'I cannot believe how gullible people are. A mould of her thingy! Quite apart from being darn right vulgar it has no, no,' he fingered the air and hunched up his shoulders, 'no soul.'

'Maybe, John, but I was so like, embarrassed,' she said, looking down at her plate. 'She's a friend of mine, you know?'

'I'm sorry, darling,' he said truthfully. Paige looked up at him with half a smile. He sounded so pompous and who did he think he was calling her 'darling'. It was as if his familiarity was drawing her into his world. She felt a sudden claustrophobic dislike for him which was compounded by his producing a monogrammed handkerchief and blowing his nose.

'Good old American snapper, sometimes I wonder if there is anything but the snapper on these shores. In the UK,' he said, lounging back on the leather banquette, 'we have a variety of fish because we have what is called the Continental Shelf – a plateau extending out to sea bathed in the warm waters of the Gulf Stream part of which, incidentally, runs along the coast of the United States meeting the arctic waters in Canada. Have you ever read Kipling?'

Freign brought in a glass of water and placed it on Mr Rhinegold's side table.

'I don't vant to zell, Robert. I don't vant to zell ze Mondrian.'

'I understand your misgivings but Mr Horovitz said the hospital bills will be quite significant and ...'

'Ze hospital bills?'

'For Mrs Rhinegold.'

'Yes, yes but ze picture belongs to Alfreda. It is a masterverk that she wants to leave to the Museum. Vat about the ... the ... Braque?'

'Something to do with your will, sir. It seems the Mondrian is the only painting you can sell without asking your daughter.'

'I should have never left ze paintings to her.'

'No, sir.'

'Zat will be all. Goud night, Rrrobert,' Rhinegold said with a sleepy yawn.

'Good night, sir.' Freign left the room silently and made his way upstairs. Once in the safety of his room he removed his suit and put on a pair of green corduroy trousers. He left his white shirt on. A few minutes later Freign was holding his tweed coat tightly about him and walking east down Seventy-fourth Street towards Third Avenue.

CHAPTER FIVE

THREE WEEKS LATER, DINNER

Dewey sat at the bar of the Odeon drinking a dry Martini, waiting for Jo. Jo was late. The Brandt show had just opened at Anna Slant's and there was a party for twelve in the corner. Barbara Repo was at a table with Ashley Bickerton, Michael Joo and Marcia Fortes. Art Spindle and Jean Maclestone were there as was Andrea Rosen with a gaggle of girls.

'What time is it?' Art asked Jean as she was arranging her lapel – the weight of her new, gold lizard brooch had pulled it down.

'Eight,' she barked looking at her watch, 'well, just after eight.'

Spindle sipped his water and looked about the restaurant. He noticed Dewey sitting at the bar.

'Bozo's here,' he said.

'Oh Dewey, that's great,' she began before Spindle cut her off.

'Let's not get him over here, Jean. He gives me the creeps.'

'You don't know him, Art. He's really a great kid.'

'It's just he keeps pestering me about this fucking show.'

Jean looked at Art and hunched up her shoulders. 'If he comes over, he comes over. Anyway, it's a great idea for a show. I think you should reconsider.'

'Jesus, Jean, these kinda shows are a dime a dozen. I get asked twice a week by eager beaver curators who think their ideas about looking at art are gonna shake the world and then what happens? You get a review or two and a big bill at the end of the show. Then, more often than not, you get stuck with a bunch of unsaleable shit which you have to insure and ship or store for ten years. Jean, you should see the warehouse – I got things which look like dog shit from the sixties because some guy like Bozo thought it should be compared with Warhol or Rauschenberg. I tell you, those kinda exhibits either make bad art look better than it is or more usually good art look second-rate. Jean, I've seen it all, trust me … Hello, Ivor. How are you?' Art ended effusively as he saw Ivor Schneider approach the table.

'Hey, Art man. Jean, yeah. This is Chelsea,' Ivor said as he moved in front of a vacuous blonde chewing on some gum.

'Is Earl coming?' Ivor asked.

'Here he is,' Jean said, smiling at the oncoming figure of Earl Magrath.

When Elaine arrives she like, kisses me on the lips but like, real hard. She looks so butch like, she's wearing this real tight leather jacket which she unzips and she's got this torn white T-shirt, you know, which kinda exposes like, a lot, you know and her jeans are all torn but in the wrong places, you know what I mean? And then she's got these like, rings through her lips, and her tongue has a like, a bolt through it as well. Can you believe that?

Elaine and Beth sat at the non-smoking table at the Harmony restaurant on 100 West Houston. Beth wore a light Anna Sui outfit. Her hair was pinned back at the sides and fell on to her shoulders at the back. Elaine wore a leather jacket and a simple white T-shirt. No bra, no make-up. Her faded jeans had tears at the knees and she had on a pair of big black army boots. Nell, the proprietress, welcomed Beth like an old friend.

'Darling, you look gorgeous,' she screamed in an Australian accent. After the introductions Elaine and Beth sat in the corner of the non-smoking section of the restaurant.

Beth looked earnestly at Elaine, 'So how's the work going, Elaine?'

Elaine leaned her head on her right elbow. 'Well, I think it's going pretty good.'

'It sounded like real interesting when you mentioned it to me at the opening.'

'Yeah?'

'Dewey rang me this morning and when I said I was seeing you, he said that your piece was going to be like, out of this world.'

'Did he? That is so great of him,' Elaine said, flatly.

'Tell me about it,' Beth said and then added half jokingly, 'sell it to me, baby.'

'Yeah, well the video itself is like a collage of situations, right? Where a combination of events that I find myself in,' Elaine started rotating her hands around each other, 'are twisted in such a way as to re-create what has actually happened, right?'

'That's real interesting. You mean like, you maybe reverse situations and kinda like, rebuild them?' Beth asked, knotting her brow.

Elaine scratched the back of her head. 'Right,' she said and paused momentarily. 'It's a collage of events which is composed to reveal the underbelly of our lives.'

'So like, what kinda situations do you video?'

'Everything, but it's divided into two main areas; one is my public life, like, the politics of it and the other is my personal life and I suppose it's how one affects the other.'

'That sounds really great.'

'Then, and this is the whole point of it in a way, while the video is running I'm recording the spectator watching it.'

'Wow.'

'And in another room the original is being shown in sync with the recording of the spectators, right?'

'This is going to be so neat,' Beth said, sipping her water. She felt a little drunk and was beginning to loose the clarity of her thoughts; the tortuous threads of Elaine's explanations were beginning to fray.

'The idea,' Elaine said, 'is that it is a continuous piece which only exists when people are looking at it but at the same time they can't ever look at themselves as spectators. In other words it's only really a work of art when you're witnessing yourself which can never be. If you see what I mean?' Elaine leaned back on the banquette and put her hand in her jacket pocket. She felt around her recorder to check it was still on and leaning across the table she whispered, 'I have a secam on me all the time and when, like, something interesting happens, right, or even plain boring, right, I put it on.'

Beth's eyes opened wide. 'You mean like, you have it with you now?' she asked.

'Yeah, I have it with me,' Elaine replied, opening her satchel and producing her camera.

'I luurved Brane's show,' Dewey prompted as he tore his bread in half.

Jo stroked his chin. 'It was a great show. It kind of reminded me of early Burri,' he agreed.

'Absolutely. Just what I was thinking, that kinda thing with material and texture.' Dewey gesticulated on texture before moving up an octave. 'Look, there's Schneider.' He waved frantically. Schneider, who was standing at the entrance next to a tall girl with black hair, screwed up his eyes and half-heartedly waved back.

Bob Maclestone and Paige Quale sat in the darkened corner of Café Luxembourg on the Upper West Side. Bob wore a baggy Issey Miyake navy-blue suit with a loose Armani turtle-neck sweater, whereas Paige wore a grey-green pleated Marc Jacobs skirt and a tight white organza top. Bob was half-way through a red snapper with lime and white wine sauce while Paige was delicately cutting through a baked sea bass with hollandaise. Bob had ordered an excellent Chassagne-Montrachet.

'So in 1966 I left 'Na-Nam and ah, came back to N-New York. I had an inheritance from my aunt and I b-bought this s-s-small building downtown on Th-Thirtieth Street. We converted it into ah, apartments, right and then we sold them.'

'Ah ha.'

'Then I bought another building on the ah, Upper West Side. It was a great th-thirties building. We c-converted that too and sold the ah, apartments to these guys from Ka-Kansas.'

'Ah ha.'

Dewey looked up at the ceiling where a mirror reflected the front tables. 'Spindle's here,' he said, inviting Jo to follow his stare.

Jo shifted uneasily in his chair. 'Oh yeah, where?'

'At Schneider's table. On the right by the window,' Dewey indicated, 'and he's with Jean. I have to say hi to Jean.'

'Who's Jean?'

'You know, Jean Maclestone.'

'Bob Maclestone's wife?'

'They have a thing,' Dewey whined.

Jo screwed up his face. 'What!' he exclaimed. 'You mean with Spindle?'

'With Spindle,' Dewey confirmed knowingly, as he took the wine menu from the waiter.

'Maclestone doesn't know?'

'He kinda does but gets off on it, you know?' Dewey said, looking down at the wine list. 'This Chilean is real good, Jo.'

'We went to the Aids benefit at the Guggenheim,' Jean began, 'and Winters spoke and he was so great. Bob bought the Drapper. It's a really great piece, one of the early ones, you know?'

'You bought the Drapper, Jean!' Spindle exclaimed.

'We did,' Jean said, turning towards him.

'Oh my God Jean, you bought that?' Earl chuckled. 'I showed him and we managed to keep the whole collection together.'

Jean looked at him quizzically. 'You did?'

'We didn't sell anything,' Earl said, to a flurry of laughter.

Beth's hand darted forward enthusiastically and she began rubbing her thumb against her fingers as if she were feeling something silky. 'His work is like, kinda surreal, right,' she said. 'Kinda weird like Bosch sort of thing, right, you know? Like weird animal-human images in jungles, you know? Like kinda post-neo-romantic, right? Real weird stuff.'

Elaine frowned. 'Totally weird.'

'Kinda reminded me of Bayou's, kinda thing,' Beth went on.

Elaine looked straight into Beth's eyes. 'Oh yeah, Bayou's, right. You mean like, real steamy and humid?' she said languidly.

Beth removed her glasses and started wiping them with her napkin.

'Yeah, real humid kinda work, you know?' she laughed.

I'm beginning to think she's being like, real flirtatious, you know, like looking at me in the eyes and leaning forward when I'm saying something so she's real close to my face and she keeps saying how beautiful I am, which is nice of her but I get the feeling that it's like, more than that, you know what I mean? Oh, and over the appetizer, when I was like, talking about the gallery and how I was like, real nervous and stuff, she stroked my face.

'I am having a show in Detroit and Dallas on the same day. I just don't know which one to go to,' Schneider said, leaning back on his chair with his thumbs dug into his trouser pockets.

'Well, Dallas is great,' Chelsea said, her lip-gloss sparkling against the raised wine glass. Ivor had brought her along to make up the table.

'Yeah, l think she's right, Dallas is great,' Spindle joined in.

'You must look up the Fishes while you're there,' Jean suggested, glancing towards Schneider while she dabbed some powder on her nose. 'They're great collector friends of mine,' she added, clicking shut her compact.

'Oh yeah,' Spindle gesticulated with the palm of his hand, 'they're real important collectors, Ivor.'

Schneider nodded his head. 'Yeah, maybe Dallas.'

'I think he would really enjoy Dallas,' Spindle said, turning towards Chelsea.

'Oh really,' Chelsea replied.

'... and I might be working with him. I'm doing this show about post-classical-post-mythological imagery.' Dewey ended his long monograph on Art Spindle.

'You mean like ...' Jo began before Dewey interrupted.

'Like, how artists have used ideas and images from mythology and Roman stuff and ...'

'You mean like Dali and Clemente and ...'

'Yes, yes, yes and ...'

'Sounds like a great idea,' Jo cut in, half listening and half mulling over whether or not he could somehow fit in with Dewey's show criteria.

'You see, I think artists are unconsciously aware of it, I mean like even Andre has a Roman monumentality which is like ...'

'I know what you mean, Dewey. It's like when I was at the Met the other day, in the Eygptian rooms, and I had this feeling, you know – kinda the weight of history and the geometry ...'

'You go to the Met?' Dewey asked, looking surprised.

'Yeah, I try to get there once a week ...'

'Then in 'seventy-two we ah, bought these buildings in Pittsburgh. Great buildings and we converted them into off-offices. That's when we ah, we started leasing.'

'Ah ha.'

'It was around about then I-I met Johns and bought a version of the map, you know? It was a great buy and I sold it in 'eighty-eight.'

'Ah ha.'

'At the height of the m-market.'

'No, it wasn't like, painful,' Beth grimaced, 'but like, afterwards it was real bad.'

Elaine pulled at one of her three lip rings. 'Gee, Beth.'

'It like, itched real bad for a couple of weeks, you know? And like, the bruising was there for like, a month, like, those rings must have hurt real bad too?'

'Yeah, but now it's cool,' Elaine drawled.

'Yeah, Elaine, they look great.'

So we were talking about her rings and studs and stuff when she like, lifted her T-shirt and showed me her boobs right in the middle of the restaurant

and like, she had rings there too and then, she asked me to like, sit with her
on the banquette, and she unzipped her fly and she like, had a clit ring. This
girl is wild. So I asked what it was like, when you like, you know, do it and
stuff and she said it was kinda painful but sexy, but for your partner it was
like, something else!

'So what are you showing?' Dewey asked.

Jo cleared his throat and laid his hands on the table-cloth, stroking the surface as if to flatten out all the creases. 'I'm doing these kinda dysfunctional objects, you know?'

Dewey raised his eyebrows. 'Hey.'

'Yeah.'

'Like ah …'

'They're kind of non-things but like, they look real,' Jo explained, rotating his index finger. 'Like a refrigerator that kinda isn't,' he went on.

Dewey cocked his head. 'Like common utility objects, you mean?'

'Yeah and cupboards and …' Jo began, before Dewey interrupted and deliberating on each word said, 'So you choose the object and dysfunctionalise it?'

'Yeah, right. I kinda play God,' Jo chuckled, 'and choose what I'm gonna make art then strip it of use.'

'And of personality,' Dewey added, before pealing into prolonged laughter.

'Right,' Jo responded equally amused.

'So, how many pieces have you got?'

'Four or …' Jo hesitated and looking up at the ceiling added, 'or five.'

'So you got the *Frigidaire* and …'

'Yeah and a real elegant cupboard, a *G E Freezer*, a single bed, and ah, ah, I gotta think of another one,' Jo said, tapping his finger against the wine glass.

Dewey pointed at him. 'How about bookshelves?' he suggested.

Jo looked serious. 'Yeah maybe, maybe.'

Dewey frowned. 'But how do you dysfunctionalise a bed, Jo?'

'The bed is made of concrete,' he replied with a twinge of self-satisfaction.

Dewey clicked his fingers. 'What a piece,' he said, deliberating on the word 'piece'.

'Thanks, Dewey. It's great, you know, I think you really understand the work.' Jo smiled.

Ivor turned to Art. 'So Art, are you gonna move to Chelsea?'

'Leo called me the other day and told me he'd seen a few spaces down there but when he told me the rents I said are you goddamn crazy. I mean I pay less on Fifty-seventh Street. Anyway if I learnt something in life it's that you don't follow people, you get people to follow you, right. I tell ya tomorrow it'll be another area of town. What do I need it for anyway? All the furs are uptown.'

'I like it though. It's different, you know what I mean?' Ivor said.

'I'm not saying it's not great but ...'

'Did I hear you're moving to Chelsea?' Earl suddenly asked.

'I was just saying to the Master here that it's a great area but ...'

'Art, it would be so great if you moved to Chelsea,' Jean chipped in.

'So I was at a Claes Oldenburg opening at the Green Room and I saw And-Andy Warhol standing ah, not talking to anybody, you know? So, I just kinda walked up to him and s-said "Hi". We talked as much as ah, anybody could, to Warhol and he invited me to the factory. Two weeks l-later my wife and I visited him. We had a ball we really did and Andy ah, decided that he wanted to do Jean and I.'

'Ah ha.'

I told her all about Hans Agnesto, this guy I was dating after Thomas Johnson. What a creep. He was this guy who worked in the like, contemporary department at Sotheby's and who I thought was like, real cool, you know, he was like, German, Italian, French and Spanish all wrapped into one. You know the type? He was real smart but a bit of a like, mommy's boy, so when we finally, like, get to the getting it together time, he freaks.

Beth pushed her arms into her side, making her bosoms jut out, and splayed the palms of her hands outwards in front of her. 'Anyway, he was like, such an ass-hole. He said he like, couldn't handle like the scars and I said they're not like, permanent right, and you know what he said?' Beth put her hands on her hips. 'In my mind they are.'

Elaine rolled her eyes. 'Oh Jesus, forget him, Beth.'

Beth threw her right hand out in front of her and touched Elaine's wrist. 'Elaine, no problem.'

Elaine looked at her sleepily. 'I like scars anyway.'

'You do, Elaine?'

'Yeah, I think they're kinda sexy. I got tattoos like all over,' she drawled.

'All over?' Beth quizzed. 'You mean like, everywhere?'

So I told her all about this like, stuff and she shows me these tattoos all around her arms and shoulders. Then she says she's got some on her ass and before she shows me I like, say to her, 'later girl, later.' Uncontrollable.

'Well, Jo, you describe it so well,' began Dewey, taking a cigarette out of a packet of Merit, 'I'm gonna write an article.'

'You will?' Jo said, leaning over and lighting Dewey's cigarette.

Dewey raised his glass as if in confirmation. 'Yeah, I'm gonna get *Translations* to do it.'

'That would be just great, Dewey. Just great.' Jo smiled and dragged at his cigarette.

'Excuse me, sir,' the waitress intervened, 'we've had a complaint about the smoking.'

'This is a smoking area,' Dewey whined.

'Yeah, but they've complained. There's nothing I can do. I'm sorry.'

Dewey slapped his hand on his forehead. 'What is happening to this country? It's like prohibition all over again.'

'I met Ivor ah, way way back in the ah, early eighties. He was having his first show at Nina Sanderson's. They were just great, you know, ah, just great. So I bought the whole ah, whole show.'

'The whole show?'

Freign peered at the ragout of lamb which had just been served to him by a young waitress. He thanked her. He always came to Le Figaro on his night off, it was a habit he had developed over the years due to the restaurant's proximity to Seventy-fourth Street, as well as its reasonable prices. French food was also particularly nostalgic to him, it conjured memories of the short period of time he spent with the French Resistance. Freign had come across them accidentally when he had been separated from his battalion in 1944. He had been hidden behind enemy lines for a tense two months and on more than one occasion his knowledge of French had been sufficiently convincing to deter some overly inquisitive SS officers.

Rhinegold's mother hovered over him with a broad lipsticked smile. She looked very pretty with that smile, he thought. 'My little Alfie,' she said, bending over him and kissing his lips. But the lips did not leave him; they lingered, and when he felt cold hands running over his body his mother suddenly turned into his wife and he gasped with astonishment.

'It's alrightee,' a voice said. The figure raised itself above him and he realised it wasn't either his mother or his wife but Dolores, and Dolores was taking her night dress off. Rhinegold woke up with a start. He shuddered. He was cold. Dolores was in front of him holding a tray with his evening medicine.

'I bought my first Basquiat from Anina Nosei. I'd first seen his work at a gallery run by Guillaeme Gallozzi and Jo LaPlaca. When I met Jean-Michel he gave me a drag of his joint and it kn-knocked me out. I couldn't think f-for about twelve hours.' Maclestone broke into a loud laugh. 'Ha-hahhaah, Jesus ahah, you should have seen me, ah ah ah.' His chest heaved. Paige hadn't seen Bob so animated before and was a little taken aback.

'That must have been so weird,' she said.

Spindle moved his leg slightly to the right where he found Chelsea Flat's calf.

'Andy used to say that Basquiat was a great artist,' Jean Maclestone was saying.

'I really liked Basquiat,' Schneider responded, 'those late paintings are so powerful, you know, they kinda blow your mind.'

Jean looked at Ivor intensely, 'I'm so glad you think so because they're my favourite,' she agreed.

The girl didn't move her leg away which boded well for Spindle's under the table tactics. He pressed slightly harder: still no reaction.

'So tell me about Spindle. What was it like working for him?'

'He was such an ass-hole, Elaine. I mean, the guy's a control freak. Everyone was so scared of him; he like, shouted all day and then like, my grandmother died and left me some money and so I like, said fuck him and decided to start my own gallery.'

'That's so brave, Beth.'

'More crazy than brave.'

'Okay, crazy and brave.'

'Yeah,' Beth laughed, 'it'll work out.'

'You know, Beth, I have a feeling that this is going to be a really important gallery.'

'You think so, Elaine?'

'Yeah.'

'Well, you know, Elaine, when you were describing me your piece I was like, thinking,' Beth paused and looked seriously into Elaine's eyes, 'I think it would be like, great if we did something together, you know.'

'That would be so great, Beth. I mean, fantastic,' Elaine said enthusiastically.

'I was also kinda thinking, you know for the opening show, when you were like, describing your piece to me, like, I have this smaller gallery off of the main one which would be like, perfect for your installation.'

'Beth, that's in three weeks.'

'Could you get it ready in time?'

Spindle leaned forward and put his hands on his knees, making sure a little more pressure was exerted on the lower calves.

'I have a great Basquiat in at the moment, one of those ...' he said, moving his little finger on to Chelsea's leg.

'You mean the one you showed me on Wednesday?' said Earl.

'Yeah, isn't it great?'

'Oh good, because the one on Tuesday was terrible,' Earl said to everybody's amusement, particularly his own.

Spindle used the short period of mirth to slide his whole hand on to Chelsea's stockinged leg.

Dewey looked across to Spindle's table. 'We should go and say hi.'

'You think we should?' Jo replied, looking down into his empty cappuccino cup.

'So, as I said to Clemente and Katz the other night, I think the Whitney Biennial is shit, you know?'

'I quite agree,' Jean said, 'it's a real bad year.'

Anticipating that any hand movement might arouse suspicion, Spindle moved only his fingers. He roamed a limited area inside her bare thigh. He could feel his own erection hard against his trousers.

'What do you think, Art?' Jean suddenly asked.

Everybody seemed to turn towards him, including the girl who gave him half a smile. He was suddenly consumed with paranoia.

'The Whitney,' he said, clearing his throat and removing his hands from under the table, 'sometimes hits the mark but generally ... doesn't.' This somewhat stilted reply was all he could manage. Everybody waited for Earl to say something funny but his attention had drifted on to another table and suddenly aware of the silence he asked, 'Who is that guy waving at our table?'

Schneider turned around towards Dewey Bozo. 'It's that creep Bozo.'

'Oh, I love Dewey,' Jean said. 'He walks my dog and everything.'

Paige felt a wave of overwhelming nausea. She fixed her sights on Bob
Maclestone's right ear and tried to concentrate on aligning her vision
which she felt was severely out of kilter. Paige's concentrated gaze discon-
certed Maclestone who began nervously touching his ear lobe.

'Can I have a glass of water, Bob?' Paige asked.

Dewey's voice rose as they approached the Schneider table. 'Jean darling,
how are you? And Ivor and Art, hi.'

'Dewey, come and join us,' Jean interrupted, giving him a smile and
throwing an inspectional glance at Jo.

'This is Jo Richards, a very good artist who I'm writing about for his
show at Beth Freemantle's new gallery in – oh, I'm sorry, this is Jean
Maclestone, and Art Spindle who you know and Ivor Schneider who you
know all about, I'm sure.' Dewey gave a broad smile as Jo shook hands with
Jean.

'This is Earl Magrath and Chelsea Flat,' Jean quickly added.

Jo began shaking hands. Art waved to the waiter to bring two chairs.
Earl made an amusing joke. Schneider took his hands out of his pockets.
Chelsea smiled flirtatiously. Dewey twittered nervously about the last time
he'd seen Schneider and how much he'd liked the last show. Jo finished
shaking hands.

'Dewey, you sit here,' Jean beckoned the waiter to bring one of the
chairs next to her, 'and Jo, you sit next to Art and Chelsea, over there.' Art
Spindle forced a smile as Jo squeezed between them.

'It's a new gallery on Twenty-second Street,' Jo was saying, 'I've got the
first show there in May,' he said, talking over Chelsea who was looking at
him with a furrowed expression.

'That sounds great,' she said, looking him in the eye.

'Yeah,' Schneider agreed, 'great.'

'So, you got shows coming up, Ivor?' Jo asked him.

'Yeah, I got a couple of museum shows, Jo.'

'I saw the last show at Annas, really impressive. It was a whole new departure,' Jo said seriously.

'Yeah, I'm real excited about the work, you know.'

Chelsea turned towards Schneider and whispered, 'Ivor, I have to go to work, do you mind if I leave now?'

'I'll get you a cab,' he whispered back.

'I'm meeting Dewey and Jo at Jackie's. You wanna come?' Elaine asked. Beth paused and looked at her watch. 'I really wanna, Elaine, you know like, everybody talks about it, but I have this like, meeting in the morning.'

'You've never been to Jackie's, Beth?' Elaine inquired. 'Jackie's is like, the best,' and then, pointing at her, added, 'You're coming, man. Dewey said he was gonna bring Jo and –'

'Okay,' Beth broke in. 'You've persuaded me but only for like, half an hour.'

Bob asked the driver to take them to Seventy-second and First, Paige's apartment.

'Bob, I can drop you off,' Paige suggested weakly.

'I p-prefer to see you home first, you just never kn-know these days,' Bob said, scratching his scalp. Paige now felt her head spinning out of control. She looked out of the window and tried to focus on the Columbus Avenue traffic.

'You don't have to, Bob,' she said. Her stomach was beginning to make its presence felt. All of a sudden, she wished Bob was not accompanying her all the way across town.

'Anybody for a drink?' Schneider asked, as soon as Art had signed his American Express receipt.

'No, I think I might retire as they say,' Jean said and looking imploringly at Art she asked, 'Will you take me home, Art?' He slipped her a forced smile. 'Sure, Jean, no problem. I have a complete day tomorrow anyhow.'

'I'm meeting my friend Elaine at Jackie's. Why don't you guys come along?' Dewey chirped.

'Jackie 60!' Earl exclaimed. 'Who could refuse?'

The chairs at the Odeon rasped as the whole party got up to go.

'Perhaps it is because,' Freign addressed the waitress, 'under a hallucino-
genic state, the pores of the mushroom ooze blood.' The waitress looked
startled. 'Oh my,' she exclaimed, picking up his plate with the uneaten
horse mushrooms spread methodically around the edges. Freign smiled as
she scuttled off. 'She would not understand,' he said to himself. In the early
sixties during training in Mexico he had been persuaded to consume a
particular type of mushroom indigenous to that area. An unpleasant
experience had ensued where he'd imagined blood pouring from everything around him. Eventually a torrent of blood covered the landscape. To
this day he retained an image of a blood-red landscape against a cobalt-blue
sky. It was not an altogether unpleasant sensation, but one which had an
irritating habit of recurring when he least expected it.

When the taxi emerged out of Central Park, Paige's sensations took a turn
for the worse; she felt as if she was being swayed in heavy undulating seas.
Bob's voice became a monotonous drone, the street lights stretched themselves into bright silver lines. As the taxi bounced awkwardly towards Fifth,
her nausea became more accentuated. She felt as if she were being thrown
off a great height and caught, seized and lifted up by a trampoline. Paige
rested her head on the back of the seat letting the wind blow on her face.
She stared at the black plastic-lined roof with its minute pores. Like dark
skin she thought. The pores started rotating. Her stomach took a sudden
leap, the taxi roof rippled and swayed, lurching forwards she grabbed the
half-open window. 'Oh my God.'

Bob leaned over, putting his arm around her. 'Driver, could you … ?'

'So, what do you think?' Art asked as he leaned back in the cab.

'Did Ivor bring it up with you?' Jean asked.

Art looked across at Baby Doll on Church. The neon lights illuminated
a group of Wall Street yuppies laughing on the street corner.

'We had a little talk. Don't you worry, Jean, I'll get him,' and he repeated under his breath, 'I'll get him.'

'Emille said that Leo offered him half a million.'

'Leo wouldn't cough up ten bucks if his grandmother was dying.'

'Well, Emille ...'

'Emille doesn't know pig's shit.'

'Maybe you're right. Art ...?' Jean started.

'Yeah.'

'Oh, nothing.'

Two transvestites welcomed Brigid Murphy at the door of Jackie 60.

Schneider, Earl and Jo walked into Jackie 60. Chelsea greeted them from behind the grille.

'Surprise, surprise,' she declared with a broad smile.

Schneider grinned knowingly. Earl laughed. Dewey put his hand over his mouth in astonishment.

So we take a cab to this crazy place full of crazy people and like on the way she sits real close and you know, kinda puts her arm on my shoulders and then on my leg and stuff. I was kinda weirded out but like, remained totally cool. Maybe I should like, say something but I don't want to offend her, you know what I mean?

As the taxi shot past Forty-second Street Art said, 'You know that Mondrian I was telling you about, Jean?'

'Er, hum,' Jean hummed mechanically.

'Well, I got a call from the lawyer representing the family. You know, I think I might get it.'

'That would be great, Art, I mean, that's a real masterpiece, right?' she said enthusiastically.

'Yeah, it's certainly that,' and, clearing his throat, he added with a hint of reticence, 'Do you think Bob would like it?'

Bob scraped fragments of orange sick from his trousers. 'I'm just mortified,' Paige was saying from next door.

Bob emerged from the bathroom smiling. 'Hey, listen, ah no problem. It ah really, ah doesn't matter.' Paige was in a white bathrobe sitting on the end of her couch looking down at the floor. Bob sat down next to her and put his arm around her. 'It doesn't ah, ah um, ah, change the w-way I feel about, about you,' he said awkwardly.

'Thanks, Bob, that's really great of you, it was just so like, disgusting, I mean Jesus that's never happened to me, you know, just like, urgh.' Bob stroked her hair. It suddenly occurred to her that he was making a pass at her.

'Alfreda,' but no sooner had he uttered her name for the second time than his will for a response receded. The image collapsed, losing itself in a deluge of broken memories. Images were the only collateral in Mr Rhinegold's world; they enabled the memories to cling to form even though the two were often unconnected, but it gave him a sense of reality and therefore some form of sanity. Ever since his wife's accident, Mr Rhinegold's memories had been melting into confusion and day by day his temporal boundaries became more blurred until the only period of his life he could recall with clarity was his youth. It was as if his mind was manoeuvring itself through a jungle and finding, through sheer determination, a clearing of extraordinary lucidity. Images from his youth flowed across his mind like an abstracted cartoon and suddenly the cold blue sky through the giant windows of the schoolroom in Charlottenburg and Werner Loeb's voice croaking mathematical equations came back to him. His voice seemed to stretch the long afternoons.

After school his governess, Frau Sauter, would take him on the tram to the Tiergarten where he would be unleashed along with a few friends. The governesses would sit on park benches and gossip for an hour or so before taking their respective sullied children back home. They had a house on the Unter den Linden. Inside it was red, velvet red; the furniture, the wall and the curtains encased within gold pelmets. Gold frames encased dark paintings. His father would bellow from his study. His father's study looked over the rich, opulent gardens with cascading rhododendrons and viridian climbers. He recalled his father's jovial, optimistic voice which was more often than not laced with a joke; it was never an angry voice, sad sometimes but never angry. He remembered lying in his bed and listening to the joyful voices echoing up the stairs from large dinner parties which, as the war dragged on, turned into lugubrious murmurs until only his parents' whispers snaked along the corridors. The cold blue afternoons in the Tiergarten. The plush red and gold house. The veridian gardens. His joking father. His loving mother. His guilt.

Brigid ordered two vodka grapefruits. Trace suddenly said, 'Hey Brigid, isn't she that girl from the other night?' pointing in Elaine's direction.

'What night?' Brigid asked, seeing who Trace meant.

'You know. "The night",' Trace exclaimed loudly.

'I've no idea what night you're talking about.' Brigid looked puzzled as she focused on several couples and groups dotted on the opposite side of the room.

'You know, the one you snogged,' Trace giggled.

Once Trace had revealed Elaine's identity, Brigid simultaneously caught sight of her. 'Ah, Jesus shite!' she said, quickly turning around and crouching over her drink as if it were somehow going to camouflage her. 'We're leavin' right now.'

Trace sipped her drink calmly. 'Sure, I'll finish me drink first, she won't see ya. She's facin' t'uther way.'

'Sure, you don't know the half of it, luv,' Brigid said.

Trace looked at her hungrily. 'What do ya mean?' she asked.

'Ah, nothin' I'm sure, just, well, I'm not sure meself.'

Trace frowned. 'Ah, right,' she said, unconvinced.

Paige got up and ran to the bathroom. Bob could hear her retching violently. 'Bob I think ...' more retching, 'I think you should leave.' This was accompanied by a distinct sound of wind. 'Please.'

Bob heard a sort of thump followed by a definite silence. 'Paige ah, are you ah, all right?' There was no reply. He got up and walked over to the bathroom door, knocking at it first tentatively and then violently. 'Paige! Paige!' Hearing no reply, he opened the door.

Paige was lying on the floor in a curled position. There was an overpowering smell. Bob flushed the toilet and soaked a flannel in warm water, then stooping over he washed the sick from Paige's chin. When he rolled her over, he saw that she had been sick down her neck. 'Oh shit,' he said to himself and leaning over again he opened her bathrobe. Bob hesitated for a moment and then started cleaning her neck and chest. He washed her breasts which protruded firmly outward from her chest, quickly at first and then gently rotating his hand over them. As he parted the lower section of her bathrobe he saw that she had shat herself.

Jo inhaled deeply on the cigar Spindle had given him earlier. He felt elated. He had made a friend of Schneider. This was the big league. A show at Freemantle's, Dewey Bozo writing on him for *Translations*. Hey, the world was his oyster; the world as an oyster, oyster feminine sexual gender, maybe there's something there.

Brigid shifted uneasily in her chair. 'Jesus, will ya hurry up with ya drink.' Trace widened her eyes and shook her head. 'Wait a sec!' she exclaimed as someone brushed her back, pushing her towards Brigid.

'Oh excuse me, honey,' a voice said. She turned around and looked at the intruder.

'That's all right,' she said, looking at the young man and then, knotting her brow, she added flirtatiously, 'I recognise you, have we not met somewhere?'

'Are you sure … come to think of it … yeah, where was it?' Dewey mused. Then in unison they both pointed at each other, 'Sky Jell,' they screamed. Brigid looked on in horror. Trace turned back to Brigid.

'Bridge, sure, you remember Sky Jell, ya big, ya big eejut,' she said.

Brigid's hand was covering her eyes as if she was shielding them from the sun. 'Aaah Jesus. How could I forget.'

'This is, ah …' Trace began before Dewey interceded. 'Dewey,' he said and then as Brigid unveiled her hand from her eyes he let out a pitched yelp. 'Oh it's you! Oh my God. Oh my God. I gotta get Elaine. Oh my God, she is going to flip.' Dewey vanished. Brigid looked up at the ceiling. 'I don't fuckin believe this. Shite, feck ... shite.'

'So I'm like, doing this like, totally great piece, like, I'm photographing this like, garbage in the Bronx, okay, and like, garbage on the Upper East side, right, and then like, juxtaposing them,' Meg said, passing her hand across her nose.

Elaine: 'That's so cool.'

Schneider laughing: 'Hierarchical social garbage.'

'Right.' Meg joined in with a snigger before abruptly breathing in through her nose.

Dewey put the drinks down on the table. 'Elaine, Elaine quick, guess who's here,' he said with great excitement.

Rhinegold woke from his slumber with an image of Aunt Anita. He now remembered how his aunts, all three of them, had come to live with his family after the war. Their husbands had been killed at Passchendaele and the Somme. By that time, they had sold the house on the Unter den Linden and moved to their summer residence in Grünewald near the Havel lakes where, as a child, he would play with his local friends. He had been particularly fond of Aunt Anita who was only ten years older than him. One summer, when he was sixteen years old, she had taken him to a boat house on one of the lakes. She had been the first woman to kiss him passionately.

Art lounged in his blue-and-white striped pyjamas on a green Jasper Morrison couch, smoking a large cigar and holding a bourbon on ice. His hair was wet and combed back. A few droplets of water had accumulated on the tufts of hair sprouting from the back of his neck. The heat and steam of the bathroom had left his face with a kind of pink-to-reddish hue and his forehead vein was noticeably prominent.

Jean sat on a precarious metal chair designed by an obscure Dutchman.

She wore a red two-piece suit. 'Art, I have to ask you?' she said, after a period of silence.

'Fire away, sweetheart,' Art replied, looking up at the ceiling.

Jean remained silent and looked down at her knees. Not hearing a reply, Art peered down his nose and across at Jean. 'What is it?' he asked with a semi-concerned intonation.

'Did you?' Jean paused. 'Did you do it with Paige Quale?'

Art burst out laughing. 'Paige Quale!' he bellowed. 'She works for me for Christ's sake,' and then he gave out a loud cough.

'I know she works for you, but ...'

'But what?'

'Rumour has it that you were seen, ah,' Jean stalled, 'ah seen, ah.'

'Seen what, Jean?'

'Well, ah, going down on her.'

Art sat up abruptly, slamming his glass down on the Diego Giacometti table. 'Jesus H Christ. Down on her, what do you mean, down on her? I mean, for fuck's sake!' he barked. A layer of moisture was developing on his forehead. 'Down on her, where?'

'Well, you know.'

'No, I don't know.'

'Between ...'

'I know what being down on her means,' he barked again.

'So you ...?' Jean whispered.

Art stood up. 'Of course not, I mean,' he stalled, 'where, what place? I mean, where the fuck was I supposed to be when I was doing ah, ah, this ah ... thing?'

'Art, you're getting angry.'

'Of course I'm getting angry. First, it's not true and these kind of rumours are bad for reputations.'

'Honey, I believe you. Just calm down, honey. Come here, my sweetie-pie. Come on, honey.'

Art smoothed his hair and sat down again. Jean leaned forward and stroked his cheek. 'I'm sorry to have upset you.'

'It's, you know, it's like a bad rumour,' he said quietly. Art gripped his hands on her knees.

She lay naked in the bath. Bob lathered the soap in the flannel and raising Paige out of the bath slipped it between her legs. 'Wads ... hap ... pen ... ing,' Paige drawled, her head on one side, hair limp over her face.

The memories of the Quale incident drifted back. How could he have done that? What had come over him? Jesus, he could have gone to jail. Fortunately, a year's wages, an apartment and a directorship of the gallery persuaded her otherwise, but it had been a close shave and now this. Who started this fucking rumour? He better ring Paige and find out.

Bob made sure Paige was completely dry before putting his arm under her thighs and carrying her to the bedroom.

Jean surveyed Art's worried face. 'Honey, what are you thinking?' she asked.
    'Oh nothing, sweetheart, just, just how I'd like to sleep with you.'
    'Art, it's been months.'
    'All the more reason to ...'
    'Has the idea of going down on Paige Quale turned you on?' Jean's tone suddenly hardened.
    'For God's sake, I, I just thought, thought it would be a great, ah ...'
    Jean got up and walked towards the door.
    'Jean,' he called out, 'come back. I meant it ...'
    'You stink.'
    'I fucking meant it,' he implored, as he got up from the couch, and in two strides he was behind her. 'Please stay. I really ...' Spindle grappled with Jean's waist.
    'So, this is what you did to Paige Quale,' she shouted and in one movement turned and slapped him around the face. Spindle rocked under the force of her hand.

Elaine made sure she still had a tape in her recorder before she went to talk to Brigid.

Bob Maclestone decided that Paige was obviously suffering from food poisoning. He rang his doctor whose only advice was to give him another call if her condition worsened.

'Hey, Brigid, it's so great to see you. You look so great. Wow! I thought I was never going to see you again.' Elaine breathed the words through her nose.

'I ah ...' Brigid started awkwardly.

'You wanna drink?' Elaine asked.

'I'm okay, tanks. We were just leaving.'

There was a moment of awkward silence.

'So what have you been up to?' Elaine drawled.

As he was making himself a cup of coffee the phone rang. The answering machine picked up and Art Spindle's voice floated across the apartment.

'Paige, are you there? It's Art.' Spindle's voice had a distinct tremble. 'Paige, Jesus, look ah, Jean Maclestone knows something she shouldn't, you know what I mean. This is real serious. Ring me as soon as you get this.' Art put the phone down and kicked the table in front of him, sending it a couple of feet across the room. 'Shit! Fuck! Shit!' he shouted.

Bob walked into the lounge and stood over the telephone listening to the tape rewind itself. 'What the hell was that all about?' he asked himself.

'Do you wanna come in?' Beth asked, running her fingers through her hair.

'Well, I should really be getting back but, okay, a quick nightcap.'

Beth led the way up the steps until they reached the second floor. 'Home sweet home,' she announced, opening the door. A small living-room presented itself. There was a couch in the middle accompanied by an armchair and two hardback chairs. A few small canvases were scattered on the walls and around twenty rusty-looking nails lay at various angles on the

mantelpiece. An invitation to an opening rested on two nails which had
been so placed to hold it.

'I have white wine or vodka?' Beth suggested.

'I'll have the vodka,' Jo replied, walking over to the mantelpiece.

'What's with the nails?' he asked.

'Aren't they great? They're Dogon money. I bought them from Kasmin's.' Beth came over and handed Jo his drink. 'Chin-chin,' she said,
raising her glass and looking into his eyes.

'Chin-chin,' he repeated, clinking his glass against hers which she was
holding nervously in front of her cleavage. She had great tits, he thought
to himself; large and firm. He knew he could score, but maybe, since she
was representing him, he shouldn't take it too far; in case it all went
horribly wrong. She looked into his eyes and smiled.

Rhinegold remembered the collection of paintings by Bleckner. His father
collected a considerable amount of this early nineteenth-century artist's
work until 1923, when reparations to the victorious Allies had such a
devastating effect on the German economy that his father had to close
down his factory and sell many possessions including the paintings. He
recalled going with his father to Brausser, the Jewish dealer of art who,
with Steimer, had cornered the art market, stripping the great collections
of their gems, and selling his father's most beloved pictures. He remembered the anger he felt seeing the pictures being handled by the gallery
porter and ferreted behind giant doors. His father, noticing his flushed
cheeks, gave him a consoling pat on the back. Rhinegold remembered
looking up at his father and vowing that one day he would buy them all
back. His father died before he could fulfil his promise.

'You know, Elaine, I think it's very progressive, art,' Dewey said flippantly.

'What do you mean, progressive, Dewey?' Elaine said irritably.

'You know what I mean, like Kelly has progressed from Matisse and ...'

'But don't you see, art isn't about progress, like when you're doing it
you're not thinking about progress or bettering something or whatever. It's

a means to an end. You can't say that the Beatles had progressed from Presley or Sinatra, or that Judd had progressed from Duchamp.'

'Oh come on, Elaine. It's all a progression, you know, a step forward.'

'It's nothing to do with forwards or backwards, Dewey, you're like an art dealer, always pigeon-holing everything.'

'Well, let's not get personal, Elaine.'

'I'm not, I'm just saying that art is like, the sum of the parts, you know, of the intuitive and intellectual parts, what have you. It's not a new car or a ground-breaking cure, it's not outdoing its predecessor, you know? I think this is the fundamental problem with people out there. I mean, they're always looking for the new thing as if it was this year's new Chrysler or something and then when something really does happen, which is like different, they're shocked.'

'Sure they are, because it's new, Elaine, it's different ...' Dewey began.

'Look, Dewey, can you imagine people being shocked by a new aeroplane or cure for something?'

'No, but what's that got to do with it?'

'Art is a revelation, not a progression. You use the imagery that you already know to explain something you already know. That is what is so shocking, I mean, it's that marriage.'

'I don't know what you're talking about, Elaine,' Dewey said, throwing his hands up in the air. Ivor was looking intensely at Elaine.

'She's saying that people are shocked by themselves,' Ivor joined in, 'by the reality which is revealed.'

'Yeah, kind of, like, take a medicine cabinet by Hirst, right, you know the image, after all you've seen it a hundred times in a thousand different pharmacists, right, and then you know the idea which is about death, the fear of death and all that stuff, right?'

'Right.'

'You put them together in an art piece and people are appalled, amazed, whatever, right? But it's not anything new as a notion.'

'I'm not sure about that, honey.' Dewey sighed, inhaling his cigarette deeply.

'You're right, Elaine,' Ivor joined in.

'But Elaine, I ...' Dewey began argumentatively.

'Oh for fuck's sake, Dewey,' Elaine yelled.

Rhinegold's uncle was the owner of a machine-manufacturing plant. They made everything from sewing machines to chronometers. Having gone to Realschulen, the University of Commerce, he had been taken on as an apprentice at his uncle's factory where he worked from the shop floor up to assistant foreman. He remembered the noise as men in blue outfits welded, hammered and drilled their way through metal. He could still recollect the distinct smell of metal.

'I don't think this is such a good idea,' Jo said as he drew away from Beth's lips. Beth's shirt buttons were undone and her breasts were noticeably heaving against her bra.

'You mean like, with me like, representing you and stuff,' she replied.

'Yeah, I think it could be kinda awkward.' He paused and dragged a hand through his hair. 'You know, in case it didn't work out.'

'I guess so but ...'

'Don't get me wrong,' he added quickly, 'I really like you but I think it would interfere with our work relationship.'

Beth was doing up her shirt buttons. 'You think so?'

Jo got up from the divan and walked over to where he'd left his black coat. 'Yeah, I think it's for the best.'

At least I know that he likes me, you know. I told him about Elaine showing in the other gallery and he didn't seem to mind but later, when I was going to sleep, he rang and voiced a few concerns. Weird about like, Elaine and Jo coming on to me on the same night. If I ever did it with a woman it would be with Elaine. No way with a woman, no way José, but I remember when I was at high school there was a girl who I kinda liked, had a crush on but that was kinda different ...

Freign observed Rhinegold. The old man lay with his mouth slightly ajar. The bedside light cast an elongated shadow on the wall next to him, which bore an uncanny resemblance to Mr Burns: head of Nuclear Power at Springfield. A book lay on the sheet covering his stomach and his thumb still gripped the binding which kept open the page he had been reading. Freign tiptoed to the bedside and bent down with his head to one side. Once he was satisfied that Rhinegold was still breathing, he delicately removed the book and placed it on the side-table. He strode quietly towards the beam of yellow light coming from the hallway.

CHAPTER SIX

TEN DAYS AGO, AFTERHOURS

May. Eleven-thirty p.m. Dewey paced his room pulling at his fingers so that they snapped, making a loud clicking noise. All of a sudden he sat down at his desk. He leaned over and ran his fingers through his thick, black, curly hair, pulling at it and eventually letting go so that the curls sprang back on themselves like wiry springs. Dewey picked up his pen and wrote: 'Perhaps Jo Richards' purpose is to empty our preconceptions of the banal object by rendering back the object to its most basic form, that is, back to the "Banal".' Dewey tapped his uniball pen on to the note-pad. He got up and started pacing again. After five minutes he lay down on his bed with his remote control and scanned all forty channels before switching the television off. Opening his side-table drawer, he took out a rugose and carbuncled object which resembled, together with its subtle, wattled colouring, the veins and lumps of a large penis. After removing his trousers and squirting baby oil on his rectum as well as the length and breadth of the dildo he eased the instrument in until it was fully inserted. All of a sudden he removed the dildo and sprang up from the bed making for the trestle-table desk.

'Jo Richards, by decontextualising the "Bed", has metamorphosed it from an inviting womb-like object which we associate with peace, rest and sleep into an abstracted, cold, dehumanised one.'

Dewey stood naked with a half-erect penis waving over the plastic swivel chair. He blew between his teeth, making a hissing sound. 'Yes, yes, yes.'

It was all going to flow now.

Spindle and Chelsea sit finishing entrées at DaSilvano. Art is telling his life story.

'My life changed when I was about fifteen. My mother took me to MOMA and we walked into the room where Picasso's *Guernica* used to hang. That picture just blew my mind and I said to her, "Mom, one day I want to have that painting," and she said, "Well, you're gonna have to earn well because that there painting is one of a kind and anything that is one of a kind is worth money." It was then that I decided I wanted to be involved in art. I wanted to deal in things that were one of a kind, unique, you know, so I applied to an art history course at New York University. After I got my diploma, I got a job as an intern at the Stella Malone Gallery. I was an assistant for about a year, until one day Bud Brewer came in and we started talking about art. Pretty soon we were good friends and when he floated Brewer Electric on the stock market he phoned up and said, "Art, I wanna back a gallery and I want you to run it." So I said, "Bud, I'll do it on the condition that you let me make all the decisions." Well, at first he didn't like that much, but a few days later we had lunch and he said he'd thought it through and felt that I was completely justified in my stipulation. The next day I handed Stella my resignation and we started looking for a space.'

I'm at the Bowery Bar and who's in there but Jo and 'The Bitch' Quale. The motherfucker. Can you believe it? He told me he was having dinner with Grave of the Observer. *So, I'm like speechless, you know, I kinda stand there like some fucking moron, right, and he goes, 'Hi, Beth' in that fucking like, dumb way he has, you know? So I said, what happened to Grave and he said Grave blew him out. Get this, Grave walks in. Paige's got that like, I got great tits, glossy lips, tight butt, aren't I sexy, I know-that-you-want-to-fuck-me, kinda look. You know what I mean? And you know what Grave said? He said, 'If I weren't gay I'd do the same.' Can you believe that? Like, Jo goes the colour of the Rothko chapel. I buy everybody a drink and pretend like, nothing is wrong, you know?*

'So, this is where I live, "home sweet home",' Jo said as he swung his front door open.

Paige gazed down the room. 'Hey, great loft.'

'Like a drink? I have a great bottle of Chablis in the fridge.'

'No, I think, ah, have you got a juice or a soda?'

'I have juice.'

'Oh great, what um …?'

'Orange.'

'I guess I'll have a soda. Can I use your bathroom?'

'Sure, right in there,' Jo said, pointing to the room within a room.

'In here?'

'Yeah.'

Jo opened the fridge and poured out the Perrier to which he added copious amounts of ice. He debated a few moments about whether to have beer or wine. He reached for the Chablis.

Paige puckered her lips and noticed that her lipstick had worn off, leaving some residue in the tiny creases of her bottom lip. She got out her rouge and ran it over her mouth.

Jo walked up to the front of his loft and after searching along the line of CDs chose Stockhausen's *Ring Circle*; always a great conversation piece.

When Paige came out of the bathroom, a good few minutes after flushing the toilet, Jo ascertained she had put on some make-up. It was kind of a good sign.

Beth sat on the couch holding a vodka tonic. Elaine sat opposite her on a hardback chair, legs apart, gripping a beer bottle. She wore jeans, a red-and-black striped lumberjack shirt and heavy black leather boots.

'You know, Elaine, it's like when I met him it was like, I felt some weird connection, you know what I mean? It's like when I met you I felt that we had this like, weird bonding, you know, it was like, right away, we kinda spilled our guts, remember? So, with him it was like we both had this kinda like, positive energy, you know, like some people have positive and others like negative? We had this positive energy, like we were drawn together. It was real weird like I was his sister or something, as if we kinda like knew each other in another life.'

Elaine took a swig of beer.

'I felt that about you, Beth, you know, like having known you from before someplace.' she said, heaving up her shoulders and trying to control an impending ruction.

'You did? That's really weird because I felt that like so strong, you know? That's just so weird, you remember, we were like so close in like, seconds.'

'Yeah, I was attracted to you immediately,' Elaine confirmed as she looked into Beth's eyes.

'So this is where you work, right?' Paige said as she looked around the loft.

Jo turned and vaguely pointed a finger in the direction of his desk. 'Yeah, I sit over there at my desk and look out on the street until an idea kinda hits me, you know,' he chuckled.

'That's so cool, I mean you don't even have to get up.'

Jo frowned as he wondered what she was insinuating.

'I guess so, but sometimes I do drawings of pieces, like prepapa, prepep ...'

'Preparatory,' Paige intervened.

A wave of embarrassment swept over him, drowning his fragile ego. 'I can never pronounce that word,' he said, cursing himself.

'I have words like that,' smiled Paige, trying to reassure him.

'Would you like to see some?' Jo asked assertively.

'You mean some preparatory sketches?'

'That's the word.'

Paige laughed flirtatiously. 'Sure.'

As they walked down the loft, Paige looked up and wrinkled her nose as though she had noticed some peculiar odour. 'Weird music.'

Jo stroked his chin. 'Yeah, isn't it great? You know, it's that guy Stockhausen.'

Although Paige had a reasonable knowledge of classical music, having had 'musical parents', she was not familiar with Stockhausen. 'Ah ha.'

As the television screen darkened to highlight the credits, Maclestone caught sight of his wife reflected in the screen. There she sat; motionless, with a kind of moronic, glazed expression. His whole life encapsulated itself in that second. He could not put words to it; it was just there in this room, the furniture, the height of the ceiling, the positioning of the door, the melancholic self-portrait of Warhol looking into nothing and Jean's deadened gaze framed in the grey-black glass of the television set. A feeling of intense nausea swept over him. He could hardly breathe. 'I'm whacked,' he said, getting up from his white leather armchair.

'Yeah,' Jean yawned.

Chelsea broke in on Art's monologue and suggested they have a Sambucca with their coffee, which Art readily agreed to. Having given the order, he leaned back in his chair and continued, 'Leo said that he knew that Broomberg had just bought this building on Fifty-seventh Street and he was looking for tenants. When Bud and I saw the space we knew it was the right one and two months later we opened with a Marc Stoppe show. What a night. The whole of New York came. But then six months later a funny thing happened, Bud had a heart attack and died. That was one of the worst periods of my life. You see Bud's wife and I never saw eye to eye and I knew she would litigate. At the time I had no money, no assets, nothing! But then another funny thing happened. She fell down the escalator in Blooming-dale's and ended up in intensive care for a month. By the time she started to litigate I had found another backer.'

'You know what I mean, Elaine? I think he was my kinda like, soul mate. We like, definitely had this like, connection, like, I knew it, you know? I like, kinda felt it.'

'You want another drink, Beth?' Elaine asked dryly as she got up.

'But you know, it's like I have this feeling like, that he's in another world, you know?' Beth said, passing Elaine her empty glass. 'Like he's not happy or something.' She raised her voice as Elaine disappeared into the kitchen. 'It's like he's holding something back.'

'Why do you think that?' Elaine shouted over the closing refrigerator.

'How do I know that? He just won't let anyone in, you know, Elaine? I feel he's really like alone, you know what I mean?'

Pinned on the wall were several drawings. Jo waved to the first one. 'This is a piece I'm doing for the Slap Gallery in Brussels. It's to do with peripheral vision, right? So it's an installation. You walk in here ...' Jo pointed to a cross-section of a room. Paige felt Jo's hand brush against her back.

'And you put your head in this device,' he said, pointing to the next drawing of an oddly shaped object which looked like a mediaeval chastity belt, 'so that you can't look around, right?' He put his hand firmly on her shoulder as he leaned towards the third drawing.

'Then to the right and left of the observer is a non-functional domestic environment.' His hand moved slowly across her shoulder. 'Part of but not the whole of which you can see.'

Paige looked puzzled and then, deliberating on each word, she asked, 'You mean you can't see all of it at the same time?'

'You got it. And you can only just see one object at a time, but if you look straight ahead you're aware of everything, right?' Jo exclaimed triumphantly.

'That is so neat,' Paige said. He was quite close to her now and she looked into his eyes. Jo was now firing on all cylinders. 'You see, it draws you into another kind of vision,' he said excitedly.

'I guess it questions reality,' Paige added.

Jo looked at her with a kinda surprised smile.

'Yeah, right.'

By now Beth, a little angry and drunk, slammed her fist down on her knee. 'Can you believe the mother fucker? He like fucking used me. Jo Richards used me to get a show!'

'He's such an ass-hole, Beth,' Elaine replied. 'Anyway, men are kinda like that, aren't they?'

'If his show wasn't in ten days, I'd like cancel the man, I'd just blow him out,' Beth said through her teeth.

Spindle wiped the corners of his mouth with his napkin. 'Fernando was a great businessman, I'll give him that, but he had one problem – women. Yeah, he had a real problem with the ladies and the next thing that happened just blew my mind. One afternoon I wasn't feeling so good and I went back to my apartment. When I walked into the lounge there they were, Fernando and my wife, fucking on the couch. My daughter was in the cot screaming her head off so they didn't hear me come in.'

Jean caught sight of Bob in her dressing-table mirror taking his trousers down. A second glance revealed a pair of white fleshy buttocks which appeared from retreating Jo Boxer shorts. As Maclestone awkwardly balanced on one leg clambering into his green-and-red striped pyjamas, she noticed the black hairs oozing from between his buttocks and spreading down his thighs and calves. Now he ambled towards the bathroom. Those short, mean, clumsy steps, shuffling towards the bathroom.

Brigid, Trace and Roberta slipped through the red rope at Nell's. They found a banquette and a waiter came and everybody ordered Sea Breezes. 'First round is on me, girls,' Brigid declared. 'This is a great place, it reminds me of the Shelbourne Hotel in Dublin.'

'I was never in that place. What's it like?' Trace asked.

'It's this big auld hotel on St Stephen's Green in Dublin. It's really lovely. It's got great settees and pictures and me and me ma used to go into the bar at the back and we'd order a couple of bullshots together. Me ma loves the oysters there. It was a big treat for us to go in there together. We didn't really have the money to go but we'd have a laugh watchin' all the American tourists askin' us whether we knew a cousin of theirs, Patrick Murphy. Jesus, aren't there a million Patrick Murphys in Ireland? What a bunch of gob shites.'

'You should get Bob to buy the place for ya,' Trace said sarcastically.

'I'm tellin' ya, gettin' Bob to buy anythin' but feckin' art would be a feckin' miracle. I mean, he buys the stuff all the feckin' time. I asked him the other day, what in the name of God d' ya do with it? And d' ya know what, he puts the whole feckin' lot in storage, and here's the good bit. Sometimes he gives it away,' she declared in astonishment, 'to feckin' museums.'

Bob bared his teeth in the bathroom mirror. His upper lip curled under his nose while the skin under his bottom lip stretched along his chin. He had a dentist appointment first thing in the morning. Fuck, he hated the dentist. He stretched his mouth wide to reveal several gold fillings running along his bottom teeth. He opened the mirrored cabinet in front of him and took out the dental floss. The angle of the door caught Jean sitting in front of her dressing-table in the other room, cotton wool soaked in cleanser between thin, claw-like fingers, dragging down her face, indenting her cheek, contorting her mouth into a mean grimace as the skin pinched against the jaw-bone. Bob noticed how her eyes separated from their sockets as she rubbed away the mascara. There she was, scrubbed and scraped, raw, with the shine of soaked cream highlighting each tiny crease of her face. Several pieces of food catapulted on to the roof of his mouth. He rinsed with Listerine and walked out of the bathroom as his wife came in.

As Jean put the final touches of night cream on her face she distinctly heard above the noise of the Park Avenue traffic echoing in the semi-distance the click of dental floss as it passed between Bob's teeth. She got up and made for the bathroom. They both hesitated at the door. The uncoordinated hesitation in close proximity seemed to embody how they had grown apart. Jean felt this was the beginning of the end or the end of the end, here, in this hesitation. It had occurred to her before but now she was decided, then and there, in that split second. 'This is crazy,' he said to himself as they shifted past each other. 'Here we are in four thousand square feet of prime real estate and we squeeze past each other in the doorway.'

'So what if you had an image on the ceiling?' Paige suggested.

'Could do, could do,' Jo pondered, 'or maybe another piece where you have an image on the ceiling which was ...' Jo looked up at the ceiling and then at the floor. 'Yeah, which is, yeah, great, which is reflected on to the floor, right? So you have the reverse image.'

'And you're looking straight ahead,' Paige added with a concentrated gaze.

Spindle and Chelsea were finishing their coffee at DaSilvano.

Elaine stroked Beth's hair and brushed a tear away from her cheek. 'He's just a jerk,' she said. 'It's not important, people like that aren't important.'

'I know, I know,' Beth replied, 'you're right, he's a totally like, unimportant jerk.' They both laughed out loud and Elaine bent over and kissed Beth on the cheek.

'Thanks, Elaine, for being here. I feel so like, connected to you.' Elaine kissed her again but this time planted her lips straight on to Beth's. Beth moved awkwardly from her slumped position until she was sitting straight-backed and perched on the edge of the couch. Feeling the mood had altered, Elaine said, 'Anyway there probably isn't anything going on, you know, maybe they were just having dinner and because he kinda knows that you don't see eye to eye he didn't want to tell you?'

'Oh come on, Elaine. She was like looking at him like ah, like some, some cocker spaniel.'

Jean flicked through the pages of *Interiors*. 'Bob,' she said, still looking at the magazine, 'I wanna divorce.' Bob took off his glasses and slipped the arm between his lips. A few seconds passed before he put his specs back on and reaching for *Business Week*, which was lying on his stomach, he said, 'Okay, Jean, if ah, th-that's what you want.'

Brigid felt the rush of blood and music replace all the idle chatter of her friends. Her muscles relaxed, the air felt smooth and soft. Her skin tingled.

'Have you noticed them guys have been lookin' at us?' Trace said. 'The one on the right's not bad.' Brigid looked around.

'Don't look,' Trace screamed. Both of them burst out laughing.

'It's beginning,' Brigid declared.

'I can feel it too,' Trace said, 'shall we go downstairs and have a dance?'

'In 'eighty-two I went to Jon Gregor's studio on Jean-Michel's recommendation. When I got there this guy opened the door and insulted me. He said, "Who the fuck are you, cunt?" I just couldn't believe it. I just stood there, right? You know he had that kinda London accent. Anyway I just stood there in disbelief and said, "I'm Art." He said, "Art, you crazy son of a bitch, come in. I've been expecting you ." Well, you had to laugh and we became great friends and now he is what he is. He made a film the other day. Did you see it? Not bad for an artist, I thought.'

The shadows flickered in the hallway and Mr Rhinegold was sure he had seen a figure going upstairs. 'Freign! Freign!' he called. There was no response. 'Freign!' He raised his voice. The elusive shadows reminded him of the human shapes enveloped in fog, moving about the port – he could see his father waving his hat at him from the quayside. He could see by her angle and posture that his mother was leaning heavily on him. The excitement of the voyage had given way to a wave of sadness. He would never see his parents again. The boat bellowed loudly. It was the spring of 1935. Ten years later he would discover that his father had been gassed at Auschwitz and his mother, having being imprisoned, died in the arms of her daughters a few months after the end of the war. He never forgave himself. He never forgave Germany. He had never gone back. 'Freign! Freign!'

'There was a lot of performance stuff and what I call "dirty conceptual", like Beuys who's a genius, don't get me wrong, but you couldn't sell it, I mean, try selling a pound of fat to a Jewish collector (laughter). But all the same, it was different and kinda exciting. I remember once John Bandor and I went to this studio in Brooklyn of an artist called Rose Laine-Peyton.

We'd met her at a Shapiro opening. Anyway, we went into this room which was covered in reddish-brown marks and on the floor there were all these used tampons. I remember she was a small, thin girl, kinda pretty, but real shy, you know, she didn't say much except what was what, like, "These marks are menstrual blood, these are used tampons." Real weird girl. I said to her, I said, "This is all very well and I think it's fascinating, don't get me wrong, but it's not going to sell." Anyway, when John and I left the studio he said it was enough to turn a man gay.'

'Just like that,' Jean barked, looking at him fiercely over a pair of gold pince-nez that balanced precariously on the tip of her nose.

'Well, you asked me, Jean. Did you ah, want me, want me to say no?' he asked. 'I mean, Jean, be r-reasonable.'

'How many years, Bob? How many years have we been together?'

'Twenty perhaps, ah ah, ah no, ah nineteen seventy-five, that makes, ah …'

''Seventy-four,' Jean interrupted.

'I think it was 'seventy-five,' Bob asserted firmly.

''Seventy-four, at Hogi Robenstein's birthday party.'

'That was 'seventy-five, we went to the Wa-Warhol later that week.'

'The Warhol was in 'seventy-four, Bob,' Jean replied angrily.

''Seventy-goddamn-five,' he said between gritted teeth. 'It was ah, also the year I had my ah, my appendix out.'

'That was 'seventy-six,' Jean said, wagging her finger. 'That was two years after we met, I remember it as if it were only the other day.'

'It was my ah, ah appendix, goddamn it, Jean. I should know when I had my a-a-appendix out.' His voice rose with the tide of the sentence.

''Seventy-six was the appendix, Robert Maclestone. Seventy-four was the year we met.'

Spindle poured some water into his glass. 'Tankador had this fifteen-foot sculpture in his studio. He'd been building the thing for ten years. When I saw it I knew it was ground-breaking stuff, right, but the problem was how to get it out, you know? Eventually we had to hire fifteen guys for two

weeks to de-construct it and rebuild it in the gallery. The French bought it.
They always get the most complicated things. I don't know why it is but
they do. One French collector bought this kinetic sculpture from us by
Franz Clatz and it kept going wrong and he tried to sue me and then when
he couldn't sue me he tried to sue the artist. I told the judge that art doesn't
come with a guarantee.'

Dewey patrolled the dark recesses of the Man Hole, occasionally acknow-
ledging a familiar face, a past affair, a frustrated suitor, unrequited loves.
After running the gauntlet of unsatisfying and unsatisfied faces he skir-
mished the bar, eventually finding a narrow path to the counter. 'Excuse
me,' Dewey apologised as he lightly bumped into somebody. 'No problem,'
the man replied in a southern drawl. 'Kinda crowded tonight,' the guy
added, looking into Dewey's eyes.

'Yeah, busy, busy, busy, so where do you hail from?' Dewey asked.

'Greg Tavali from Houston, Texas, you wanna drink?'

'A drink of what, honey?' Dewey squealed. Greg laughed as they turned
towards the bar.

'More vodka, Elaine?'

'Yeah, and then I did this piece at Visual Arts, right, based on Duchamp's
Woman Falling Down The Stairs, yeah, and that's where I hit on the idea,'
Jo said, pouring himself another drink. Paige was resting on her elbows
next to him on the bed as there were no other seats in the apartment except
Jo's desk chair but that was on the other side of the room. She hadn't
minded reclining on the bed and he seemed cool anyway. 'That's real
interesting, Jo.' He thought it was time to make a move but tactically Jo
was in a quandary as to how to go about it. They were both using their
elbows to rest on which meant he could not use his hands, leaving only eye
contact as a means of seduction, but this meant straining his head around
and he felt uncomfortable with the angle. Finally, Jo decided to get up so
that he could reposition himself more advantageously when he lay down
again.

Beth stumbled on to the couch. 'Wow!' she exclaimed.

Elaine laughed. 'You know, Beth, I watched you go get the drink and you know, you have a great figure.'

'A great figure?' Beth slurred into her glass. 'Elaine, are you serious?'

'I'm perfectly serious, Beth. You have a great body.'

'No way.'

'The cutest butt, slim waist, and those tits look just ...'

'Silicone, honey.'

'I've never seen silicone.'

'Oh come on, you have.'

'It's weird, but I haven't. I mean, not in the flesh.'

'Well, you know they're like, well, you know, like tits.' Beth and Elaine burst out laughing.

So, Elaine and I are reeling. She is so like, great, you know. I'm so happy that I'm representing an artist who is so cool and understanding, you know what I mean? Elaine says that Jo is good-looking but kinda like dry, you know, kinda cold, she said. I guess she's right, but I still really like him. So, I have my tits out, right, and she kinda holds them and I'm thinking 'weird', and she like, starts stroking them in a kinda provocative way, you know? I do my buttons up and she asks if I wanna see her tattoos, right, and so she takes her T-shirt off and wow, they're tattoos like, all over and nipple rings and a belly button ring – totally weird.

'Don't they kinda feel weird?' Beth asked. Elaine looked down at her bosoms and taking one of the rings she said, 'Hold it.'

Beth tentatively held the ring.

'Pull it.'

'That's weird, Elaine.'

'Pull it,' she demanded.

'Come on, Elaine.'

'Just do it!'

Beth pulled at the ring gently so that the nipple extended away from the bosom. 'Go on,' Elaine urged.

Beth tugged at it until the bosom was now stretching away from her body.

Elaine closed her eyes and bit her top lip. 'That is so sexy, Beth,' she whispered.

'I'm sorry, I can't do this, Elaine. It's too weird,' Beth said, getting up from the couch and looking at her watch.

'Do what, Beth?' Elaine asked quizzically. 'I'm only showing you my rings.'

Spindle and Chelsea were in a taxi driving uptown to his apartment.

'You know, I've always loved art, Chelsea. It's the primary reason in this job, it has to be. You are responsible for bringing art to the public. This is our *raison d'être*. It's us who are the bridge between the artist and the public. We are the educators. Sometimes it's not what the public wants, but eventually they get it. Then suddenly in the early eighties there was a *Zeitgeist* and then that's when the gallery really got going. People just went crazy. I remember selling a piece in the morning and being offered it later that day after it had changed hands five times. The fucking thing was still sitting in my office.

'Well, when Warhol died, you know, it was like when Kennedy got assassinated, I remember exactly where I was, the weather, the time, everything, as if it was yesterday. When I heard he had died, I remember thinking that was the beginning of the end. It was then collectors became dealers and suddenly everything was for sale. That was the other turning point, when people realised everything was for sale. When it finally happened it was a real disaster. Prices collapsed. They just avalanched. Just unbelievable. I couldn't sell a fucking thing. All these artists with mortgages ...'

'You wanna drink, Chelsea?' Spindle asked, turning on the lights in the living-room.

Between two large windows was a small photograph by Matthew Barney framed in wax. On the adjacent side of the room, next to some shelving laden with art books, there was a Basquiat and on the main wall opposite the window was a written painting by Landers. Several pieces were scattered amongst the furniture including a Marc Quinn sculpture, a Damien Hirst sheep and a Michael Joo piece stretched across the room like the beginning of a giant cobweb. On another wall was a pinky-white painting, the texture of which resembled flesh, with a naked girl emerging out of it. 'I'll have vodka, if you have it,' she replied, looking around the room. 'Do you mind if I smoke?'

'No problem, I'm gonna have a cigar.'

'That's a divine "Ivor",' Chelsea said, standing in front of another flesh-coloured painting. It was a large Minimal painting with a hint of a nude body emerging from it.

'Isn't it just great?' Spindle affirmed. 'I'm real pleased with that work. Real pleased.'

Jo was now only six inches away from Paige's lips. She looked into his eyes and he into hers. Three inches and closing. Lips meet, stroking, moving like plasticine, the tongues probing and dancing in unison. The passion mounting. The tongues move deeper, penetrating deeper. Their bodies close together until they're against each other. His hand curves around her hips and up her back. Her right arm is trapped awkwardly against his chest, the palm of the other hand splayed outwards before it shyly strokes his shoulder. He gently pushes her on to her back. She places her arms around his neck, filtering her hands through his hair. His hands move along her side, meeting the gentle curve of her bosom which lies under black cotton cloth. She runs her hands down his back. He slips his hand under her top, smoothing her ribs and finding her nipple. She pushes her pelvis against his, frees one hand and explores his thigh. Both his hands slither under her top, and then, drawing himself up, he slips it off her, kissing, licking, sucking her nipples. She slides her hand into his trousers, searching.

'Jesus,' she whispers, upon finding an abnormally large prick.

'I think Ivor is at a point in his career where he needs an established dealer. I mean, it's all very well, but unless someone looks after the fella he's in danger of fucking up.'

'What do you mean, Art?'

'Well, Ivor is an established artist but, you know, he's not cutting edge, right, you gotta sustain a reputation. You have to manipulate, make sure he's in the right collections and so on,' Spindle said, walking over to the sofa.

'That's real interesting, Art, but don't you think he's doing just fine right now?'

'Yeah, but with all these young artists coming up, the attention shifts, you know. I mean, the guy's already thirty-seven, right?'

'That seems young, Art.'

'Yeah, but collectors like the new thing, the next Koons,' and then, giving out a chuckle, he added, 'Or Hirst.'

'He told me he's had like, offers but he thinks he can do it alone, with a cool PA.'

'Oh yeah, that's good, that's good, do you ah, know who's offered?'

'Move into Art's? Are you out of your mind?' Jean screeched. Bob looked away and walked towards the window. 'You guys seem, ah seem ...' he mumbled. Jean's public affair with Spindle had been implied but not discussed freely between them. It had been an unwritten law between them that certain aspects of their private lives had restricted access. Bob was about to break the taboo, 'seem to be very ah, very ah, happy together.' Jean Maclestone was dumbstruck. It had never occurred to her that he would bring her relationship with Art into the open.

Elaine is suddenly on top of me. I'm totally freaked. I mean, can you imagine? One minute I'm like, holding a nipple ring and the next she's got me pinned down, holding my hair and like, kissing my neck and ear. I'm so surprised I don't like, react for a second.

Elaine's half-naked body lay on Beth, trapping her head in the corner of the couch. Her tongue roamed up her neck, gently biting the lobe of her ear. 'Elaine!' Beth exclaimed. 'What the hell are you doing? Jesus Christ!' She tried to get up but Elaine was holding her hair and resting her whole weight on Beth's chest. 'Just relax,' Elaine whispered into Beth's ear, 'reelaax.' Elaine's tongue moved down to her shoulder. 'I'm not this way, oh please, please.' Elaine stretched Beth's bra away from her breast and began delicately sucking her nipple. 'Oh Jesus, oh Jesus, oh my God, oh Jesus, oh my God,' Beth said, holding on to Elaine's bald head and trying to draw it away, but it stuck to her like a limpet. Elaine moved her thigh between Beth's legs and started rotating her hips. She then kissed her repeatedly on the lips and tried to slip her tongue into Beth's mouth while sliding her hand down her waist and under her dress.

This is just like, so embarrassing. I'm going to have to push her off me. Jesus, this is like rape. You know what I mean? But like, I don't know.

Paige rolled her tongue down Jo's cock until she got to the base and then she slowly moved up gently nibbling the edges and, opening her mouth as wide as possible, she placed the whole head into it. As she rotated her tongue around his crown, she wrapped her fingers three-quarters of the way down his cock and started massaging it. Jo grabbed her hair and moved himself deeper into her mouth. After a while he announced he was about to come. 'I'm coming.' Paige sucked him more fervently, quickening her rhythm. Jo's sperm hit the roof of her mouth. She could feel it slipping down her throat but continued sucking until the last drop had come out. Paige opened her mouth, letting the remaining cum fall out into her cupped hand.

Elaine began to stroke Beth's breasts.

'Elaine, Elaine, please,' Beth whispered as Elaine moved forward.

'I know this is real weird for you, Beth,' Elaine replied, undoing Beth's shirt buttons.

'Elaine, don't do this,' Beth said under her breath. Elaine undid her bra and gently caressed her nipples with the palms of her hand. Beth looked down and bit her lip. She suddenly clamped her hand on to Elaine's wrist but Elaine shook her hand free and placed it back on the inside of Beth's thigh. Elaine could feel her wetness.

'You're real wet, Beth,' she whispered, 'just stay cool and let me touch you, okay. How does this feel?' she whispered as she lightly massaged her through the gusset of her pantyhose. 'That's good, isn't it, Beth?' Elaine leaned over and kissed Beth on her open mouth.

Chelsea sat down on the couch. Art followed suit and sat next to her even though there were several options scattered around the room. 'I would look after Ivor, you know, but if he wants to do it himself, what can I say?' he said, nodding his head sadly.

'Is that why you took me out this evening, Art?' Chelsea queried. Art laughed heartily, bringing his hand down on Chelsea's knee. 'Of course not. I'm sorry, Chelsea, if that's what you thought, no no no,' he hooted. 'I ah, well, I took you out because ah, because ...'

'Yes, Art?'

'Well, you know when ah, we had dinner with Ivor?' he asked awkwardly.

'Yeah.'

'Well, I kinda thought, you know, that ah, that ...'

Chelsea laughed. 'You mean when you were stroking my leg under the table in front of everybody?'

Art laughed again, going a peculiar shade of purple. 'Yeah well ... ah, I ah, felt that ah ...' Art's hand moved around Chelsea's knee. She looked at him, waiting for him to continue his explanation. 'I have been ...' he hesitated, 'this is totally out of line, Chelsea,' he continued, looking down at the floor, 'you mustn't tell anybody, please.'

Chelsea smiled. 'I'm intrigued, Art, wait, no wait, I'll tell you,' she said, suddenly getting up from the couch. 'You sat next to me at the Odeon, right?' She turned around facing the window. 'You thought I was some kinda dumb model who was fucking Ivor that night, right?' she said, walking around the back of the couch. 'You put your hand on my leg and I didn't resist, right, so you thought that I was like maybe on for it, okay, and like, you have been horny ever since, but Ivor is an artist you want in your gallery so you think, well, let's take Chelsea out and maybe talk to her and she might persuade him or something pathetic, but then you get horny again and you have to balance wanting Ivor and wanting me. So you're going to proclaim some kinda love when in fact you just want to push your ugly little body between my thighs, am I right?'

Spindle sat motionless, his mouth open, bottom lip quivering. 'Jesus, where the hell did that come from?' he whispered.

Chelsea's legs were a little apart, hands on hips. She looked down at him with a self-satisfied smile. 'Harvard.'

'We have always been good friends, you know,' she said quietly.

'Jean, do you ah, take me for an idiot? All th-those weekends. The collectors' tours Art organised in Eur-Europe. The weekend in Tulsa when you said you were on a "Friends of the Gu-Gu-Guggenheim" trip in New Orleans.'

'How did you know about that, Bob? I mean how the hell did you know?'

'Is that ah, important, Jean? How I know?'

'Yes, it is,' Jean said.

'But why?' Maclestone asked.

'Because it means,' she started, and clenching her hand brought it down hard on the bed, 'it means that you didn't trust me,' she wailed.

Bob emitted a sharp yell. 'I don't believe what I ah, I'm hearing.' His voice was laced with cynicism.

'You had me followed?' Jean asked, trying to shift the advantage and repeating for effect, 'You had me followed, didn't you?' Her voice trembled with a combination of indignation and disbelief.

Elaine brushed her fingers lightly and slowly drew her finger along the lips until she found the small swelling of Beth's clitoris. She softly pressed her fingers on to and around it until the passages were wet with desire.

I don't believe this. Oh shit, I don't want this, man. She's a girl. I don't
believe I'm like, doing this. Maybe I should let her do it. No way.

'Elaine, my God, Elaine, oh God,' Beth moaned as she leaned against her.
'This is totally weird, oh Jesus Christ, what are you doing? This is enough,
man,' she said, grabbing Elaine's hand and sharply removing it from
between her legs. 'Elaine,' she said sharply, looking straight out in front of
her and doing up her shirt buttons, 'I am not like, I am not a lesbian, okay?'
    'Oh shit,' Elaine said, 'I'm real sorry, I ah, I don't know what came over
me, will you forgive me?' she pleaded. 'I'm just going through this heavy
shit with my friend, you know? I kinda, you know, Beth, I wanted, I feel
like so ...' Elaine put her head into her hands.

'That was so great, Paige,' Jo said breathing heavily. 'But I really wanted
to make love to you, you know?'
    'Wrong time of the month,' Paige said, smiling at him as she stroked his
hairy chest. 'Next time, okay?'
    'Yeah, sure thing,' replied Jo as he averted Paige's oncoming lips. In
truth he didn't want to taste his own semen, so he moved away from her
puckered lips and kissed her cheek instead. Paige ran her fingers around
his shoulder and down his arm, her eyes blinking with satisfaction.

So, I'm like, standing there and Elaine is kinda upset 'cos I'm not like, gay
and stuff, but like what was weird, was that she'd really turned me on, you
know?

Beth lay back on the couch. Her legs were about two feet apart, knee to
knee, and slightly bent. Her panties were tautly stretched around her ankles
and her stocking lay entwined around her feet like a boa constrictor curled
about its victim. Her bare white legs were mottled and goose-pimpled.
Elaine kissed her neck while sliding her fingers between Beth's legs and
caressing her clitoris. Beth felt Elaine's finger penetrating her. 'Elaine,' she
groaned as she arched her back. 'Oh Jesus.'
    'Does that feel good, Beth?' Elaine asked.

There is a point of no return and it happened. I just like, let her do her thing, partly because I was like, curious, I guess, partly because I like her and partly because, well, she like, turned me on. Elaine is kinda forceful, overpowering, but gentle at the same time. She knows how to touch a girl in the right places at the right time, you know what I mean, and although it was totally weird it was also totally great.

Elaine stepped back off the sofa and getting on her knees removed Beth's knickers. She then put Beth's right leg over her shoulder and kissed her belly button.

'Elaine, I don't think I, I want this. Elaine, God. Oh. Jesus ah. Oh my God. Oh God, ah ... Elaine.'

Elaine licked the inside of Beth's thigh. She placed her lips over her vulva and probed her tongue around Beth's clitoris. Beth raised her pelvis, moving to Elaine's rhythm.

Here's the scene. It's the back room of the Man Hole club around 2.30 a.m. The main chamber is barely lit, several men are patrolling the area. There's a strong smell like a mixture of body fluids and chemicals, as if someone had used Palmolive as a deodorant. A small crowd gathers around the entrance of one of the cubicles which line the perimeter of the room. A large black guy holds a flashlight illuminating the dank cupboard-size room and highlighting the gyrating flesh. A prick is wending its way with some force into Dewey's ass. His hands laid flat on the wall in front of him, legs apart and knees resting on a small bench in front of him. Dewey looks out of the cubicle. Two guys have their pricks out and are wanking each other off. Dewey holds a metal bar on the wall to steady himself as Greg rams hard against his butt.

She had the perfect ass, Jo thought; rounded and firm with a cute gap where he could bury his finger. He moved his middle finger between her buttocks and finding her anus pressed his finger in a little.

'What are you doing, Jo?' Paige murmured into the pillow.

'Do you like that, Paige?' Jo whispered.

'It's kinda weird,' she said.

Jo leaned over and opening his side drawer retrieved a jar of Nivea. Having covered his cock with the cream he got on his knees and holding it firmly in one hand he reached down with the other, parting her cheeks. Manoeuvring his prick with the other hand, he found the indentation in her skin. Then, letting go, he slowly slipped the head of his cock into her.

'Jo, ow, Jo, it hurts, Jo. Jesus!'

'Just relax, Paige, just relax.' Jo felt Paige's sphincter muscles loosening. He picked up the pace a little, moving his whole cock into her.

'Jo, Jo, my God.'

He slid his hand under her thigh and finding her clitoris started to massage it.

'Jo, get out. It hurts, it really hurts ...'

Jo half withdrew and continued to rotate his hips gently. Paige gave out a pained whimper. He felt his orgasm coming and penetrated deeper into her again.

'Get out,' she screamed, but Jo had gripped her pelvis and was forcing her against him.

Chelsea sat in front of Spindle, provocatively stroking the inside of her thighs. Spindle nervously flattened his hair with the palm of his hand.

Jean squeezed her make-up bag into a small Gucci leather overnight case. Bob was now at the end of the bed and wearing a dark red silk dressing-gown. He started pacing the room. 'Jean,' he began before pausing briefly, 'this is ah, ridiculous, absolutely ridiculous. We've had rows before. You don't have to be so extreme. I mean, can't we talk about this sensibly?'

'Bob, I am leaving you,' Jean muttered as she zipped up her bag. 'I've thought about it, and it's just not going on between us any more. We're miles apart.'

Bob wiped his brow and looked at her. 'We might be going through a difficult moment, ya know?'

'You see, you don't know. I mean, you don't even know whether we're having a "difficult moment," she said miming quote-marks with her index fingers, 'or not. You're totally oblivious to ...' she hesitated and hunched her shoulders up, 'to everything to do with our life together, you have been for years.'

'Jean, that's just not true. I have always loved you,' Bob began.

'Don't give me that, Bob. Tell me how many times have you been unfaithful? Ah, how many times?' Jean asked, hands on hips.

'Are you in a position to ask me that, Jean? Bob retorted.

'Bob, you just hide under a thousand excuses, you have done all your life. You will never come to terms with yourself.'

'I suppose that's what your a-analyst told you, right?' Bob interrupted.

Jean walked into the bathroom. 'I have a brain of my own, Bob. Maybe you missed that as well.'

Bob followed her in. 'I am not saying that you don't. It's just a-analyst talk that bugs me, Jean. I can't stand it when you qu-quote a-analyst jargon.'

'Well, you won't have to worry about having to any more, Bob,' Jean replied, picking up a toothbrush and dropping it into her handbag. She walked back into the bedroom.

'Well, I do, Jean, I do. I know that it's been difficult at times but we've built a l-life together and two children, and yeah, what about the kids eh, what about them?' Bob asked, raising his voice somewhat. 'I mean, Jean, have you thought about the kids?'

'Listen, Bob,' Jean said calmly, 'the kids are at college, they'll be just fine.'

Bob looked at her incredulously. 'Your a-analyst advised you, didn't he? Advised you it would be just, just fine, did he?'

'I'm their mother, right? I should know, I know my children. I don't want to spend the rest of my life with you and they will understand that,' Jean shouted, picking up her case and walking out of the room.

Bob turned after his wife, his body lumbering over the bleached maple floor. 'They will never forgive you, never, you fucking se-selfish bitch,' he bellowed. The door opened. He came to a standstill. The door slammed in his face.

Art kissed Chelsea's parted knees and then slowly moved up the inside of her thighs. She looked down on his bald head and smiled. He shuffled forward on his knees, adjusting position to allow for his progress. Chelsea opened her legs wide to accommodate his beady head. Finally, Art arrived at his destination. His tongue extended out like a lizard, searching for the partition, the dividing line, but the skin did not part under his probing tongue and instead of the soft indentation he was expecting, there was a hard fleshy protuberance.

Jo's cock slackened and flopped melancholically out of Paige's ass, sliding carelessly over her thigh as he moved over her to lie on his back. He looked up at the ceiling and blew out through pursed lips. Paige curled up into a ball and stared out into the roomy loft. She bit her lip and closed her eyes. Soon tears were oozing from between her eyelids and trickling down on to the pillow.

Elaine's fingers wrapped around Beth's temples and her palms pressed her eye sockets. Between Elaine's spread thighs Beth's tangled hair fell carelessly over stomach and hips. Beth's tongue roamed around her clitoris. They both turned so Elaine was positioned over her face, then lowering herself she gently slid over Beth's mouth, nose, cheekbone, eyes and forehead.

She's over my face. I can feel her sliding all over. My face is totally wet with her. I let her dig deep into my face, my face is soaked with her. I can feel her coming over me.

Elaine's tongue bolt rubbed against Beth's clitoris. She sensed that Beth was climaxing and clasped her around her thighs so she couldn't move away. Beth gave out a staggered moan.

Then I come – with a woman. I mean, can you believe that?

'Oh gee, I didn't ah, know, I mean, I didn't realise. I just ...' Spindle stuttered as he stared at Chelsea's prick rising majestically over him like a crucifix.

'I'm flattered,' Chelsea replied, undoing her shirt buttons.

'I don't think I can go through with this.' Art began getting up. Chelsea smiled down at him as she slowly opened her black chiffon shirt revealing a pair of perfectly formed breasts, the nipples of which stood out arrogantly from their surgical dependents. Spindle hesitated.

Chelsea rubbed her black leather stiletto heeled shoes into his shiny two-tone crotch. 'Something is going to be disappointed,' she said, feeling his erection on her ankle.

'What are you doing, Paige?' Jo asked sleepily.

'I gotta go, I have to be at work tomorrow,' Paige answered, snapping her bra on. Jo detected an air of nonchalance in her deadpan delivery, maybe she was just tired, he justified. Nevertheless he felt something was amiss.

'I want you to stay, I mean, can't you stay?' he asked weakly.

'I gotta get ready in the morning, you know, I gotta go to work early,' she said, sliding into her Agnes B pleated skirt.

'Are you sure you can't ...'

'Quite sure, honey.' Paige's reply was firm and Jo discontinued his feeble attempt at persuading her. In truth he preferred she went; he hated getting up in the morning and making polite conversation. He enjoyed being alone with his thoughts and coffee, anyway he hadn't gotten enough milk.

'Is this gonna hurt?' Art asked.

'It's a sexy kinda pain, Art. Just don't worry about me, okay?' Chelsea said.

'Oh Jesus Christ,' Art muttered as Chelsea placed his condom-lined prick against Art's anal orifice but just as he was about to push it in, the door-bell echoed around the apartment.

'Oh my God,' Art panicked. 'Who the hell can that be, oh Jesus, you

gotta go, right now, oh my God.' He sprang off the bed, reached for a towel
and swept it about him.

'Art, don't panic,' Chelsea said, smiling up at him. 'Just don't answer the
door.' She rolled her tongue along parted lips and stroked her nipples
seductively.

'The doorman knows I'm in for Christ's sake, get dressed for Christ's
sake, hurry.'

Chelsea got off the bed. 'Men are all the same, it's all in their balls,' she
sighed. 'So where's the spare room?' she asked.

'Spare room!' he gasped in disbelief. 'You gotta leave, Chelsea.'

'Are you throwing a young girl out on the street? No way Jose. I'm
staying right here,' Chelsea declared, as the door-bell went again.

'This could be my daughter.'

'Or girlfriend, you mean,' Chelsea replied, as she obstinately sat on the
edge of the bed.

'Oh please, please,' Art implored. 'It could be Jean, you're right. It
could, look, okay, okay, you can sleep in the spare room, just don't make
a noise, please.'

As Paige walked down the stairs of Jo's apartment building she felt a warm
wetness between her legs. Stopping in mid-flight she put her hand up her skirt
and slipped her hand down her knickers. Paige delicately probed her aching
ass-hole. On retrieving her finger she found it was coated with blood.

'Oh my God,' she whispered between clenched teeth, 'the fucker,' and
drawing out some tissue from her bag she cleaned her bloodied finger
before continuing her climb down the stairs.

Jo touched the water as it rushed into the olive-green basin and finding it
to his satisfaction he washed himself thoroughly until certain he had
cleaned away every unpleasant residue.

'I've just walked out on Bob, Art,' Jean said triumphantly.

'You've just walked out on Bob?' he exclaimed, shutting the door behind
her. 'Jesus, isn't that a bit extreme?'

'I've had enough, Art, I'm forty-five years old, I don't want to be kicked out on my butt when it's all too late, you know. I don't wanna be left when I'm old and cranky and look like the butt end of a rhino, you know what I mean. I don't wanna stagnate in some Park Avenue apartment watching my husband screw secretaries and then one day, when it suits him, leave me and marry one of them. Art, I am not going to discuss it right now, okay, I am tired, tired of twenty years of marriage, twenty years of putting up and trying to make it work. I don't think you know what it's been like, Art, I couldn't go through another Sunday with his mother stroking his hair and telling me what he was like aged six for the millionth time or grimacing each time she eats my food, complaining about the weather, contemporary art, politics. I wanna live, Art, I wanna go to bars, museums, I wanna go to Paris, Moscow, Cambodia. I want my own apartment, my own friends, I wanna stay up all night. I don't wanna hear about the latest property deal or the basketball score or Matisse's coiffure, or have long discussions about how he met Warhol and how many inches of space the Basquiat should have around it, you know. I've had enough. I guess we've grown apart, miles apart, we've nothing in common except two internet freak kids and taste in art.'

'Right,' Art said, falling into his customary armchair. This was going to be a long night, he thought to himself. Jean removed her heels and curled her calves under her thigh.

'You know, I am sure we've met; you're so familiar. Maybe it was in the club or someplace. Have you ever been to Miami? I went there last winter and the summer before,' Dewey fired in an effeminate fashion.

Greg Tavali sat down on the kitchen chair. 'Perhaps,' he yawned. 'Kinda pokey,' he added, looking around the room. 'You always lived here?'

'It suits me fine, honey. Anyway, rents are so expensive in New York, you know, I couldn't afford anything bigger, not for the time being anyway. Maybe when I curate more and do more articles. I got this show I'm curating next month, it's going to be so great ...'

'Right,' Greg broke in with another yawn. 'You know, you talk a lot,' he added wearily.

'Honey, I …' Dewey began.

'I'm staying the night.'

'Well honey, of course …'

Brigid was off her head. Her arms were swaying back and forth to the rhythm of the music. Sweat was pouring off her face and made dark pools under her arms and back. A rastafarian held her tightly from behind and gyrated against her ass, his hands on her thighs holding her firmly against him. Another rasta guy came up to her and started gyrating from the front.

At about 3a.m. Elaine woke from a deep sleep. Beth was down on her. Half in a dream she stroked Beth's head and opened her legs wide.

Dolores Ballesteros was dreaming that Mr Rhinegold's house was ablaze. Rhinegold himself was unable to move from his bed. She tried to pull the curtain down from its support but it was not giving way. She suddenly saw Freign behind the flames. He was smiling at her and pointing at Rhinegold. Dolores woke up in a sweat. The electric heater was full on and the room was stiflingly hot. Having got out of bed to switch it off, she turned on the television. Ren and Stimpy were chasing a fart which Ren had delivered and had kept as a pet. The fart had escaped the house. Eventually, after looking for the fart in every nook and cranny, they found it in a trash can in the form of a half-eaten fish. They brought it back to the house where it dawned on Ren and Stimpy that the fart had grown up and must be allowed to go its own way in the world and presumably meet other farts and procreate. By the time the fart had flown the nest Dolores was fast asleep.

CHAPTER SEVEN

LAST NIGHT

Rhinegold lay in peaceful stillness, mouth open, jaw resting on his throat, lips curled about his gums; his hands clasped the blanket like a child would a teddy bear. His lined face had smoothed out and small shiny pools of reflected light from the bedside lamp highlighted his grey-white cheekbone and forehead. His head made a shallow dent in the pillow.

Freign opened one eye. He'd left his reading light on. It was three in the morning. As he shifted over to turn the light off, the book which he'd been reading fell from his bed and a faded envelope dropped out from between the pages. It contained a letter which his father had written to his mother in Burma in 1934. He had been a Sergeant-Major in the Tenth Indian Fusiliers. His parents had met at a music hall in Hackney in 1931. She had a part-time job as an usherette and he was a young foot soldier on leave from Aden. As soon as they were married he was posted to Burma. Freign was born in 1936 in Bethnal Green. After the war his parents applied for a job at a school just outside Boston called St Francis. His mother, being a keen Sunday painter and teacher at a local Catholic school, applied for the post of art teacher and her husband for physical education instructor. It was the perfect application and they both got their respective jobs.

Dreaming is like watching a movie, thought Jo as he leaned over and switched on the side-light. A crazy movie full of familiarities and yet completely alien, like a science-fiction movie, but with your whole family and all your friends roaming around odd spaces which are equally familiar, yeah, a paradox within a paradox, he conjured dreamily. Maybe life was just like that; the brain serving to put events into sequences, um, hey, how about that; like a paradox within a paradox. There must be a piece in there somewhere. He should write all this down before he forgot. Maybe he could include it in a piece. Fuck. No pen. Jo switched the light off and turned on his side. Yeah, this was going to be a great piece. It was going to make him. Perhaps for the next show. He must remember a 'paradox within a paradox'.

Joany sat, legs apart, smoking a cigarette on a fifties chrome kitchen chair. She leaned a thick white arm on a yellow vinyl table. She had bleached hair greased back, a powdered white face, dark red painted lips, thick black mascaraed lashes. A black tank-top stretched across a pair of large bosoms. A short black leather skirt hovered over a pair of bare sturdy legs which were cut below the knee with black socks. Joany came in at about one hundred and sixty pounds. She was just under six feet tall. The room was lit by a single light bulb, high wattage. Behind her was the kitchen counter and sink piled high with dirty plates and saucepans. A poster of a Frida Kahlo self-portrait hung on the wall to her right. She chewed noisily on bubble-gum.

'Where the fuck have you been?' she slurred drunkenly.

'Oh you know, around and about,' Elaine replied.

'You mean fucking around and fucking about,' Joany said coolly as she stubbed her cigarette out, 'you fucking midget slut.'

'Whatever,' Elaine replied. 'I gotta show tomorrow, in case you didn't know.'

'I gotta show tomorrow,' Joany imitated her slow Californian accent. 'You couldn't fucking show a fuckin',' Joany hesitated, 'a fuckin' duck.'

'A duck, Joany? Can't you do better than a duck?' Elaine looked up at the ceiling and half closed her eyes. 'Can't you get proper lighting here?'

Joany lit another cigarette and spat, 'Don't you fucking patronise me, you undersized fucking whore.'

'Listen, Joany, I haven't come here to be pissed on, I've come here because I love you.'

'Because I love you,' Joany mimicked her voice again and then, 'Because I love you. You couldn't love your own fucking baby.'

'Joany,' Elaine started.

'No, I'm wrong, man, you only love yourself.'

'Well, make up your mind,' Elaine said, blowing smoke through her nose.

Joany waved her hand at Elaine. 'Look at you! Your fucking tattoos. Your little dyke lip rings and nipple rings and clit ring. You're just a self-adoring, self-obsessed, selfish, second-rate, so-called artist, you couldn't even fuckin' draw a fuckin' straight fuckin' line.'

'Listen, Joany, let's not get into this, right? Anyway, I do videos.'

'So, she does videos now,' Joany whined. 'Don't tell me, of yourself, right?'

Elaine sighed and threw her jacket over her shoulder. 'As a matter of fact, yeah. Do you want to see them, Joany? Being fucked real good.'

Joany got up and crossed the room to where Elaine was standing. They looked at each other for a few seconds in silence.

'By a man,' Elaine whispered, looking straight at her. Joany looked away. Elaine lowered her head. Joany punched her in the face. Elaine staggered back and held her nose, partly covering her mouth. Blood began seeping between her fingers. 'Jesus Christ, Joany!' Joany moved forward and, grabbing Elaine's hair in her pudgy fist, pulled her towards the door. An anglepoise lit the top right hand corner of an unmade bed, which was scattered with clothes of various sizes and colours, sheets, pillows, make-up-soiled towels. A black cupboard loomed in the corner, spilling more debris out on to the dirty yellow ochre carpet. Joany threw Elaine on the bed. Elaine tried to get up but Joany slapped her down.

'Look, Joany, I'm sorry. It was a joke, Joany. Please, Joany!' Elaine implored as she sat up amongst the carnage.

Joany picked up a leather belt from the floor.

'Joany, please don't. I don't need this, please,' Elaine pleaded, holding out her hands, her fingers spread wide like cobwebs through which she could see Joany towering menacingly, partly silhouetted against the side-light.

'So, it's perleaze now? I'll give you perleaze,' Joany half shouted and threw the belt across Elaine's shoulder.

'Joany, no!' Elaine shouted, trying to scramble off the bed.

Joany jumped on to the bed and grabbed Elaine's neck. She dug her knee into Elaine's back. Once Joany had her pinned to the bed she tugged at her jeans until both jeans and underwear were around her thighs. Joany then raised the belt high above her shoulder and brought the leather thong down swiftly across Elaine's butt. Elaine screamed. Joany continued hitting her in rapid succession. Joany stopped after the sixth beating, abruptly got off the bed and went strutting out of the room. Elaine lay on her stomach weeping into the pillow.

Beth was running through a scraggy, bushy savannah-type landscape. Two lionesses appeared behind her. She ran faster but they were catching up. A door suddenly appeared and she jumped in, closing the door behind her. The hole became a cell and she opened the door of the cell and looked down a narrow corridor stretching down to a caged exterior. She was in a zoo. The lions roamed up and down the corridor except at mealtimes when they would be thrown legs of lamb by the zoo keeper. Beth realised this was the only time she could escape. She stayed in the cell until she plucked up enough courage to open her cell door. She ran down the corridor past the lions in the enclosure, who were voraciously eating their dinner, and jumped up, grabbing the iron bars of the enclosure. She couldn't haul herself up.

Beth woke and looked at the clock beside her bed. 3.30 a.m.

'Fuck.' She passed her hand over her forehead.

Young Freign was devoted to his mother. He would spend his afternoons with her, drawing on pieces of brown paper which they would find drifting across the streets around Spitalfields market. His father would play soccer with him and tell him stories of the Empire: in each pink area of the map of the world his father had his own heroic tale to tell.

Freign had been both terrified and in awe of his father, who was prone to a short temper that would manifest itself with a kind of implosion: shaking his huge belly and colouring his face to a dark purple, he would bellow an array of expletives of one kind or another assembled in a curiously disjointed order as if the blood flooding his brain were somehow forcing the whole lot out at same time. But these outbursts would fade as quickly as they had emerged, and the recipients, who were now usually frozen to the spot, would find themselves being drawn into the warmth of the rotund belly of their interlocutor. The pupils of St Francis' were on the whole fond of their physical education teacher, until one day in the spring of '48, after barely two years in the job, he was to be seen lying prostrate on the sports field where he had been coaching the school softball team. He had died instantly of a heart attack. Freign was a spindly sixteen-year-old adolescent.

At first his mother bore the pain with admirable resilience, no doubt attempting to shelter her family from the effects of their huge loss, but soon the cracks began appearing; Mrs Freign would shut herself in her room in the early evening, which soon became the late afternoon; finally she would disappear as soon as her classes had finished. Her two children were left to fend for themselves. They would pack her off to work in the same way she had packed them off to school before her curious behaviour began. This latent grieving lasted for a year or so until one morning, during breakfast, she appeared with an uncharacteristically demonic smile on her face, a smile which had been absent for so long that her children mistook it for the symptom of an unnerving mental condition. Freign still shuddered when he remembered the stretched mouth over her neglected teeth. From then on Mrs Freign acted as if nothing had ever happened. She never mentioned her deceased husband and on the occasions when his name slipped into conversations, she would glide over the reference with some agile observation or other. It was almost as if she had completely erased him from her memory.

'I'm sorry,' Joany begged when she came back in. 'I'm sorry, honey.' She rolled over to where Elaine lay and stroked her butt with an ice cube. 'I love you, you know that.'

'You bitch,' Elaine choked in her tears, 'you fucking fat bitch.'

Joany continued sliding the ice cube over Elaine's ass and thighs and then, bending down, she ran her warm tongue over her welts.

'You know, Greg, this apartment is like a little small for two, you know what I mean?' Dewey yawned and ran his fingers through his hair. Greg looked forlorn. 'Dewey,' he said quietly, 'I got nowhere to go.' Dewey tugged at the refrigerator door and stumbled awkwardly towards it. 'Greg honey, why don't you go back to Houston?' he suggested, looking around the shelves. 'Sell your place and buy in New York,' he said, as he eyed a yogurt from among the half empty jars of jam, pickled gherkins and several indiscernible yellow and green condiments. 'It would be just so great.' He was sure Greg wouldn't mind if he had the last yogurt, he thought to himself as he went to pick up the orange and yellow container.

Suddenly Dewey felt himself lurch forwards into the refrigerator. He crashed on to the shelves sending bottles and cans spilling out on to the floor. 'Jesus Christ!' Dewey shouted, as he tried to pick himself up. 'Greg, what the fuck ?' As he looked up he saw Greg looking down at him with a Gustav Emil Ern kitchen knife in his hand. 'Oh my God, oh my God.'

'Just keep quiet and come over here, sweetie-pie,' Greg ordered in his slow Texan accent. Dewey straightened up and casting a stern look at Greg said, 'Just,' 'what,' 'the,' 'hell,' 'do,' 'you,' 'think you're doing?' pronouncing each word deliberately.

'Sit here, honey,' Greg motioned, pushing a chair into the middle of the room. Dewey stared uncomprehendingly. 'This is my place. I'll sit where I like.'

'Just sit down,' Greg repeated, waving the knife provocatively. Dewey got up from the debris around him and sat down. 'Now put your hands on the arms of the chair, that's right, sweetie.' Greg tied Dewey's forearms against the chair.

'Is this some kind of sex thing, Greg? Because if it is, I don't like it.'

'Move your leg back, honey,' Greg demanded. 'That's right, against the chair, sweetie-pie.' Greg tied both ankles to the legs of the chair.

'Greg, this is not funny any more. I'm going to scream. Do you hear me?'

'If you scream, honey, it'll be for the last time.'

'Look, if this is about the apartment, you can stay as long as you want.'

'Don't worry, honey, I'm leaving very soon,' Greg said calmly. 'Open your mouth wide.'

'Oh ...' Dewey began before a drying-up cloth plugged his mouth.

'That's better, much better, now just you relax. What a day it's been.' Greg wiped his brow. 'Now it's just you and me,' he added, drawing up a chair of his own.

Freign's headmaster had taken special interest in him after his father's death and, seeing that he wanted to follow in his father's footsteps, managed to secure a place for him at the local Military Academy. After a gruelling three months during which Freign was put through a gamut of physical exercises, he failed to qualify for the succeeding semester. He had always been a delicate child and his manhood had not strengthened him. He went back to live with his mother and, unable to motivate himself after the humiliation of the Academy, he spent a year working in various establishments in and around town. He was a petrol attendant, a newspaper delivery boy, a washer-upper in the local bar and then in the town's only coffee house. Then in 1955 he applied for a job as a caretaker of a house just outside Boston.

Mrs Rhinegold smiled benignly at Spindle through a pair of horn-rimmed spectacles. Her mouth seemed unusually large. Her teeth, like a horse's, moved up and down rhythmically. She was saying something but he couldn't really make it out. Then Jo appeared from nowhere, like a ghost, a ghost with a knife. He had a leering smirk but Mrs Rhinegold went on chomping and Jo continued smirking.

Spindle turned to run away but was confronted with a grey wall and he ran along the side of it, aware of all its rivets and nodules. When he heard Jo's breath behind him all seemed lost, but suddenly a hole appeared in the wall through which he scrambled and scurried, the claustrophobic narrowness almost suffocating him. The level tilted sharply and he felt himself falling and it seemed endless, like an elevator shaft, twilight and grime clinging to the unevenness of the wall, and stretching his hands out he felt the moss like velvet. His fall was broken and then he was in a grey room and although it was a small room he couldn't reach the other side. It was his gallery, but there was no exit and he unsuccessfully tried to climb the walls. They were wet because there was a leak from the skylight and it was dripping on the Mondrian. He picked it up and watched the water run off and then the paint slid off in one piece on to the floor. His heart raced. He picked up the paint which now had the consistency of a piece of paper in a puddle, but it began tearing in the middle, so he tried to join the edges, however the paint started chipping and dampness made the colours run on to the floor.

Art Spindle woke up in a sweat. His quilt was wrapped awkwardly around him and he had to get out of bed to unscramble it. 3.45 a.m. The garbage men were outside throwing sacks and stuff into a gaping mouth of steel. Art lay back, listening to the revving of the engine as it worked the hydraulics which squeezed its burgeoning belly.

The Arrowsmith family owned a large portion of Boston as well as huge estates in Vermont, a Caribbean island and numerous other properties in New York and Mexico City. Mr Arrowsmith's father had managed to unshackle the family from its huge wealth and had left his son and heir the task of unscrambling the disparate pieces of his empire, the character and interests of which were so removed from each other that he spent the rest of his life endeavouring to rearrange the business. Disused mines were sold off, old dance halls were torn down to be replaced by tenement blocks, land was traded, fishing fleets discontinued, Californian wineries liquidated. In other words, Mr Arrowsmith dismantled all his father's whims. It was in the twilight of his employer's life that Freign was installed in a small bungalow at the foot of a large house that was built entirely of wood in the style of a small Scottish castle.

A life-long smoker, Mrs Arrowsmith had developed emphysema and was slowly becoming less mobile and more truculent. She was, to say the least, quite a handful, and one by one her employees capitulated to her unrelenting neediness and rigid expectation until Freign was unceremoniously left to deal with her as she steadily regressed into senility. Towards what seemed to be the end of her life Mrs Arrowsmith's eldest daughter came to visit her. When Alfreda Arrowsmith arrived at the door of her ancestral home she was met by Freign. It was love at first sight.

Hotel Costes, Paris, France. 10 a.m. Jean Maclestone leaned across her dressing table and inserted her contact lenses. There was a knock at the door.

'Yes?' she shouted.

'It's Ivor,' a numbed voice answered, 'can I come in?'

'Give me fifteen minutes?' she shouted back. 'I'll meet you in the lobby.'

Beth turned over again. She looked at her bedside clock. Four fifteen.

Am I doing the right thing? I've spent the whole of my grandmother's like, inheritance – fifty thousand dollars! Fuck. What if the gallery doesn't work? What if it's a total failure? What's everybody gonna think of me? My parents will like, kill me. What if nothing sells? I owe the construction guys ten thousand dollars. This is so bad! I must have been like crazy to think I could have opened a gallery. Fucking crazy.

'You see, Dewey, it's guys like you that fuck it up for everybody, you know? You know what I mean? You just go out and fuck anything that moves. Anything. And one day you fuck the wrong guy. Like me.' He broke into laughter. 'Right, and that's it.'

Dewey mumbled and wriggled in his chair.

'There's no point you attempting anything. This, sweetheart, is it. *Finito*. The end of the road. You see, I'm going to die because bastards like you exist.' Leaning over, he took Dewey's right hand and smiled at him. Then, spreading the fingers, he cut the tendon between the first and the second digit. Dewey's eyes bulged as a muffled scream came out of the cloth.

'I'm sorry, did that hurt, sweetie-pie? Oh dear, all over my shirt.' A spurt of blood had dribbled over Greg's white T-shirt. 'Let me tell you a story.'

Joany undid the dildo straps and removed the apparatus from around her hips. She fell on her back, giving out a long sigh.

'That was great, Joany,' Elaine said. 'Can you do it again?' Joany laughed as she placed the dildo in her mouth and slid it in and out.

'Don't do that, Joany. It makes you look like, so hetero,' Elaine said.

'Elaine, you've just had the symbol of maleness thrusting in and out of you and you're saying this makes me look too hetero?' Joany giggled and drew the wattled instrument across her extended tongue. 'Anyway,' she continued, 'it's my turn.'

'I'm beat, Joany, maybe tomorrow, you know, after the show,' Elaine suggested.

'There's always an excuse with you, Elaine, you know, like always a fuckin' excuse, anyway I'm not going to your fuckin' show.'

'Joany, it's like, four-thirty in the morning and I ...'

'You see I used to go to The Mineshaft. You remember The Mineshaft days.' Greg leaned over and cut between the second and third digit. 'I remember seeing you there,' he said, leaning back on his chair and looking up at the ceiling. 'It was quite some time ago of course,' he whispered, looking at Dewey again. 'You fucked me – don't say you remember because I know you don't.' Leaning over again, he unravelled the remaining uncut fingers of Dewey's right hand. 'And some time later we met again and became friends,' he added slicing another tendon, 'but what you didn't know, sweetheart, was that I was looking for you. Yes, that's right, for you.' Four of Dewey's fingers had now been cut open and the blood seeped rapidly out, flowing down the legs of the chair and forming a small pool at its base.

'It took me some time of course, but with a little help from my friends,' he paused, 'and some of yours.' He now unclenched Dewey's left fist and, like a sushi chef, started cutting the tendons between each finger joint. Dewey was shaking his head and whale-like noises were coming from his throat.

'We managed to track you down,' Greg continued.

Spindle was in a burnt landscape, the wind howled. Up at the top of the field was a Frank Lloyd Wright bungalow. He recognised it as belonging to one of his clients and started to walk towards it. His feet were heavy and then he was on a porch and he opened the door of his own house. Two policemen stood in the hallway. What were they doing? Paige came down the stairs with Jean Maclestone. Jean looked angry and Paige smiled at him and pointed at the policeman who turned into Jo. Paige was stroking his chest. Jo threw him into a room and it was his gallery where Jean stood screaming at him.

'No, no. You don't understand,' he shouted, but Paige looked at him with a sneer. She pointed at him. Someone was taking paintings away through the doors. Art woke up with a start. Five to five. This was no good. He got out of bed and staggered to the bathroom.

Beth sat up in bed. It was five in the morning. *How can she do this to me for Christ's sake. She makes love to me a couple of times and tells me she's like, in love with me and then she disappears. Can you believe that? She's probably fucking somebody else. How can she do this to me?*

Beth fell down on to her pillow and then smothered her face with it. 'I have to sleep!' she shouted to herself.

Greg stood by a small window looking out on to a dirty red brick wall with a shaft of night light casting down its walls. He sighed. 'Kinda pokey apartment, you didn't really think I wanted to live with you here, did you, honey?' Dewey's eye sockets were compressed, waiting to burst; the lids were shut tight and tears oozed from between them, trickling down his cheeks.

Greg got up and poured himself a glass of water from the kitchen sink. He started to sing 'Y.M.C.A.' and, laughing, made the letter signs with his arms.

Paige woke up. It was quarter past five. Her mouth was dry and she had a sharp pain in her side. She went to the bathroom and searched for her codeine. The pain had come and gone several times over the last few days. She had a doctor's appointment the next day. Paige filled a glass up with water and threw two pills to the back of her throat.

Greg drank some more water and went back to sit down with Dewey.
'Then you fucked it up.' Dewey was nodding his head back and forth.

'Yes, yes, Dewey, you did, you did, you fucked it up.' Greg scrutinised
Dewey's wrist and inserted the point of the knife into the white flesh, and
then eased it under a tendon. The phone rang in the background. Greg
hesitated and waited for the machine to pick up. Elaine's voice recorded
itself: 'Dewey, it's me. Hello, Dewey, helloooo.' Greg watched the liga-
ment slither like a worm up Dewey's arm. 'Ring me,' the voice said.

'I don't think so,' Greg laughed. Dewey fainted.

Jean looked into the mirror at her left side before turning forty-five degrees
and inspecting her right side.

'Do you wanna take in a show before going to the gallery?' Ivor
suggested.

'What's there to see?' Jean drew a hair away from her eye.

'There's the Ropac Gallery and Templon, those kinda galleries, or we
could hang out in that café where those crazy guys hung out, The Two
Maggots or something.'

'What crazy guys, Ivor?'

'You know, Picasso, Sartre and all of those guys.'

Jean pouted in the mirror. 'That sounds great. I don't feel like art this
morning – maybe later. Do I look okay?'

'Just great,' Ivor smiled.

Marie-Therese dreamed. Her head lay at a slight angle on a red armchair,
her yellow hair cut by a violet-white shoulder which extended down to
alabaster bosoms and arms, clasping white-violet, white-green hands on a
cobalt-blue skirt. Dreaming. Below Picasso's voluptuous pale figure of
Marie-Therese, Brigid lay, arms stretched back behind her head, elbows
clasped, rich red hair falling with abandon over face and pillow, eyes
closed, mouth slightly open with a protrusion of teeth biting on her lower
lip. A shadow from the coned lampshade covered her neck and cut her
plump breasts just above the nipple. A ray of light accentuated her brown

sun-bedded ribcage and hips and highlighted a nest of curly black hair rising up between her open legs; where a pair of hairy hands clawed each thigh as they reclined over Bob's white rounded shoulders. His body curled like a giant mollusc over the edge of the bed and on to the floor where his knees were tied by a pair of blue-and-white striped pyjama bottoms. This heaving mass of white flesh suddenly jerked forward like a samurai wrestler heaving over its victim. Meeting the occasion, her calves locked around his ribs, feet buckling like a belt over his back until a quick succession of movements completed Bob Maclestone's intentions.

Brigid lay squashed but satisfied. After they had breathed heavily over each other, Brigid said, 'Bob?'

'Yes, honey?'

'You're flattening me.'

'Oh, I'm, I'm sorry, honey.' He rolled over to the other side of the bed, revealing a flushed face covered with a thin film of sweat.

Brigid shifted across the bed and rested her head on his shoulder. 'I'm mad for ya,' she said.

'I love ah, love you too,' he replied.

They lay in silence for several minutes, contemplating all the implications of their feelings.

'What ah, do you think, what shall we do?' Maclestone agonised.

'I wouldn't know,' she replied in her Irish accent and added with a sigh, 'but I havta look after Mr Rhinegold tomorrow morning, so I better get some sleep.' Looking at her watch she said, 'Feckin' hell. It's half past five.'

'I thought you ah, had a day off.'

'No rest for the wicked.'

'Rhinegold? Rhinegold? I know that ah, name.' Bob furrowed his brow.

Brigid drew herself out of bed. 'Sure he doesn't know it himself, I tell ya that much,' she said merrily.

'Mr Rhinegold?' he pondered. Brigid disappeared into the bathroom and soon the noise of flushing water drowned Maclestone's thoughts.

Mrs Rosemary Schwartz, Mr Rhinegold's daughter by his first marriage, woke up with a start. An uncannily warm breeze drifted across her face.

She felt a strange sensation of unease. She tried to concentrate on her throat chakra but no amount of diaphragm breathing could relieve her of the tension that was building up there. Her husband Tom snored loudly beside her.

Jean Maclestone and Ivor Schneider were finishing a late morning coffee at Les Deux Magots. Schneider was in a particularly ebullient mood. As they sauntered down the rue des Beaux Arts, he hummed the first few bars of 'O sole mio'. François Delraye had asked him to meet him at the gallery to install the show. When they arrived at number sixty-three rue des Beaux Arts, instead of finding the gallery, they were confronted by a dingy antique shop which looked as if it had been derelict for months. Nevertheless Schneider rang the bell. An old lady slowly made her way to the door and greeted him. He mustered up all his charm. 'La Galerie Delraye?' he asked politely.

'*Non, non, ce n'est pas une galerie*,' she brusquely replied.

'Oh ay, La Galerie, si vous plaît,' Jean intervened impatiently. The old lady shrugged and pursed her lips, making a raspberry noise, before closing the door in Jean's face.

'These French are so impolite, I mean, did you see that?'

'This is real weird,' Ivor said, turning to Jean who was now glaring through the dusty window at the old lady's blurred silhouette. Schneider's note-book confirmed the gallery address as number sixty-three rue des Beaux Arts.

'Let's walk down the street. Maybe I got the wrong number. You know, he kinda had a weird accent. Maybe he said fifty three.'

Greg shook Dewey without any response. 'Dewey,' he whispered, shaking him again and then raising his voice, 'Dewey, wake up, honey.'

'I haven't finished, I haven't finished,' Greg shouted and, in one quick action, like a conductor in a particularly fast movement, he grabbed Dewey's hair, and pulling back his head he sliced open his windpipe. 'That's for not hearing me out. Sweet dreams,' Greg said, unclenching his fist. Dewey's head lunged back. A spurt of blood arched across the room.

Jean and Schneider had walked up and down the rue des Beaux Arts twice. Most shops and galleries were closing for lunch.

'What is this place?' Jean finally asked. 'I mean, they close for lunch, can you believe that?'

'Maybe we should ask the old lady,' Schneider suggested. The woman signalled from her chair at the sign on the door, *'Fermé'*. Schneider pointed at his mouth and then at the old lady, which could have been loosely interpreted as, 'I want to be sick on you', but was, of course, an innocent appeal for verbal communication. The old lady continued pointing at the door.

'Jesus Christ, what's wrong with that old bitch?' Jean said under her breath. Schneider joined his hands as if in prayer before again wagging his finger to and fro. Finally the old lady struggled out of her armchair and with an exaggerated limp came waddling to the door. She held a half-eaten sandwich which oozed a powerful garlic cheese and a necklace of crumbs hung precariously about her chest. *'Alors, on peut pas manger tranquillement?'* she asked irritably, waving her sandwich under Schneider's face.

'We look for eh,' Schneider gesticulated wildly, 'La Galerie Delraye, Madame, pas trouvée, vous ... What's the word? Fuck, man!' he swore, stamping his foot on the ground with frustration. 'La Galerie Delraye, eh, you know?' He pointed up and down the street.

'Pariscope,' the woman replied.

'What?' He looked at her quizzically.

'The woman's crazy,' Jean whispered.

'C'est touristes,' she said, waving her sandwich at him again. 'Pariscope,' and then deliberating on each syllable, 'Par-is-scope.' The old lady shut the door firmly.

'Periscope? What is she talking about? She's nuts,' Jean said, tapping her head with her index finger at the retreating figure.

It was nearly 6 a.m. Freign turned off his side-light. His love affair continued thoughout Alfreda's mother's illness until one day Mr Arrowsmith discovered the lovers in the Grecian folly beside the lake. Freign was fired immediately and Alfreda was told that she would be disinherited if she continued the inappropriate liaison. It was not long after her mother's death that her father also passed away. His will stipulated that she would only inherit if she married a man of her own social status. This so-called status would be assessed by two appointed trustees of the highest Bostonian pedigree. By this time Alfreda had installed Freign in her New York apartment. It was not long before she realised she would have to find somebody appropriate to marry if she was going to be able to continue her illicit relationship. It was then that Mr Rhinegold was chosen. He had been pursuing her for some time and fitted in well with the necessary criteria. Freign masqueraded as the butler, enabling the lovers to continue their romance and providing the mundane discipline necessary to fuel his military fantasies.

The entwining floors of the Guggenheim gleam with an intense whiteness. Jo sees himself standing in front of Giacometti's *Woman with her Throat Cut* and as he raises his hand to his neck in sympathy he notices an unfamiliar coloration on his hands. On closer inspection he discovers that his fingers are made of luteous wax with a kind of ossification coming through at the joints. He must have been infected by a Rosso; the inner plaster mould oozing through the split wax could have had a toxic or viral property and contaminated him. He should walk away from the infected area. By the time he reached the Gaudier-Brzeska his arms had turned to plaster and hung away from his body like a shop mannequin's. They swung to the rhythm of his steps which themselves seemed to be becoming stiffer with each stride. His shoulder sockets were making a grinding noise as if two pieces of rusty metal were rubbing against each other. Not far to go now, he must be nearing the top of the circular walkway, after all he had just passed a Caro, but what was this? – it couldn't be – but surely Arp was before Caro and yet, there it was like a lizard's tongue curling, slipping up to the ceiling. Jo felt his own tongue enlarging and sliding like a large slug through his open mouth. He now understood that somehow he had ingested all the sculptures he had walked past and was being partially transformed into them. This presented a problem since the only way down was past two thirds of the show he had already seen, by the beginning he would have completely metamorphosed. His tongue was growing at an alarming rate; it made a perfect semi-oval and curled up between his legs where it probed his testicles. Its appearance was not dissimilar to that of a Senufu fertility totem. As Jo lumbered past Henry Moore's *Reclining Woman*, he began to feel a curious undulating sensation together with a strong gravitational pull which had him almost pinned to the floor. His movements become part of a larger movement. His steps are the steps of nature; time becomes part of the movement, for each second an eternity passes. His body is now composed of the things of nature, the components of the earth, and as he lies there feeling part of the whole a river rushes along his spine.

CHAPTER EIGHT

TODAY

Rhinegold lay in peaceful stillness, mouth open, jaw resting on his throat, lips curled about his gums, hands clasping the blanket like a child would a teddy bear. His lined face seemed to have smoothed out, small shiny pools of reflected light from the bedside lamp highlighted his grey-white cheekbone and forehead. His head made a shallow dent in the pillow.

Freign groomed himself, first combing then patting down his hair with gel. He brushed down his black suit. Indenting the polish with a yellow duster, he coated his black walking shoes and buffed furiously until the matt black turned to a dull gleam. He dried his hands, now washed of the minuscule nodules of shoe polish, and dolefully looked in the mirror. A throaty cough, the turn of the door handle into the kitchen. Rhinegold's morning cup of tea noisily arranged itself on the tray. Dolores' souvenir cuckoo clock struck eight a.m. Freign cleared his throat, the kettle boiled, he walked out into the hallway, stooped, collected the letters and the daily paper. **BLAST IN JERUSALEM.**

The headline reminded him of that balmy evening when he had been shot at while patrolling the streets of Jerusalem. The bullet whistled past him, hitting the lamp-post in front of him. It had been a close call. In one move he turned, and seeing the sniper on the roof between two chimneys, aimed from the hip and fired. Having arranged the mail on the tray he marched towards Rhinegold's quarters. The sniper rolled down the roof and fell to the ground.

Art rolled, slid, lathered a bar of soap over, through, into each crevice; washing away yesterday. A step back inside the torrent of water, the soap slid down his body like old snake skin, rolling down to his ankles, collecting, accumulating and finally disappearing into the plug-hole. Spindle slithered through the plastic curtains, emerging from the steam, squinting into the mirror, lathering, shaving the bristles, slapping his cheeks with sandalwood, coating his armpits with deodorant.

Jo's loft was hardly light; the sun managed a glimpse in the late afternoon though this was reduced to a blink during the winter months. Mornings were virtually nights. Jo jumped out of bed knowing he had dreamt of something. He remembered waking up in the middle of the night aware that his dream held some sort of revelation. A cockroach darted along the edge of the kitchen sink and dived under the bread board. What the fuck was it? He tried to concentrate but the vague images of his dream refused to cohere into anything tangible. It occurred to him that his mind was like a Surrealist mechanical contraption of no apparent purpose. The water boiled. 'Goddamn it,' he muttered and brought his fist down on to the bread board.

Ready for the suit; pale, dark, chequered, two-tone, pin-striped, mohair, corduroy. Today was a two-tone kinda day, with a blue shirt and the cravat of course. Every day was a cravat day. Otherwise people wouldn't recognise him, or so he had come to believe. Spindle without the cravat was Spindle without character. Spindle without Spindle.

Eight-thirty a.m. and Beth pushed her quilt back down the bed, across like a drawbridge landing on the carpet, bent, hugging herself as she stumbled to the bathroom. Blinded by the light, squeezing her eyelids, focusing through last night's make-up, scrubbing off the night's spittle, washing the night away, drying, dressing for the day. *Today is the day. The day.*

Paige stood naked in front of her bedroom mirror rubbing body lotion into her bending, curving, arching figure, smoothing her skin from top to toe and scrutinising her legs, stomach, bosoms, shoulders and face in the reflection. Turning to her left she concentrated on her butt and thighs. Then on her right side, she observed her back, shoulder-blade and neck.

'Good morning, sir,' Freign said as he lowered the tray on to the side-table. 'Sir?' He looked down at Rhinegold and raised his voice, 'Sir?' Bending over he put his ear to Rhinegold's open mouth.

Paige snapped on her bra and climbed into Calvin Klein underwear, another twirl before the mirror. Opening her cupboard she walked in to meet an array of clothes. A short Donna Karan was the first to be pulled out, followed by Armani, Galliano and Jacobs. Galliano was tempting but too evening. Armani was always a safe day outfit. Paige felt a sharp pain on her left side. 'Perhaps the black Chanel,' she thought to herself, as she held her abdomen in pain.

Paul Devraux hated blood. When he was in close proximity to it his body would buckle under a wave of nausea and he would have to steady himself against the nearest available prop. When he got down to the second floor of his apartment building, there, seeping under an apartment door and covering the pale green linoleum landing, was a pool of blood. It had managed to drip down to the next step where it had formed another, smaller pool. Paul Devraux stared in disbelief.

A Surrealist mechanical contraption, Jo thought. No beginning, no end. A paradoxical thing. What the fuck was it? For some reason he was convinced that his dream the night before had contained something of real importance: a revelation of some kind. Jo strolled up to the front of the loft with his newly made coffee and sat down at the desk. He put his feet up and stared out of the window.

'E die very peacee,' Dolores said. 'No soundi, nuthee,' she added, looking down at Mr Rhinegold. A single tear flowed down her cheek followed by another. Then, lowering her head on Rhinegold's bed, she sobbed uncontrollably.

'We better call the nurse, Mrs Ballesteros,' Freign said solemnly.

'Señor, señor,' she wept. As Freign turned away it occurred to him that he had never before seen a dead body.

Brigid lay in the bath surveying Mrs Maclestone's collection of bottles perched on the glass shelving. It reminded her of the strange encounter with Elaine the year before. A few things had come back to her from that evening and, although she was still shocked by her recollections, they were now removed enough for her to be able to look back at the occasion with some fascination. Like reviewing something from the wrong end of a telescope: distanced and abstracted.

Elaine surveyed Joany's buttocks which rose like two large rounded mountains sloping between the peaks of her own knees and beyond. Sitting on the table on the other side of the room, she could make out the silhouette of her secam video-camera. A tingling sensation was beginning to move like an electric current up the inside of Elaine's thighs. She arched her back so that the back of her head was touching the wall. The current spread into the lower diaphragm. It imploded and her pelvis moved up against Joany's face. A second spasm jolted her again. In order not to move out of frame she held the pillows beneath her. Joany quickened as did Elaine's involuntary movements. The climax was virtually upon her. Joany's tongue moved up to her clitoris. She felt fingers moving into her. She felt her vagina opening and closing with the movement. The fingers moved more rapidly. The tongue became like butter. Everything contracted.

'Hi, Jean. How's it going over there?' Art asked cheerfully, rolling his tongue over his top lip. As he went on listening his expression changed dramatically.

'What!' he exclaimed, his face becoming noticeably stiffer. 'What do you mean it doesn't exist?' The tone now became grave and concerned. 'Well, did you look him up in the directory?' He moved the phone away from his ear as Jean's voice, now a rat's squeal, became deafening. 'Okay, Jean, Jean, look, now calm down, honey.' Art's hand splayed out in front of him before falling limp on the desk. 'The rue de what, des Beaux Arts? Yes, okay, look, Jean, no, this is what I'll do.' Spindle's hand raised itself again. 'I'll ring up the shippers and find out where they delivered the paintings, ask Ivor who the shippers were ... yes, are you at the hotel? Okay ... okay. How's Ivor taking it? ... Yeah, I bet.'

'I'll see ya this evening, okay?' Brigid said, folding her arms around Maclestone's neck. 'Don't do anything I wouldn't. Be good now,' she added, kissing him on the lips.

'Around ah, around eight-thirty?' Bob suggested as he automatically looked at his watch. When they had said their goodbyes Bob went back to the bedroom and lay on the unmade bed. He rubbed his scalp with his fingertips and looked up at the ceiling. A few minutes later he was fast asleep.

'Roebuck & Roebuck? I've never heard of them. I'll get Paige on to them when she gets into the gallery. Listen, Jean, how many times do I have tell you, there is nothing between us. I mean, she could be my daughter. No, I will not fire her. Jean? Jean? Hello? Jean?' Spindle put the phone down. 'Jesus Christ!'

A moustachioed fireman, clad in a voluble synthetic uniform, splintered the door with his axe. Two blows were sufficient to break the lock. Despite Paul's aversion to gruesome spectacles, he had retained enough morbid curiosity to place himself in a position which would afford him a view into Dewey Bozo's apartment. Dewey, whom he knew only as a brief greeting on the stairwell, sat in a chair, head thrown back with a bloody mass around the neck. Paul promptly fainted and fell clumsily to the ground.

Paige slipped into work five minutes late. Clara Dupont, now a part-timer at the gallery, was already at her desk. 'Morning, Paige, how are you?'
    'Okay, I guess. Anybody call?'

'Art was asking for you. He's in his office. So this is the big day for Jo, right?'

'I guess so. Shall we go together?' Paige asked, putting her coat into the closet.

Beth looked at the carpenter with disdain. 'Goddammit, you gotta finish it! I like, open this evening! You're under a goddamn contract!' she shouted, as Jo Richards came into the gallery.

'Jo, you're late! Been tied up with "Bitch Quale", I suppose?' Beth snarled. 'I got Maclestone coming in like, this afternoon – the show has to be installed.'

'Look, Beth, Paige and I are not an item, okay?'

'Paige and I, is it?' she sneered and then, noticing a table being misplaced, she shouted, 'Hey you, not in there, over there, right? Where's Elaine for fuck's sake? Jo, I think the refrigerator should like, go here, what do you think? Cindy, get me Elaine on the phone and have you booked at Luncheonette? Well, do it for two. The desk over there. Peter, paint that wall again, it's got like fingermarks all over. Look at this. Look! Not there, to the right of the window. Right, you got it, Jesus! Cindy, have you got Elaine yet? Jo, you know I think like, the bed should be like, the centrepiece. What do you think? She's not there? It's a quarter to ten. Where the fuck is she? Cindy, where's the equipment for Elaine's piece? ... Jesus Christ, it hasn't fucking arrived? Well, get on to it.'

'Roebuck & Roebuck. Are you sure? Thank you.' Clara put the phone down and pressed for Spindle's office. 'Art, there is nothing under Roebuck & Roebuck. I've tried everywhere, nothing.'

Paige turned towards Clara. 'I feel so weird today, you know?'

'Oh yeah, what's the matter, Paige?'

'I got this real weird pain in my side. I don't know, like period pains, you know? Maybe it's just that, but it's just kinda sharp, you know what I mean?'

'You should see a doctor, Paige.'

Spindle leaned back on his chair as he talked to Ivor Schneider. 'You got any paperwork? He arranged the whole thing. Have you a number for him? Have you rung the operator? Yeah. No shit. Well, Ivor, how did you get to know him? At the Gagosian opening. Why don't you go to Laurent and find out if they know anything about this guy, and Ivor, don't mention anything, this kind of thing could harm you. If you'd joined the gallery this just would never have happened.'

'I just don't know what to do about him, Clara.' Paige sighed. 'It's just like weird, you know?'

Clara looked at her earnestly. 'What's the problem, Paige?'

'I don't know, he's kinda so great, but like, kinda weird too, you know?' Paige said, looking down at her nails.

'Well, he's an artist, Paige. I mean they're weird people. They're supposed to be,' Clara sympathised.

'I guess so but it's just ...' Paige paused.

'Just what, Paige?' Clara's attention was now fully concentrated.

'Well, it's kinda embarrassing, you know?' The lift doors opened and the first customer of the day came through. 'Good morning.'

'Dewey, it's me. Hello, Dewey, helloooo,' Elaine cooed sleepily down the telephone. 'Ring me, I'm at Joany's.' She put the phone down and glanced at her watch. Ten o'clock. She reached down to the floor where her clothes were sprawled and grappled with various zips and pockets, finally managing to extract a cigarette and an old crumpled packet of Sky Jell matches. She blew the smoke up at the ceiling and gave out a series of short staccato coughs, inducing a tear to well up and moisten her eye. 'Jesus fuck,' she groaned, stubbing the cigarette out. A few minutes later she lit another with less traumatic consequences.

Paul came to as Dewey was being carried out by two ambulance men. Several tubes were coming out of Dewey's arm and a man was holding up what looked like a quart of blood. Paul's vision blurred. 'Oh Jesus, oh my God,' he said, dragging himself up.

'So what's so embarrassing, Paige?' Clara whispered.

Paige went red and looked down at the desk. 'Oh Gad, I don't know, maybe it's not so weird, I don't know,' she said quietly, before Art Spindle's voice resonated down the intercom.

'Clara, have you sent Mrs Brandenberg's flowers and can you get all the available Brane transparencies for me? Ask Paige to get me Laurent in Paris.'

Beth rushed to the bathroom, slamming the door behind her. She buried her head in her hands. 'Fucking Jesus,' she sobbed. 'Where the fuck is she? Get a grip, get a fucking grip.' She looked in the mirror and wiped the tears away.

'Fucking bitch! I'm stronger than this, man. I'm stronger than that fucking dwarf bitch.'

'You think this video shit you're doing is art, Elaine?' Joany asked as she lay back in the bed.

'I don't know, Joany, I guess it's the way you look at it, you know.'

'The way you look at it?'

Elaine inhaled her cigarette deeply and then used it as a pointer. 'Yeah, if you were looking at it like a family video, then that's what it is, right, but if I said to you that the video was a work of art or like, if you saw it in a gallery, right, you would look at it in a completely different way, I mean you kinda look at the like, camera work, story, meaning and all that stuff.' Elaine ended her sentence by stubbing out her cigarette in the Cinzano ashtray next to her.

'So you're saying the video is art?' Joany asked in such a way as if Elaine had clearly contradicted herself.

'I'm not consciously making a work of art.'

'Oh Jesus, Elaine, either you are or you're not.'

'No, I'm ...' Elaine began before Joany interrupted her. 'How can you say that it isn't a work of art when you're showing it in an art gallery?'

'I'm not defining it as a work of art, Joany – the gallery is.'

'Yeah, but you made this thing knowing that it is going to be exhibited in a gallery.'

'Yeah, but there's so much shit shown in galleries that perhaps it doesn't mean anything any more, you know, like the pope made whoever saints.'

'So?' Clara looked inquiringly.

'So what?' Paige replied.

'You know, you were about to say, about Jo?' Clara said impatiently.

Paige sighed. 'Oh God, here goes. Like, he's into like, anal sex,' she whispered.

'Up the ass!' Clara exclaimed. 'I just don't get that anal thing – you know what I mean? It's like totally, totally weird.' Clara gave out a muffled giggle just as a visitor was leaving. The lady, who was wearing what appeared to be an airline scarf and hat, looked around and glared at the two girls. Paige, bent double, tried to restrain herself from laughing but a sharp, brake-like noise managed to escape. The lady looked around again and started walking towards them.

'Excuse me, but may I ask what you find so amusing?' An upper-class English accent whipped across the room.

'Oh, we weren't ...' Hysteria now had control and the two girls broke into spasmic giggles. Paige held her side, half in pain and half in laughter.

Joany had started shouting over Elaine's explanation. 'That's not what I'm saying, Elaine.'

'How can a black box and a screen be an art piece just because I put it in a gallery?'

'That's the nature of it. You go to an art gallery to see art. Basta. You just said it yourself.'

'Let's say as the artist I didn't intend it to be a work of art, okay. Let's say I was just making a document of myself, right, surely I have some say over what I'm doing?' Elaine's voice became irritated as she tired of the conversation.

'So what are you fucking doing?' Joany shouted.

Elaine lit another cigarette. 'It's like a project, I guess,' she said, coughing on 'project'.

'You mean like a school thing?'

Elaine sighed pointedly. 'Yeah, why not.'

'I think you're full of shit.'

'Do you have to be so aggressive? We're only discussing it.'

'You're a fucking narcissist, Elaine. It's all about you at the end of the day.'

Elaine looked at her and frowned. 'Sure it's about me. It's a fucking self-portrait.' She got out of bed and started picking up various items of clothing which were scattered around the bedroom floor. 'It's about me, it's about my relationship to people, to the art world and it's about the art world and how we can never quite attain ...'

'Yawn yawn.'

Elaine rolled her top over her body and threaded her arms through the sleeves and then dragged the T-shirt down over her torso. As her face appeared through the blue-and-white striped collar she said, 'Anyway, perhaps art doesn't even exist any more.'

Joany coughed into her mug of coffee. 'What!'

'Well, perhaps art's become like a parrot, it imitates and then repeats itself so much that it's become like any other mass product.'

'This is too much, man. Are you being serious?'

'Well, I like the idea. After all, it's as easy to say that art doesn't exist as it is to say that it does. I mean, if Duchamp could say, by identifying a urinal as an art piece, that anything could be art, by the same token, one could say that nothing is.'

'You're crazy.'

'Maybe, but I like it. Yeah, you see that Frida Kahlo in the kitchen?'

Joany sighed. 'Whatever, Elaine.'

'It's just an object. It's just an object to decorate the wall, hide the trash, reflect the light ...'

Elaine leaned against the bedroom door. 'So you're not coming tonight?' she asked Joany who was still lying in bed.

'I'll think about it,' Joany replied with a yawn and then in one movement she threw the comforter off herself and stepped out of bed. Elaine made a square out of her thumbs and index fingers and used it as a viewfinder to follow Joany's weighty form lumbering across the room. Her whole body seemed to quiver and vibrate with each heavy step she took.

'Sure, he had a good run for his money,' Brigid remarked, sipping her tea. Freign nodded his head in agreement. 'What are you going to do now?' Brigid asked.

Freign coughed gently and looked out of the kitchen window. 'I've worked here for thirty years,' he said quietly. 'I haven't thought about it.' He scratched his head thoughtfully. 'I could go back to Boston. I have ...' He paused. '... I have relatives there.'

'I thought you were a Brit?' Brigid queried.

Flag Boogie-Woogie, one of the last two paintings by Mondrian, was hanging in his office. *Victory* had sold in '98 to the Gemeente Museum in the Hague for forty million dollars. Spindle could hardly believe it. This was the greatest masterpiece ever to have graced his gallery, or at any rate the most expensive. And today he was to sell it. 'Forty million dollars,' he said under his breath. And to think that a year ago he was going to sell it for seven million, double that alone would be his profit. 'Fourteen million dollars,' he said to himself as he clenched his hands into fists and threw them into the air as if he'd scored a touch down. As he mulled over the profit margin a small wave of guilt swept over him, but it was shortlived. After all Mr Rhinegold would not have to worry himself about the financial consequences of his wife's coma and he would also have plenty of money to spare. Just as he was justifying his moral dilemma, Clara's voice came through the intercom.

'I have been assured a stipend for my services to the family,' Freign was saying. 'It will be sufficient to allow me a certain ...' he hesitated and looked out of the window, 'a certain freedom.'

'To do what?' Brigid asked.

'I am very much taken by the art of painting,' he replied. As Freign talked he realised that he was being unusually candid about himself. At first he thought it was a result of the emotion of the moment but then it occurred to him that he was experiencing a feeling of release, as if he had been unshackled somehow. 'Yes,' he continued. 'I am very much looking forward to a life of painting.' Freign felt momentarily ecstatic. Brigid was not aware of Freign's sudden elation.

'I went to that museum down the road, you know, the Frit.'

'The Frick Collection, ah yes, a very great collection. I often go when I am on leave.'

'You sound as if you were in the army,' Brigid laughed.

'The terminology may be incorrect but to run a household is like a military operation and as you might expect, it requires discipline and order ...'

Elaine took the subway home. Several messages were on her machine. Most were from the Freemantle Gallery but one was from Detective Lopez of the NYPD. A strange sensation swept over her, something had happened. She rang Lopez. 'Yes, I do know him. Is he okay? What? Multiple lacerations, Jesus. Oh my God. Which hospital? Sure, yeah, I'll be there as soon as I can.'

'Oh my God, Elaine,' Beth was saying on the phone, 'I just don't like, believe it. Oh my God, my God. Drop by before going up there. Yeah. Yeah. Jesus shit. See you later. 'Bye.' Beth slammed the phone down and shouted, 'Jo, hey Jo, Dewey Bozo's in intensive care.'

'What?' Jo questioned.

'Yeah, isn't that weird?' Beth shouted across to her secretary. 'Like, where are the lights, Cindy? Oh and Cindy, the video-machine and the projector, where the hell are they?'

'Intensive care,' Jo said to himself. He was suddenly aware that his feelings of concern for Dewey were mixed with those on whether or not Dewey had finished his piece on him for *Translations*.

'I think we'll move the cupboard a little to the left, yeah, a touch more, great.'

'Forty-five million bucks is a lot of money, Art,' Tucker Grasple said.

'Well, it is probably one of the last great masterpieces of that period in private hands. You know, if you get this, Tucker ...' Art paused, 'you will have ...' another pause, 'one of the great seminal paintings of the twentieth century.' A long silence ensued. Art could hear Tucker breathing down the telephone. 'When can I see it?'

'It's here waiting for you,' Art said.

'Just hold it a minute, willya.' Art could hear Grasple asking his secretary what he had on that day. 'Okay, Art, I'll fly in this afternoon. I'll be in town about four o'clock this afternoon, so how's five for you?'

'Great, Tucker, five is fine by me.'

Dolores dabbed the corners of her eyes with a handkerchief. As Dr Grout signed the death certificate he asked, 'Has ze family been informed?' Freign confirmed that Mr Rhinegold's sister, Frau Ebelstein, who lived in Munich, had not as yet been informed but that Mr Rhinegold's daughter by his first marriage, Mrs Schwartz, had been. The doctor nodded and then asked who was to be responsible for making the arrangements. A silence followed interrupted by Freign saying that he would inform Mr Rhinegold's lawyer. The doctor continued nodding his head. 'Who vill inform de undertaker?' Freign replied that he would but expressed reservation about choosing the appropriate coffin, suggesting that Mrs Schwartz should perhaps make the choice. 'Yah, yah but ze undertaker vill have to embalm him before Frau Ebelstein arrives from München, vat about ze daughter, Frau Rosemary?'

'Mrs Schwartz,' Freign intervened. 'Unfortunately she is in Santa Fe. I cabled her and she is getting the next plane at ...'

'Yah, yah, I see. Goud, goud,' the doctor interrupted. 'I should be on my vay, yah, there is an undertaker on Madison and Seventy-ninz, now I fink of it, also on Third and Sixty-five.'

'The undertaker on Madison is perhaps more appropriate,' Freign replied.

'Yah, but I hear that ze Third Avenue eese verry goud and most rrreasonable.'

'I will try the Third Avenue parlour,' Freign decided. The doctor looked down at Rhinegold and sighing mournfully murmured, 'I haf looked after Alfred for over vorty ears. He vaz a grreat man.' With that he patted Rhinegold on the cheek and after an awkward silence broken only by Dolores' sniffles he repeated, 'Yah, a grreat man.'

Dr Grout picked up his hat and old leather case. 'Keep me informed of ze arrangements, Freign.'

'I will indeed, sir.'

'Adios, señor doctor,' Dolores choked, as the doctor made his way out of the room.

'I shall see you to the door, doctor,' Freign said.

Jo stood back from the installation with an air of satisfaction. Pete the electrician was fitting the last of the lights, directing them on to each piece so they glowed imperiously like ancient royal tombs. Beth stood next to him, her lips curled into a faint smile. 'Wait till like, Roberta Smith sees this show. She is going to like, flip.'

A few drops of rain slid down the window and crept out on to the sill. They gathered and eventually trickled their way down the grey asphalt into a gurgling Paris gutter. A ray of sunshine momentarily lit up the room and then vanished, leaving Ivor and Jean in the grips of mid-afternoon gloom. Schneider looked forlorn and his steady gaze hovered over the ashtray in front of him. Jean sat impassively reading French *Vogue* in a new grey-green Christian Dior two-piece suit. Schneider remembered the sense of foreboding he had had that morning on arriving at rue des Beaux Arts. He tried to imagine finding the gallery and putting up his show, before realising these thoughts were just too perverse. There would be other shows, he said to himself. What would New York think? It suddenly dawned on him that he would be the laughing stock of the art world. He would ride the waves. The rain was falling steadily now. Jean placed *Vogue* on the glass table in front of her and smiled at him. It suddenly occurred

to him that she was kind of attractive. He liked all the power-dressing and
red lip stick, maybe something weird like, if she kinda got hold of his dick
without warning; like kinda raped him violently.

This is like, the most exciting thing that has ever happened and the worst at
the same time! I mean look, I have my own gallery, right, but I have to make
it like, work. I have like, artists to look after, you know? They're going to
be my babies. They need to earn a living and I'm the one who is going to be
like, responsible, right. Shit. I think Jo is pleased. The show looks real strong.
Maclestone is sure to buy something, you never know, right? Elaine won't
show me her video. She says it's going to be like, a self-portrait kinda thing.
This is so fantastic. Weird about Bozo.

Jo moved the viewing device, occasionally bending down and fitting his
head into the metal contraption. Once he had placed all three devices in
their designated places, he and Pete moved the screens between them. Now
you could only see the installation between three thin gaps the size of a
human head. Jo placed instructions on the screens next to the devices.

Freign opened the door to the attic. Several paintings leaned against the
wall. Brigid deliberated over each one, nodding her head in approval. It
reminded her of home. 'They are so quiet,' she said. 'So peaceful, I love
these paintings.' They were her cup of tea. 'Lovely the way they're painted.'
    'Thank you, thank you,' Freign replied. He was quite taken aback by
Brigid's effusiveness. Clearing his throat he said quietly, 'You are the first
to see my paintings, apart from Mrs Rhinegold of course, who was always
so supportive.'
    'You should show them,' she suggested. He mumbled that he couldn't
possibly. 'Why not ? They're only brilliant! What's wrong with you? There
is so much crap out there. I mean, have you seen it all? Have you seen all
that shite in Soho? They're all mad,' she said excitedly.
    'I don't know, I've never thought about it,' he said. 'They're a bit
old-fashioned, wouldn't you say?'

'It doesn't matter a shite, I'm telling ya. If it's something that's now, it's modern. Go for it!'

Her down-to-earth logic inspired him. 'I wouldn't know where to start, how to go about it, where to go.'

'Well, maybe Bob will be able to help? You know he collects Picasso and all sorts,' Brigid suggested.

'Who's Bob?' he asked. Bob was her boyfriend. He collected art. He's great. He'd really like him. So knowledgeable and all. She'd get him around, she said. No, he couldn't do it. It would be embarrassing, a modern art collector, out of the question he said.

'No, no, no he'd love them, sure I know he would,' she said. 'He's very open-minded.'

Freign hesitated, he felt nervous, embarrassed by the adulation but proud as well. His confidence escalated by the second.

Elaine and Beth were standing in the doorway of the smaller gallery. 'I think the two monitors would like, look great on this wall, Beth,' Elaine was saying.

'Maybe like, one on each wall,' Beth replied.

'No, they gotta be on top of each other.'

'Umm, okay,' Beth said, unconvinced. 'I think this wall is better so that like, when you come in you're kinda like, confronted with it, you know?'

'Yeah, maybe. We'll have to black out the window in any case,' Elaine said, pointing to the window.

'Well okay, what like, with paper or ...?' Beth poked her head out of the door. 'Hey! Peter! Peter!' she shouted.

'Coming,' a voice boomed down the corridor.

'Yeah, Peter, can you black out this window like, with something?' she went on shouting.

'Maybe that black felt stuff? You know?' Elaine suggested as Peter walked into the room.

'Sure, I can get that stuff. We could put it around the windows and stick it with black tape,' Peter suggested, with boyish enthusiasm.

'Make it so,' Beth pointed, imitating Picard of the *Enterprise*.

Elaine smiled. 'I want it totally dark in here, right, Pete?'

'Totally dark?' Peter grinned back.

'Totally,' Elaine whispered seductively.

'Get to it, Peter,' Beth intervened with a cold stare and watched him leave the room. Visibly flustered, she turned to Elaine. 'What was that about?'

Elaine lit a cigarette and inhaled deeply. 'What was what about?' she asked coolly.

'You know damn well, Elaine.'

'What the fuck are you talking about, Beth?'

'Talking to Peter like that.'

'Like what?'

'You know, like that.'

'No, I don't.'

'Oh, fuck you, Elaine.'

'Hey, Beth.'

'You were flirting with him.'

'No I wasn't.'

'Yes you fucking like, were.'

'I just don't like, believe this. Anyway, what if I was?'

'He works for me.'

'So?'

'I just don't like, believe this, Elaine.'

'What's gotten into you, Beth?'

'Okay, okay. Look, like ten days ago you seduced me. You made love to me. I'd like, never done that before, you know, like with a ah, a like, female, right?'

'Yeah?'

'Well, I have feelings, you know.'

'Look, Beth, I'm sorry if I kinda hurt you, we just got into an intimate situation, that's all, and anyhow I know Pete from way back, man.'

'That's all? That is all? I just don't like, believe this.'

'What is your problem, Beth?' Elaine yelled. Beth burst out crying.

Jo catches the end of this as he walks into the room. 'Oh Beth, can I ...' He stops short his question as Beth rushes past him. 'What's wrong with her?'

'I think it's the pressure of the first day,' Elaine replied.

'I guess it's kinda weird for her,' Jo agreed.

'What I ah, I don't believe is that she had already made ah, a list before she announced she wanted a di-divorce,' Maclestone was saying.

'Well, Bob, in my experience women are pretty methodical when they make a decision of this kind,' Hal Volta said.

Maclestone pursed his lips and sighed wearily. 'Well, you b-better hit me with it.'

Volta put on his reading glasses. 'She wants the Brancusi.'

'She wants the Brancusi!' Bob exclaimed. 'I just don't be-believe it. I ah, ah, mean she hates it. Why the hell would she ah, want the fucking Brancusi?'

Volta sat across from Maclestone looking down at some papers. 'Well, it's worth a million or so, that's probably why, and the Warhol of Joseph Beuys, the Hockney in the hallway and Groover photographs in the first-floor bathroom.'

Maclestone got up and paced the room. 'Ar-Art Spindle's behind this. I know it.'

Volta went on reading. 'The Alex Katz cut-outs on the stairs, Mapplethorpe photographs on the landing, Matthew Barney in the living-room, the two Schneiders, the Koons, Currin, Landers and the Bickerton in the library. She also wants the Dogon piece as well as the Picasso sculpture together with all the art books. Moving on to the dining-room, I thought that room was on the first floor?'

'It was but she moved it up to the second.'

'But the kitchen's on the first.'

'It's crazy. She built one of those dumb-waiter things.'

'Sounds nuts. Did you approve?'

'No, I didn't. I just don't believe she wants the K-Koons.'

'So you had a row about it?'

'What?'

'The dining-room.'

'We sure did, in fact one hell of a row, and months of di-disruption.'

Hal Volta had now picked up his pen and was writing quickly on a note pad. 'You could say that she disrupted your work schedule among other things.'

Two men in white mackintoshes walked into the room.

'*Bon après-midi, Madame, Monsieur,*' the elder of the two greeted with a bow. He had a thick, black, Iraqi-style moustache and grey-black, unkempt hair.

'Parley pas Françay,' Jean attempted with an elaborate sigh.

'Madame, I speck a little Inglish, I am, how do you say, detecteev. My nam is Dunont and thees is Inspector Xavier.' He indicated his younger and shorter companion who also sported a black moustache but whose head, apart from a little hair above the ears, was bald and shining as though he had waxed it. Everybody shook hands. The detectives took off their coats. Jean ordered room service. They all sat down.

'As Ma always said, "Don't trust older men". But sure when you're in the nursing profession you learn not to make judgments because everyone is so different. We're all in the same boat, do you know what I mean? All this business where you're from and where you're not from. When you're on that bed dying aren't we all the same? No amount of money is going to change that, is it? I mean, take poor old Mr Rhinegold – he had all the cash in the world, but he was stuck in a wheelchair for forty years. Anyway, Bob is thirty years older than meself but he's a great man, very kind and concerned. He doesn't care where the hell I come from. I think that's why I'm so mad for him. Do ya see what I'm saying, Robert?'

'Si, si, all man the sami,' Dolores said from the kitchen sink. Freign sat morosely at the end of the kitchen table. It was not his opinion. The down to earth sentiment was all logic and reason but he felt Brigid's optimism and eagerness to be positive about everything undermined the validity of her opinions about his work. Suddenly Brigid's opinions on his work seemed irrelevant.

Although Beth knew she was about to be glorified, esteemed as the new young, forceful art dealer, she felt emasculated. Elaine had undermined her ambition, her desire to perform, to be. Tears were running rivers of mascara down the sides of her nose.

'Beth, Beth,' Elaine shouted through the bathroom door. 'Are you okay, Beth?'

'Just go away,' Beth's muffled voice came through the door.

'Beth, just let me in.' Beth needed no persuasion and turned the handle. Elaine slithered in.

'Look, Beth,' she whispered, stroking her hair, 'it's kinda like, pretty simple. I like sex with girls, right, you know that. I don't dig boys, right, that's the first thing, okay? The second is like, I don't want relationships, okay? Like, you know, I really had a good time with you but that's as far as it goes, okay?'

'Is that it, Elaine, just like ...' Beth's muffled, hesitant voice questioned, 'just like that?'

'Listen, Beth, we'll like, talk later. I just haven't the time right now,' Elaine said impatiently.

''Laine, I love you, man.'

'I know, Beth,' Elaine whispered softly, putting her arms around her, 'and I really like you but I don't wanna have like, flowers sent to me and stuff, that's just not my scene okay? Maybe like, we could like, you know, get it together occasionally, okay?'

Beth sniffled and then blew her nose on some toilet paper.

'Now, let's get this make-up back on.'

'Let's move on to East Hampton. She wants the house, Bob.' Volta moved uncomfortably in his chair.

Cupboard is now. A wave of doubt engulfed him. Maybe the *Bed* looks a bit too much like Rachel Whiteread's *Bed*. Elaine walked past the gaps. 'Later,' she smiled. 'Yeah, later,' he replied.

'Let's move on to East Hampton. She wants the house, Bob.' Volta moved uncomfortably in his chair.

Maclestone's eyes bulged out, his chest expanded. 'She wants the fucking house!' he shouted. 'J-Jesus Christ!'

'The problem is that the judge is going to want to let her have one or the other home, right. I don't think we're going to get round that one, Bob.'

Bob had his head in his hands. 'She can have the New York apartment but I want East Hampton.'

'I thought you preferred the New York apartment and ...'

'Exactly,' Maclestone interrupted.

It occurred to Schneider, as he considered the two detectives, that Inspector Dunont shared certain comical mannerisms with Inspector Clouseau of *The Pink Panther*.

'Gagosian,' Jean affirmed.

'Gargisian,' the Inspector repeated.

'Gag-os-ian.'

'Gug-oos-yum.'

'G.A.G.O.S.I.A.N.' Jean spelt out irritably.

'Gagosian,' the Inspector repeated quietly and wrote the name down in his note-book.

'Right, anyway, so then he said to Ivor to meet at the gallery.'

'And one final thing ...' Volta paused.

'What's that, Hal?' Maclestone stifled a yawn and buttoned up his Armani jacket.

Volta closed the folder in front of him. 'She wants the dog.'

'She wants Matisse,' Bob whispered. 'Oh Jesus, not Matisse. She knows Matisse is ah, is my dog. I bought fucking Matisse.' He raised his voice alarmingly. 'How the hell could I've married that bitch?'

My gallery is opening today, this is too fucking crazy. No way am I in love with Elaine, just like no way. I have a major outfit, there's no time for this. I look like shit. My eyes are like, completely fucked. Shit, look at that mascara. What a bitch. How could she flirt like that? I suppose it's not his fault but you can't like, employ somebody who's going to like, flirt with the artist, you know what I mean? I'll fire him tomorrow. I've gotta get ready for the Maclestone lunch. I gotta look real good.

Inspector Xavier was busy writing down notes while Dunont paced the room firing questions. 'Monsieur Schneider, you say François Delraye meet you at harf past eleven?' he inquired, smoothing his moustache and chin with his hand. 'Ess thees correct?'

'Yeah,' Ivor said. 'Eleven-thirty and then we were going to have lunch.'

Dunont had a manic pitch in his voice lending a sense of urgency to the proceedings. Xavier would look up from time to time with a stern, uncompromising look as if he did not believe a word Schneider was saying. Most of the questions seemed irrelevant anyway, but although Schneider was the victim of the crime, he couldn't help feeling as if he were the one being accused of it.

Oddly wizened and in black, the undertaker bowed solemnly and with a curiously pitched, almost castrato voice, introduced himself. His rotund young assistant's watery and doleful eyes gazed upon the floor.

'My assistant, Mr Salamander.' Mr Salamander's eyes acknowledged Freign with a glance accompanied by a mumbled greeting before retreating back to the floor.

'This way please, gentlemen,' Freign signalled. All three men glided across the marble hall towards Rhinegold's bedroom. Dolores, who was sitting at the end of the bed, got up as Freign and the two men walked into the room. A few seconds elapsed before the undertaker emitted a church-yard cough. 'Has the deceased a suit we could dress him in?' he squealed.

'Si, si, Señor Rhini has mani suiti, I gette I gette.' Dolores scurried into the dressing-room leaving Freign alone with the two men. 'May I get you anything, gentlemen?' he asked, but just as the undertaker was about to answer Dolores reappeared with a black suit draped over her arm together with a white shirt and a dark blue tie sporting a yachting insignia. As the undertaker took these from Dolores he asked in a noticeably more enthu-siastic tone whether he could also have some shoes and socks. 'Of course, sir,' Freign replied before Dolores could do so herself. 'If you don't mind, sir, I will polish the shoes.'

'That would be just fine,' the undertaker replied, turning towards Rhinegold and almost as if it were an afterthought, adding, 'Oh, and how would you like the deceased positioned?'

Both Freign and Dolores looked puzzled.

'We can have him lying down or sitting up. Most of our clients opt for the lounging position. It is generally thought to be the most casual, but if you prefer ...'

'Monsieur Schneider, the pantin' werse ... *comment vous disez ... eh assuré?*'

Schneider screwed up his face in incomprehension. 'Ass u ray,' Inspector Dunont repeated.

'I think he means insured,' Jean intervened. Schneider looked up at the ceiling, folding his bottom lip over his top one. 'I am not sure whether my insurance covers this,' he replied finally.

'You are not sur, Monsieur?' Inspector Xavier piped up.

'No, I'm not,' Schneider replied. A few seconds of silence followed before Dunont said, 'Monsieur Schneider, we like you to stay in France for a vew day.'

'Is that necessary, Inspector? I have a lot of work back in the States.'

'We will contact le FBI,' Dunont continued, getting up from his chair, 'and Monsieur, I think I have your passport for le moment.'

'My passport!' Schneider exclaimed, suddenly becoming indignant. 'But why?'

'His passport for Christ's sake! What the hell do you need that for?' Jean asked.

'Madame, we have to look en tous sens,' Xavier said. 'We look at all possibilities, yes?' He smiled.

'Are you suggesting that Ivor may have set this whole thing up?' Jean raised her voice in disbelief. Inspector Dunont looked uneasily at Jean Maclestone.

'Madame, please.'

'I'm gonna call the embassy. This is an, an outrage. A complete outrage.'

'Jean, calm down. Just don't make it worse, okay?' Schneider said, as he removed his passport from his jacket. He handed it over to Inspector Xavier's waiting hand. 'Et Madame?' the Inspector asked with hand outstretched. Jean's make-up changed colour and consistency like a rare lizard. 'I, I have never been, been so insulted in all my life, no I will not, do ya hear,' she gasped and then breathing in for air she yelled, 'I will not give you my passport.'

'Madame, is the French law that.'

'Inspector, I am a citizen of the United States of America, do you know what that means?' she shouted.

'It means, Madame,' Dunont said respectfully, 'that you are on French soil under the loi of the Fifth Republic. I am serry, Madame, you mus geeve me votre passport.'

'Jean, just give it to them for Christ's sake.'

'No, I will not.'

Beth's smile opened like an umbrella. 'You made it.'

Maclestone murmured an apology as he manoeuvred himself into the chair.

'What a tie, Bob,' Beth said, adjusting her glasses and looking intently at his butterfly-covered tie. 'Isn't that like, a swallow-tail?' she asked, pointing at a yellow-and-black striped butterfly curled around the knot like some gaudy Christmas packaging. Bob attempted to look down but the butterfly was too high up. 'I ah, I guess so,' he replied, as he quickly unfurled the rolls of his chin. 'I bought it in the ah, UK.' He stifled a yawn and continued, 'At ah great little shop, you know, in the ah, the Kings Road. La-Latchky told me about it. He gets all his ah, shirts and ties there.'

'Just like, great,' Beth said, still concentrating on the tie. Bob yawned again.

Freign and Dolores sat across from each other. A cerulean-blue formica table stretched between them on which sat two green tupperware bowls.

'Me canni beelee ee,' Dolores cried. 'Mista Freign, me canni beelee.' She clasped her hands together while looking up at the ceiling. Freign couldn't help noticing that a piece of salad had embedded itself between her two front teeth covering the top half of the right-hand tooth.

'What are you going to do now, Dolores?'

'Me go,' she started, before a tap on the door interrupted her.

'Mr Rhinegold is ready,' the young assistant announced. Dolores and Freign looked at each other and slowly drew themselves up. They were not quite sure what was expected of them, but, presuming an inspection of some sort was required, they followed the young assistant out of the room and into the library. Mr Rhinegold lounged on the settee with his head perched on a pillow, his tinted glasses looked out into the middle of the room. Somehow the lines on his face had disappeared, taking away the omnipresent malevolent expression and turning it into a smile. His grey complexion had transformed to a pinkish hue and his hair was brushed forwards and glistened with some kind of ointment. Mr Rhinegold in death had evolved into a carefree *bon viveur*. Dolores' reaction was instantaneous; a sort of hysterical wailing, originating from deep inside her, filled the room with an alarming resonance.

A Surrealist contraption like a dysfunctional computer printing out all sorts of false information but with some kinda disorderly purpose. Like chaos. Feed the computer with random information which affects the final outcome – the butterfly theory. Jo sipped his coffee. A girl two tables away smiled at him. He smiled back. Everybody was feeling his high. He was infallible.

'I think he is like, a great artist,' Beth was telling Bob. 'Like those colour gradations in his last show on that laminated metal, that was like, so far out, and the piece you have in your collection? Like, the best.' Beth's eyes bulged out and she brought down her hand in a karate chop to affirm the point. 'Did you see the review in the *Times*? That was so like, you know, just so great, and,' Beth raised her voice in astonishment, 'your piece was illustrated!' She hunched up her shoulders and splayed the palms of her hands out in front of her. 'I remember,' she added excitedly.

'Yeah,' he replied, wearily scratching his designer stubble.

'I'm gonna put him in a group show next season, Bob.'

'Oh yeah?'

'Yeah, it's a show on post-classical imagery and modernism. I'm gonna call it *Deviant Mythology* – isn't that great? What do you think of the title, Bob? You don't think it's like, too pretentious?'

'No, ah Beth, I think it's kinda good. I mean it's to the p-point. *Deviant Mythology*,' he repeated. 'Yeah, great.' He yawned again.

'I'm pleased you think so,' Beth replied, smiling. 'Dewey Bozo thought of it.' Then, without drawing breath and as if she had remembered something of tremendous importance, she leaned over the table. 'Oh my Gad, did you hear what happened to Dewey?'

Bob stuttered to attention. 'W-what?'

Elaine walked down a long white corridor past white doors with framed grey frosted glass windows, her leather jacket thrown over her shoulder. Each door was numbered in black with a dark grey capital letter next to it. A goofy intern looked curiously at her rings, studs, short hair and nipples pressing against her white T-shirt.

Paige emitted a guttural rasping noise through clenched teeth. She clutched her side and keeled over on to the floor, eyes shut tight.

Clara brought a hand to her open mouth. 'Paige, oh Gaad, Paige, are you okay? Shit.' She picked up the phone and spoke urgently. 'Art, something's wrong with Paige. I think you'd better call an ambulance.'

A black nurse sat behind the counter chewing gum and reading the *National Enquirer*. Elaine tapped the knuckle of her index finger on the counter top. The nurse looked up. 'Can I help you?'

'Yeah, a Mr Dewey Bozo?'

'He's in 10A, miss. Are you a relative?'

'Kinda.'

'You have to be a relative.'

'So, I'm a relative.'

'You will have to fill out a form.'

'How is he?'

'You'll have to ask the doctor.'

'Who's his doctor?'

'I'm not sure.'

'Can you find out?'

'I'm not the duty nurse.'

'Who's the duty nurse?'

'She's having her lunch right now.'

'When will she be back?'

'About two o'clock, I guess.'

'This is unreal,' Elaine said under her breath.

'Excuse me?' the nurse asked.

'I said this is unreal,' Elaine repeated with an air of resignation as she turned around, heading for the plastic chairs.

Paige' s head was nestled in Spindle's lap. 'Close the gallery, Clara, tell Jack to get me a cold wet flannel.'

Clara picked up the phone. 'The Spindle Gallery ... No sir, Mr Spindle is in a meeting right now, yeah, sure, I know ... He is very busy. I'm sure he has seen them, yes I will, I will, goodbye, Mr Toon. The Spindle Gallery. Oh hello, Mrs Maclestone, well he's kinda caught up at the moment. It's that urgent ... I'll see what I can do.' Clara held the receiver away from her ear. 'Art, it's you know who.'

'Jesus Christ, tell her ...' Art held his forehead in his free hand. 'Tell her I'm tied up ... I'll ring her right back.'

'Art will call you right back, Mrs Maclestone. I can't do that. I'm sorry I just ca ... Mrs Maclestone, Mrs Maclestone.'

'She hung up, Art. She said something about being detained.'

Spindle's eyes widened. 'Detained?'

Elaine wondered whether Brigid was on duty today. It had been a while since she had videoed her. Maybe she didn't even work at Sinai any longer.

'Let go of me! Let go of me now! I said now!' Jean screamed. The policemen held her arms as she tried to push them away from her. Eventually they picked her up and with legs battling in mid-air she was propelled towards a holding cell. 'I'll sue you, you ... My father liberated you from the Germans, you fucking bastards. Let go! If it weren't for us you'd be fucking Nazis!'

Elaine liked the white transparent synthetic material the nurses wore. Awesome. She was just imagining the material rubbing the inside of her thigh when the bitch nurse beckoned her over.

'You didn't fill out the form.'

Elaine retrieved the yellow paper. 'Thanks,' she said and walked back to her chair. She could feel the nurse's stare boring through her back.

Paige was lifted on to the stretcher. Art, Clara, Jack and Anne watched as she was delivered into the waiting elevator. The doors closed tight and she was gone. Art mopped his brow and, turning towards his office, bellowed, 'Let's get the show back on the road.'

'No, no, no, this is on me,' Beth insisted. Bob leaned back in his chair. 'Well, thank you, Beth, you know it's not often one is taken to lunch by a beautiful girl.'

The waiter slithered up and whisked away the little wicker basket containing Beth's Visa card. 'Well, thank you, Bob,' she replied flirtatiously.

'Mr Maclestone, you have a telephone call,' a voice broke in. Maclestone excused himself. The waiter brought back the card, Beth signed, he parted the slips and handed the relevant one to her.

Maclestone reappeared with an unfamiliar grin. 'Something has come up, Beth, I'm afraid I won't be able to come to the ga-gallery right now.'

Beth managed to hide her disappointment with a broad smile. 'Oh, that's too bad, ah you sure? I mean it won't like, take a minute.'

'I'm afraid it's important,' Maclestone replied seriously as he scratched his stubble.

'I understand, maybe later, Bob, you're coming for the opening?'

'Yeah, I'll be there, Beth.' He yawned lazily.

Jo crossed Ninth Avenue and started to walk up Twenty-second. He popped a mint into his mouth. Beth's gallery was between Tenth and Eleventh so he had plenty of time for the small white disc to dissolve. He had only met Robert Maclestone once before but thought the meeting was a total disaster. Jo's impression was that the great collector had been and was still utterly disinterested in him. A wave of paranoia engulfed him. As he walked up the stairs of the gallery he crunched up the remaining mint in his mouth. On the other hand Maclestone may have forgotten about that previous meeting.

'People are so feckin' strange,' Brigid was saying, 'I mean, imagine doing that, it's worse than that gobshite the General.'

'The General?'

'He was a vicious bastard, he drove feckin' nails through the hands and feet of people he didn't like very much. Didn't ya see the film? Feckin' great.'

'It's hard to believe he's still with us.'

'Yeah, he should have bled to death. I tell ya what though, I wouldn't want to be the surgeon. Can you imagine? The state of his hands must be like a bowl of spaghetti bolognese.' They both broke out into laughter.

Dolores sat in the gloom of the library. She brushed away the tears with a kitchen towel held tightly in both hands. After a few minutes she got up and crossed the room to where Mr Rhinegold lay. She looked at his ruddy face and attempted to untwist the curl which the undertakers had fashioned so neatly on his forehead, but each time the curl was straightened between Dolores' pudgy fingers it curled up again. Was it a particular kind of wax the undertakers had used, or had Alfred always had this stubborn twist on the right side of his temple? Bending down she placed her lips to his.

Although Nurse Magrath spoke quietly, pronouncing each word in a lilting Irish accent, she could not disguise the slight squelching noise her chewing gum made as she clenched her mouth around certain syllables. 'Dr Dix will be able to inform you of Mr Bozo's condition as soon as he has made his rounds, Miss ah, Miss?'

'Yoon,' Elaine aided the faltering Irish nurse. Nurse Magrath was a stunning brunette with pale blue eyes – she had great fuckable potential, Elaine thought.

'If you follow me, please, Miss Yoon.'

Dolores sprayed the glass cabinet with Windolene and proceeded to wipe it vigorously. Meanwhile Freign climbed the marble stairs in the hallway and made for the guest room which was soon to be occupied by Mrs Schwartz, Mr Rhinegold's daughter from his first marriage.

'The oesophagus was punctured and all the finger tendons cut.'

'Shit,' Elaine uttered as she looked down at Dewey. Several tubes were disappearing into various parts of his body. He would have liked the restraints, she thought to herself.

'It's awful what people do these days,' Nurse Magrath whispered.

'What's that ?' Elaine asked, getting perilously close to her.

'I said,' she whispered, getting even closer to Elaine's ear, 'it's awful what people do these days.' Her soft Irish accent snaked itself around Elaine.

'Yes,' Elaine replied, 'it's like, so weird.'

'We better get going,' the nurse said.

'Already?'

'Visits to Intensive Care patients are limited.'

'Oh shit.'

'You can come back later, Miss Yoon.'

'Can you give me two minutes with him, please?' Elaine looked at her as imploringly as she could, gazing into her open face.

As soon as Nurse Magrath had left, Elaine set up her video camera on the table so that Dewey's bed was in frame. She took off her clothes and manoeuvred a chair on the other side of the bed and in front of the camera.

'Art,' Clara said down the intercom, 'a guy called Robert Freign rang, he said that a Mr Rhinegold passed away last night. Did you hear me?'

Spindle brought his fist down on to the table. 'Shit,' he said. 'Shit! Shit, shit.' Spindle realised he had to sell the painting before any complications arising from Rhinegold's death affected the sale of the picture. He had to work quickly. Very quickly.

At five-fifteen in room 10 J, Mrs Rhinegold's life-support machine broke the three-month rhythm. Her breathing became coarse. Her eyeballs rolled under her eyelids. A nurse swung into the room with some urgency.

'Where the hell am I?' Mrs Rhinegold croaked delicately.

'Mount Sinai,' the nurse replied.

Mrs Alfreda Rhinegold's voice crackled with alarm. 'In Israel?'

'You'll be hearing from the embassy. You don't know who you're dealing with, ass-holes.'

Jean Maclestone stormed out of the police headquarters. Several cabs ignored her frantic hailing. A group of people who were waiting for a bus began laughing. Jean turned and stared at them angrily before one of them pointed to the taxi rank on the other side of the square.

Maclestone chuckled to himself as he dialled Jean's lawyer.

'Yeah, Mr Jon Grafton,' he asked with a broad smile on his face.

'I've just heard the ah, the news,' he said with a deliberate mocking intonation, 'Jean is stuck in Paris. Yeah, yeah, ah ha, well, I don't know how I could help, I'm sure that Mr Spindle is more than c-capable of dealing with that, ah ha, yeah, I see. Well, you may tell my wife that I would be more than ha-happy to help, but employing l-lawyers on such matters is quite a fi-financial proposition and one that I feel, given the demands she is making in the settlement, is slightly out of my re-reach.'

When Bob had put the receiver down he felt quite pleased with himself and highly amused at his wife's predicament; but, on the other hand, he was concerned for his Schneiders – they might depreciate in value if the story hit the headlines, after all an artist couldn't be so dumb.

'Shit ,' Jo said under his breath.

'Yeah, just a bummer,' Beth joined in, 'still, he could come later, he said he would. I think he's like, a man of his word.'

'Anyway, I think I might move things around a bit, Beth, I'm not that happy with the installation.'

'Okay, Jo. You haven't seen Elaine?'

'Nope.'

Nurse Magrath came back into the room five minutes later. Elaine sat on the chair naked with her feet up on the side of the bed. 'Holy mother of Jesus! What do you think you're doing, young lady? Get dressed right now before I call security.'

Elaine pretended to cry.

'Now, now, now, that's enough of that. Come on now, young lady, let's get you dressed.' The nurse's voice softened. 'Oh Jesus, ya pierced all over, may the Lord forgive you.'

Paige Quale's trolley rolled down the corridor towards and past Brigid Murphy and Nurse Klasic and Flo. They walked down the corridor towards the waiting room where Elaine was talking with young Dr Dix. Elaine's back was turned towards them as the three nurses walked past.

'The cartilage is sliced between the first, second and third joints of all the fingers, as well as the tendon on both wrists. Luckily, his oesophagus was punctured, which prevented him from suffocating – the attacker gagged his mouth with a towel.'

'Is he out of danger?'

'He's in shock, but he should pull through. I do warn you he will have to have several operations to sew those tendons together.'

'How many?'

'Maybe thirty. I gotta say, I've seen terrible things in my time but this is the worst.' Dr Dix wiped his brow and then put his hand back into his pocket. 'Just who would do something like that?' he half-questioned himself.

'Some freak,' Elaine replied.

'Yeah,' Dr Dix affirmed, 'some crazy son of a bitch.'

A rich red-and-gold square was left where the Mondrian had hung for forty years. This sharply contrasted with the rest of the wallpaper where the gold was now a dirty ochre and the red had faded to a yellowing pink.

'This picture definitely needs a surface clean,' Spindle remarked as he drew a wet finger across the surface of the Mondrian.

It was three-thirty when the hospital rang and informed Freign of Mrs Rhinegold's condition.

Jean and Ivor sat across from each other in the dining-room at the Hôtel Costes.

The surgeon was removing a tumour the size of a melon from Paige's stomach.

Beth was barking at the management of Bar D'O about how many guests she was expecting at the party after the private view.

A few toes stuck out of what looked like veined liver, a jaw bone, a half-made eye, a mouth with no lips. It looked like something between a foetus, a car accident, an alien, a Bosch demon, a boshed Bacon, a miniature devil.

'They could be anywhere by now,' pondered Ivor Schneider, as Jean delicately slid a forkful of ratatouille into her mouth. 'I mean what the hell are they going to do with them? They can't sell them. They can't show them. It's just so fucking weird.'

A minute's silence ensued before Jean slanted her head sideways and furrowed her brow. 'Perhaps,' she started quizzically, 'perhaps a dealer who's trying to make a point.'

'What do you mean, Jean?' Ivor asked.

'I mean, you've been adamant about dealing with your own affairs, perhaps a little too adamant, this might be a way of drawing you into their net or maybe,' and she laughed, 'just teaching you a lesson.'

Ivor motioned to the waiter. A whisky was needed to fend off an impending attack of paranoia. 'I see your point although I think it a little far-fetched,' he said, still flapping his hand in the air.

'Or,' Jean continued, 'a disenchanted rival, a jilted girlfriend, a ...'

'Okay,okay, I get the point,' he said impatiently. 'Un whisky, si vous play,' he asked a haughty-looking waiter who chose not to pay attention. Why was it, Schneider thought to himself, that waiters never noticed him?

Jo tested his contraption again. He bent over and placed his head in the device. *Bed* was to the far right with *Cupboard* near it, the *Frigidaire* to the far left and *Television* in the middle. All were at the limits of the space defined for the installation. If you looked at *Television* in the middle of the room, what he called the vanishing point, four items were within peripheral vision. He could just see the second device against the same wall as *Bed,* but the third was out of view. He liked the idea of having the human element in the fray. It was a good balance with the make-believe aspect of *Television.*

As Schneider sipped his whisky a deluge of enemies, ex-girlfriends and even jealous artists swirled about. Who would play such a trick? It was true he was a successful artist and one who maybe was an easy target. He was perhaps a little arrogant in his dealings with people. There had also been a string of broken hearts over the years. Mrs Allenberg, for example, was rich enough to set the whole thing up.

'I never trusted that Allenberg woman,' Jean said suddenly, reading his mind as he was mulling over the possibility. He had ditched her for her sixteen-year-old daughter, creating a scandal in the art world a few years back. Mrs Allenberg had even sent him death notes.

'Mary Allenberg.' Ivor rubbed his left eye. 'Yeah, I guess she had reason but you really think, I mean, she's determined but not that bright, you know what I mean? She couldn't have thought of it.'

The second device afforded him the view of *Frigidaire* and *Bookshelf* as well as the first device. He would like more space between *Cupboard* and *Frigidaire* but perhaps it would imbalance their relationship with *Sofa*. The third device excluded the second device. Where the hell was Elaine with her video? It was important that the video was good enough to hold the attention of the public on *Television* as an object, his vanishing point, but not good enough to distract them from the installation as a whole. He had only agreed to Beth's suggestion of using Elaine's video because, having met her, he was convinced she would make something fairly banal. In the meantime, however, he had substituted for Elaine's impending video Orson Welles' *The Third Man* which was now being projected from the ceiling across the gallery and on to *Television*.

This is just so great. The Richards installation is like, fabulous. Elaine's video is like, nowhere to be seen. She said that like, it shouldn't distract Jo from installing the piece. I see her point but Jo is kinda nervous and talking of nerves I'm like, right on the edge. I cannot believe I started this whole thing. I must have been nuts, you know, completely fucking nuts.

Elaine had downloaded the rushes from the hospital. She put her video on the monitor and began splicing the hospital scene and incorporating it with her art piece. This was going to be some weird motherfucker of a video, she thought to herself.

In fact, it was Paige's sister. Her twin wrapped inside of her since birth, curled, autonomous, cocooned, asleep, alive, helpless.

'This is a highly developed teratoma,' Professor Zilke muttered, as he peered at the object on the table. 'The heart is beating normally and here there seems to be a respiratory system,' he said, pointing to a small sac curled around the jaw bone. 'This is quite the most developed specimen I have ever encountered,' he repeated.

'Do we keep it alive, professor?' the surgeon asked.

'I cannot think of a precedent but I presume with such an advanced case it would technically be Miss Quale's parents' decision whether or not to terminate the teratoma.'

'Not the twin's?'

'Umm, I see your point,' Zilke agreed.

Spindle beamed. 'So what do you think?' he bellowed as he shut the door behind the advancing Jamie Lawrence.

'Well, well I never,' the restorer piped in a jaunty, upper-class English accent. 'What a jewel, a veritable jewel, and in,' he cleared his throat and peered at the canvas, 'excellent condition, would you not say? Just a few cracks over here,' he pointed to the lower left hand area of the canvas, 'but this is often the case with Mondrian. Needs a bit of a scrub, don't you think? On the whole quite excellent, yes, quite excellent.'

Freign, although in some way relieved that his position was, for the time being anyway, secure, could not help but feel disappointed. He had grown accustomed to the idea of a new chapter, a new beginning to his life, and Mrs Rhinegold's lazarine rise from the dead had scuppered his fantasies. Another unexpected feature in this turn of events was a sudden emotional shift concerning Rhinegold. Freign's indifference to his employer's death now changed to feelings of regret. Life was going to be somewhat tedious, he thought to himself, without the old man's bad temper and eccentric behaviour. Dolores, on the other hand, could hardly contain herself. 'Incredebli, incredibli, me donna beli ee ...' she ranted.

'It's all very well, Mrs Ballesteros, but she does not know about Mr Rhinegold and furthermore when she finds out Mrs Schwartz is here it will be a most uncomfortable experience for her. You know how she feels about Mrs Schwartz?'

As Elaine watched the final edit she became decidedly horny. The edit room was too public. Once in the cubicle, stained and condensed with the smell of urine and the faint odour of excrement, she took off her jeans and sat on the cold, white, plastic toilet seat and, leaning back on the rubiginous piping which snaked up to an old-fashioned cistern above her, she opened her legs wide. After a few seconds her hand quickened and, vibrating like a standard eight movie, shook her whole body. Elaine arched her back, the shoulder-blades drawing together, eyes clenched, front teeth dug deep into her lower lip. She pulled the chain. The water, churning, frothed against her skin as the gurgle of a thirsty cistern drowned a ruckled sigh.

Maclestone woke up from a heavy slumber. He had only drunk one glass of wine at lunch but as was always the case when he drank during the day it had knocked him out. And he felt decidedly groggy, a headache hammered away at him and there was an unpleasant acrid taste in his mouth.

Normally, at this time of the day, Freign would be giving Rhinegold his heart pills but now he was quite at a loss as to what to do. He had an impression of seeing himself from the outside in without the ability to do anything about anything, 'a goldfish bowl of inertia', he reflected rather cleverly. His day-dreaming was broken by the door-bell. Mrs Schwartz had arrived.

Dolores was more excited by the extraordinary coincidence than she was for its consequences. Only a few hours before she had grieved for the death of her master as well as having contemplated the possible financial benefits arising from it. Now she juggled with the metaphysical phenomenon of Mr Rhinegold's spirit passing on the breath of life to his comatosed wife. It wasn't until the door-bell rang that her highly charged theory faltered. Mrs Schwartz had arrived.

Spindle thanked Clara and glanced at her tight butt as it sprang out of the door.

'So, I go back into the room and there she was stark bollock naked. I couldn't believe my feckin' eyes,' Nurse Magrath was saying. Brigid and Nurse Klasic both laughed. 'So then what happened?' Brigid asked.

'I said I was going to call security and didn't she start crying? So I took pity on her and she got dressed but didn't I notice she'd been videoing the whole thing. I felt disgusted. I told her to get out, I did.'

'They're all mad over here in this country. I mean, imagine strippin' off in Intensive Care in Dublin? You'd be sent straight to John O'Gods asylum, you would,' Brigid said.

'Another strange thing was that she was covered in tattoos and there were rings all over the place ...' Brigid's expression hardened, her spine straightened. She looked down and fidgeted with the corner of her synthetic white uniform.

The faint smile forced by the undertakers and set by rigor mortis lingered unconvincingly but nevertheless steadily and consistently on his frozen lips. Mrs Schwartz observed her father from across the room. She had not seen him since the early seventies. They had corresponded on certain legal matters pertaining to an educational trust he had set up for her children but no visual contact had been made. She tried to conjure up memories of her youth – before her mother had left him and taken her to live in New Orleans. His peaceful countenance reminded her of the lighter moments during her childhood years.

She had been six years old when her parents had asked her to make a choice between them. She had not been able to exorcise the experience. Fifteen years of anti-depressants had not succeeded in shedding the past and even to this day she felt betrayed by her parents; by her father because he had never forgiven her for choosing her mother and by her mother for putting her in that position.

Jean and Ivor sat in the oak and velvet bar of the hotel. The cataclysmic events of the day had transformed themselves from disbelief into accepted fact. These facts now wallowed uncomfortably within Ivor's consciousness where they induced, together with the bottle of Châteauneuf du Pape and a second whisky, a state of self-pitying melancholia. Jean, who had recently rebelled against years of self-control, was also feeling the same melancholic effects, although she had only drunk half a bottle of Puligny-Montrachet and one glass of Malibu. She ordered a second. Ivor continued talking about himself. His art, he felt, was his spiritual centre, his *raison d'être*, he explained, without which he would be lost. Jean nodded while raising her cocktail to a pair of recently rouged lips. His friends didn't understand him, he felt that he was an enigma. He now leaned back on the plush red armchair with hands wrapped behind his neck to support his head. He stared at the ceiling. Maybe he was doing the wrong thing in life, maybe he should go to Kenya and forget the art world, forget art. He ordered a fourth whisky. Maybe he should get married and have babies. Jean was thinking about the time she, Bob and the family went on vacation to Hawaii and Bob had slipped on a mango; how they had laughed. That was the year her son Luke had discovered Game Boy. Through the haze of memories she heard Ivor say, 'The world's crazy anyway, we're destroying ourselves.' For an instant Jean felt he might stop talking about himself – but no such luck, Ivor continued to yarn about his plans to travel for a year before it was too late, go to Australia before the Chinese took over. Still gazing at the ceiling, he smiled to himself. Jean got up to go to the bathroom. As she left the room two models sauntered in. Ivor's upward gaze fell like car headlights on to the exiguous figures gliding towards him. He grinned at them hopefully but their expressions remained bland and haughty. They huddled in a corner with their backs to him. He felt old.

Mrs Schwartz rushed from room to room like a gun dog smelling out game. Cupboards were unlocked, drawers opened, pictures scrutinised, sculptures caressed. A few minutes after the initial shock at seeing her dead father lying angelically on the sofa, she'd started on her pre-meditated quest. Mrs Schwartz rifled through her father's desk. She read letters, notes and business correspondence. Rhinegold, after a turbulent career in manufacturing, had ended up with a chain of pharmacists on the East Coast. The business was sold in the early seventies when the oil crises had threatened to undermine the whole economy. He felt that he'd earned enough to see him and his wife through to the end of their lives. Rhinegold had given his daughter a lump sum in the sixties believing that it would be more than sufficient to last his lifetime. He had been left nothing by his parents and therefore saw no reason why she should get anything from him, besides which he assumed her mother, his first wife, would provide for her. She had after all received a very large settlement from him. Mrs Schwartz had firmly held on to her father's gift. Her mother had been married for the sixth time to a retired Frenchman who had been a director of a bottle plant in North Carolina. They lived frugally in Florida. The Schwartzes lived in a large adobe on the outskirts of Santa Fe. She owned a shop in town selling furs and artisan products such as beaded necklaces and miniature wooden statuettes carved by local Indians.

'Mr Freign,' Mrs Schwartz shouted from the library as he was entering the kitchen, 'the Mondrian, where is my father's Mondrian?' Freign appeared as she was scrutinising a Fung mask bought by Rhinegold from Perl who had originally bought it from Derain, and which was an artifact Freign had quite often let his wildest recollections loose upon.

'The painting is presently at the Spindle Gallery,' he replied.

'What the hell is it doing there?'

'I believe it was at the request of Mrs Rhinegold's lawyers,' he said blandly before being cut off.

'But they have no right to sell my father's painting. What the hell is going on?'

Tucker Grasple walked into the Spindle Gallery with a sense of purpose. Like many rich and dynamic men he was encompassed by a powerful aura. People looked up from whatever they were doing to stare at this aura as it leaned towards Clara Dupont.

'I'm here to see Mr Spindle. My name is Tucker Grasple, thank you.'

Within a few seconds Spindle was effusively greeting the great man. 'It's just so great to see you, Tucker, you're looking ten years younger. I donna how you do it.'

The two men walked into showroom one where the Mondrian now hung imperiously.

'Well, well, well, there it is,' Grasple said, going up to the picture and scrutinising each box of colour.

Spindle said, 'I'm just so excited to have this painting, you know? It's these little moments, as Cézanne said, that make it all worthwhile. I mean, have you seen a Mondrian like it outside of a museum?'

'Even inside a museum,' Grasple said, thinking out aloud. Art had wanted to say inside of a museum but felt that it would have sounded too much like a pitch, however, now Tucker had suggested it, he agreed wholeheartedly. 'You know,' he said before pausing briefly, 'you're absolutely right.'

'I am sure that Mrs Rhinegold will be able to enlighten you on the sale of her painting.' Freign made sure there was not a hint of gloating in his delivery.

'What are you talking about? Alfreda is in a coma.'

'I have been informed that Mrs Rhinegold has come out of her coma.'

Rosemary Schwartz's estrangement from her father stemmed from an incident in 1968. Before she had met her current husband, Rosemary had been a prominent member of the early hippie movement. Her community had pitched camp outside of Santa Barbara in what appeared to be a disused farm. A neighbour happened to have witnessed the group, which averaged about fifty hippies, dancing in what seemed to him to be a drug-induced state. He reported the incident to the local police who rang headquarters in San Francisco. The messages, having been handed from person to person, arrived at the captain's desk with the grossly exaggerated figures of at least a thousand anti-Vietnam protesters, all of whom were performing strange devil worship. When the police arrived, accompanied by the press, they found only a small group of stoned and naked hippies dancing Indian fashion around a small fire. Unfortunately a photograph was taken of Rosemary, naked, her long blonde hair glued to her scalp with a flowery bandanna, handcuffed to a moustachioed policeman in full riot gear. The startling photograph was splashed across every paper in the US, and while papers of high moral tenor had the decency to disguise her nudity, those of New York – which indeed were also those read by Alfred Rhinegold – fostered no such restraint. The photograph soon became an icon of its time: it was even on the front cover of *Time* together with a short interview in which Rosemary Rhinegold eagerly condoned the legalisation of drugs and the abolition of private property. Her opinions, together with the ubiquity of the image, so enraged Mr Rhinegold that he vowed never to talk to his daughter again.

'Can you do anything on that?' Grasple asked, falling into the chair.

'It's tight, Tucker. Real tight. I tell you what, though, we could give you three per cent off the price and stagger the payments over one year. Let's say you give me eight to begin with and we could work the rest out over monthly payments. How about that?' Spindle did up his jacket button. Tucker Grasple stroked his chin and looked out of the gallery window.

'Yeah, that could work out, yeah, but wait, how about if we came to an arrangement over let's say my De Kooning and maybe the Pollock you sold me a couple years back.'

'You wanna sell the Pollock, Tucker?' Spindle exclaimed, undoing his jacket button.

'It's a great painting but it kinda doesn't fit in with the rest of the collection.'

It was five-thirty-five and Bob Maclestone was contemplating getting ready for the Beth Freemantle opening. There had been quite a lot of talk about Jo Richards and he quite liked a self-portrait by Elaine Yoon, a transparency of which was lying on his desk. She was kinda sexy and the photo was upfront, strong and resolute; he liked that – he liked that kind of art. Perhaps Brigid would enjoy it.

As he was mulling this over the phone rang. Brigid would pick him up at the gallery in a couple of hours. Time for a shower and maybe a quick visit to Billy's Topless. For some reason Jean came to mind and he wondered what she was doing. He kind of missed not being able to talk to her; but on the other hand it was a relief not to have to.

Rosemary Rhinegold had been thought of as a great beauty among her peers. To sleep with her was a desire that most members of her group, including girls, tried to satisfy at one time or another but although she partook in every kind of drug, took her clothes off at the slightest opportunity and danced with provocative abandon, she was strangely prudish about sex. In fact, she had remained a virgin up until her wedding night; despite the wait, she found her defloration really quite unpleasant.

Tom Schwartz was a Hell's Angel biker whom Rosemary had met in a roadside café. After five minutes of monosyllabic conversation she was on the back of his Harley Davidson electro glide speeding towards Woodstock. It was July 1970. After two months on the road, Rosemary Rhinegold became Mrs Schwartz.

'I could take the De Kooning and give you the Mondrian for eighteen. The Pollock I'll give you two for, which makes ...' Art was using his fingers for the thousands and his thumb for the millions.

Tucker pointed towards the ceiling. 'I bought it for three, Art.'

'You did?' Spindle did up his jacket and then drew his hand up over his head.

In the following year Tom and Rosemary Schwartz appeared on the steps of her father's Seventy-fourth Street mansion. She was seven months pregnant and wore a psychedelic pattern dress which was so short that it barely covered her butt. Tom wore his leather jacket and oily flared blue jeans with a pair of well-worn cowboy boots. His handle-bar moustache was now joined by thick black sideburns and his stringy, knotted hair collapsed over his sloping shoulders. All in all, very few of Tom's facial features were visible. Freign had timed their audience with Mr Rhinegold as four minutes and thirty-three seconds.

Spindle crossed his legs and then uncrossed them. 'Fifteen million. The Kelly, De Kooning, Pollock and the Bacon.' Tucker narrowed his eyes and spoke from the back of his throat. 'I wanna keep the Bacon.'

Spindle rubbed his forehead and blew out his cheeks. 'You drive a hard deal, Tucker.'

'That's business, Art.'

Jo washed, bathed, shaved, put on his favourite cologne and his best suit and then spent the next few minutes twisting and turning in front of the mirror. Then it occurred to him that dressing up for his own opening was perhaps a little geeky, not at all cool, so he took the suit off and slipped a pair of jeans on instead together with a simple black T-shirt and an orange mountaineering puffa jacket. After all, he thought to himself, he must be seen not to care too much. The phone rang. Spindle said he had some good news. The painting was in his office and a major collector was very interested. They got talking about his impending opening. Art said he would be down later – of course. Incidentally one of the girls was having emergency surgery. Jo's heart missed a beat. 'Who?' 'Oh, Paige Quale, intestinal or some other shit,' Art laughed. Jo accompanied Art automatically just to please him, but deep inside he'd been hit hard. Did he know which hospital? He thought Beth should know, they were friends, Jo explained. When Spindle called off Jo punched the air and yelped but then bit his bottom lip and wondered what was wrong with Paige. Perhaps it had something to do with the anal sex. He decided against the puffa jacket.

Disheartened by the lack of parental understanding, the Schwartzes moved to a commune in Santa Fe where their first child was born. Meanwhile Tom worked part-time in a car dump where he developed an already substantial understanding of mechanics. After a couple of years he persuaded Rosemary to invest in a car rental business. She had not touched her nest egg since her father had given it to her at the age of twenty-one. Sex and money were Rosemary's only real hang-ups, the former being rarely performed and the latter being rarely spent, but seeing the potential in Tom's idea and since he had never asked her for anything in the past, she agreed to back his endeavour. Finally, after insisting on some unusually stringent clauses in her contract with the newly formed company, she deposited her investment of twenty five thousand dollars. Tom began salvaging car parts in the dump, building them into road-worthy wrecks and renting them cheaply to tourists. They now owned a chain of companies throughout New Mexico, Arkansas and Texas. Tom had lost all his facial hair and had become a large, robust, balding, middle-aged man, who wore shiny blue suits on all occasions. He was known as the 'blue man'.

Even though she had been briefed about the gravity of her situation, Paige came out of her anaesthesia feeling quite light-headed, almost to the point of euphoria. The nurse informed her that a doctor would shortly be visiting. Paige asked the nurse if she knew anything about the operation. She didn't. A few minutes later the euphoria wore off and developed into intense anxiety and deep depression.

When Jo finally found somebody in the know, he was told that all information regarding the patient was privy to family or legal guardians. Jo became indignant and for the first time admitted that he was 'kinda the boyfriend'.

'I'm sorry, sir. You will have to come to the hospital and talk to the registrar.'

Jo was in a quandary. His show opened in half an hour. He couldn't go to the hospital now. Paige would surely understand. Anyway, they weren't an item in the proper sense. Just fucked a few times.

'Shit,' Beth said. 'First Dewey, then Paige. So fuckin' weird.'

Jo walked hurriedly down Eighteenth Street. It couldn't be anything to do with having fucked her anally? They'd only done it a few times. He'd heard semen sometimes caused constipation. It was probably an appendix or a hernia. However, it was the last thing he needed on the opening night. Jo walked into the flower shop and chose a bunch of lilies. He wrote a little message on a greetings card which read: 'My thoughts are with you. Wish me luck for tonight.' After some hesitation he added, 'Love Jo', with a little x beside it. This he slipped into the miniature envelope and asked the florist to send them to Mount Sinai on 100th Street.

Paige held her father's hand and smiled. 'That's so weird, Pop.'

Elaine still hasn't arrived. Can you like, believe that? I give this like, student, a show and she doesn't even have the courtesy to fucking like, come on time. Jesus, I hope Maclestone shows up. He'll go crazy for it. Matthew Marks came in to congratulate me. Can you believe it? He's so great.

Bob had decided to go to Harmony instead of Billy's. Harmony was a joint where the girls wandered around half naked until a customer responded to their seductive stares. Some asked for fifteen bucks, others ten. Once the transaction was made the girl would mount the client, who would be sitting in a large plastic armchair, or a stool if he preferred, and writhe on him or her for the duration of one song. Occasionally clients put on prophylactics in case they ejaculated. Bob always liked the black girls or Chinese if there were any. Tonight he picked up a Chinese girl who turned out to be Japanese. She sat on his crotch, smiled and brushed her cheek against his bristling lips. Soon she was holding her breasts and inviting him to suck her nipples. Bob didn't go in for prophylactics – it was too messy.

'Thank God for that,' said Jo after Beth had relayed the circumstances of Paige's operation. 'I've never heard of a teraloma.'
'Teratoma,' Beth corrected him.
'Yeah.'
'Hirst could make a great piece out of it,' she laughed.
Jo looked serious and shook his head. 'No, it's too obvious for Hirst.'

Elaine had had her head shaven. She wore a black Agnes B suit with a white shirt, black tie and English leather shoes from Church's. A sort of lesbian Gilbert & George look.
'Where have you been?' demanded Beth.
'Working,' Elaine replied, looking over at Jo's piece. 'You've changed it, Jo, it looks great. What's the video?'
'I put it on in case you were held up at the hospital. It's one of my

favourite movies, you know, *The Third Man*,' Jo said, putting his hands in his pockets.

'I never heard of it.'

'It's an Orson Welles movie, you know, from the Graham Greene book?'

'Who's Graham Greene?'

'*Brighton Rock, Our Man in Havana, The Quiet American, The Comedians* ...'

'Right,' she broke in languidly and then looking at the video she added, 'Great lighting. Well, here goes,' she said, handing Jo her video. 'It's for Dewey, Jo. It's for his fucking life, man.'

'How long, nurse? I have a right to know,' Mrs Rhinegold croaked.

'The doctor will be here shortly,' the nurse whispered soothingly.

'This is very disturbing. Where is everybody? Why can't I move? I feel so weak. Oh dear, this is all very worrying. Why haven't I got a phone? Where is the doctor? This is very distressing. Why can't I move? Nurse, I want to talk to my husband. What is happening? Oh dear, oh dear, I can't move. Is the doctor coming? Where is the doctor? Oh dear me. Get me a phone. I feel so weak, so weak. Where is the doctor? Nurse, nurse, where is the doc ...' Mrs Rhinegold's voice weakened into a whisper, her eyelids fluttered against the burden of sleep, finally closing, and with a light breath she fell into a deep sleep.

Jean's coat of lipstick had smudged over her lips. As she pottered out of the bathroom a dark-skinned, shortish man with a bristling moustache, not altogether unlike her husband's in '81, sidled up to her. '*Madame, vous avez l'air d'être perdue*,' he said. Jean focused on the little man. He could be the manager, she thought to herself. 'Hi, I'm sorry, don't understand a word,' she slurred.

The little man suddenly entwined his arm under hers and led her proprietorially back to the bar. 'Well, thank you kindly,' Jean crowed flirtatiously. However, before she knew it he had seated her at another table, away from Ivor's, whom she could just make out lounging on the settee looking up at the ceiling. 'Drink perhaps?' the man asked, with a strong Arabic twang.

'Pernod,' she found herself saying, even though she'd never tried it before. The peculiarity of her situation seemed to necessitate something adventurous with a view to erasing the memory of the day's events. The little man clicked his fingers at the waiter who came scurrying over. He said something which she did not catch.

'You know, I have a friend over there who ...' she motioned with a kind of uncoordinated abandon.

'No problem, no problem,' the man replied, turning to the waiter. He fired an order, accompanied by various gesticulations aimed at Ivor who was still lounging oblivious to the unfolding scenario. Jean was finding it hard to concentrate, which she needed to do in order to understand what was happening to her. A bottle of Crystal champagne arrived. She looked at the precious bottle with surprise.

'Crystal is so tempting,' he said, smiling as he handed her a glass of champagne, 'and so why not?' he added quietly, looking into her eyes. 'My name is Abdullah.'

'Jean.' They clinked glasses. The models looked over and giggled. Jean thought he looked like a miniature Omar Sharif.

The Japanese girl had already taken thirty bucks. They had struck up a general conversation about Japan. The girl turned out to be an aspiring writer. The discussion turned to Japanese writing. Being a voyeur, Bob's favourite writer was Tanazaki. He described *The Key* where a man fantasises in his diary about his wife having an affair with a colleague at the university. He leaves the diary out so that she reads it and she in turn writes about the affair that he wants her to have in hers and he reads it. Mariko liked Mishima and Kawabata. Meanwhile she gyrated slowly on his semi-erection. 'You ver nice, I li you.'

Bob smiled up at her. 'I like you too.'

'Maybe we mi layta,' she said.

'Sure, Mariko.' Bob's heart raced, he couldn't believe his luck. 'Where do you w-wanna m-meet?'

'Where you wan, Bo,' she said, moving seductively. 'I give you goo tie, only five hundra dolla.'

Bob's face collapsed. 'Oh I see, I didn't realise ah ah ...'

Mariko bit his ear lobe. 'Too ma? Four hundra, I fuck you goo, real goo,' she whispered.

'I don't know, I ah, don't think, I mean it wasn't what I ah, was thinking.'

'Let cock thin for yoo, and I do res.' Mariko made a well-pitched sigh in his ear. 'I blow you, I fuck you goo.' Bob's urges were now getting the better of him. His desires were becoming difficult to control.

Ivor slept on the sofa in the bar. It was midnight. Abdullah was telling Jean his life story. His Lebanese background. His first business, his second business. He described the beauty of the Lebanon, the cedar forests, where you could both ski and look out on to the Mediterranean at the same time.

'If you don't get shot in between,' she slurred. Abdullah laughed.

'I'm getting divorced,' Jean started. 'I was married eighteen years, can you believe that? I can't. Two kids, two houses, two cars.'

'I married three time,' Abdullah joined. 'One Arab, one Jew, one English.' They laughed. Abdullah leaned over and filled their glasses.

Elaine put her video on. An image emerged of Elaine naked on the concrete screen of *Television* and on the lower monitor of Gallery 2.

'Is there an image?' Elaine shouted.

'Got it,' Pete shouted back.

'Now switch on the video camera.' A birds eye view of Gallery 1 appeared on the upper monitor. Jo looked at the video through his head contraption. 'It's great, Elaine,' he enthused.

Elaine sipped some water from the plastic glass. Jo noticed the elliptical shape the pressure of her grip made. Any fears that he'd had about her video now faded. It was as he thought: fairly banal kinda art school stuff but she was kinda sexy in a boyish sort of way, yeah, like an adolescent boy.

He asked her, 'So why did you choose video?' and she replied, 'Why did you choose installation?'

Elaine watched Beth's reaction as she peered across at *Television*. The first ten minutes' footage spliced her pursuit of Brigid with what looked like a murky porn movie: the images clearly outlined moving bodies but they were too dark and out of focus to reveal their identity. 'You know, 'Laine, it's ... it's real, you know? It's kinda, it's so like, in your face, you know? It's so interesting how you've done that.' Beth paused and gave her a hug of approval.

'Thanks, Beth,' Elaine muttered awkwardly.

Bob drew up his coat collar so it covered the side of his face and adjusted his hat so it fell over his eyes, and then calmly pushing at the exit door, he slipped furtively out on to Twenty-third Street.

People were beginning to come into the gallery.

'It's about how peripheral vision determines our view,' Jo was saying to a young critic for *Art Forum*. The critic, who wore dark spectacles, nodded his head. 'You mean like taking things out of spatial reality?' he said earnestly.

Jo stroked his chin and thought about this for a while. 'Yeah, I guess you could say that the contraption prevents peripheral vision, so that the viewer can only see a partial aspect of the installation,' he replied confidently.

'I'm sorry, I don't see what you're getting at.'

'Well, the idea is to get pure focus on one thing which ...'

'You mean by taking out the peripheral you're concentrating on the image ...'

'... by taking it out of its context,' Jo added.

This whole thing is like totally bizarre, I mean really, really weird, you know? Oh my God, my God, oh my God, Mom and Pop have just arrived, I told them not to come. Oh Jesus, I'm so embarrassed. They're not going

to like, understand any of it. I mean, it's like, too contemporary, you know?
Shit. Elaine naked is going to totally freak them out. 'Hey, Mom, I don't
believe it, you guys, you came over.'

The Beth Freemantle Gallery was rapidly filling up. Michael and Nikki Joo,
Matthew Barney, the Currins, the ubiquitous Haden-Guest and Adrian
Dannatt, Neville Wakefield, Chris Brooks, Marcia Fortes, a gang of Brazil-
ians, Jeanne Greenberg, Peter Fleisig, Jessica Craig-Martin, the Force girls,
Adam Fuss, Daniel Wolf, Daisey Garnett, Tim Hunt, Gary Simmons,
Vincent Katz, Michele and Sean Landers. Earl Magrath and Paul Kasmin
were just arriving through the door.

Maclestone walked in and gave the room a quick once-over. He immediately recognised Clara's stooping form looking down through the second
view-finder. He went over and gently slapped her butt. 'Ohhh,' she cried
out and stood up straight, 'Bob, you bad boy!' she said with a giggle.

'I have penthouse suite, four bedroom. It look over Paris. Come, Jean, we
see Paris now,' Abdullah smiled.
    'I should really be going to bed, Abe,' Jean said, looking at the floor for
her bag. 'I hope you don't mind me calling you Abe? Abdullah is so long
at this time of night.' Her eyelids half closed.
    'No problem. You come, I show you and you go bed, okay, is it a deal?'
Abdullah suggested excitedly.
    'What shall we do with Ivor?' asked Jean as she turned towards
Schneider's recumbent form on the other side of the room. Abdullah
clicked his fingers at the waiter who came scurrying over. He said something rapidly in French and turning to Jean said, 'The staff arrange
everything, no problem.'
    Jean attempted to get up but at half-way she slid back into the chair.

Art pinched his nose and frowned. He bent over the first view-finder.
Television was placed in the middle of the contraption with this kinda
lesbian scene interwoven with street scenes and so on. 'Jesus fuck,' Art

muttered to himself. Embarrassed, he stood up and adjusted his tie. 'Jo did this?' he muttered to himself. Seeing the artist across the room, he walked up to him and broke up what seemed to be a heated discussion.

'Hey, Art, glad you could make it,' said Jo, putting his arm familiarly around him.

'Kinda extreme video you've made, Jo.' Art laughed heartily; a man-to-man laugh.

'Well, actually I didn't. It's more of a collaboration ...'

'Honey, we are so proud of you,' Mrs Freemantle was saying.

'Didn't think you had it in ya,' Mr Freemantle grinned.

'Well,' Beth shrugged, 'here I am.' She smiled triumphantly. Her parents gave her a kind of bear squeeze from both sides. It was a clumsy affair, with Beth squashed awkwardly between them.

Elaine vaguely noticed Beth's parents giving her a congratulatory hug but was too engrossed in her conversation with Clara whom she'd met at Audrey's Karaoke night at the Elbow Room. Clara told her about Paige Quale and Elaine told Clara about Dewey Bozo. The girls were taking it in turns to hold their hands over their mouths in astonished ecstasy.

Now Bob bent down to the view-finder. Every item in the installation was arranged like an appendage to it and yet each was part of the whole. Interesting. He particularly liked the solidity and austerity of the installation. The video went from an interior shot of the Guggenheim to a murky scene two girls making out on a bed. Bob was sure that there was a still of Beth performing cunnilingus on a heavily tattooed girl whom he recognised as being the artist. He straightened up with a look of surprise. Not being quite sure he waited for the vertical and horizontal lines to clear again. Several frames of other girls appeared but none of these was Beth.

'Where is she?' Art asked, lasciviously searching the gallery.

'Talking to Clara,' Jo replied, pointing towards the animated couple.

'She's kinda cute,' Art thought out loud. 'Will you introduce me later, Jo? I'd like to meet her.'

'Sure, so what do you think?'

'I think she's great.'

'I mean the work.'

'What?'

'My show ...'

'So Beth, I guess you are the dealer and the artist, eh?' Maclestone grinned.

'The artist, Bob?' Beth looked puzzled.

'You seem to figure, if you know what I ah, mean.' Bob went on smiling. Beth laughed, not quite knowing what Bob meant. 'Oh yeah, I guess the dealer is like, part of the art process.'

'I like it. Can you give me ah, an idea on ah, the prices, Beth?' Bob pushed on. Beth's whole persona changed as she geared up for what could be her first ever sale.

'Fuck me,' Clara said.

'You like it?' Elaine asked.

'It's totally bizarre, Elaine.' Clara was bent over her long legs. 'I'm amazed Beth let you do this! I mean, Jesus Christ, look at you guys!' she continued in astonishment as the two videos simultaneously showed Beth going down on Elaine and Beth working on Bob Maclestone next door.

'What ah, about ah, *Television* and Elaine Yoon's video piece? Can you give me something on ah, on those, Beth?' Bob asked, turning back to look at his impending acquisition.

'Sure, Bob, I can give you 15 per cent,' she replied enthusiastically. Bob's attention seemed to be completely focused on *Television* where Brigid was now entering a Betsy Johnson store. The video cut to Elaine masturbating in the hospital.

'I'll take them,' Bob mumbled.

As Beth's father was talking to Art, his daughter was down on Elaine, her face firmly placed between her legs, her hands wrapped about her butt. The footage then evaporated into a haze of interference.

'I'm not a contemporary man myself, Art,' Mr Freemantle was saying.

In Gallery 2 Mrs Freemantle had caught sight of her daughter on the video performing sex with another woman. She looked up to the second monitor and identified her daughter in the crowd; she wondered whether all those girls over the years who had stayed with her, on some pretext or other, had in fact been her lovers. Could she really have been so blind to her daughter's lesbian tendencies? Had those so-called boyfriends just been an elaborate ruse to divert attention from the truth?

Beth took Jo aside and whispered in his ear, 'Maclestone's bought *Television* and an edition of Elaine's video. Isn't that great?'

Jo stroked his chin. 'Cool,' he replied calmly.

Art could not concentrate on his conversation. He had just seen Beth have an orgasm and now he was talking to her parents.

'Did you see Tiger Woods' tee shot from the fourteenth? ... just exquisite,' Mr Freemantle was saying. Quite a number of people had gathered in front of the installation and all three viewing stations were occupied. A middle-aged lady with curly red hair in a pin-striped suit suddenly appeared next to them.

'Mother,' Mr Freemantle yelled effusively over the noise of the crowd, 'this here is Art Spindle, remember? Who Beth worked for a few months back ...'

'You want some charlie to celebrate my first ever purchase, Elaine?' Clara asked.

'What?'

'You know, cocaine,' she whispered.

'Oh right. Why not?'

'Is there a bathroom around?'

'Yeah, follow me.'

Beth caught her mother staring at her and she smiled back, giving a confident wave suggesting that all was well. Mrs Freemantle smiled anxiously in a way only a daughter could interpret.

Dad's probably like, boring the shit out of Art. This is so awesome, like everybody is here and they're all real interested in the art. Clara Dupont wants to buy an edition of Elaine's video. Isn't that just great?

Joany was wearing a leather biker outfit with yellow stripes down one side. She scoured the gallery for Elaine. Not seeing her immediately, she decided to look at the exhibition. Soon she was witnessing her lover's infidelities.

'You must be Beth Freemantle,' an English voice asked dryly. He was tall with short black hair, black framed spectacles and a pristine dark grey Savile Row suit.

'I sure am,' she replied confidently.

'Jay Jopling,' he announced, extending a long arm. 'I am delighted to meet you. I wanted to congratulate you on your splendid gallery.' He smiled, looking directly into her eyes. 'It is a very brave thing to do,' he added, finally letting go of her hand.

'Well, thank you, Jay, like coming from you that's a real compliment. I'm so pleased you could make it.'

'I was just admiring the Jo Richards installation next door; I very much like the austere arrangement of the work, I think it lends itself very well to the space,' he continued as he followed the line of Beth's gaze which was glued to the lower monitor – a quick succession of images of Brigid walking across streets and into shops had been suddenly broken by a murky image of Elaine kissing her. Beth froze.

Joany raised herself from the device and placed her hands on her hips. Elaine was nowhere to be seen but she recognised the girl through the doorway talking to a tall young man with glasses and a flamboyant lady in a red-and-green spotted suit with a black dog.

Mrs Freemantle edged her husband towards the exit.

'Do we have to go right now?' he pleaded.

'I'm not feeling too good,' she replied weakly, 'I told Beth we were going home.' She exerted enough pressure on her husband's forearm to make him realise that no form of persuasion was going to delay their departure.

'It's a marvellous space. Don't you think, Clarissa?' Jay was saying to his companion.

Joany barged into the group. 'Who are you?' she blurted angrily.

'I am Beth Freemantle,' Beth replied, noticeably taken aback. 'Can I help you?' she added cautiously.

'Oh,' Joany exclaimed sarcastically, 'so that's why Elaine has a show. I get it now.'

'What do you mean?'

'I think it's pretty fucking obvious, lady,' Joany sneered.

Jay excused himself, leaving Beth under the looming figure of Joany FitzPatrick.

Antony Haden-Guest, Ashley Bickerton and Art Spindle stood facing the video monitors, 'This is great,' Haden-Guest was saying, 'it reminds of that piece you showed in 'seventy-seven. Do you remember, Art? ...'

Elaine was bending over the toilet cover. A snorting noise accompanied Clara's opinions on Art Spindle's selling techniques. 'He has this like, crazy energy and like, tacky charm, you know?' she was saying. 'But you get the feeling, you know, Elaine, like he doesn't like, give a fuck about the work.'

The sentence was broken by a sharp knocking noise followed by Beth's muffled voice. 'Elaine, are you in there?'

Elaine rose from her crouched position. 'Shit,' she said quietly.

'Elaine,' Beth repeated, 'I know you're in there.'

Jo had now understood why there was so much attention to the video. His feelings for Beth changed dramatically. He'd obviously been wrong about not reciprocating her advances. They could have had some fun together. Shit.

Beth slapped Elaine hard. As she cowered back holding her smarting cheek, Beth punched her on the other with her left fist. Elaine sat abruptly on the floor as Clara tried to manoeuvre herself between them. Beth turned and walked back into the gallery.

Something strange was happening to Jean. Abdullah was not just double but triple. 'What's happening to me?' she slurred and fell into the armchair. 'I think I'm passing out, oh shit.'

Ivor was being shaken violently by an irate waiter. 'What the fuck?' he said sleepily.

Clara bathed Elaine's cheek with a tissue and cold water.

'Jesus, Elaine, I think she's real mad. Here we go. That looks sore. Open your mouth. Oh yeah, Jesus. Here, let me dab it.' Elaine's lower lip was swelling fast. Her upper lip was still swollen from Joany's punch the night before.

'Can you take these rings out, I think they're going to make the swelling very painful.'

'Yeah, but I prefer to leave them in,' Elaine mumbled.

'But why?' Clara asked.

'I like the pain,' she replied matter of factly.

Abdullah was having trouble with Jean's bra. His attempt to undo the invisible hook was failing miserably. Meanwhile Jean was trying to hold the little man off.

'Abdullah, for God's sake,' she slurred. 'I have a husband and my boyfriend downstairs, I mean, not my boyfriend but friend. I mean for Christ's sake. Get off me! Bob! Abe!' She finally managed to dislodge herself from his firm grip but not before one of her silicone bosoms sprang out of her bra with some urgency.

'I would never have guessed,' Art sniggered.

'Nor would I,' agreed Jo.

'And displaying it in the opening show. Quite a thing to do. I think she's going to be good, yeah.' Art said, scratching the back of his head.

Jo hadn't thought of it this way. 'I guess you're right, Art,' he agreed.

Art moved away and placed his head in the device. He peered at *Frigidaire*. If Bob had bought *Television* maybe he should buy something. You never know. But as he was contemplating an acquisition a pain shot up his back and seized his muscles. He couldn't move.

Abdullah had a pathetic, pleading look, like a hungry dog. His trousers were entwined around his ankles together with a pair of voluminous white boxer pants, revealing socks that were held up by garters elasticated below the knee. His erect penis hovered horizontally beneath a large stomach, which in its thick, short, door-knob-like quality was in keeping with the rest of him.

'Abdullah, for God's sake put it away,' Jean said, doing up the buttons on her blouse.

Jo caught Elaine by the arm. 'Isn't it great about Maclestone?'

'Yeah, Jo. Can you believe that?' Elaine tried to smile.

'I was thinking, Elaine, maybe we should collaborate more often?'

'My work is always a collaboration, Jo.'

'Oh yeah. I suppose it is,' Jo responded quietly as he realised how ill thought out his eager suggestion had been.

'Art seems ah, to be en-enjoying the show,' Bob said as he observed Art Spindle's posterior. 'Yoon's video must have turned him on.'

'He's been like that for ten minutes,' Clara said. 'Do you think he's okay?'

Elaine was talking in whispers to Pete, Beth's assistant. 'How do you think it's going?' she asked.

'People love it, Elaine.'

'You really think so?'

'I wish you were straight,' Pete grinned youthfully.

'Honey, the problem is that girls do it ten times better.'

Jo Richards and Pete helped Art Spindle out on to Tenth Avenue and hailed a taxi.

'Thanks, guys,' he said painfully.

'Are you going to be all right, Art?'

'Don't worry, Jo. It happens sometimes. I'll be fine tomorrow.' Art fell into the back of the taxi and stared out of the window. It had been a tense day. The Mondrian deal had really taken it out of him. But this was going to be the deal of a lifetime.

Freign sat reading the *Times* while Mrs Rhinegold dozed serenely in the bed across the room.

'Robert,' she said, waking up with a start, 'where am I?'

Freign sat up abruptly. 'You are in hospital, Alfreda,' he whispered.

'Oh, I see.' She paused. 'Well, what is wrong with me?'

'A slight concussion, my dear, you fell ... in the bathroom. It was my fault. I startled you while you were in the shower.'

'How clumsy of me, Robert.'

'Bathrooms are minefields.'

Spindle was suddenly engulfed by a repulsion for everybody and everything. 'What's the point of all of this?' he muttered to himself. The strain of being Art Spindle, of always having to be mildly fraudulent, of having the responsibility of these ego-driven careers and being at the mercy of people's fickle taste. He felt deeply depressed and alone.

Jean stumbled out of Abdullah's suite and into the brightly lit corridor. She leaned against the wall and adjusted her shoe which had slipped away from her heel. She walked along the corridor until it ended abruptly.

'Shit,' she slurred and turning around she fell clumsily on to her knees.
A few minutes later she was pressing at the elevator button.

'How long have I been out, Robert?' Mrs Rhinegold asked.

'Three months,' Freign replied slowly.

'Three months!' she exclaimed, quite startled.

'Yes, it has been quite some time.'

'Robert, how is Alfred?'

Freign hesitated for a second. 'Mr Rhinegold …' His voice rose an
octave on 'gold'.

'He's dead, isn't he, Robert?' she intervened.

'Yes, I'm afraid he is.'

A moment of silence ensued before she looked across at him and
whispered, 'You won't leave me, will you, Robert?'

'We shall always be together, Alfreda.'

It was only when the taxi had passed Forty-fourth Street that Spindle
reminded himself that it was uncharacteristic to wallow in such pessimism
and self-pity. After all, he was a career maker, a man of the moment, not
some crummy door-to-door salesman living each day with precarious
intent. And anyway, he should be celebrating, he had just made several
million dollars. It had been the deal of a lifetime.

Dolores replaced her house slippers for a pair of sturdy, ochre leather
shoes which she always parked next to the radiator in the laundry room
and then, unhooking her grey nylon coat from behind the door, she slipped
into the hall. Once in the open space she reached down into her plastic bag
and produced a yellow scarf, and, having covered her head with it, she tied
the corners firmly under her chin. As she walked past the library, where
Mrs Schwartz sat in vigil next to her father, she crossed herself and made
for the front door. She closed the door quietly behind her.

Jo talked to Paige from Beth's office.

'Jo, I'm so sorry for all of this,' Paige said sadly, 'I wish I could be there,
I'm so like, pissed off.'

'How are you feeling, Paige?'

'Kinda weird.'

'Yeah, I guess you would be, did you get my flowers?'

'I'm looking at them right now, Jo,' she said, looking across at the lilies on the side-table.

Jean searched her bag for her key-card. She couldn't find it amongst the debris of American Express receipts. Finally she tipped her bag out on the floor and getting on her hands and knees parted each item until the key-card appeared between two Coffee Republic loyalty cards. She then scooped everything back into her black leather Gucci bag and inserted her key-card into the wall. The door clicked open.

Beth escorted Bob into her office. A self-portrait light box by Yoon hung on one wall and a No Entry sign hung behind her desk.

'So this is the nerve centre.' She flung her right arm in the air.

'I like the No Entry sign,' said Bob.

'Isn't it great? It's by Todd Vatec. My next show. He's like saying that every No Entry sign in the world is like, art. Like a signature, you know?'

'Can you buy it?' asked Bob.

'You know, Bob, he has said that to like, buy it would be to like, alter its use, its like *raison d'être*, so it becomes something other than what it is, right? But he does say if you steal one he'll sign it for you.'

'But what's the difference,' Bob wondered, 'between stealing and selling?'

'He said by stealing it you're creating a need to replace it and so the piece becomes like, self-propagating.'

'So the ah, more are stolen the more are made?'

'I guess so,' Beth said triumphantly.

'Very ah, good. I like it but I ah, want it.'

'Go out and steal one, Bob.'

Bob went up to the sign and unhooked it from the wall.

'What ah, like, are you doing, Bob?'

'I'm st, stealing ah, your sign, Beth.'

Wrapped in a towel and devoid of make-up, Jean stumbled into the bedroom. Ivor lay naked on the bed. Jean gasped. Ivor woke up and smiled sleepily.

'How did you get in here?' Jean gripped her towel.

'Someone brought me up from the bar,' he slurred.

'Look, Ivor, we've been friends for too long, I really don't think this is a good idea.'

'I'm sorry, Jean, but they brought me to the wrong room. What do you want me to do? Sleep on the floor?'

'I'm sorry, Ivor. I ah, I ah …'

'We can sleep in the same bed, can't we?'

'Well, okay.' Jean turned the light off and slipped into the bed. 'Good night, Ivor.'

'Night.' A few minutes went by before Ivor pulled Jean over on to her back.

When Rosemary Schwartz turned on the light for the walk-in cupboard she was confronted with two doubled-up lines of clothes about twenty or so feet deep. She unhooked an early fifties Givenchy evening dress and put it up against herself. 'Oh my,' she gasped. In no time, she had stripped off her clothes and begun to try on a multitude of dresses, all of which fitted her like a glove. When a dress was particularly to her liking she would go down to the library and twirl in front of her father saying, 'Daddy, see how pretty your little girl is?' or, 'How does this look, Daddy?'

As Brigid walked into the Beth Freemantle Gallery, Joany stormed through the crowd towards her and introduced herself aggressively. 'I'm Joany.'

'Brigid Murphy,' Brigid replied with some surprise. There were a few seconds of silence. Brigid looked at Joany inquiringly.

'Don't give me that fucking who-the-fuck-are-you look, bitch,' Joany said, waving her hand in front of Brigid.

'I think you got the wrong person,' Brigid replied calmly.

'You better keep away from my girl, you fucking whore. *Comprende?*'

Beth, who had witnessed the beginning of this conversation, asked Pete to throw Joany out of the gallery. He went up to the couple and grabbed Joany's arm. 'I'm sorry, lady, but you will have to leave.'

'Get off of me, ass-hole,' Joany said angrily. Pete strengthened his grip around her arm. Joany's right fist swung across, landing just below Pete's jaw. He fell against the screen and collapsed on the floor.

'Next time ask politely,' she said, looking down at him. Brigid made to leave but Joany snatched her hair, heaving her back.

'And where do you think you're going, young lady?'

Brigid turned around and slapped Joany on the cheek as hard as she could. Joany took two steps back but before she could react Brigid followed with another slap. Matthew Barney and Michael Joo separated the two girls and under the instruction of Pete, who was still on the floor, threw Joany out of the gallery.

Beth rushed into Gallery 2 where she found Elaine looking impassively at the commotion in Gallery 1. 'Elaine, don't you think you should be dealing with your friend?' she asked.

'She'll get over it,' Elaine said and then, seeing Jo coming towards them, she added, 'Beth, I wanna talk to you, in private.'

'Hey guys, what a fight. I mean did you see that whale being thrown out?'

'That whale, Jo, happens to be my girlfriend,' Elaine said, staring at him coldly.

'Oh I ah, I ah,' Jo stumbled awkwardly.

'I think ah, I think you have some ah, explaining to do,' Bob said, looking at Brigid who was looking down at the floor.

'It was long before I met ya, last year sometime, I ah, Jesus, she must have followed me. The bitch. I just don't feckin' know. Honest to God. You gotta forgive me, Bob. It meant nothing to me. She's a right shite. Believe me, I swear it.'

Bob looked across at Elaine and smiled. 'She's ah, very attractive.'

'I want to get out of here. This has bin the day from hell.'

'Let's go and talk about it and celebrate another ah, ah, acquisition,' Bob said, taking Brigid by the arm.

When Spindle got home he hobbled to his answering machine and pressed the replay button. The first message was from Tucker Grasple: 'I've decided to accept the terms. I'll send a deposit this week and get the shippers to send you the Pollock, the Bacon and the Rothko. Hey, I hope my wife likes it!' The message ended with a loud laugh.

The second message was from Freign: 'This is Robert Freign. I thought you would like to know that Mrs Rhinegold has come out of her coma. As you can imagine we are overjoyed.' Beep beep beep.

'Oh, Art, it's Tucker again, err … I just spoke to my wife and well, err … she reckons the price is too high. Maybe you could ring me, err … I'll be in all evening.' Beep beep beep.

'It's Jean,' her voice slurred down the phone, 'I want you to know that I'm having a great time despite the fuck up.' The phone knocked about before cutting off.

'Mr Spindle, this is Brad Quale. Paige wanted me to ring you to thank you for the flowers and all your kindness today. She's doing just great. We should do a round of golf some day … Oh, my wife wants me to say how grateful she is too … What's that? … Paige wants a word … Hi, Art, I'm sorry about all of this. The doctor said I should be back at work real soon. Thanks for the flowers and all your like, support. I really appreciate it. Bye.'

Art fell back and placed his hands over his face. Beep beep beep.

'Hey, Art, how you doing, sweetheart? It's you know who. Give me a ring sometime. Let's hook up this week.'

Art looked at the phone for a minute before reaching over and dialling a number from memory. 'Chelsea, it's Art. What are you doing tonight? I feel like celebrating big time.'

Elaine closed the door of the office and leaned against it with her hands behind her back. Beth sat down at her desk and dropped her head in her hands.

'Why did you do it, Elaine?' she sighed despairingly. Elaine lit a cigarette and let the smoke pour through her nose.

'It's a game, Beth,' she drawled. 'It's about the art game and the art of the game.' Beth looked at Elaine through her fingers. Elaine took another drag of her cigarette. 'Does this have a lock on it, Beth?' she asked, looking down at the door handle. Beth cleared her throat.

'So how did I score?'

'A perfect ten.'

'Elaine ...' Beth paused and let her hands fall slowly on to the desk, 'is this off the record?'